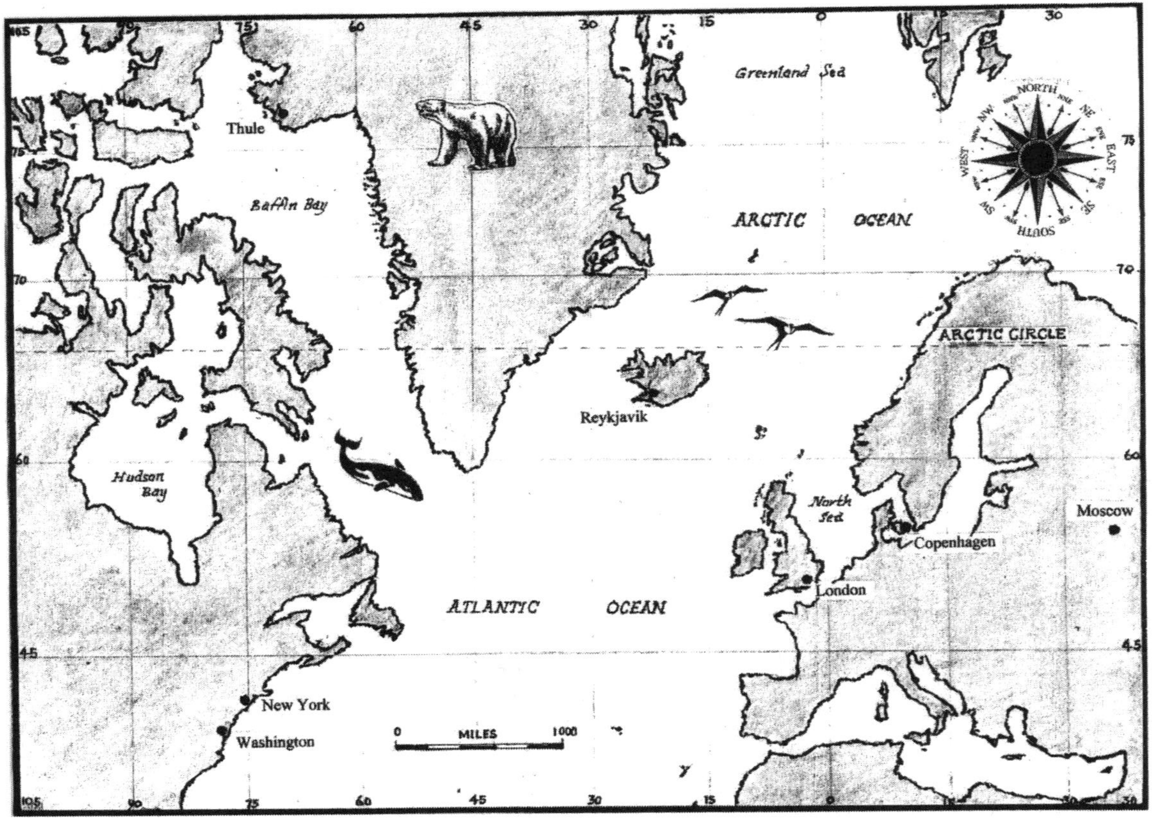

Greenland Sea
Thule
Baffin Bay
ARCTIC OCEAN
ARCTIC CIRCLE
Reykjavik
Hudson Bay
North Sea
Moscow
Copenhagen
London
ATLANTIC OCEAN
New York
Washington
0 MILES 1000
NORTH
EAST
SOUTH
WEST

CRIES FROM

THE FROZEN NORTH

COLIN BEAZLEY

Published by
Four Boys Books
Heywood House, Chulmleigh, Devon. EX18 7QS
www.fourboysbooks.com

Printed in Great Britain by
Imprint Digital – Academic Printers

While this book is a work of the author's imagination, it is inspired by real events.

A NOTE ON NAMES

Icelandic names can be confusing to non Icelanders.

Icelanders always address each other using first names since most people have a patronymic name, rather than a 'proper surname', which ends in -son for a son and -dóttir for a daughter. Eva's full name is Eva Jóhannesdóttir taking her father's first name and adding dóttir. It is not unusual for the surname Jóhannes, pronounced Yóhannes, to be shortened to Hannes. Her father is commonly known by his middle name Magnús as in Jóhannes Magnús Sigurdsson. Some Icelandic families however, do have traditional surnames from the Danish. First names are used extensively, not only in listings such as telephone directories, but also throughout the police heirarchy when referring to one another, such as Andri and Hinrik.

The Greenland settlement of Thule is pronounced "too-lee".

THE COLD WAR

For over fifty years after World War Two and until the collapse of the Soviet Union in 1991, there was a period known as The Cold War. During that time the United States and the Soviet Union each held vast nuclear arsenals capable of inflicting unimaginable damage upon the other.

This was an era without parallel, when an attack by one on the other would almost certainly result in complete annihilation of them both.

'Now, I am become Death, the destroyer of worlds,'
quoted J Robert Oppenheimer, father of the Atomic Bomb.

REYKJAVIK – ICELAND
Friday April 13th, 2001 10pm

CHAPTER ONE

There was the piercing squeal of locked wheels as Eva's car ploughed into the lone dark figure, hurling the body into the air. It bounced over the car's bonnet, arms and legs flailing in all directions like some possessed rag doll.

From the very moment of impact Eva's heart felt as if it would burst, panic gripped her and adrenaline flooded her whole being as the car lurched to a final stop. The crumpled body slumped in a heap – motionless. The VW's engine protested as Eva instinctively moved the gearstick into neutral. With her hands tightly gripped onto the steering wheel she sat frozen, mesmerised, and a sickness welled-up deep from the pit of her stomach. Her car's headlights reflected yellow pools of light ahead on the flooded road while the rain pounded relentlessly. Nothing moved except for the wiper blades which frantically scribed arcs across the screen. Eva strained to see what she had hit. What was the dark shadow that had suddenly appeared then vanished into the filthy night? She sat there desperate for something to happen, someone to come, anything, anyone.

With the movement of the wipers, blood smeared back and forth across the windscreen. Then, and only then, did the reality fully hit her. Eva screamed as loud as she could and slammed her hand on the car's horn. She was now shaking with terror; she had never killed anyone before.

A flashlight's beam wheeled round, circled about her car and finally came to rest. In the gloom she could make out a stocky figure, dressed in a drab grey rain-cape and hat, holding the light and crouched over the crumpled form. Eva couldn't move.

A patrol car, siren wailing, lights flashing, mounted the curb and pulled up beside Eva's stranded car, its headlights illuminating the figure bent over what appeared to be a body. A burly patrol man approached the driver's side of the VW. He opened the car door and lifted Eva's hand off the horn. She turned towards him, saw the black uniformed officer and cried out. A shout came from the figure by the body, "Get an ambulance, he's still breathing!" A feeling of relief flooded through her.

The police questioned Eva then cautioned her not to leave the city. They still needed to speak with the witness as well as the man she had almost killed, and at present he wasn't talking. For Eva, this was the beginning of her worst nightmare. In all her years of driving she had never been involved in an accident and had always regarded herself as a careful driver. She knew her route through the city well, travelling it as she did most days to attend rehearsals and performances in the concert hall, but today she had been late, driving faster than usual. The appalling road conditions hadn't made her journey easy as she struggled to keep control of the car.

Having left the police station she made her way to the hospital, where she lied and successfully convinced a member of staff that she was related to the patient. Consumed by her emotions she had no idea what to expect or, indeed, why she was even there. Eva had been sure the man couldn't have survived, but it seemed luck had played a kind hand that night. Even though the nurse had explained that the patient was in a coma, Eva was shocked to see his motionless body surrounded by medical paraphernalia. Monitors bleeped as brightly illuminated dots shot across a screen. Hardly making out his face beneath the bandages, the passing reassurances from the nursing staff that he was stable did little to quiet her concern. It was all proving too much for her. She so wanted, no, needed, this stranger to live. She couldn't get out of her head that the only reason he was like this was because of her.

Eva sat by his bed staring at him, wondering to herself who this man was. Where was he from and did he have a family? The name, Nathan Trent, on the bed-head told her he was no Icelander. Maybe that's why no one else was with him. Eva stayed close, only briefly leaving his bedside. She waited, wanting to see even the smallest movement, any sign of life, willing him to wake. For thirty-two hours Eva diligently sat talking to him, sometimes in English, sometimes in Icelandic, not always conscious of what she was sharing and not thinking of what she would say to him when he did wake. Just wondering if he ever would.

CHAPTER TWO

Nathan found lying in a hospital bed, kind of dead yet half alive, a very strange state to be in. He didn't know, in his semi-consciousness, how bad a shape he was in. He could hear machines bleeping and people talking, some of which he understood. Voices were saying calmly that he had been in a car accident and that he needed to rest but would be alright. They kept on telling him that.

He remembered a sudden impact, hurting all over, and being wet and icy cold. Moments of understanding were disrupted by surreal and horrific dreams. One minute he saw himself walking on stars, the next lying on a hospital bed in the centre of a huge white room. It was hard to tell whether it was a dream or reality in this strange world he inhabited. He could feel his body being moved and needles being pushed into him but he felt no pain. A woman was there talking to him in a muffled voice, asking him, in English, to wake up, but trapped between life and death, he was helpless to reply. Frustration was too inadequate a word to describe what he felt. Time seemed to have slowed and then suddenly, something changed like a sharp flash of consciousness and reality started washing back. When finally he came to, Nathan screamed, but this time he could hear himself and he realised others could as well.

Gripping his shoulder a nurse kept repeating, "It's alright, you're in hospital," but somehow her words weren't reassurance enough. He shouted again and struggled to push himself up. She restrained him, calling out for help. Moments later a well-built orderly came to her aid, closely followed by the duty doctor.

"I'm going to be sick," Nathan yelled and retched into a bowl. He began fidgeting, writhing in his bed. A woman who was at his bedside tried to calm him, laying her hand firmly on his arm and continuing to reassure him. Nathan saw tears roll down her cheeks. The duty doctor blurted an instruction to the nurse, "5 mg of Diazepam," then turning to the woman explained that Nathan needed to rest and it would be best if she left.

The next morning Nathan woke early. He had slept for a full fifteen hours and somehow things seemed clearer in his head. The routine of the hospital day was already underway. Through the half-glazed door of his room Nathan spotted an official-looking entourage conducting their rounds, a young, bespectacled man wearing a white coat and green trousers at the helm. The group eventually entered, surrounded his bed and, before Nathan had a chance to think of something useful to say, the young doctor smiled the broadest of grins and said, "Welcome. It's good to have you back with us, Mr Trent." Nathan's charts seemed to prove a momentary diversion for him, then he continued, "Well, I expect you're wondering how you got here and how long you'll be enjoying our hospitality?"

The group respectfully acknowledged his humour. This, however, wasn't the most prominent question at the forefront of Nathan's mind, but before he had a chance to share it the doctor said, "I will drop by at the end of my rounds and explain what we know, and answer any questions you may have. I am sure you must have some questions?"

Within the hour the doctor returned, an air of confidence accompanying him.

"I am Dr Thorirsson and you are in Lanđspitali University Hospital. You were admitted three nights ago, do you remember?" A puzzled Nathan shook his head as Dr Thorirsson continued, "That's perfectly normal after the kind of trauma you've suffered. Paramedics were called to the scene of a vehicle collision at about 10 pm. They found you unconscious at the side of the road; you had been hit by a car. We kept you in a coma for two days to allow your brain to recover." He paused, then in a gentle voice enquired of Nathan, "Can I ask you some questions?"

A confused Nathan nodded. "Yes, of course. Of course you can."

"Good. Can you remember my name?" Nathan looked blank, lost.

"Never mind, what about the date?" This proved no easier. "The day then?" He waited for Nathan's answer but nothing was offered. "Then the year?"

"1991?" Nathan said after a long pause, lacking any conviction.

"You're not far out, 2001," Dr Thorirsson said. By now Nathan was becoming uneasy, concerned about what might really be wrong with him. "That's okay, episodes of short-term memory loss are not unusual, nothing at this stage really to worry about."

"What's wrong with me, doctor? What if my memory doesn't come back?" Nathan pressed, wanting to stop this game in which he was clearly having little success.

"I am pleased to say, Mr Trent, it would appear there's very little wrong with you looking at your scans and X-rays. That is, apart from cuts and bruises and a few cracked ribs. Your head took quite a blow, but there is no evidence of significant brain injury or bleeding; the cross-sectional images confirm the trauma has not damaged your spinal cord and you'll be pleased to hear your vitals are normal. The cuts are mainly superficial and the bandages can soon come off. We will need to monitor you to ensure all is well, but you've been extremely lucky."

A silence rested over the room, each looking at the other for a minute or more. Finally Nathan spoke, "What exactly happened? Do you know?"

The incident was recounted, but from a detached medical perspective, and what Dr Thorirsson was sharing came as a shock and a complete surprise to Nathan. However, the greatest news that unsettled him was the revelation that a woman had sat at his bedside for two long days, waiting for him to regain consciousness.

Nathan had many questions he wanted to ask about the woman, but before he had gathered his thoughts Dr Thorirsson said, "We need to know something about you, Mr Trent, for our records, you see. All we have are the papers, documents and books you were carrying. I gather you are a scientist?" Nathan looked confused. "You are the author of one of the books in your possession." Smiling, the doctor raised a clipboard and, clicking a ballpoint, looked Nathan in the eye. "What else can you tell me about yourself? Take your time," Dr Thorirsson encouraged. "Where is your home?"

"I am from England. London." He was quite certain of that.

"Yes, well, you hold a UK passport which has your date of birth as February 1954. By my reckoning that makes you forty-seven, Mr Trent. And are you here on holiday?" Dr Thorirsson prompted.

"No. No, I don't think so."

"Perhaps you are working? Your papers suggest you hold a professorship at Aberystwyth University in Wales and that you are visiting our university."

Nathan's expression eased.

"We're making progress." Nathan didn't respond. To Nathan, Dr Thorirsson seemed to be asking him endless questions.

"No matter, the authorities can soon establish that; they will hold onto your personal effects for a while. Maybe you have just flown in? The accident took place near the bus station for the airport shuttle."

Nathan nodded whilst trying hard to work out the sequence of events.

"Do you have any family or friends here in Iceland?" Half under his breath the doctor muttered, "Perhaps not. That would explain why no other visitors come and no one else asks after you." He coughed as if to regain Nathan's attention. "If there is anyone you want us to contact for you let the nurse or myself know. The police wish to speak with you when you are fit enough. You may find that too much just now so I think we will keep them away until tomorrow, and anyway, I want to monitor you for another twenty-four hours at least before we think of discharging you."

There was little Nathan thought he could tell the police that would be of any use since he really couldn't remember anything about what had happened.

"It's just a formality with incidents such as this," Dr Thorirsson added in an attempt to allay any anxiety. "Do you have any more questions you wish to ask?"

His invitation was unnecessary and Nathan interrupted him. "The woman, why was she here?"

Dr Thorirsson waited, carefully considering his response. "I believe she was the driver of the car and was, understandably, concerned about you."

An elderly auxiliary nurse bustled in balancing a small meal-tray and, acknowledging the doctor's welcome, slid the tray onto Nathan's side-table. Dr Thorirsson stood to take his leave. "I am sure you have had more than enough of my questions. You must eat now to help regain your strength, then rest, and I will be back later to check on you."

The following morning two burly men in black jackets entered Nathan's room accompanied by a nurse.

"These officers wish to ask you some questions, Mr Trent. Don't over-tire him," she said firmly to them both.

One of the officers turned to the departing nurse and explained that they would only be a few minutes. Nathan's concentration was distracted by the second officer who, taking a notebook from his pocket, asked him to relate his account of the accident.

After what Nathan considered to be a futile interview, one of the policemen fixed Nathan's gaze and suggested, "When you're better you may want to consider pressing charges against the driver."

"The woman who tried to kill me? What's her name?"

The two glanced at each other and the one who had done most of the speaking explained, "On Friday night last, just before 2200 hours, you were hit by a black Volkswagen Beetle which mounted the pedestrian-way at the junction of Njarđargata and Gamia Hringbraut. Thirty-six year old Eva Hannes was at the wheel of the car. She was alone. More than that we cannot disclose at present whilst we pursue our investigations. Do you know her?"

"No. No, I'm sure I don't."

Once they had left he stumbled from his room to the adjoining toilet. He ran the hot tap and a smell of sulphur made him wince. Staring into the mirror above the hand basin, confusion overcame him. He looked beyond the grazes and the bandages and he just saw the face of a lonely, bewildered man that he didn't recognise.

"You should be in bed." The words came from beyond the half open door. "A visitor is waiting outside. She asks if she can see you?"

Nathan grabbed the dressing gown off the door and replied to the nurse as he headed back into his room, "Is she alone?"

"Yes, she has always been on her own. What do you think . . . should I tell her to go?"

"No, I guess I'll see her." Immediately he wondered if this was a mistake. After all, he was convinced that she was the one who had put him in this hospital bed.

Nathan couldn't help but notice how young she looked as she stood in the doorway. The woman's short, blonde hair beautifully framed her finely-sculptured features. Her dark eyes stared at him, offering no hint of a smile. Her red lips, closed in concentration, punctuated the paleness of her skin. Wearing a white blouse beneath the jacket of an austere black trouser suit she looked quite uncomfortable, and he wondered if she was unwell.

Tentatively smiling, she spoke. "You know, I was so scared. I couldn't stop in time, I thought I had killed you."

Nathan sat down. He needed a moment to gather his thoughts; her appearance and words had thrown him. He wanted to grab hold of her and shake her and shout, *What on earth were you doing?* But he didn't. "Sit!" and he gestured to the other chair.

Eva said, "This is the moment I've dreaded, I knew I wouldn't know what to say. Friends told me I was crazy to come. I am so, so sorry. I would change things if only I could."

There was no let-up in her pleading, and he couldn't help notice her sincerity and innocence. He managed a half-smile.

"Do you believe in good luck?" Nathan said.

She looked up, surprised at the question. "I don't know. Yes. Well, I suppose so, why?"

He smiled again, the warmth reaching his eyes this time. "The doctors say that, in spite of your driving, I will be okay."

For fifteen minutes or more Eva talked with Nathan, but he struggled to come up with any real answers to her questions.

He was beginning to doubt if he truly was okay.

CHAPTER THREE

For the last two days Eva had sat keeping vigil, fighting exhaustion, waiting for him to wake, and now he had she didn't know what to do. The thought of how useless she was haunted her as she walked down the corridor and out into the hospital car park. A gust of icy air bit into her face and the rain was torrential. Eva opened the door of the car and slumped into the passenger seat. It was a few moments before her girlfriend spoke.

"Well, is he alright?" and turning to her exclaimed. "Hell, you look shattered, I'll get you home."

Eva never uttered a word. She didn't really hear her, she just sat there, her clothes soaked and her face wet with rain, picturing Nathan with his bandaged face and eyes that looked possessed. Sabina started the engine, drove out of the car park and, checking the junction, pulled out into the traffic.

"What the hell's wrong with you, Eva?" Sabina shouted so loud that all in the neighbouring apartments couldn't fail but hear. "You've been there every day, you've talked to him, he's okay, so leave it, move on, don't kill yourself over it. It was an accident."

"It's not like that, he lost a lot of blood. I just want to know that he will be alright. You don't understand, I nearly killed a man," Eva screamed, tears rolling down her face.

"But you didn't, and now everyone's paying for it."

"Just stop, I can't take any more." Eva fled into the bathroom where she rummaged in the basin cabinet for some aspirin. The front door slammed. Sabina had gone. Eva cursed, collapsing into an armchair, sobbing.

* * * *

As Eva entered Nathan's hospital room he woke.

"I've come early today because I have a rehearsal at three and I won't be able to come tonight, is that okay?"

There was an awkwardness in her manner, an uncertainty of her reception. Nathan looked her up and down. It was the same young woman but this time she was impatient, agitated.

"Do you want me to go?" she asked, sounding tense.

"No . . . stay."

"Are you sure? Only I can't stay long, I have a lift. My friend Sabina is waiting to take me to the concert hall but I wanted to see you again." The words tumbled from her.

Dr Thorirsson entered, a folder clasped in his hand. He gazed at Eva then at Nathan.

"Mr Trent, I wish to discuss with you your discharge." He again looked at Eva, making it obvious that he wouldn't say any more until she left.

"I will be late and that will never do," Eva said. She looked across at Nathan as if asking permission, and he nodded. She turned to the doctor and smiled briefly, then hurried out leaving Dr Thorirsson explaining to Nathan what would happen now.

Across the city, Eva's journey with Sabina was proving anything but straightforward. A lorry had jack-knifed on Bústađavegur with a build-up of traffic for several hundred yards, just what she didn't need. By the time they arrived rehearsals were well under way, much to her annoyance. Leaving her bag, concert dress and violin case in her locker, she waited until there was a loud passage in the music before attempting to sneak in. Sabina had been able to slide into the back row of the 'cellos almost unnoticed. For Eva, being the leader of the second violins and seated directly in front of the conductor, this proved impossible. As she crept onto the platform, the conductor's hands, which had been gesticulating every note and nuance, expressing the heart and passion of the piece, came to an abrupt stop. The orchestra stumbled and ceased playing. There was a deathly silence, with the exception of the noise of falling coins. Loose króna were being tossed to the floor by the brass players. This they always did to mark the late arrival of a musician and it was the ultimate insult. The conductor looked to the brass section and said in a commanding tone, involving more than a hint of sarcasm, "Perhaps, ladies and gentlemen," at which point he glanced down from his rostrum to Eva, "we could proceed without any further interruptions. That is, when we are all quite ready. As for the offerings, they can be collected later." He tapped his baton and paused, "We'll go from bar 120," then raised both hands slowly and, with his up-beat, the orchestra began to play. The deep mellow sound of the violas, 'cellos and basses filled the auditorium. He nodded to the woodwind and brass sections, then turning to the strings, the impassioned eloquence of Rachmaninov's Second Symphony in E minor began to breathe.

Eva adored this piece with its poetic string melodies. The haunting romanticism and melancholia of it came to her afresh with every playing – the symphony was just wonderful. The violin transported her to another world, a world unlike any other, making her feel as if she was flying, lifting her spirit above the mundaneness of everyday life. Eva had hoped that during the break before the evening performance she could avoid her colleagues' cutting remarks. They, however, were less than accommodating.

"Couldn't you get away?"

"You say he's on his own but you've been there every day."

No matter what she said they didn't believe her. "Face the facts Eva, you're obsessed with him."

The start of the concert performance came as a reprieve for her. For an hour or more she escaped from the complications of the past few days. She was totally immersed in Rachmaninov's symphonic work – the broody and mysterious intensity of the first movement, the wild energy of the scherzo, the melodic serenity of the third with the beautiful clarinet solo, and the drama of the final movement's grand sweeping style. The concert continued after the interval with the dreamy Reverie by Scriabin and concluded with Mendelssohn's menacing and brilliant Piano Concerto No. 2. The conductor invited the soloist to take his bow, then shook the pianist's hand, nodded to the orchestra's leader and turned to the audience. The orchestra rose as one and the auditorium erupted to the ecstatic applause and enthusiastic shouts of "Encore, encore". The soloist returned and Scriabin's early piano piece Opus 8 was sensitively performed to a rousing ovation, after which the audience seemed delighted and content to head on home.

Sabina, struggling to negotiate the late evening traffic, suggested they stop off at a bar for a drink on their way home. As Eva expected, the talk quickly turned to Nathan. She didn't really mind, having known Sabina for years, and she was quite capable of telling her when to shut up. Eva decided the easiest thing was to level with her: after all, it was late and she was too tired to play games.

Sabina retorted, "What on earth is up with you?"

"Oh, I don't know. What with the accident and Father obsessed with this thing over Ernst and their time in Thule, I just can't cope. I feel responsible and guilty, and wanted to say I was sorry, but the more I see Nathan . . ."

"What?" Sabina interrupted.

The temporary silence provided an opportunity for them both to drink their beers, but Sabina was clearly not letting go that easily. "So it's out of pity?"

Eva ignored her.

"I'm not sure. It's strange, but I feel for him."

As it got later and the empty glasses collected on their table, all Eva wanted to do now was to go home and sleep.

The next day she was free: free of rehearsals and concerts. She made her way across the city by bus, annoyed that the police and garage still could not tell her when they would be done with her car. Deciding to call in on her father Magnus, on the way to the hospital, she was anxious to find him so stressed. His place was turned upside down. Papers and files covered the floor, photos were spread across the table and he was obviously in the process of studying some letters.

"What on earth are you doing, Dad?"

"For years I've been meaning to get to the bottom of this and now's as good a time as any," Magnus burbled while shuffling documents.

"Bottom of what?"

Ignoring her, Magnus said, "Someone needs to answer for all that went on up there, they can't hide forever." Eva could see where this was going. Greenland, she thought to herself.

"Dad, I've got to get to the hospital, but you must put a stop to this because it's insane; no good will come from it." She hesitated, "It will destroy you."

She entered the hospital, heading up to the first floor as she had so many times over the last few days. Passing the ward's reception station a young woman, whom she had not seen before, enquired who it was she had come to visit.

"Nathan Trent, he's in . . ."

But before she could finish her sentence the woman spoke in an authoritative tone. "Are you a relative?"

She'd never been asked this before, but there again the woman appeared new to the job and clearly conscientious.

"I've been visiting him since he was admitted after the accident." Her response was unexpected and left Eva cold. "I see, so you are not family are you?"

The directness threw Eva, "As I explained, I have been visiting regularly and I saw him yesterday."

Ignoring her pleas the woman continued, "When did you say you last saw him?"

"Late morning yesterday, why, does that matter?"

"You must understand he is not well." The young woman, realising that Eva was not fully aware of the situation, added, "Let me call the doctor."

In a matter of minutes the duty doctor appeared and, recognising Eva, he took her to one side. "I am afraid you can't see him." He explained that Nathan's health had deteriorated during the night and his condition had become unstable necessitating his transfer to a different ward where he was being monitored more closely. He had collapsed several times during the evening and complained of dizziness, and seemed very anxious. They were in the process of carrying out more tests to ascertain what exactly was wrong.

Eva stood speechless, shattered by the news, her eyes full of panic. The doctor, appreciating her distress, attempted to reassure her. "We will know more once we have the results of the tests," and with further consideration added, "leave your contact number with reception and we'll let you know if and when you can visit."

The telephone had rung twice before Eva managed to get the key into her apartment door, and by the time she got to the phone the caller had rung off. Her initial thought was that it was the hospital and she was annoyed with herself for having missed the call. Then she realised how ridiculous that was because even if they had managed to do further tests on Nathan, they wouldn't have got the results yet.

The phone rang again disturbing her chain of thought and, to her surprise, she heard Sabina's voice. "I thought I'd ring and see if you're alright?"

In a moment of honesty Eva confessed that she couldn't really think straight. "They wouldn't let me see Nathan, the doctor said there could be complications."

Sabina's momentary silence was broken, "You're besotted with him, aren't you?" Eva knew her well enough to realise she was jealous.

CHAPTER FOUR

The duty nurse pulled back the curtains and the invited morning sunlight filled the room with a warming glow. She checked the monitors and drip and then, once content, turned her attention to the patient himself. His disturbed night had taken its toll and an exhausted Nathan, still half asleep, restlessly turned in his bed. The initial tests had revealed no reason for concern and all his readings were normal.

Dr Thorirsson entered the room and demanded Nathan's attention. "It would appear your symptoms have abated and from what you have said, your memory is gradually returning. Nothing suggests to me we should alter our plans. We will keep you in for another forty-eight hours and if there is no change, you can leave." The doctor continued, cautioning Nathan, "It will be vital that if you have a recurrence of these or similar symptoms, you contact us immediately. Sister will discuss with you your discharge and she'll arrange for an appointment at the end of the week."

He paused, allowing what he had said to sink in. Formalities out of the way, Nathan was left alone to think about what his future might hold.

He was beginning to realise that maybe he had been naïve to come to Iceland, believing that such a trip would offer a distraction from the sad memories that burdened him at home. In his own way he had seen it is an adventure and, with a degree of apprehension, had been looking forward to it. Nathan would be the first to admit that he and the idea of adventure were not natural bed-fellows. Time and again his father had tormented him, accusing him of being feeble and pathetic – a man in name only. Mother had so often tried to calm the waters and build bridges between her husband and her son, but time and his father's tyrannical ways proved more than she could bear. Lost to periods of deep depression, she increasingly withdrew into herself, to a world none of them understood. As far as his father was concerned, Nathan knew that his own marriage to Lindsey had been the final act that sealed his fate. Not that Father violently disliked her. What in truth he loathed was the fact that this barren daughter-in-law would never give him a grandson, a child to continue the family line.

"Welcome to another day, are you alright?" a nervous Eva asked Nathan.

"Sure, they say I'm fine and I can leave."

"That's great news. I was so worried about you when they wouldn't let me visit."

Nathan seized on her remark. "They wouldn't let you visit?"

"No, they said you weren't well."

"I thought you'd just decided not to come."

"No," she said, then added, "What are you going to do? Where will you go? Who will look after you?"" The words flooded from her as she impulsively took his hand.

He told her he honestly had no idea. He had spoken with his contact at the university and they had obviously had to cancel his first lecture but were keen to reschedule when he felt up to it. The accommodation he'd booked had been lost so he would need to find somewhere else in the city, and quickly, although he hadn't as yet decided how long he would be staying.

Eva broke in, "You're welcome to stay with me until you sort yourself out."

"I don't know if that's a good . . ." His voice trailed off.

"What about your family," she said. "Have you spoken with them?" Nathan appeared to be lost in his thoughts. "Is there someone you need to contact?" she persisted.

Nothing she had said seemed to prompt an answer. She squeezed his hand and, as if by magic, his vacant gaze vanished and he was back with her. "What did you say?"

"Your family. Do you need to talk to them?" Recognising her

concern and wanting to keep nothing from her he attempted to appease her, sharing that he'd spoken with Jane and the boys in England, who now knew all that had happened.

CHAPTER FIVE

Eva's alarm beeped softly but it was still an annoying sound; any disturbance for her at 7:30 am was. Although the spring days were now lengthening, the uninviting cold black sky wouldn't see daylight until well after 8am. Showering, she dressed and gathered together her things for the morning's rehearsal whilst the life-saving coffee pot was percolating. There was a rap at her apartment door, Eva hurried to let her visitor in to avoid any further disturbance. Sabina was prompt as usual and burst in sharing her thoughts on the morning's traffic then adding, "When did you say you are getting your car back?"

"I didn't," confirmed Eva in a quieter tone, "but it looks like tomorrow. Can you keep your voice down," she said, glancing towards the spare bedroom door, hoping it wouldn't open.

"Why, who's here?" Sabina pressed in a half whisper.

A cough came from the room.

Eva said she would explain outside, but first she had to leave a note. Sabina was clearly frustrated, desperate to know who was hidden away. Eva, whilst writing the note, thought it was amazing that Sabrina had no idea and feared what her reaction would be when she told her.

"So tell me who it is?" came Sabina's words before they had even reached the stairs.

"Nathan." Eva thought this straightforward admission was the best way.

"Nathan?" Sabina was stunned. Reluctant to let Eva's admission go, Sabina repeated his name, "Nathan?" The disbelief in her voice was clearly evident.

"He's got nowhere else to go and the least I can do is to offer him a place to stay for a few days."

Sabina was speechless, a rare occurrence Eva thought.

Sabina's silence was too good to last, "So now you've shacked up with a complete stranger who you only met a week ago and who's eleven years older than you."

"It's not like that. He's just stopping over for a few days whilst he's lecturing at the university, and anyway, he's married with children."

They were now in the car and the busy traffic was proving an unwelcome distraction for Sabina as she tried to manoeuvre through both the congestion and the conversation on what was another rainy April day. That, however, didn't stop her exclaiming, "Married?"

An irritating car horn burst from behind them, a rude and impatient noise. Sabina responded with her horn and Eva saw this as the moment to end this increasingly difficult cross-examination. "Don't you think you should concentrate on the road?"

"Just tell me it's none of my business," Sabina shouted, "but don't ask me to get you out of a fix when it all goes wrong."

CHAPTER SIX

Nathan emerged from the bedroom dishevelled. Pressing a towel against his chin, he tried to stem the flow of blood from a cut made by his unsteady razor. Arriving late the evening before he had had little chance to familiarise himself with Eva's apartment. She had been out and left a spare key with a neighbour. The silence of the apartment now struck him, just the slow, deep sound of a clock. He called to Eva and was surprised when there was no answer. He stood in the middle of the spacious room, studying every aspect of her lounge. Cream walls were hung with landscapes, plaster cornices decorated the high white ceiling, and the woodwork, perhaps oak, was finished with varnish. Heavy drapes hung at the two large windows, the material of which matched the cushions on the brown leather sofa. On the mantel above the empty grate sat an old pendulum clock. A dozen or so photographs were arranged either side of the timepiece; probably family portraits, he thought. The alcove shelves were loaded with books and an untidy heap of music scores was piled beside a wooden table on which was an old computer. There was an all-pervading smell of furniture polish.

Exploring the room, he noticed a handwritten note trapped under a coffee-stained mug. *Gone to rehearsals, be back later with some lunch. Make yourself at home, bread and milk in kitchen. Hope you slept well. Left early and didn't want to disturb you. Eva.*

Nathan's attention was drawn again to the photographs. There was one of a young child, Eva he assumed, in the arms of a woman bathing in an outdoor pool, great plumes of steam rising from the water. Another was of a family group in a garden somewhere and one of a teenage girl, clearly Eva, dressed in a smart coat, bent over feeding a group of ducks on a lake. Several of the photographs were of groups, but one in particular caught his eye. It was a black and white print in a silver frame of two middle-aged men dressed in padded fur-lined jackets, arms about each other's shoulders, clearly enjoying themselves as they smiled at the camera. Thick snow lay everywhere and it looked as if it was still falling. What particularly interested Nathan was a massive sign behind the men upon which was the word, THULE. He was unfamiliar with it but assumed it was a place. He studied the back of the frame but that showed nothing more.

Curiosity led Nathan to the bookshelves with book after book in Icelandic, and just as he was about to give up hope of finding anything of interest, there, nestled amongst a batch of unpronounceable titles, was a map of Iceland. From a young age maps had held a fascination for him. He had spent hours studying his father's collection, imagining far-away lands and discovering hidden places nearer home. Spreading the map out on the floor he remembered that he'd left the tea still brewing in the kitchen. Tipping it away he started again. On the countertop was a newspaper, *Morgunblađiđ.* As he flicked the pages a photograph on a page entitled 'INTERNATIONAL NEWS' caught his attention. It showed a smiling-faced cosmonaut doing a thumbs-up. The Icelandic caption was translated in English below and read, 'The World's First Space Tourist'. Perhaps one day, Nathan thought to himself.

Nathan settled on the sofa and, sitting forward, he could easily see Iceland's rugged northern coastline in dramatic detail on the map. Encircling the whole island its only road clung in the south between Iceland's largest glacier, the Vatnajokull, and the ocean, while the fertile land to the west was home to the island's capital Reykjavik, Nathan's temporary refuge.

As his eyes travelled over Iceland's mountains and fjords, the apartment door burst open, and in barged an overloaded Eva struggling with a soaked coat, her music bag, violin case and a very damp smile.

"It's absolutely falling down again. They said there was a low to the south-west coming in from the Atlantic, perhaps a storm." She stopped abruptly and stared at Nathan who was by now standing, amused by her entrance. "You're bleeding, are you okay?" she said.

Nathan returned a puzzled glance, then realising he was still holding the bloodstained towel replied, "Oh, I cut myself shaving, sorry about the towel." Eva smiled, relieved.

"Have you been alright? Did you find some breakfast?" Nathan held up his cup as proof.

"Where was this photo taken, Eva?" He went across to the mantelpiece and picked up the one showing the girl in the pool. Eva, busy rearranging the bags, looked up.

"That one Father took: it's of Mother and me at the Blue Lagoon in mid-winter. We had great fun back then, they were good days and I miss her so."

Nathan sensed wistfulness in her reply as she disappeared into the kitchen.

"And what about this one?" He knew full well she couldn't see so followed her. "Who are these guys?"

Eva stopped what she was doing. "That's dear old Dad sporting the pipe with Uncle Ernst beside him. It was taken when they were in the military, way back in the sixties I think."

"Where's Thule?" Nathan asked with more than a passing interest. "I tried to find it on the map but without success. Whereabouts is it?"

Eva's answer surprised him. "Oh, it's in Greenland."

"What were they doing in Greenland?"

"It's a long story and not a good one. It's history, but being a stubborn old man, he won't let it go. I'm sure one day he'll bore you with it if you really want to know."

Humming, Eva busied herself in the kitchen, putting a ready-meal into the microwave. She stood and watched its turntable revolve behind the glass door. Some minutes later the bell of the microwave tinged like some fairground side show, and she smiled. She carried a tray loaded with bowls and glasses into the lounge, propped it on the corner of the table, cleared a space and laid up lunch.

"Eat it whilst it's hot." Nathan was uncertain what 'it' exactly was. It looked like a stew or broth but it smelt like nothing he had come across before. He could see various vegetables floating around, and his first few mouthfuls told him all he needed to know. Hard and somewhat stringy they all tasted much the same. The pieces of meat were surprisingly chewy considering how thinly sliced they were. He had no idea what meat it was and decided it was probably best he didn't know.

Eva looked up in between mouthfuls. "What do you think, is it okay?"

Nathan disguised well his indifference. "It's certainly filling," he managed to say as he tried to swallow a mouthful of doughy bread.

Misunderstanding the sentiment, Eva took it as a compliment and said, "Good, eat up, there's plenty more."

Retiring to the sofa with their glasses of beer they spent the remainder of the afternoon enjoying each other's company and talking.

"Have you always lived here?" Nathan said, glancing about the apartment.

"No. Home was a small off-island to the south. When Mother died I moved to the city and bought this apartment; I couldn't see a future for myself in that isolated spot. Reluctantly, Father soon followed and quickly made a new life for himself here. Mother would have loved Reykjavik, the vibrancy, energy and spirit of the place, but Father had always resisted such a move," Eva said. "Even now he says he still misses the angry seas and wild weather that buffeted our island home."

"What was your mother like?" he asked.

"Special," Eva replied without hesitation. "You would have loved her, everyone did. She never had an ill word to say about anyone, and somehow coped with dear old Dad and his peculiar ways. They doted on each other and after she passed away he was completely lost; it was sad to see him like that. Over time he began to fill his life again but he was never the same man."

Eva's earlier explanation that her father's story about Greenland was *not a good one* was enough to further fire Nathan's interest. "Tell me about Greenland," he said.

Her posture straightened; any appearance of being relaxed was gone. She glared. Nathan didn't feel it was at him but more through him. "Why do you want to know?" came her baffled reply.

"Oh, no particular reason, it just sounded interesting." He could see she was unsettled. "Is something worrying you? It's not the accident, is it?" he risked.

"No," she replied. Nathan sensed she was lost fleetingly in her own thoughts.

"Then what is it? Can you tell me? I know we hardly know each other but sometimes that makes it easier."

"It's my father," she said. He could hear the tension in her voice.

"What about him?"

"I don't know how well he really is. He doesn't seem at peace these days and I think it's this Greenland thing playing on his mind." The look of bewilderment that had occupied her face dissolved into an expression of amusement as her mood lightened. "Dad always described Greenland as one of the Americans' more crazy ideas." She sipped her beer. "Perhaps whatever he and Ernst were involved in turned out a bit crazy," she said.

"That sounds cynical," Nathan said.

"Being cynical is one of the talents Dad says I've inherited from him," she admitted.

"What other talents have you inherited?" he said.

Eva frowned, "I don't know."

"Music?"

"No, certainly not my music. In many ways I think of myself as quite ordinary. The only thing I feel strongly about is my music, some think almost obsessively so. Mother always said my creative flair and sensitivity originated from her side of the family, while Father attributed my sharp intellect as down to him, but I'm not sure about that. I've never been great with people I don't know well. I suppose I'm a fairly private person."

"Certainly our first meeting couldn't be regarded as a complete success could it?" Eva didn't answer him. "I was joking," Nathan added.

"And that's something that's not a strong point of mine – humour," she said through a half-smile. "Enough about me, what about you?"

"There's not much to tell. Apart from the usual student jobs in restaurants and as a ski instructor, I've been an academic all my working life. As the years have moved on I've found myself undertaking more consultancy."

"What's your subject or should I say specialism?" she asked.

"Glaciers."

"Right." He sensed she didn't know what to say.

"Over the past few years I've attempted to reappraise my life and work out what I should do in the future."

"That sounds dramatic," she said. "What have you in mind?"

"That's the problem: as yet nothing, to be honest," Nathan said, aware that Eva was trying to read between the lines.

"You don't like talking about yourself, do you?" she said, taunting.

"There's really not much to tell, I'm not that interesting."

Eva dismissed his reply with a shake of her head. "What about your mother and father? What are they like?"

"My mother was the exact antithesis of my father – selfless, unassuming and loving, fighting hard to keep our family together and happy, while Father did all in his power to pull us apart. I don't know if that was intentional but, nevertheless, that was how it was. Whether she truly loved him, or held on to the old fashioned principle that the head of the family was the man, I'll never know." Nathan became aware of a harshness in his voice and he wondered if Eva, this relative stranger, had detected the deep disdain he had felt towards his father.

"You didn't like him much, did you?" Eva cautiously ventured.

"He's dead now, but no, I didn't." This young woman's intuition had led her directly to the truth. He felt his whole body tense and what seemed like a stifling fog fill his head. "I don't know why I'm telling you this."

Nathan thought he would need to be more guarded in future.

"Is there anyone close to you, Eva, other than your father?"

She considered how to answer.

"No, not now. I had a boyfriend back along but he found it impossible to share me with my music so we agreed to split. It never would have worked out, we weren't good for each other. And you? Forgive me for saying, I know England's a long way away, but why has no one come to see you?"

A sudden strong gust of wind rattled the window panes and the sound of the pounding downpour seemed louder than before. Something told Nathan that this was a storm that was just beginning.

CHAPTER SEVEN

Across the city, nestled next to the British and German embassies on Hellusundi, stood a small red, wooden building, in front of which a substantial red rock had been erected. Here seventy-one year old, wizened Magnus Jóhannes Sigurdsson, Eva's father, had been busy threading the leader of a 16mm cine film through the gate of the Eiki projector. This was the Red Rock Cinema and Magnus, the Volcano Man, was busy with the projector, rewinding the film ready for the next performance. The noise of the rattling spools meant he was clearly taken by surprise when Eva appeared with Nathan.

Magnus looked up. "If it isn't my dear Eva, and who's this fellow with you?" he challenged, and before she had a chance to answer he continued, "He's not a spy is he?" and laughed as his attention was drawn to the projector where the film leader was now flipping against the housing. Eva smiled at Nathan looking somewhat embarrassed. But Magnus didn't give up. "Oh, this isn't the fellow you tried to kill?" Glancing at Nathan he said in cynical tone, "You didn't do much of a job, he looks very much alive to me," and chuckled. "So to what do I owe the company of my beautiful, wayward daughter?"

Eva said, "We thought we'd say hello and see if you wanted to come for a coffee after the show? But if you're . . ."

Magnus could tell she was about to excuse him, but he wasn't going to let her off that easily. "Sure, grab yourselves a seat and enjoy the show."

As the two of them sat down Eva apologised for her father's humour and Nathan asked her, "What's this about being a spy?"

She dismissed his comment, saying, "He's completely hung up about something that happened years ago."

The hundreds of performances that Magnus had orchestrated had taken their toll. Magnus's unemotional voice boomed out from the front of the tiny auditorium and the audience listened attentively to his welcome; words he had repeated so many times before.

"Our world is violently changing. Every year there are one and a half million earthquakes worldwide, and fifteen hundred electric storms that chase over our planet. Every three months a tsunami races across the Pacific Ocean, every six hours a tornado tears across our lands and each second eleven lightning bolts strike the earth. There are over five hundred volcanoes in Iceland alone and here an eruption occurs every two weeks. Each year we are subjected to hundreds of earthquakes, fortunately many are minor.

"One of the last times we had a quake close to here, near Hekla, was the summer of 2000, during my afternoon show. The violence of the 6.5 quake shook our little cinema and the audience, who felt the whole place tremor, thought it was part of the performance. Oblivious to the real occurrence they congratulated me on the realism of the special effect!" There was a laugh of acknowledgement amongst his audience.

Ensuring the film was engaged in the projector's sprockets, he flipped on the motor and lamp switches and, with a clatter, the projector came to life. The reels whirled and another masterpiece from the renowned Icelandic filmmaker, Knudsen, began to reveal the spectacle of nature's amazing creation. The Volcano Show had begun, transporting not only Nathan and Eva but also the dozen or so curious and eager tourists into *'Iceland's Volcanic Adventure'.*

The magic of cinematography was rudely interrupted when the picture shuddered on the screen, and the film jammed and broke. Magnus stirred himself from his chair and, muttering under his breath, announced to the expectant audience that, like the real volcano show which had been running for millions of years, nothing was going to stop today's performance. His fingers worked nimbly and, to a feeble round of applause, the performance recommenced. Magnus settled down again next to piles of dusty film canisters containing Knudsen's life-time work. Eva explained to Nathan that the films held little interest to him these days as he could visualise in his mind's eye every scene and knew

Knudsen's impassioned narration by heart, and anyway, at his age regular naps had become second nature to him. While the echoing eruptions of volcanoes and the mighty rumblings of earthquakes captivated the cinema goers, Magnus managed to doze.

The tourists mingled in the foyer, briefly discussing the dramatic presentation with one another and, on thanking Magnus, headed out into the bright daylight. Having straightened the *Fire and Ice* wall map and rearranged the literature display that one of the children had fiddled with, Magnus announced, "Coffee."

Magnus pushed open the door of the cafe and called out to the waitress, "Three coffees please, Kristjana," as they settled at a table.

Wearing baggy blue overalls, which looked two sizes too big, and wiping his nose with a handkerchief he took from a torn trouser pocket, Magnus said, "So Mister —"

"Nathan Trent," Eva interjected.

"What are you doing in Iceland, Nathan Trent?"

Nathan smiled and, as he replied, Eva edged forward on her seat as if preparing to be enlightened.

"Well, to be completely honest I'm not totally sure. I was going to be lecturing at your university and, I believe, involved in some joint research."

Magnus turned to his daughter, "Maybe you've done a better job than I thought. What sort of research?" he said once again addressing Nathan.

"Glaciology, that's my area of specialism."

"When you say joint research, what exactly is it that you do?" Magnus asked, inquisitively. "And who for?"

Eva could see a puzzled and confused expression creep over Nathan's face as he searched for the answer. Magnus, aware that Nathan was struggling, eased any momentary embarrassment. "No matter, my daughter's often been likened to an interrogator, so if anyone can help you through your mental haze, she can."

"Dad!" but Eva's exclamation was short-lived.

"I know one thing, I am certainly not a spy," Nathan said to Magnus with a twinkle in his eye. "You're worried that people are watching you, aren't you?"

Magnus glared at Eva, "What's she been filling your head with?" In an instant any playfulness had gone from his voice and the old man's demeanour had, like the swirling Arctic wind, changed.

CHAPTER EIGHT

The air smelt clean and invigorating as Nathan stepped out onto Stangarholt. The morning rain had refreshed the city. Within a few minutes he was strolling along the narrow Main Street, joining locals, their bags tightly gripped, scurrying purposefully home before the next shower.

Reykjavik had grown on Nathan and he felt an affinity for this place. Its provincial character was something he hadn't expected from a European capital; the city's charm came as a surprise. It was as if he had fallen into a time warp; nothing around him held any resemblance to his family home in London or, for that matter, where he lived now in Wales. What had been a lecture trip and a chance to promote his latest book was turning into something very different. The close encounter with death had heralded what he now considered to be a journey of discovery, in a land he was unfamiliar with.

Reaching the reception hall of the university, he enquired of a young woman the whereabouts of the Department of Earth Sciences, mentioning his appointment with the faculty head. She phoned through and, within a few minutes, a man who looked to be in his late sixties descended the stairs and, in a perfect English accent, was greeting Nathan as if he was a long lost friend. Nathan couldn't help but think that Professor Arni Schott looked like a one-time member of a sixties rock band who, although finding himself well into his golden years, had decided not to move with the times. Schott's face bore all the scars of a misspent youth, and he celebrated the fact with his silver tumbling locks gathered back in a ponytail. His stature was upright, proudly so, and his movements were deliberate and steady. The once rock star's attire had given way to a black suit, white collarless shirt and brown brogues.

"You must call me Arni," Schott said insistently as they chatted. Nathan quickly warmed to the man, recognising him as a cultured and refined academic. He couldn't but wonder if Arni's years of study bore any resemblance to his own and, as they made their way through the maze of corridors, Nathan found himself reflecting on his early life.

Academic study had come naturally to Nathan. One of two children to Charles and Elizabeth, his early years were full of marvellous memories: glorious summer garden parties, extravagant family holidays abroad and fabulous birthday and Christmas celebrations. Whilst his mother's love had to be shared two ways, there was only one child as far as his father was concerned – his son, who he would parade at all the social functions much to Nathan's annoyance. Father's career in the Army necessitated Nathan's parents being abroad for long stretches of time so consequently, he and his older sister, Jane, were packed off to boarding schools. This, for Nathan, was a life of mixed blessings: he missed his sister with whom he had been so close. He rose to the academic challenges placed upon him and suffered the brutality of the school bullies and rugby toffs. Over and over again his father's words would haunt him: *you mustn't let the buggers grind you down, boy. Unless you toughen up you'll never rise in the ranks – we need real men out there running our wars.* Nathan's unfailing commitment to his studies ensured that any experience or knowledge of the worldly kind was delayed until university, where a new-found freedom awaited him. Nathan seized on this with a renewed appetite and wasted no time in making up lost ground.

Meanwhile, Jane, whilst training to be a nurse in Cambridge, fell for Duncan, a paediatrician with an eye for the women and sports cars. They were wed and, within twenty months, twins, Christopher and Phillip, were born. With Jane very much the committed home mother, Duncan's roving eye soon focused on some American bio-chemist visiting England on a year's sabbatical. When she left to return to the States Duncan went with her. Nathan was devastated for his sister and nephews, so much so that his farewell meeting with his departing brother-in-law resulted in a fight from which neither emerged unscathed.

Nathan subsequently graduated with a first and went on to study for his doctorate, balancing his research so that he could spend as much time with his sister and the boys as his studies at Aberystwyth University allowed. Here he met Lindsey, a fellow student, and fell helplessly in love with this wild beauty who, on the 29th February 1988, proposed marriage to him. The following years were the most joyous of his life.

Over time Jane and Lindsey became like sisters and, after the passing of Nathan's parents, the three of them and the boys became even closer. Not blessed with children, Nathan and Lindsey threw themselves into their careers. Lindsey's expertise in Environmental Engineering ensured a successful placement in a top London consultancy, while Nathan pursued research with Aberystwyth University and the Open University. Much to Nathan's delight and peace of mind, his sister came out of the break-up stronger and more independent than before. Once the boys were settled in school she got herself a part-time agency job and, in her own right, became firmly ensconced in the 'Hertfordshire Set', joining the women's team at the local golf club.

It was shortly after Nathan and Lindsey's move to Hertfordshire that they were given the dreadful news. Nathan was devastated. Lindsey's prognosis was without hope – six to twelve months, but as is often the case, the prognosis was too optimistic. During her last weeks Nathan and Lindsey were even closer than they had been during their seven brief years of marriage. Jane dedicated herself to nursing her beloved sister-in-law to the end, and fulfilled a promise she had made to Lindsey to be there for Nathan and help him rebuild his life.

Jane and the boys were Nathan's only family now: they were his life.

"Our university is an old institution, but of course, not as old as some of yours in England, but we are proud to be rated within the 'Top 300' in the world." Arni's words brought Nathan crashing back to reality.

"That's a tremendous achievement," Nathan said. "The university is far larger than I anticipated."

"Oh, well, we employ some fourteen hundred staff on our ten hectare site," Arni shared.

Making themselves comfortable in the burgundy leather easy chairs that sat before Arni's grand oak desk, a spidery, middle-aged woman in her mid-forties efficiently served them with tea and some sort of rye biscuit, then departed as quietly as she had entered.

"All Englishmen drink tea, is that right Professor?" Arni said, and laughed.

"Yes, Professor," Nathan replied, and laughed too.

Arni settled back and studied his colleague. "First Nathan, you must tell me all that has happened since you arrived on our shores. When we couldn't contact you ahead of the lecture, we had no alternative but to cancel. We even got hold of Aberystwyth but they could throw no light on what had happened."

Clearly, Arni had all the time in the world, Nathan considered, and he began to tell his story. He went into great detail about his flight, and how arriving at the airport bus terminal in Reykjavik there were no taxis available to take him to his hotel; they were ferrying other poor souls who didn't want to get soaked. He described his stay in hospital and the visit by the police, the temporary loss of memory as well as his initial impressions of the city, but he failed to mention about Eva. Nathan tried to convince himself that Arni wouldn't be interested.

After fifteen minutes Arni chose to speak.

"It doesn't sound to me like our usual Icelandic welcome, Nathan, but I'm glad to see you survived. And now, are you up for this lecture?"

"Sure, if you can re-schedule," said Nathan.

"Don't worry, I have already taken that liberty: next Friday evening is your second lecture date. Is that okay with you?"

Nathan had no need to confer with his diary and agreed.

"Now our business is out of the way, let's have a proper drink before I show off my department to you."

For the next two hours Arni and Nathan relished each other's company, jostling intellectually, sharing their research findings and discussing future global challenges. After a relaxing light lunch together the two parted company. A mutual warmth and respect had developed between them, a real friendship, the intimacy and depth of which surprised even Nathan. However, what was unclear in Nathan's mind was how he would cope with delivering his lecture.

Nathan arrived back at Eva's apartment before she had returned from the concert hall. He let himself in with the spare key and dumped his bag of food on the counter in the kitchen. He had no idea if Eva was bringing a meal home so he started to explore the possibilities with the few groceries he had got. Nothing immediately came to mind. *That's the problem when you just grab what you fancy rather than what you need,* he thought to himself. A quick study of her kitchen appliances told Nathan that the safest bet was probably the microwave. He thought it looked pretty ancient and, after a quick play with its controls, realised it was nothing like his one at home. The microwave tinged and he felt obliged to open its door although he knew nothing was on its turntable.

He heard a key in the apartment door and, to his relief, Eva's voice, "Are you back already?" She entered, arms straining under the weight of bulging shopping bags. "I've picked up some fish and vegetables for supper." Then, seeing the array of produce on the counter, she enquired, "What delicacy did you have in mind?"

After the meal they shared the events of the day: Nathan's mooch around Reykjavik in the mist and rain, and for Eva, the orchestra's run-through of a piece by a composer Nathan had never heard of. An unexpected knock at her apartment door startled Eva. The rap came again, this time with greater urgency. It was apparent to Nathan that Eva wasn't expecting anyone. She rose, looked towards him then, mumbling something under her breath, made to answer it. For the third time the caller rapped. Their impatience was clearly irritating Eva who called out, "Okay, okay," in an annoyed tone. As she opened the door to the communal landing, Nathan could just make out what appeared to be two official looking men, the taller of the two resting his shoulder on the door frame. He straightened and spoke, "Eva Jóhannesdóttir?"

"Hannes, yes, and you are?" she said. Before either had the chance to respond Eva had opened the door just wide enough for the men to be aware that she was not alone.

"Police Officers Andri and Hinrik," one announced. Nathan saw each in turn flip open a pass and the glint of their badges. "We wish to talk with you; can we come in?"

Reluctantly Eva beckoned them in. Closing the door she challenged them, "What is this all about, why are you here?"

Hinrik, the taller, athletic-looking officer, acknowledged Nathan then turned to his partner, who addressed Eva.

"We have been going through the record of your interview that you made at the police station following the recent accident you were involved in."

Giving him no time to continue she said, "Yes?"

"We wouldn't normally do this but we were passing by and there was something we wanted to clear up."

Eva nodded, but Nathan couldn't help notice a look of annoyance on her face.

"And who is this gentleman?" the crabby-faced officer, Andri, asked turning to Nathan.

"This is a friend, Nathan," she explained firmly. "So what else is it you need to know?"

Nathan considered that both policemen greeted the confirmation of his identity with a measure of satisfaction. Andri, without a word, settled in a chair and, in an authoritative voice, told Eva to sit down. He coughed, clearing his throat, and looking towards her for clarification said, "Before we discuss anything I need you to explain exactly what your relationship with this," he paused and glanced towards Nathan, "gentleman is?"

"I told you," she hesitated, "a friend," then added, "from England."

"Have you known him long?"

"No, not long."

"Maybe no more than a couple of weeks?" Andri suggested fixing her with a precise glare.

"Yes, maybe."

Hinrik's next question was unexpected. "This wouldn't be the Englishman that you were involved in a road accident with, would it? Mr Nathan Trent?" Standing opposite him he eyed Nathan for any reaction.

Nathan quickly interjected, "Yes, but it wasn't her fault."

"I see," replied Andri appearing to be totally unsurprised at the answer. "We know you had no intentions of pressing charges, is that still the case Mr Trent?"

"Yes," Nathan replied emphatically.

Turning his attention to Eva the officer said, "You will I am sure, Miss Hannes, be aware that officers have already spoken to Mr Trent.

You may not, however, realise that a witness to the incident has also made a formal statement."

With that it was apparent to Nathan, that Eva was becoming increasingly agitated.

"Who?" she insisted.

"The old man at the scene. Our officers who attended the accident took his details and, subsequently, he made a statement at the station." As if further clarity was needed he added, "He was the man trying to bring you around, Mr Trent." Andri paused, as if waiting to measure her reaction.

"So what was it you wanted to clear up?" Eva said.

"Oh yes," Andri said, "we have your mobile phone. After confiscating it from you following the accident we checked it for calls to establish you were not using it at the time. That being the case we've finished with it," and he handed it to her.

While the officers edged towards the door, Officer Hinrik said in a low hoarse voice, "As things stand we don't believe you committed any offence but the garage hasn't as yet finished inspecting your car."

"You surely don't think I hit him deliberately?" she said in despair, but the two men were already heading for the stairs.

Nathan saw confusion and disbelief haunting Eva's face. He attempted to reassure her. "You've no need to worry, I know it was an accident."

She looked at Nathan and opened her mouth but no words came out.

That night Nathan experienced the most terrifying dream. He visualised himself naked, half buried to his waist in snow. In every direction there was nothing but an endless white expanse. He had no sense of place, no sense of being, imprisoned and freezing in this icy grave. He could faintly hear in the distance the creaking sound of giant cataracts fracturing from monolithic ice cliffs and calving into the sea. Above him the endless whiteness was bearing down upon him. Try as he might, he could not free himself from this icy tomb; his clawing fingers were numb and without feeling. Nathan's chest burned with exertion. Finally fatigue overcame him, and with it feelings of inadequacy and helplessness filled his head. Despair seeped through his body. Slowly the snow was taking him and now it had come for his very soul.

A singular, haunting howl penetrated the void. Then, filling the air around him, came the savage barking of hungry wolves. They drew nearer, their endless wailing cries resounding in his head. Beasts leapt from nowhere, falling upon him, clawing, digging at the snow packed around him. As they began to loosen it so Nathan could sense their ravenous excitement and anticipation. Long trails of yellow glutinous saliva dripped from their mouths as they snapped their jaws, first at each other, tearing their flesh, then at him. Doomed, Nathan could see his body slide from him, down through the thick pack ice into the freezing depths of the ocean. The bitter cold squeezed the air from his lungs like a vice and ate deeper into his frigid bones. And then, in that lonely grave, floating beneath a frozen sky, all was silent, except, that is, for the racing beat of Nathan's own heart. Anger consumed him as he battled against the overwhelming grief of his end.

As suddenly as the twisted irrationality of Nathan's dreams had crushed him, so it left him. Soaked in sweat, and lying exhausted, his disorientated mind raced, trying to make sense of anything.

Standing before the bathroom basin he washed. Steam clouded the basin mirror. He took a towel, wiped the misted glass and looked at himself long and hard. He rubbed the centre of the mirror, this time with the back of his hand. The glass squeaked. Not liking what he saw, he splashed his face with cold water, soaking the floor. Water ran off his chin as he dragged his hand down his face. Finding aspirins in the bathroom cabinet, he put three or four into his mouth, intending to wash them down with water cupped in his hands. He looked again in the mirror then spat the tablets into the basin, running the tap to wash them away.

"Welcome to another day," Eva called from the doorway as she set down his first coffee of the morning on the chest of drawers. Some sort of classical music was playing in the background. "Breakfast in ten minutes, okay?" she added as she returned to the kitchen. In an attempt to recapture reality, Nathan grunted in agreement.

Over breakfast Nathan sensed that Eva's frustration of the day before had almost melted away and he decided to make no mention of it.

"Today is a special day for you, I believe possibly the start of a new adventure," Eva said coyly. "You have been summoned by the great Magnus."

"Why? What for?"

She continued, "Well, you obviously made a big impression on him. Oh, and I told him that you wanted to know about Thule."

"What did you say that for? I just asked about the photograph. What made you mention it?"

"Nothing," said Eva indignantly, surprised at Nathan's over-reaction, "but I think you might get answers you weren't banking on. It would be good if you could get him to drop his foolish campaign."

Nathan's head started to pound and he felt an unexplained tightness throughout his body, it passed in a matter of minutes but left him wondering and anxious.

* * * *

Magnus refused Nathan's outstretched hand as he stepped into the old man's kitchenette. Magnus put the sharp blade and partly gutted fish on the drainer, washed his hands under the flowing tap and, having wiped the worst off on a towel, gripped Nathan's hand firmly.

"It's good to see you my boy, although I've got to say you don't look too well." Magnus's iron grip belied his aged and feeble appearance.

As Nathan's face gradually gave birth to a grin of acknowledgement, Magnus let go and turned and smiled at Eva. Now that the vice-like sensation had ceased, Nathan noticed the all-pervading smell of the ocean, the stench of fish.

They sat opposite each other in easy chairs, Eva to the side of them. Nathan had wondered how he would start this strange conversation but, unprompted, Magnus spoke.

"You asked about Thule, so, if you will humour an old man I will recount an episode that took place there that many would wish to forget. To begin we will have to go back thirty-three years; that's when the true horror of what happened deep under the Greenland ice cap was discovered. For many that dark day changed their lives forever."

The old man struggled to gather his thoughts, obviously fighting off his emotions. For forty minutes Magnus related the story as it happened whilst Nathan sat silent, hanging on the old man's every word.

At the end Magnus said, "Can I read you my brother's letter? I think it will be of interest to you." Magnus turned to Eva for the first time since he had started to speak, "I know, my dear, you have never heard Ernst's last words," and picking the letter up from the table he began to read.

When you read this I will be no more. It had never been my intention to write about my time in the army as, for heaven's sake, who would be interested, but after those dreadful events I felt duty-bound and unable not to do so. Reliving my frightful memories of those days at Camp Century and Thule, a wretched sickness stirred inside as I recalled those that had gone, gone forever, now only names.

I was certain that one day their end would equally prove to be mine. I wrote this knowing that whoever should read it would no longer be able to ask me what happened. So it fell to me to set to paper what did really happen in 1968, far up in the frozen north of Greenland. It may well be that no one else has ever told what happened. Some may have wanted to but were too ill to coherently relate the events of that time. So that's why I began to write my account, each day adding to it as the memories returned.

At the outset I had prayed that I would be able to sustain my strength long enough to complete the task, but over time, as I became increasingly frail and weak, it was harder. I pressed on knowing that the full story needed to be told. I don't know who would be the last to see me alive, but that, in many ways, is immaterial. What is important is that you are hearing my final words.

Along with this letter is the account of those days that led up to that fateful event, and a photograph of me taken long before I fell ill, when I was full of life. Although, over the following years, life was slowly sapped from me, I want to be remembered as I once was.

Ernst Sigurdsson

Magnus handed Ernst's account and photograph to Nathan. It showed a strapping young man that Nathan clearly recognised as the fellow standing beside Magnus in the picture on Eva's mantelpiece. Passing it to Eva he glanced at the account: forty-three pages of neat handwriting in English, on narrow-lined foolscap.

"It's in English," Nathan remarked, as he slid it back into its envelope.

"Yes," Magnus said, looking exhausted by the ordeal while managing a smile of recognition. "I believe an old friend wrote it out for him; Ernst wanted everyone to know what happened.

Nathan said he would study it closely – that was the very least he could do, he assured him.

On their way back to her apartment, Eva began to share some of her fears about her father.

"Ever since Dad started trying to search out their gang from the old days, he has become paranoid that he is being observed and that someone is interested in what he's doing; tell me, how preposterous is that?"

Nathan, thrown by this revelation, attempted to clarify things. "Who does he think is following him?"

He needn't have bothered because Eva just dismissed what she considered was a stupid idea. "It's an over-active imagination," she said. "He's got too much time on his hands, but if you really want to be bored for hours on end, I'm sure he'll tell you."

Eva clearly had no intention of discussing it further, yet Nathan thought it might prove interesting to take it up with Magnus when he had the opportunity. He wondered why anyone would be interested in what an old man like Magnus got up to: an old man who, Nathan considered, from their brief time together, was level-headed and not prone to imagining things. For a fleeting moment Nathan had the most ridiculous thought that maybe this was a chance to bring some excitement back into his life; his father had persistently accused him of lacking any sense of adventure. He had long been finding university life getting him down – endless policies and procedures, mundane research projects, sponsorship dinners and irritating, immature students who wanted to spend their academic year drinking and having sex. Britain could be a pretty bleak and miserable place, Nathan mused. Surely Greenland can't be any worse, he said to himself.

That evening Eva attended rehearsals leaving Nathan to his own devices. He settled himself in an armchair, a glass of whisky close to hand, and began reading Ernst's bold and moving account. Three hours later Eva returned to find him dozing. Amazingly he hadn't touched a drop of the whisky. Nathan was, once again, lost to this world, dreaming, but this nightmare was very different to his last. This one felt real. This one scared him.

US AIR FORCE BASE, THULE – GREENLAND
Sunday January 21st, 1968

CHAPTER NINE

As Roy switched on the radio the power indicator glowed and a deep hum vibrated the cabinet of the set. He spun the tuning knob of his shortwave transceiver and the noise of static and interference assaulted his ears. Turning down its volume, he played with the band control while waiting for the valves to heat up before he fine-tuned the frequency.

This January afternoon was much like any other up in the far north of Greenland: dark as night and a whistling wind whipping up the fresh powder snow, piling it against Roy's squat hut. The base was normally dead on Sunday, however, today was different. A bright yellow-orange aura flared on the horizon created by burning wreckage out towards Wholstenholme Fjord. He had felt and heard the impact. It took a couple of telephone calls to realise this was no engineers' blast as they surveyed the ice sheet. This was the downing of a bomber, a fully armed American B-52 Stratofortress equipped with four nuclear warheads.

His ears tuned into a burbled wireless message, Roy concentrated, fiddling with the dials. He flicked the transmit switch on the table mic and began to speak, giving his call sign. Within a matter of minutes Roy's revelation was being sent, bouncing off the ionosphere, to distant lands, to whoever was listening. He heard no response: it was as if it had been swallowed by the silence.

Not until the early hours of the morning of Monday January 22nd 1968, did the first news of the disaster break. The persistent overnight rain had cleared and a bright balmy day was in store for Londoners. At the London premises of Reuters in Fleet Street, an operator was busy receiving a message over the telex network from their North American office. The Olivetti teleprinter chattered away as the news flash came in, and punched paper tape reeled from its heart. As soon as the printer had stopped, the operator began transmitting the message to subscribers.

Five hundred yards down the street a portly sub-editor of a second-rate tabloid stirred; the click-clacking of the office teleprinter had disturbed his early morning meditation. The carriage of the machine jerked from side-to-side like some demented loom. He grasped the edge of the typed paper and tore it against the slit of the machine. As he started to read so did scores of other newspaper hacks spread halfway around the world; Reuters' mainframe computer had, once again, worked its magic. He huffed a half interested huff and, tossing the sheet into the 'transmissions receival' tray, thought to himself, *Is there nothing new, nothing that hasn't happened before,* and slumped down in his leather swivel chair to study the weekend's sport pages.

The following day the *Petersburg Times* in the US ran the story. The brief report was lost somewhere between a smash and grab in the local shopping mall and a developer's fraudulent land deal. *'Crash on Sunday near Thule sending shudders through nuclear-nervous Denmark and raising the spectre for the missing bomb under the polar ice.'*

The Pentagon was quoted as saying, there was *'no danger, the bomb's not armed'.* Several papers revealed that The Atomic Energy Commission were to despatch three experts to help locate the weapons, purely as a matter of routine. The front page headlines of the day were given over to the Apollo 5 launch from Cape Kennedy, and the unmanned lunar module's 'fire in the hole' test as the Americans ventured to land on the moon. The Danish press made no mention of the Thule incident, perhaps because they were too pre-occupied with news of their national election. Maybe some external pressure had been brought to bear in an attempt to suppress the disturbing news.

REYKJAVIK – ICELAND
2001

CHAPTER TEN

The black Mercedes weaved through Reykjavik's Friday rush hour traffic, alongside Lake Tjörnin, heading for the university campus. Seated in the rear, an anxious Nathan was poring over his notes. The car pulled up onto the concourse in front of an austere, white three-storey building which was home to the School of Engineering and Natural Sciences. The driver directed Nathan towards the entrance of the Askja Building. Inside, a young man approached him, checked his identity and explained that Professor Schott wished to be informed immediately upon his arrival.

The Main Lecture Hall was vast. He nervously asked Arni how large an audience he anticipated.

"Give it forty minutes and we will see," Arni replied smiling. They climbed the steps to the platform and Nathan surveyed all before him. The red upholstered seating tiered steeply, and high at the back of the auditorium a trickle of guests was beginning to arrive. Behind him, stretching the full width of the platform, a screen displayed an image of Athena's head, which Nathan recognised as the university's emblem. Beneath it were the words, *The Institute of Earth Sciences Lectures, Professor Nathan E. Trent.* Nathan stepped up to the glass lectern and began to arrange his papers, taking particular care with their order. He adjusted its light, but in the process was distracted by a general hubbub in the hall. Glancing up again he was surprised to now see sixty or more faces looking at him. Arni touched him on the shoulder and, turning, Nathan saw an attractive woman, smartly dressed in a black trouser suit, standing beside Arni. Nathan was sure he recognised her.

"I would like to introduce you to the sponsor of tonight's lecture, and our 'anchor', as they say in the business." Arni was clearly enjoying his joke. "Kirstin, this is Professor Nathan Trent."

The young woman beamed, "Professor, I am delighted to meet you and so glad that you are able to honour us tonight."

"It's my pleasure," Nathan replied.

"Kirstin is one of our more distinguished graduates," Arni glanced towards her, "of a few years back now," she acknowledged him, "and is something of a major celebrity here in Iceland." Nathan's interest in the woman was further heightened. "A journalist, documentary film maker, Left Green Party politician, and author – like yourself Nathan. You may well have seen her presenting our weekly television news programme. Kirstin will say a few preliminary words then introduce us both and, as we agreed Nathan, initially we will begin with an informal interview, mentioning your new book, then it's over to you. Are we all okay with that?" And in the absence of an objection Arni added, "Good," as they left the platform.

Fifteen minutes later, to rousing applause, Kirstin stepped into the spotlight before an audience of five hundred or more. "I am truly excited to be able to welcome you all to what I know will prove to be a most thought provoking evening. It is a great honour to be asked to introduce Professor Arni Schott, Director of The Institute of Earth Sciences and the Nordic Volcanological Centre here at the University of Iceland. Professor Schott will be in conversation with our keynote speaker, the highly distinguished glaciologist, Professor Nathan Trent, discussing his latest book and his work with The Centre for Glaciology, at Aberystwyth University in Wales. Professor Trent's lecture will focus on his research of glacial dynamics – identifying, measuring and interpreting glacial change in the Arctic region, as well as its actual and projected environmental impacts. A field of work I know many of us have a profound concern for as we speculate on the future of our earth. Ladies and gentlemen, it is with great pleasure that I welcome both Professors Schott and Trent, tonight's speakers, onto the platform."

The hall echoed to a warm welcome as Kirstin gestured across the platform to the two men, who were now busy settling themselves in black leather chairs across a glass coffee table upon which microphones and a water jug and glasses were arranged.

Arni was first to speak. "Breaking with tradition, many of you will be aware that tonight's keynote speaker and my new-found friend and colleague, Professor Trent, is the only speaker we have felt worthy to invite back for a second time before he has addressed us once." The crowd awarded Arni's humour with warm laughter. "I know, Nathan, it was no fault of yours that you were unable to attend your first lecture, but we are all delighted that you are well enough to be with us tonight." Spontaneous clapping broke out.

"Thank you," Nathan said, acknowledging Arni's playfulness with a nod.

"Firstly, I'd like to talk about your new book, *For the End of the Earth.*" As Arni spoke an image of the book's front cover was projected onto the screen behind them. It featured a giant, blue ice-cliff breaking away and sliding into the sea. Dwarfed below was a tiny sailing ship floating perilously close.

Arni went on, "Before I ask you to introduce us to this work, I must share a quote from the pen of no less an individual than the internationally respected politician, campaigner for the environment and climate protection and past US Vice President, Andrew Gerri.

"Professor Nathan Trent's latest book, is both an amazing and extraordinary work. In a clear and concise way Professor Trent describes how glaciers work, how they live today on the cold of past ages, and how the processes of glacial erosion impact on our changing earth, bringing together numerous state-of-the-art research contributions from around the world. This book is a unique and invaluable wake-up call of what lies ahead in our beautiful and dangerous world . . . an alarm call for all of us."

A chorus of applause rang out.

"That's high praise from somebody of such stature and influence," Arni said.

"Yes, but I really must explain," interrupted a slightly embarrassed Nathan. "You see, my publishers approached Andrew to write the foreword for my book knowing that, when asked to write a review for the media, as undoubtedly he would be, it would be a glowing one." The audience were laughing, having already guessed where this explanation was going. Nathan continued, "The insane scale and power of glaciers are beyond our wildest dreams; we must prepare for the inconceivable and the inevitable. I believe that it is vital that each of us recognises the significance of these creations and their impact on our changing planet."

"Nathan," Arni said, "would you share with us an extract from your book, from the prologue, to set the scene on this freezing world?"

Nathan moved closer to his microphone and, opening his book, began to read.

"At the peak of the Arctic winter its freeze spreads across the Arctic Ocean for some 5.8 million square miles, yet the evidence shows that the ice is thinning. Historic aerial reconnaissance demonstrates that the Arctic's ice edge is retreating further north, and so are the creatures that inhabit the High Arctic as they compete with reducing coastal harvest areas for food and survival.

"As the sea ice declines, so does the earth's natural reflector that returns the sun's heat back into space. The more the ice melts in the Arctic summer, the more heat is absorbed by the ocean. Because the melt water is cold and fresh and caps the North Atlantic, it prevents warm water moving north, disrupting the earth's current system – the *global conveyor belt.* Eventually, when the waters warm and the melt reduces so the conveyor will be stimulated, then life as we know it will begin to dramatically change.

"We, the so-called superior life-form on the planet, the planet we are rapidly filling, can but only speculate as to what the future holds for each one of us."

A silence rested within the hall.

Arni spoke next. "I know, Nathan, we would be interested to hear something of your up-bringing and how you got into this area of study."

Nathan shared a glimpse of his early years in England, his schooling and studies at university and what it was that attracted him to this field of work. Arni's questioning neatly led Nathan into explaining, in a few words, about the car accident and his time in hospital. Arni then handed the proceedings over and invited him to deliver his keynote lecture.

An air of expectation fell over the assembly. Nathan positioned himself behind the lectern, adjusted his notes and, as the hall lights dimmed, he began. All listened intently, and for forty minutes he captivated his audience. He concluded his lecture with the following moving appeal. "Ice first appeared on our planet over two billion years ago, and since that time it has been growing and melting, advancing and retreating. Glaciers have the power to spectacularly change the face of our earth, and at an alarming rate, with the potential of raising sea levels, changing our global ocean currents and flooding massive areas of land. However, in spite of centuries of research we are still uncertain as to what the 160,000 glaciers, which cover about 10 percent of the earth's land area, will do next. Nor do we know what will be the consequences for us, and every living creature, on our planet. Whilst the snow keeps falling, so also will glaciers continue to move across the face of this earth. Native Inuits have a saying: *glaciers eventually give up their secret, but none know when or what that will be.*

"Whether we like it or not we are all playing the waiting game, and the stakes couldn't be higher."

The whole hall erupted in applause as the audience, initially one by one, then in groups, responded with a standing ovation. An eager chatter broke out as the applause, louder than before, continued for many minutes. Nathan had thought that was the end of his part in the night's proceedings but that couldn't have been further from the truth. For thirty minutes people came to him, bestowing praise, admiration for his work and wishing to discuss aspects of his research, all of which he accepted with great humility, deflecting where possible their compliments and tributes. Arni stepped in and brought the evening to a close and, after a swift whisky in his office, Nathan was unwinding, seated in the back of the Mercedes, on his way back to Eva's apartment. As adrenalin seeped from him, a heavy tiredness engulfed him and all he longed for was his bed.

The news Nathan heard from Eva when he got back to the apartment surprised him. "The police have been in touch and they want me to report to the station at ten o'clock tomorrow."

"Why? What for?" he asked.

"They wouldn't say. Will it ever be over?" The pain was evident in her voice.

CHAPTER ELEVEN

Officer Hinrik was standing by the front desk at Police Headquarters on Hverfisgata when Nathan and Eva arrived.

"No worries," Hinrik said to the desk clerk, "this is the woman I was telling you about."

He led them down a dimly lit corridor full of the sound of chatter as policemen and detectives hurried between offices.

"In here please." He pushed a door with the name plate *Lögreglufulltrúi Briem*, and ushered them in.

"This is our boss's office," Hinrik declared.

Andri, already seated behind the desk, looking very much at home, said, "Please sit down."

To Nathan, Hinrik's face appeared to contort into a disconcerting smirk. "At this stage, Mr Trent, we must ask you to wait outside," and he ushered an anxious Nathan out of the room.

"We have now had a chance to study the only witness's account, your statement, Miss Hannes, and our engineer's report. Let me tell you what we know," he continued, drawing Eva into the conversation, "and you fill us in if we've missed anything."

Finding it impossible to stay quiet, Eva began to speak, indignantly pleading, "It was an accident, I'm telling you."

Andri instantly shut her up. "Please listen to what we have to say."

Officer Hinrik, who had been pacing around the room, spoke. "Allow me to remind you what you stated during your interview and tell you what we know."

Eva's head was thumping and her hands felt clammy.

After some ten minutes sharing the pertinent details of the old man's witness statement, the findings of the vehicle engineer's inspection of her car, and confirming the results of the test for alcohol in her blood, Hinrik concluded by asking her if she had anything to add. Eva shook her head and said no.

"Good," he said. "Now I believe we're getting somewhere. I'll ask Mr Trent to join us."

Eva and a confused Nathan both sat speechless, looking at the cops and waiting on their next word. Andri spoke. "So, Eva Hannes, we have no grounds to believe the incident was anything other than an accident and as Mr Trent here is not pressing charges you are free to go." As if an afterthought, Andri's next words were directed to Eva, "But let me assure you, that should there be any future developments, and we feel it necessary to talk with you further, we will have no hesitation in bringing you back in.

"The garage workshop has finished with your car so you can pick it up."

Nathan and Eva arrived at the garage to collect her car. The reception was empty. Nathan peered into the office and looked on what he considered to be a shocking mess of papers and parts; a lingering smell of oil filled the room. Again no one was around. Heading towards the workshop, they could hear the noise of machinery. In a dimly lit shed a man was bent over a whirling grinder, its wheel sending showers of orange-yellow sparks into the air. The sight made Eva start back, screwing her face up. A taste of what seemed like burnt toast clung in Nathan's mouth. The mechanic, on noticing them, straightened up and switched off the motor.

Eva spoke and repeated herself, louder the second time. "I've come for my car."

The mechanic, an elderly man in brown overalls, unshaven and with smudges of grease on his face, stood before them. He lifted his goggles to his forehead and said, "Which car's yours?"

"The VW," Eva said, pointing.

"Right, yes, it's done; a fair bit of damage. Whatever you hit must have taken a hammering," and he sort of smiled.

"Yes," Eva replied, embarrassed.

* * * *

Eva and Nathan headed north on Route One. They were desperate to get away from all the hassle of the past few days. Above all, Nathan needed time to think: so much had happened, things he could never have imagined when he first set out from the UK. The road was fairly free of traffic as they left the city. To the west, the bay opened up revealing a cold, milky-blue sea with streaks of reflective sunlight on its surface, glistening and moving like sea snakes. To the east, a glacial plain gave way to a low mountain range; ice lay thick along its ridge, strikingly white in the noon-day sun. The peninsular of Akranes stretched out before them across the still waters of Whale Fjord, a sea haze hiding the far shore from clear view. Heading inland they traced the southern shore of the fjord. Occasional isolated farmsteads nestled close by the water's edge or tucked in the sculptured folds of the range, protected from the Atlantic weather. With every twist and turn of the road he became increasingly impressed by the splendour and rawness of the landscape.

A group of chestnut horses cantered alongside the road, then came about and headed for the hills.

Eva broke Nathan's concentration. "As children we would spend hours exploring the rivers and mountains on horseback, and each year we joined the local farmers as they rounded up hundreds of sheep from the highlands. Our horses were bred for this land," she added longingly. "For generations my family have owned a cabin on the northern shore of Whale Fjord: it was their retreat." Nathan knew little of this part of Iceland, and certainly nothing had prepared him for its wild beauty. The cabin was waiting at the end of a short dirt track, no more than two hundred yards from the water's edge. The plain timber walls were of rich pine, aged by the sun and rain. Red brick-coloured sheets of tin covered the roof and a raised, boarded balcony over-looked the fjord and the lush, green meadowland that reached down to a small bay. The water was almost completely still. A glassy, shimmering expanse of silver-white rippled gently, creeping towards the bay's tiny black sand beach.

As Nathan got out of the car he noticed a chill in the air but the tranquillity of the place immediately struck him. In the distance he could hear the shrill call of Arctic terns circling over the meadow grass.

Above, massive cloud formations towered high into the azure blue sky, their passing gradually masking the sun's bright rays. The whole mood of the fjord changed; a sense of mystery, even menace prevailed.

Nathan noticed Eva beam as she took in the little cabin and the scene before her. It was clear that the place held only fond memories of precious family times.

"Nothing ever seems to change," Eva said, "but every time I visit it feels like one big surprise."

Eva unlocked the cabin door, and as they entered Nathan imagined that the retreat's interior had probably remained virtually untouched for years, apart from some swish new pantry cupboards. The table appeared to be fashioned from one large block of wood and the smell of pine and new wax greeted him. Antler wall-lights and a central horned chandelier held stubby, half-burnt candles, and a bundle of dry moss beside split logs rested in the fireplace.

Having unpacked and settled in they sat beside each other on the balcony savouring a glass of wine, then Nathan asked Eva what childhood memories she had of being here.

"I was always excited when we came. My days here were very different from being on the island. The summers were often hot and I'd play outside most of the time. There was no school so I'd spend my time with the other children, chasing around in and out of the water, and lying in the long grass day-dreaming, watching the fishing boats and whalers. I loved it, it was fun. The days were long and the sun hardly went down. Dad caught plenty of fish so each evening we ate well, then I would try to sleep even though it was still light. In the early autumn the neighbouring farmers brought the sheep down from the mountains and we helped separate them up into pens for the various farms. I joined friends on the nearby farmstead bringing in the harvest before the weather turned bad." She paused, reflecting on those times. "Staying here on the fjord we never needed pictures in our cabin because every window presented a fresh scene each day.

"When the snows came it was harder to get here but we managed it. I remember well the winter days being very short and the daylight being strange. Occasionally we were treated to a magical firework display – the Aurora Borealis; the fantastic clouds of psychedelic light that painted the sky. If the generator failed it got very cold in the cabin and we had to rely on the stove for warmth. Practising my violin by candle-light was not so easy.

"The birds and seals returned in the spring, hundreds of them, and soon after, a profusion of colour burst forth in the meadows. I can still recall the perfume of the fresh grass and flowers, and the feel of soft turf underfoot. Every time I stroll beside the city lake those memories come flooding back to me. I had a wonderful childhood spending my holidays here and I will always be thankful for this place.

"Father was not a religious man but he loved nature. His first words when we arrived were, *'He makes me to lie down in green pastures: He leadeth me beside the still waters. He restoreth my soul'.*" Eva's eyes appeared to sparkle in the light.

Eva shared, with a hint of remorse in her words, "I was born on the isolated Vestmannaeyar island of Heimaey, off the south west coast of Iceland, but Mother had been increasingly disillusioned with life in what was a small fishing town and yearned for something more – Reykjavik. Its stores, theatres and dance halls would have held a new-found excitement for her. On the island I had learnt the rudiments of the violin but Reykjavik's Music Conservatoire gave me the opportunity to study and develop my skills."

It was clear to Nathan that music was now her life.

"When Mother died, Father sold our island family home which was far too big for him. I bought my own small apartment in Reykjavik and he concentrated his energies on refurbishing his new flat in the city, his work in the cinema, and throwing himself into researching the old days when he was stationed in Greenland. Something from those times haunts him," Eva explained, "but I've never been totally sure exactly what it was."

The few days Nathan spent with Eva in the cabin overlooking Whale Fjord, marked the start of an emotional journey, one which he hadn't planned. Having been lost for so long following Lindsey's death, it was a chance to find his true self, and together they stumbled along this journey of physical and emotional discovery. He, a diminished man, tied to his past and she, insecure and unsure of her future.

Their time was interrupted by a call on Eva's mobile. He listened, then wished she hadn't answered.

"They want me back for an extra rehearsal; it seems the guest conductor is anxious about one of our concert pieces. He has the reputation for being a perfectionist. I'll be back tonight at the latest, but I need to go. You understand, don't you?"

"I won't go with you," Nathan said.

"No," replied Eva, pre-occupied with gathering her things. "Anyway, you've got a pile of stuff to go through," she said, tossing a tied bundle of papers onto the table.

"What are these?" asked a puzzled Nathan as he started to flick through them.

"Dad dropped them over to my place for you. I haven't a clue what you'll find. It's probably more of his ramblings and conspiracy theories."

CHAPTER TWELVE

As he attempted to doze in the heat of the afternoon, Nathan couldn't get out of his head the frightening images that were beginning to appear, the shadows and ghosts of Thule filling his restless mind.

The bundle of papers included extracts from journals and old newspaper articles describing the terrible accident. *The Times* 24th January 1968, declared: *'RADIATION LEAK ON GREENLAND ICECAP B52 Bomber crashed off Greenland on Sunday, wreckage is found by search teams. The B52s on North American patrol normally carry four hydrogen bombs. Military sources say that the prospect of recovery is small. US Navy and Air Force patrols were reported to be using dog teams and helicopters today in the search for the missing hydrogen bombs.'* Official photographs and diagrams showed the US Air Base at Thule, way up on the north west coast of Greenland where the accident happened.

As Nathan became increasingly absorbed in the story he found himself starting to study the documents more closely, even taking notes. Piles of papers began amassing on the table, organised by date, location or subject. Time and again Nathan rearranged the piles, changing his mind as he found new information. Delving deeper, similarities and common links emerged, as well as worrying contradictions. What he had at first considered to be an innocent collection of vaguely related documents, was proving anything but.

Amongst the replies to Magnus' letters, many furnished no useful facts, offering only suggestions of others who might be able to help with his enquiries.

The Air Attaché's office at the US Embassy in Copenhagen suggested contact with Thule Air Force Base itself in Greenland. Magnus was redirected to the Royal Danish Embassy who stated that *'it was with regret the specific information requested was not available'* but he should try the Dansk Polarcenter in Copenhagen. They, in turn, couldn't send any information but proposed the Department of Defence, US Strategic Command, Bolling AFB, Washington DC. Bolling recommended contact with Maxwell AFB, Alabama, as did the National Archives and Records Administration, Maryland, but all Maxwell said was *'material and/or information requested cannot be provided because they are classified or under some restriction'*, and there this particular paper trail went cold. There were lists of organisations, and some individuals that clearly Magnus had approached, but no evidence of any replies.

Within three months of the crash, the Americans had conducted, under the guise of an environmental impact survey, a comprehensive but fruitless seabed search with a mini-submarine for the lost bomb. The bomb of which the Danish authorities had been unaware. According to the account of a BBC journalist, a document dated July 1968, read: *'The fact that this operation includes search of an object or missing weapon's part, is to be treated as confidential – NORFORN, meaning not to be disclosed to any foreign country or distributed to any foreign national'.*

Nathan once before had seen such a smoke screen, officials avoiding the truth. When his wife, Lindsey, had initially been diagnosed with cancer, a catalogue of delays, incorrect treatments and negligence had followed. Nathan fought hard alongside her, but the long-running battles had claimed their victims: his beloved wife and the turning of Nathan into a bitter and despondent man.

In the package that Ernst left Magnus a file caught Nathan's eye marked, 'The World Uranium Hearing of 1992 in Salzburg'. A note appeared on the front sheet. *'We dedicate this manifestation to all children throughout the world and to their future, free from the physical and psychic contamination which has been caused by disturbing uranium's timeless sleep in our earth.'* Included was a document about the Thule Association which had two names added to its front sheet, in what Nathan took to be Ernst's hand: Sally Schnell and Hanne Danielson. Nathan read an attached statement by Hanne Danielson.

'My husband was at Thule Air Base in Greenland in 1968, where a B-52, loaded with four H-bombs, crashed on the sea ice. He left Thule Air Base 14 months after the accident. Already in 1972, he got his first symptoms. His left leg looked like a thick-skinned, purple-coloured birthmark from his knee to his foot. In 1975, it started with impairment of memory and also with reduced power of concentration and continued until death. There were also some changes in his natural behaviour. In April 1987, it started with a pain in his back, and on the 19th of April he went to a hospital and he died of cancer the 30th of April, and in those eleven days he lost 30 kilos. Years back when we talked about Thule, my husband got very aggressive. I think it was caused by his fear.'

The puzzle before Nathan was far from complete, but he could see the outline of its fearful picture taking shape, this spider's web of intrigue and deceit. The words of his father came to him once again, playing on his confused mind: *we need to talk the only language they understand, son, nuclear force.* Disapproved of as a weak-willed failure by his irascible father when he didn't become a soldier, Nathan remembered how he had spent his youth battling against Father's demanding ways. A father who seemed to find intimidation deeply satisfying. For many years his old man had succeeded in making him feel inferior, worthless; a legacy which, at times, stilled burdened Nathan.

Nathan tried to convince himself that his difficulty in concentrating, keeping focused, was just a sign of getting older. That's what he told himself. Moments of depression that he had previously experienced had, as yet, not returned, but he feared it was only a matter of time.

Sleep overtook Nathan, stealing his consciousness and transporting him back into the grey world of bombs and destruction that was beginning to consume his waking hours; but he could only begin to imagine what it must have been like.

On the morning of Sunday 21st January 1968, at 0730 hours Eastern Standard Time, Captain John H. Haug reported to the SAC 528th Bombardment Squadron Briefing Room for a pre-take off briefing for a Chrome Dome Mission, code name 'Butterknife'. At the briefing crew E-14 were directed to take off ten minutes early due to forecast wind conditions and a last minute change of aircraft. Following the briefing, the seven members of the crew proceeded to the Personal Equipment

Section, then on to the aircraft. The aircraft's pre-flight checks had been undertaken by another crew, which was on alert duty. On arrival at the aircraft, Captain Haug's crew loaded their equipment and at 0844 hours started the eight turbo jets of their Boeing B-52G Stratofortress from the 380th Strategic Aerospace Wing. At 0929 hours their 200 ton bomber lifted from the runway of Plattsburgh Air Force Base, NE New York, close to the Canadian border. Call-sign HOBO 28, the US Air Force's ultimate cold war warrior, was en route for the north west Greenland coast, one of four daily B-52 missions, guarding the top of the world.

The flight was uneventful except for a minor auto-pilot malfunction which necessitated air-to-air refuelling with a Stratotanker to be carried out manually. Two years earlier, almost to the day, a collision between a B-52 and its air tanker had resulted in the loss of both aircraft, eight aircrew, four nuclear weapons and the instigation of an enormous recovery effort. The crew of HOBO 28 were very conscious of this disaster, as well as the need to maintain their range capability of 12,500 miles to enable them to deliver a strike against any target in the world. As they reached 75°O'N, 67°30'W over Baffin Bay, they entered a figure of eight holding pattern at some 35,000 feet above Thule and Baffin Bay.

Approximately one hour after refuelling, whilst maintaining their secret mission over Thule, Captain Haug reported to Thule air traffic control that he had an uncontrollable fire, suspected to have been caused by a faulty heater in the cabin, and required clearance to descend immediately. At 1527 hours the fully loaded and armed bomber started its descent for an emergency landing at Thule Air Force Base. At 1535 hours a complete electrical power failure occurred, smoke filled the cockpit and within two minutes a bail out order was given.

At 1539 hours, in clear weather and nine miles visibility, HOBO 28, crashed into sea ice covering North Star Bay, at a speed of 560mph. On board were four B28 F1 thermonuclear bombs, each with a yield of 1.1 megatons of TNT. The impact triggered an explosion of the aircraft's 35,000 gallons of jet fuel as well as detonating the high explosive onboard, causing widespread radioactive contamination, but a nuclear explosion did not occur. The United States declared the accident a 'Broken Arrow', meaning it did not present a risk of war! But one of the bombs, roughly equivalent in explosive power to all the bombs dropped by Allies in World War Two, and nearly one hundred times greater than that dropped on Hiroshima, was missing.

* * * *

Eva burst into the cabin. The disturbance shook Nathan from his frightening world, a world where the past was insidiously overtaking the present. As she put on the light he saw her standing in the doorway. Papers and folders tumbled to the floor as he pushed himself out of the chair. He took hold of her but Eva resisted him.

"You'd better get your head down," he said finally.

"You're right," she replied in a timid voice, appearing annoyed, and without another word she disappeared into her bedroom. What Nathan didn't know was, that in truth, Eva so wanted a deeper relationship.

He hardly slept unable to settle, struggling to get Eva out of his head and the way she had treated him. He sat up in bed, sweat clinging to his body. Nathan was totally confused. Only once before had he felt this way for someone and that had been someone he cared for, someone he loved. He had no idea how Eva really felt towards him. After all, he'd never asked her. And anyway, he was still finding it impossible to forget Lindsey.

The following morning, having showered and dressed, Eva called out to him, "I'll make us breakfast, then we must head back, I've rehearsals. Did you sleep alright?"

Nathan was still standing out on the veranda where he had been for the last hour, gazing across the fjord, lost in another world, contemplating what he should do with what he had learnt.

CHAPTER THIRTEEN

Magnus sat alone on his couch. The late evening's sunlight had given way, albeit briefly, to the half-light of night. To anyone else his cluttered flat would have seemed depressing and dreary, but to Magnus he felt at ease surrounded by his dust covered mementos, memories of a past life. He drew deeply on his cigar, inhaling its sweet, woody fragrance before puffing out swirling smoke into the room. As he sipped from his glass of brandy, he cast his thoughts back to the good days that he had shared with his dear brother Ernst and a single tear welled in each eye. He always tried hard to forget the moments of hopelessness they had known, the bad days they had shared and those end days. For so long Ernst had fought hard, battling against the effects of exposure. The accident at Thule, and its radiation fall-out, had claimed yet one more victim.

Like so many other nights, once he had finished his cigar and brandy, Magnus would ease his aching body deeper into the couch and try to escape in sleep and, like so many other nights, this tired old man rarely did.

Midsummer in Reykjavik finds the sun never quite setting. At night the city is illuminated by a purple-blue haze; an extraordinary half-light that merges one day into the next. On nights such as this, Magnus stood at his window watching ghostly shapes move in silence about the street below, weaving between the parked vehicles and trees like lost souls. He found it hard to express what it was that made him love this land, but what he knew was that, he just did. The truth is, it was his memories that made him restless. Memories that, in a matter of an hour, were not going to be his alone.

*   *   *   *

"It's good of you to come, Nathan. No Eva?" Magnus said, knowing full well she had rehearsals. Eva had told Nathan she had been short with Magnus when he had asked if Nathan would see him. She wanted to be there as well to find out exactly what it was her father had on his mind.

Magnus tipped away a half cup of coffee from the night before and made two fresh cups. He encouraged a puzzled Nathan to sit, then moved his own chair to be opposite him. For the first time Nathan was somewhat unsettled in the old boy's company. Magnus' manner was determined, his face giving little away. A broad, wrinkled brow below his receding silver hair, appeared to exactly match the prominence and squareness of his chin. His eyes hadn't dulled with the years as one might expect; to the contrary, they were sharp and piercing like the eyes of a man who was trying hard to assess what Nathan's reaction would be to what he was about to say.

"Did your stay up at the cabin go well?"

Nathan mumbled, "Yeah, sure . . . thanks."

Magnus put his coffee cup to one side, mopped his brow with a handkerchief. "I have been worried about Eva and how this dreadful thing is affecting her." He didn't wait for Nathan to respond but with a hesitant note in his voice, said, "Did you get a chance to look over Ernst's papers, and those I gave to Eva for you?"

"Yes." Nathan's enthusiastic response brought a change in Magnus' demeanour. The old man moved back from the edge of the chair, sighed and said, "It's been painful holding onto my secrets all these years. Secrets that others may have long since forgotten.

"My parents could hardly have known that their two sons would be born into an age of war and unrest. By the mid-fifties the Cold War was tightening its icy grip, the Western World was becoming increasingly fearful that the Soviets would invade. It was a time of terrible darkness.

"The jet age was upon us, along with the escalating arms race, delivering weapons that could cause massive and far reaching destruction. The Soviets would soon have the capability to hide their submarines beneath the North Pole's ice sheet, break through and fire their payload of missiles which, within a matter of minutes, could reach America. At that time Cuba was becoming the new USSR on America's doorstep, threatening the country with its Russian-backed nuclear missile base there.

"To counter the advancing threat of the communist east, the US needed more than just their British missile sites: they needed to be able to reach Soviet cities with their long-range heavy bombers. To help locate their strategic targets for elimination, intelligence was crucial. Your RAF pilots flew along with the CIA spy plane missions, cruising on the edge of space, overflying Soviet targets. Anyone at that time could have been forgiven for believing that the world was on a crazy collision course of self-destruction – Armageddon. The world was a truly dangerous place. You too, Nathan, would have feared for your future." Nathan was now fully on board, hanging on Magnus' every word.

"In those early days the US had established a network of over sixty Early Warning Stations in the northern hemisphere, stretching 3,000 miles from Alaska to Baffin Island, monitoring the launch of any intercontinental ballistic missile. To ensure a credible deterrent, a strategically located Combat Ready Defence Force was needed to react quickly to any alert. An Air Force Base at Thule, north west Greenland, midway between Moscow and New York, was ideally placed to deliver an American nuclear attack to the Soviet's heartland. The powers that be hoped that the theory of mutual destruction would be a catalyst for peace.

"During the mid and late sixties, both Ernst and I, like many others, were chasing the money, jumping from contract to contract. It was the time of the Space Race, Cambodia and the war in Vietnam and there was plenty of work around. Thule was a so-called jointly operated defence area between the governments of Denmark, who had sovereignty over Greenland, and the United States. The Yanks provided flight, defence and security personnel, whilst the Danes and Greenlanders supplied the support staff. Much of my time, initially, was spent working for the Radio Corporation of America with engineers, helping maintain the giant Ballistic Missile Early Warning System tracking antennae.

"Each of our four static radar antennae was the size of a football pitch, arranged in an arc and facing north, with a moveable scanner housed in front of it. A tunnel, stretching for over a mile, allowed us to access the entire complex of buildings, regardless of weather conditions. It was a five billion dollar installation and provided 160 degrees of detection over the Pole, a warning of every missile firing from the Soviet mainland as well as their Arctic and North Atlantic submarines."

Nathan sat immersed in this strange world Magnus was painting for him.

"Thule," he said, "what was Thule like?"

Magnus hesitated to answer Nathan, appearing to gather his thoughts.

"It was an amazing place, seven hundred and fifty miles inside the Arctic Circle. Thule was the most secret of places – well, that is what we thought. It served as a hub for all the clandestine activities there at the top of the world. In 1951, US military, under a code name called *Blue Jay,* began constructing the huge air base. It would be the hub serving the development of the early warning radar net, the Cold Regions Scientific Research facilities and the staging of Strategic Air Command's bombers and fighter interceptors. As well as all this there was the construction of an enormous city, hundreds of feet under the ice – Camp Century – some one hundred and fifty miles out on the ice cap. An armada of over eighty ships, with twelve thousand men and nearly a third of a million tons of cargo, arrived in the July. Within a hundred days Thule Air Base was fully operational and home to ten thousand service personnel!

"Living and working there was hard, it was an effort to keep one's wits while coping with some of the world's harshest conditions, I can tell you. You needed considerable personal fortitude to keep going. There was little on the ice cap to sustain the base, so everything was brought in either by plane or ship during July and August when the Coast Guard icebreakers cleared a way through the block ice.

"While the spring, like summer, is brief up there, offering a balmy sixty or so degrees, the winter soon returns with a vengeance: little sunlight, temperatures below minus 40°C, winds in excess of 150mph and blinding snow storms. Mentally and physically it was a real challenge, but it's funny, you know, there are times here in my little flat in Reykjavik when I find myself desiring the stillness and solitude that I experienced in Greenland.

"It's somewhat surreal to be out hiking across a frozen fjord, thousands of miles from civilization, and look up to see a B-52 leaving contrails overhead, on its way to the Russian border!" As if reconsidering his words, Magnus said, "Forgive me, I've rambled on long enough at the risk of boring you."

"No," Nathan said. "But they're not the painful secrets you can't forget, are they Magnus?"

"No." Magnus shuffled uneasily in his chair. "I will tell you."

He explained about the crash of the B-52 bomber, reiterating for Nathan much of what he already knew. What Nathan did not know, however, was how massive the American clean-up operation was after the accident.

"All of those involved were told that what we were doing was completely safe," Magnus said, "and we assumed the US military would never knowingly kill their own." He sneered. "I am an old man, far older than many, but I'll not live much longer. The documents I signed way back then have no meaning now, they had no meaning for Ernst and the many others that have gone.

"I've been living in a nightmare knowing what really happened. For years I've felt as if I've been drowning in a sea of deceit. I'll not take this with me to the grave: others need to know the full truth."

His troubled words weighed heavily on Nathan. "I knew from the very first day we met, Magnus, there was a fear within you; I could see it in your eyes, but I had no idea what it was. I never fully realised why you were so afraid." For a moment each rested in the other's silence before Nathan spoke again. "Why are you telling me this?"

"Because there is no one else." Magnus eased forward in his chair, "The truth must be told but I'm an old man, too old now. If I had a son I would ask him. I sense, Nathan, that you're searching for something; would you do this thing for me, would you be the son I never had?"

CHAPTER FOURTEEN

Eva and Sabina's friendship went way back. They had joined the orchestra at a similar time and shared a love of the same music. They became instant friends and, over time, almost inseparable. Sabina's way of wanting to know everything Eva got up to surprisingly didn't bother Eva. Having someone interested in her, in a funny way, felt good. Eva was aware that Sabina found her own indecisiveness and reluctance to try something new irksome, seeing it as a flaw in her character. One big difference between them was Eva's passion for her music. As soon as she started to play, leading the second violins, she became alive, she felt the music lift her as if on wings. Her whole body reflected the mood and rhythm of the piece and it was as if her instrument became a part of her. Sabina never acknowledged Eva's outstanding gift and, much to her annoyance, failed to receive the same praise and adulation Eva enjoyed.

Sabina parked outside Háskólabio Hall in time for rehearsals. Just as Eva was getting out of her car she called to her, "Do you reckon Eva, now you've got your car back, you'll use it occasionally?"

They both laughed, but for different reasons. Eva realised she had become a nuisance, perhaps even taking Sabina for granted. She knew she would never have felt like this in the old days.

"Why didn't you get your new man to hire a car? After all, he's more or less moved in."

Eva hated this bitchiness in Sabina. It was a side of her she'd only seen since things had changed between them. Magnus had never taken to Sabina and had made that abundantly clear whenever Eva talked about her. At one time Sabina's attitude would have irritated her to the point of anger, but less so these days.

"Well, you won't need to worry about a lift back, thanks. I'm meeting my *new man*, if that's okay with you?" Eva didn't expect, or want a reply, and left Sabina fumbling with her 'cello case.

"How did rehearsals go?" Nathan greeted, pleased to see Eva.

"Fine thanks," she said, trying to put the earlier incident behind her. "So, what have you been up to?"

Nathan hesitated, seeming reluctant to elaborate. "I've been chatting to Magnus, listening to his story, and then we grabbed some lunch. He's an interesting fella, your old dad."

"Really?" said Eva, feigning amazement. "He's stubborn and belligerent, that much I know."

"That's as maybe," Nathan said, "but he believes in the truth."

"So what was it you spent so long talking about?"

"Oh, this and that," said Nathan, attempting to deflect Eva's interrogation.

"This and that . . . what?"

"Actually it was about his time in Greenland and what went on, but you knew that was why he wanted to see me."

"Sure, and what else?" Eva aggressively demanded, insisting there was more to their meeting.

"I had some time before I was meeting you so I've been looking around your stunning cathedral. I was captivated by the place. The sunlight flooded through the windows and uplifting organ music filled the whole building. I felt completely at peace there. Before I entered that place I was unsure what I should do, but now I've made a decision."

"You're leaving?" Eva said, trying to mask her fear.

"Where did that come from?" Nathan countered.

"Are you?"

"Yes."

In a faltering voice Eva tried to hide her tremendous disappointment. "You're going back to England, to your family and your work. I knew one day you would but didn't . . ."

Nathan stopped her ramblings, "What on earth are you talking about?"

"To your wife and children, although I don't know why, they never came near you in hospital."

"I haven't got any children"

"What?" Eva said pathetically.

"My wife died four years ago and I never remarried. I don't have a wife. Where did you get that idea?"

"You talked to her – Jane. You were talking about the children, the boys."

This was getting silly, Nathan concluded. "That's my sister and the twins, my nephews. You heard me talking about them."

A sense of relief surged from deep inside Eva. "I'm so sorry," but still she had the nagging question going around in her head, *Why is he leaving?* "Is it your work?" Eva asked.

"No, since my wife's death my role at the university has been as a consultant, providing me an income while allowing me time to get over what happened. It's something Magnus said."

"Did Magnus tell you about Sabina?" Eva said, almost biting his head off. "He never did like her."

"Sabina?" Nathan questioned.

Eva then opened her mouth and, totally out of the blue, her confession came tumbling out.

"I had a relationship with Sabina." There it was, Eva had said it.

"Who?" said Nathan.

"Sabina, she plays the 'cello and gave me lifts to rehearsals."

"An affair do you mean?" Nathan said, looking directly at Eva.

"No . . . not exactly an affair, more of a very close friendship."

"How close?" he chirped, like a reporter who was about to get his first scoop.

"At the time we were both lonely and depressed, and she and I were between relationships. One evening when we'd drunk too much we spent the night together."

"So what happened?" Nathan persisted.

Eva screamed, "Damn you, Nathan Trent! I don't know, I was far too drunk to remember anything. I wasn't myself. Anyway, why do you care?"

"I don't," he said in a matter of fact way. "It just doesn't sound like anything much happened. More like one of those moments when you're alone and low and end up doing things you wouldn't normally." In his naive way he tried to reassure her, but then ruined it. "You're not sleeping with her now, are you?"

"Hell no."

"You're friends, right?"

"Well, we were until we rowed."

"Rowed about what?"

"You." Eva came back bluntly. "Anyway, if it's not that, why are you leaving?"

"It's something your father said, something he asked me to do."

"Yes, and what's that? What's so important you have to leave now?" she challenged with an agitated note in her voice.

"It's Greenland, or rather, it's about the time he and Ernst were working at Thule Air Force Base for the Americans in the late sixties. You know about the bomber crashing on the ice with its load of nuclear bombs?" Eva nodded, still trying to reason what this had to do with Nathan.

"The bomber caught fire and exploded, radioactive material was spread over an enormous area and one of the four bombs burnt through the glacial ice, sinking to the seabed. Immediately a top secret American operation was put in hand to clean up the contaminated snow and ice. You see, the Danes didn't know nuclear bombs were on Danish soil. Magnus and Ernst, along with hundreds of others, took part in the clean-up, but they were lied to. They were told it was safe."

"So what?" Eva said.

"Since your Uncle Ernst's death, Magnus has discovered many others who have died mysteriously. Died of radiation sickness – cancer. The compelling evidence he has gathered points to the fact that the Americans knew full well what they were doing, risking hundreds of lives to avoid a major international incident. He is convinced top politicians in Denmark were fully aware of what was going on in Thule as well but, as it was only days before their national election, they decided to keep it from the Danish people. News that neutral Denmark was, in fact, a nuclear power threatening Russia would have been a disaster for the government."

"But what's it got to do with you?"

"Only by going back to Thule to discover what really happened after the crash will the full truth ever be known. Magnus is no longer a young man. The memories and ghosts such a journey would resurrect are more than he could bear, but he'll not rest in peace until then."

"But why you?" Eva said.

"He asked if I would go in his place, believing that I could discover the truth. My father never thought anything of me. Some don't say what they mean but father had no such problem. He thought I would never do anything worthwhile, even when I got the university job. I knew different and this is the chance to prove it to myself."

Throughout his cold explanation Nathan had avoided looking Eva in the face. He had not seen the emptiness reflected in her eyes. Eva drew herself up to ask the question that had been running through her head all the time Nathan had been talking.

"Will you come back . . . back to Iceland?"

Then she waited, dreading what the answer might be.

CHAPTER FIFTEEN

"I was told that this was my best bet if I wanted to get to Greenland in the next few days."

Nathan had come to a downtown hotel bar adjacent to the City Airport.

The barman looked long and hard at Nathan over his newspaper without saying a word, summing this man up. Nathan started again, "I understand no scheduled flights are going out of Keflavik for Greenland in the next few days and my only hope is—"

He was cut short by the barman's words, "Yes, here."

Nathan was becoming increasingly unsure as to whether this man of few words was ignorant or just rude.

"What's your poison?" the man said as he put down his newspaper in readiness to serve Nathan.

"A beer."

"A beer it is," said the barman. Clearly any conversation was going to need working at, Nathan thought, but before he'd considered his next question the barman came back. "If anyone can help you, he will." He pointed to a large figure, half in shadow, seated in the corner of the otherwise empty bar. "Chas," the barman called across, while precisely arranging the glasses above the bar, "there's a fella here who wants a chat."

Nathan could have sworn the man let out a moan in reply but what was evident was that he made no attempt to acknowledge him, his concentration fixed on his paperback. What the hell was this place – a library!

As Nathan anxiously approached, Chas placed his paperback to one side and looked him in the eye. What adventures and conflicts had this hearty man experienced, Nathan wondered, this veteran of the air, and was he really as old as he looked?

"Is it a good read?" Nathan broke the ice with.

"What, this?" Chas flipped over the paperback to reveal its cover, Harlan somebody or other, *Silence of the Dead.*

"Any good?"

"Yes, it's okay," Chas replied, "the usual stuff, but good God man, you didn't disturb me to discuss books."

Nathan immediately warmed to this broad-shouldered Canadian's direct manner. "No, you're right, I came looking for a flight to Greenland."

"Really," Chas said, "and why do you want to go to Greenland? It's pretty if you like snow, but there ain't much else there, just miles and miles of nothing, and more nothing."

"I need to find something out," Nathan said rather pathetically, believing there was no point in selling this one a line: he was clearly too clever for that. Chas eased back from the table, filled his chair and put both hands behind his head.

"So exactly what is it you want to find out?" Chas said with a mere passing interest.

"What happened at Camp Century and Thule in the sixties."

Chas's weathered face gradually moulded into a smile. "So it will be Thule Air Force Base you'll be heading for, am I right?" Nathan nodded. "Well," Chas went on, "for a price I can probably oblige. I run a regular freight air service between Keflavik and the west coast of Greenland. Our next trip is light on cargo, so if you want a seat to Thule. . ." He stopped short for a response. Pre-empting Nathan's next question regarding the fare, Chas made his offer, "One large bottle of fifteen-year-old Laphroaig. Do we have a deal?"

"Mmm." Nathan couldn't help but think that this was too good to turn down, but appreciated his response probably lacked the conviction Chas might have hoped for. "So, what is it you fly Chas?" Nathan asked, hopeful such information would see his confidence grow.

"An Aero Commander," and Chas gestured to a group of aircraft sat on the periphery of the airfield. "The white and blue one," he added, realising Nathan had no idea which one he meant.

Nathan squinted, his eye drawn to a sleek, twin-engine craft some thirty-odd feet long, parked to one side of half-a-dozen light aircraft. "She's a fine-looking bird," Nathan said, floundering for something to say.

"You're damn right she is," Chas asserted. "No spring-chicken, but a beast, and flies like a dream, and that's what I've been doing for the past thirty-three years, man and boy."

Nathan thought he needed to sound interested if he was going to hitch a lift. "What can she do?" He knew little about aircraft and had no idea what answer such a question might bring.

Chas was in his element. "Her two engines deliver a maximum speed of 215mph. Our service ceiling altitude is around nineteen and a half thousand feet, but will cruise below ten thousand unless we hit bad weather."

"Are you expecting bad weather?" said Nathan, anxiously picking up the prompt.

Chas' reply came with an air of frivolity. "No, it's looking good for the next few days, though even up here the MET boys don't always get it right." Nathan could have sworn he could see a twinkle in Chas' eye. "So what do you say?" Chas pressed, "are you up for it?"

"Yeah," was the full extent of Nathan's response.

"Grand. I'll get Liam to sort a seat for you. After filing our flight plan with control, MET and pre-flight checks, I'm aiming to be away by 1500hrs tomorrow. I want you on board twenty before, no later, is that clear?" Nathan nodded.

"Good," Chas acknowledged. "Our flight time is about four and a half hours, dependent upon head winds which are forecast. When we're some eight hundred miles out we'll put down over-night at a small strip near Kangerlussuaq Fjord to deliver part of our pay-load, check the plane and re-fuel before heading further north. We'll shadow the west coast north to Thule Airbase and I anticipate our flying time for the second leg will be five or so hours. I suggest you get your head down early tonight: you've a long day tomorrow, and who knows how it will go?"

Squeezed inside the cramped, noisy aircraft, Nathan couldn't help but wonder what on earth he was doing there. The idea of journeying to Thule with Chas had been impulsive, seized during one of his weaker, more reckless moments – and probably after one too many beers. Here he was, heading for the top of the world.

For hours on end it felt as though they were being helplessly buffeted at who knows how many thousand feet. Only the occasional breaks in the engulfing grey cloud revealed glimpses of the endless icy sea. Breaking waves, whipped by the wind, tossed up slithers of foaming white spray. The drone of the aircraft's engines and the freezing rain pounding against its fuselage made it hard for Nathan to clearly think of anything else. Eventually sleep overcame him. He woke suddenly to what sounded like rocks hitting the aircraft. He could see through the window that ice had formed on the propeller and wing, splinters of which were breaking off and hitting the fuselage. The aircraft was descending through the dense cloud-filled sky and an enormous expanse of cracked drifting ice was far below them.

The wilderness that was Greenland rose up before them. With the changing pitch of the engines, Liam frantically scrambled past Nathan and the lashed down cargo crates, to the rear of the craft where a large reserve fuel tank was stowed. A pungent smell of kerosene filled the cabin. The engines roared again and they turned and climbed. Moments later the plane came steeply round, the whine of the engines changed, they slowed and the plane gradually dropped onto a black gravel strip. It bounced and swung from side to side before coming to a stop.

Nathan breathed a sigh of relief; he was on the ground again.

As Chas was leaving the cockpit Nathan caught his eye. "Was that touch and go?"

Chas chuckled, "Touch and go? Hell no, just a bit tricky for a minute or two; I try not to do touch and go's up here." A radio crackled from the cockpit and Chas was distracted.

Liam arched in the cabin doorway, wearing a parka and a fur-lined hat with ear muffs. "Over there you'll find the hotel," Liam said as he pointed into the far distance.

Nathan ventured down the steps onto the icy ground – his first steps onto Danish soil.

A collection of brightly coloured huts and block-houses marked the only settlement in sight and, slinging his canvas hold-all over his shoulder, Nathan made tracks. For him the journey to Greenland felt as though the clock had been turned back a whole season. In Iceland vegetation was bursting with life, here it was just wintery desolation. The acid-cold air took his breath away, the sheer effort in staying on his feet and making headway in these conditions demanded his total concentration.

Albeit few strangers visited this place, he was surprised how little interest there was in his arrival. He'd booked the only accommodation – Friendship Bay Guest House. The young girl didn't seem surprised that this Englishman had come so far and was really only intent on assuring him he had the best room. It was Spartan, plainly furnished with nothing more than a bed, table and chair. The walls and ceiling were white, as startlingly white as the landscape viewed from its first floor window. To Nathan this seemed a world far removed from Reykjavik – he could have been on a different planet. A feeling of emptiness consumed him as he stared into the pale Arctic sky. There was no hint of anyone else here; the snow-covered shacks looked cold and soulless. He drank the thick sweet coffee she'd made him, lay on the bed exhausted, and slept.

The stark light woke him. He looked at his watch – eight, he'd slept for a full eleven hours. The morning sky was crystal clear and the far-sweeping snow-covered horizon glimmered in the dazzling sun. He thought he could just see a glacier reaching out into the grey-blue bay, with fragments of pale blue icebergs and frozen ice floating in its waters. A pair of snow geese circling lazily overhead caught his attention, and he realised that they were the only living things he could see: it was one of the more disturbing feelings he had experienced.

"Morning. Coffee?" the girl asked at the breakfast table.

"Yes, with no sugar, please," he said without thinking. The dining room was empty except for a big old dog whose long tangled brown coat equipped him well for this environment. The beast stretched between yawns and did little else all the time Nathan took to eat his breakfast.

"Chas asked me to tell you that the weather is good," the girl said, as she poured fresh coffee on top of the dark sludge that remained from the previous cup. "He'll be loaded, re-fuelled and on the strip ready to go just before ten. If you want him to take you on to Thule, make it fifteen minutes before, he can't afford to hang around."

The idea of yet another flight didn't fill him with excitement, but there again, he had promised Magnus that if they wanted to find the truth, this was probably the only way.

The engines were already running when Nathan boarded. Mumbling something over the radio, Chas boosted power and in no time they were in the air, skirting Greenland's west coast, heading north, further into this godforsaken no-man's land.

"I never realised Greenland was so vast," Nathan directed at Liam.

"Yes, a load of treeless nothingness, nearly ten times the size of your old Blighty."

The flight of over 700 miles proved uneventful; noisy and cold, but uneventful all the same. In the absence of any buildings it was impossible for Nathan to appreciate at what height they were cruising.

"Thule is coming up on our port side," Liam prompted an aching Nathan. "We've picked up the homing beacon and will be landing in five or so minutes."

Soon Thule slid into view along with the great flat-topped Mount Dundas, its guardian. A network of runways and taxi-ways with huge hangars were arranged in a grid formation, while row upon row of similarly-sized, regimented buildings and fuel tanks stretched from the runway to the sea. In each corner of the base stood a missile launch pad, reminders that even here peace was fragile. The plane dropped onto Thule's two-mile runway and came to a stop.

An Arctic breeze whistled through the aircraft's door as an anxious Nathan stepped out into this unfamiliar world. A large paint-peeling sign extended a greeting, 'Welcome to Thule Air Base – 76,33°N 68,6°W', as he entered the tired-looking terminal building. Hardly fitting, he thought, for a multi-million dollar military project, nine hundred and forty-seven miles from the North Pole. The vivid splash of ochre in the otherwise pale townscape was the four-storey North Star Inn. It stood alongside other similarly unimpressive block buildings, lining what he could only assume to be the main street. He doubted if it had ever enjoyed days of glory; characterless buildings like that didn't.

The interior entertained an air of functionality and despondency. Rows of boots and damp coats marked the reception, and his meagre room and shower on the second floor did nothing to change Nathan's mind. One thing in its favour, however – it was warm. He didn't know how you kept somewhere warm up here but equally, he didn't care. Outstretched on his lumpy mattress he slept through the remainder of afternoon.

Within an hour of rising he had devoured a bowl of steaming meat stew, several chunks of doughy brown bread and downed two beers. The atmosphere in the hotel bar seemed subdued, and after a few minutes he concluded that hangovers amongst his fellow drinkers were probably to blame. The middle-aged redhead behind the bar had a certain charm about her; there was a beauty in her freckled face. He caught her eye.

"A whisky please."

She took a bottle of Glenmorangie from the glass shelf and, smiling, poured him a double.

"Could I have a little water and ice please?"

She looked at him quizzically, "Surely there's plenty enough ice around here already for anyone's taste."

Each warmed to the other.

"This your first time in Thule?" she said in a deep, mellow voice.

"Yes, first time in Greenland."

"We rarely get first-timers, just the MET boys, power engineers and military, they keep coming back. So what brings you to this inhospitable wasteland, if it isn't a rude question?"

Nathan thought quickly. "Research."

"And how's that?" she said, while drying a dozen or more glasses.

"I'm interested in glaciers."

She smiled, "We've got a fair few of those for you to research."

One of the old boys stirred, sidled up to the bar and, taking a foul smelling pipe from his mouth, ordered Aquavit. She gave him a litre bottle and money changed hands.

Glancing at Nathan he said, "Good on yer, Sissel," put a match to his smouldering pipe and returned to an occupied table in a shady corner of the bar where he topped-up his colleagues' glasses.

"They're scientists from up at the station," Sissel said, noting Nathan's interest.

Sissel obviously knew everyone up here, Nathan thought to himself, wondering if she would prove useful in helping him get closer to the truth.

A powder-blue sky, shot through with swirls of pink clouds, greeted Nathan at the start of a new day. The wet snow covering everything glistened in the rays of the warm sun. Having showered, he grabbed a coffee and began to plan his next move. Four days, that's all he had before his return scheduled flight with Grønlandsfly Air. Chas was already long gone, needing to get back to Iceland for the engineers there to check out the wing struts. If Nathan missed the flight there wouldn't be another for at least a week – weather permitting. He needed no convincing that another week in this place was a week too long. He had to find out if anyone remembered what happened here; their secrets. He couldn't waste any time. The odd remark here, the cautious question there, but so far nothing useful had come his way. His chain of thought over lunch was broken as Sissel poured him another coffee.

"They say you've been asking about the old days," and she looked towards a crowd in the restaurant who were tucking into what smelt like curry. "We get few travellers here asking lots of questions and you must understand, it's not something that's welcomed."

Maybe he'd misjudged the woman as she sounded almost menacing.

That afternoon Nathan spent his time reading in the small library of the Greenland Institute office. It wasn't extensive in its reference stock but the collection, concentrating on local history, proved useful. Of particular merit were the articles and documents regarding the US military presence during the Cold War. At the hotel he enquired as casually as he could of the young girl who served him dinner if Sissel was off, or away. His spirit lifted when she told him that, as it was quieter tonight, she was only needed on the bar.

He washed, shaved and changed into a fresh shirt. Country and Western music emanated from the dimly lit bar, Tammy Wynette or Loretta Lynn he guessed. The place was empty except for Sissel who was seated on the edge of a stool, one leg stretched out in front of her, the other bent and resting on the bar's foot rail. She was oblivious to him, concentrating on painting her finger nails. It wasn't just the smell that immediately struck him but also her appearance. She wore a white shirt, black quilted trousers and black knee-length boots. The auburn-red of her nail varnish almost exactly matched that of her long hair.

"All alone tonight? he ventured.

She looked up, "Oh, hi. Yep, the boys won't be in until later," then returned to finishing her nails.

"Can I take the other stool?" He didn't wait for an answer and slid onto its padded seat. She nodded, screwed the brush into the small glass bottle and stowed it in her bag.

Stating the obvious, he said, "You've been doing your nails."

"Yes, I'm often doing my nails. When I get bored I clean it off so I can paint them again! Can I get you a drink? A beer or a whisky?"

He smiled warmly. "Yes, thanks, a beer please, and you?"

She put the beers on the bar then came around to sit beside him. There was more than a passing interest evident in what she said next.

"You're not just an adventurer are you? There's something more to it than that."

He found the woman's frankness refreshing and concluded that, as time was short, he needed to find out if she was willing to help. As he explained why he was in Greenland, he couldn't help but notice her growing interest. At the end of it she got up, went behind the bar and poured two whiskies. Sissel edged her stool closer to Nathan.

"There are people here who could help me, who know what happened; am I right?" He was clearly taking a chance.

"Sure. Maybe, but do you think they will trust you, an Englishman, a stranger?"

"But they'd talk to you."

"Perhaps, but you can't go around pretending to be interested in glaciers and asking those sort of questions. You need something more plausible or else they won't understand why you're asking such questions and they'll not trust you, they won't talk."

"What about a journalist? I've written syndicated pieces before for news bureaus," he paused, "what do you think?" His wait seemed ages.

"Yes, that could do it," she eventually responded with a wry smile, "say, twentieth-century life in Greenland."

They drank and talked late into the evening with only the occasional interruption by a demanding punter. The longer he spent with her the more he found himself drawn to this unknown woman.

That night Nathan spent in a restless half-world between being awake and asleep, turning over and over in his head the previous day's events. Eventually the coming of the morning released him. In the bathroom mirror he saw a weary, haggard man with baggy, bloodshot eyes who had a splitting headache. He breathed deeply to try to clear his head, showered, towelled himself and looked again in the mirror for an improvement. The weather was also taking a turn for the worse. He stood in the hotel entrance and looked gloomily out at the snowstorm that was beginning to engulf and hide everything before him. The low grey cloud that blanketed the sky earlier had now been lost, and as he opened the hotel door a bitter wind cut into his freshly shaven face. The thermometer was reading –14°, but he had no idea how cold the wind chill made it.

A smiling Sissel served him a mug of hot, strong coffee and a large plate of bacon, sausage and fried potatoes. In spite of his lingering headache and the bad night, he found it impossible not to return her smile.

"What plans have you for today?" she asked.

"I really don't know," said Nathan.

"Good. I've spoken with three locals who I think can help you. One is an old man of this land who was here when the Americans came, then there's an American that worked on the giant antennae, and finally, a Danish widow who stayed on and settled here after her husband's death. Reluctant as they are to dig up old memories, I am certain they know something. You've just got to convince them to tell you."

CHAPTER SIXTEEN

Roy Abrams lived on his own a little way outside the main settlement, on one of the many side tracks that led into the centre of Thule. His home was fabricated from timber panels under a metal clad roof looking much like many of the other neighbouring boxes except, that is, for its bright red door and a twenty-foot aerial mast erected in the back yard.

Abrams had been a science officer from the mid-sixties working at the secret US base out on the ice cap. He had retired back in '83, having completed his service career at Camp Century, then for several years working on the BMEWS antennae. He had no desire to return to the States but decided to see out his days here in Greenland. Maybe Sissel had got the measure of Abrams, Nathan thought, and, for that matter, others up here.

"Many come here to get away from something, even themselves. You don't come through choice, but you often remain here because you have no choice," she had said.

Abrams had told Sissel he was more than happy to have a chat with Nathan about old times, but as soon as he realised that Nathan was not a veteran this quiet man became even quieter.

"I don't know there's anything much I can tell you," Abrams said as he shuffled across his over-furnished lounge and set down a tray of coffees.

Nathan realised the approach he had considered taking was not going to work. He changed his tack.

"As I think Sissel said when she called, I am really interested in the early days at Camp Century for my article," Nathan tried, hoping this innocuous enquiry would get things rolling.

"Oh well, I can certainly tell you what Century was like when I was there. What do you know about it?"

"Nothing much really," sharing a half-truth, "only that it was a research facility way out on the ice cap, wasn't it?" Nathan replied. Sissel eased back in her chair, prepared for a long session.

"Yeah, 140 odd miles from here, way up on the cap. One of my lasting memories was the weather; if you think Thule is bad it's got nothing on the conditions at Century. Winds of 125, 150mph and temperatures down to minus 57°C. It was a hostile place if you were top side. You felt like a pioneer on a quest to conquer the elements.

"If I hadn't seen it with my own eyes I would never have believed it possible to build such a city 200 feet under the ice. Who in their right mind would do that?"

Nathan didn't answer, regarding this as a rhetorical remark.

"Construction started in the early summer of '59, as soon as the Coast Guard icebreakers could cut a channel through the six feet of sea ice in North Star Bay. Four thousand workers were needed to build the airbase and Camp Century, and more than six thousand tons of materials were hauled on special sleds, which crept along at a couple of miles an hour towed by caterpillar tractors. For us service men, the trip took half a day in an articulated pole-cat vehicle, twisting around crevasses and snowdrifts.

"In the first weeks of construction we lived on top of the ice cap in wood-framed canvas shelters. It was bitter. Interconnected trenches were cut into the ice by giant rotary milling machines. The longest trench, Main Street, 1100 feet long by 28 feet high, stretched the entire length of the camp's complex like its back bone, with a series of lateral trenches. These trenches were covered with arched corrugated sheets then buried with snow, hiding the whole city. We were completely self-contained with labs, a communication centre, infirmary and a chapel, as well as accommodation for two hundred all year round; and, for privacy, a hundred man latrine." At this Abrams laughed, "Necessity is the mother of invention, we soon got used to that."

"What about water and power?" Nathan said.

"Down a deep ice well, sunk half a mile, we pumped steam which melted the ice and produced our water supply, thousands of gallons of fresh water daily, allegedly from snow that had fallen nearly two thousand years before. At first we were dependant on diesel generators and great quantities of fuel hauled by tractor train from Thule. Hardly practical, so the US Army's first portable nuclear reactor was installed. As well as supplying two megawatts of electricity, the nuke plant also provided steam for the water well."

"The whole project must have cost a fortune?" Nathan said.

"You're right," Abrams agreed. "The talk was around eight billion dollars and that was way back in 1960."

"What was your job, Roy?" Nathan said, wanting to keep the conversation flowing.

"In the early days it was unloading and shifting materials and fabricating the plywood buildings. Many of us were occupied cutting back the snow in the sixty-three tunnels, almost two miles of them, in freezing temperatures. We looked like overstuffed deadly teddy bears in Arctic gear, wielding chainsaws. As time went on I became more involved with the research work, deep ice core drilling, bringing up continuous cores from over 4,500 feet for the physicists to study. My other work was involved with the Snow, Ice and Permafrost Research Unit, studying the techniques needed to create secret Arctic bases and how troops might live and fight in such demanding and arduous conditions."

"It's hard to imagine something on that scale," Nathan said.

"We'd joke that we were living in the largest deep freeze in the world. In fact, we were the very first city to be entirely powered and heated by atomic fuel."

"Sure, and a city that could probably outlive all other cities," Nathan surmised.

"No," Abrams was adamant and quick to reply, "it was eventually abandoned in 1966. I heard that the constant movement of the ice cap and the ice build-up in the tunnels, which we had been fighting against, had almost completely destroyed the complex and wrecked the buildings."

"What happened to the reactor and all the radioactive waste?"

"The solid waste was shipped back to the US for disposal while the liquid waste was discharged deep into the ice cap. As for the reactor, it was successfully shut down in '63 and dismantled, hauled across the ice cap and loaded onto a ship called *Victory* at Thule Harbour. We were told this was the first time a nuclear plant had been closed down, let alone in somewhere like Greenland. The Navy were keen to get their investment back: they said it had something to do with the development of nuclear submarines."

For Nathan, Abrams' explanation was both fascinating and frustrating. Although Nathan was certain the man knew a lot more than he was telling, for some reason he wasn't sharing it. Nathan steered the conversation in another direction.

"Were you here when the aircraft crashed?"

Abrams' willingness to discuss what happened surprised Nathan.

"Yes, it disappeared east of the air base and we all got turned out to try and find it. The weather was horrendous – twenty-four hour darkness, an ice-fog white-out, minus 65°C and gusting up to 50 knots. Our search was useless, conditions were so bad. To my knowledge the pilot was never found and the wreck was soon covered in snow."

"When was that, Roy?"

"It was the winter of 1962/63 when the F-101 fighter went down."

"Right," said Nathan. "Actually, I was thinking about the B-52, that accident."

Abrams looked at Nathan, then at Sissel who was showing no sign of surprise at Nathan's remark. Abrams sipped his coffee while considering his response, but the brew was cold and he put the cup to one side. Abrams' voice changed, it was faltering, hoarse. "Nobody talks about that one, that was a time wrapped in secrets."

Nathan stayed silent, wanting him to go on but Abrams sat perfectly still, appearing to be lost in his thoughts. When finally he spoke his voice was soft, almost a whisper.

"I survived, but many didn't."

"What actually happened?" Nathan said slowly and deliberately. Abrams waited a while before replying.

"They say that when the angle of impact of a nuclear weapon is severe but not direct, the explosion scatters most of the non-fissile material rather than blowing it up. It becomes a dirty bomb."

"And is that what happened when the B-52 crashed, it was a dirty bomb?"

"Yes. They said about thirteen square miles of ice was contaminated. Sirens wailed out over the air base when it happened. I knew from practices the sound of an atomic alarm. We heard a massive explosion out on the ice in North Star Bay. We soon learnt that one of the SAC's B-52s had crashed, making an emergency landing on the sea ice of Bylot Sound, eight miles from Thule, loaded with four hydrogen bombs.

"In spite of the Army being desperate to get to the downed plane first, it was actually the Inuit who arrived at the scene on their dog sledges ahead of them. They'd heard the bang and winds had driven smoke from the burning aviation fuel south, five miles to their settlement. Like us, they didn't know the danger that awaited them. Nuclear weapons were prohibited by the Danish government from being stored or flown over Greenland, a Danish territory, but the Pentagon clearly had other ideas. Experts came from the Atomic Energy Commission labs in New Mexico and investigators from SAC Headquarters; the place was awash with 'specialists' and radiation. An area four hundred feet wide and extending for two thousand feet, was blackened by the burning aircraft sliding over the ice. Three of the bombs had smashed on impact, spreading nuclear waste; the fourth was missing. Immediately a clean-up operation was launched – Project Crested Ice. It made it sound as if the whole thing was planned, not like an operation close to panic. The pressure was on to complete the clean-up before the ice melted in the spring, carrying more contaminated waste into the sea. Within hours an airborne bridge of supplies was in operation between the States and Thule. Hundreds of us, along with Danes and Greenlanders, worked endlessly day and night, month after month, in appalling conditions. Temperatures dropped as low as minus 60°C and the winds were up to nearly 90mph. Only after three weeks did the sunlight start to gradually begin appearing.

"Within four days of the crash a Zero Line surrounding an area of alfa radiation contamination, one by three miles, marked the decontamination boundary. An ice road was constructed from Thule along with a second route to the site, and igloos, huts and buildings, a heliport and communication centre were established. Heavy machinery and graders were brought in to begin the task of scraping the blackened area and the top of the surrounding ice.

"The Danish authorities insisted that no nuclear material was to remain in Greenland. Well over half a million gallons of contaminated liquid was moved to a holding area near Thule Air Base – the Tank Farm. From there the full tanks were shipped to the States.

"Project Crested Ice was wrapped up after nine months, when they said everything had been recovered . . . but we knew better; we knew that wasn't true."

"What happened?" Nathan asked.

"Everything happened, everything changed."

"In what way?" Nathan pressed.

"Officials and scientists arriving from all over the place, hundreds of them. Many workers involved in the clean-up became ill. Fishermen and hunters started catching dead and deformed animals. Flights out of the base reduced dramatically as did the service personnel, and I no longer saw the B-52s overhead on their missions. A canopy of secrecy descended and we were all cautioned never to talk about what happened," he paused. "I suppose I really shouldn't be talking to you. I wish I could forget what happened but I can't, I never will. If I stay silent I might as well be dead."

"I suppose everyone feared the Soviet's response to nuclear weapons over Greenland?" Nathan said.

"Hell, that's when I started to see sense. I knew something momentous was happening . . but I didn't know what."

"What do you mean?"

"I started to nose around a bit and subtly ask questions and slowly things fell into place. The innocuous US Army Polar Research and Development Centre – Camp Century – was the location for far more sinister Cold War work."

"Yes?" Nathan said.

"The extensive research undertaken into sub-ice construction and water, power and waste solutions, along with the psychological research into isolation and morale problems on an underground workforce, were all in preparation for 'Iceworm'."

Nathan had never heard this name before. "Iceworm?" he repeated, with more than a hint of uncertainty.

"I'm not surprised you've never heard of it," Abrams said. "I discovered that Project Iceworm was the code name given to a massive network of missile sites under the ice sheet. The Army was planning to base newly designed 'Iceman' missiles in six hundred silos dug into Greenland's ice cap, close enough to strike targets within the Soviet Union. Whilst Century was known and approved by Denmark, it seemed they knew nothing of the planned Iceman Network across their land."

Abrams sat in his chair, staring out through his window onto this strange world and the storm that raged outside.

"I spoke with someone who worked at the BMEWS site at Thule," Nathan said, trying to re-engage with Roy. "He said it could detect an object no bigger than a door if it was launched from the Soviet Union."

Abrams, oblivious to Nathan's comment, muttered under his breath, "The place that had been my home under the ice for so long was a miniature atomic city full of secrets." He continued to stare, lost in another world. He didn't turn to speak, "It felt to me like being in a submarine out in the middle of a frozen sea with a time bomb hidden on board."

Driving back with Sissel, Nathan watched the swirling black clouds race across the threatening sky, hiding the pale sun. The monotonous landscape of this brutal country was lost from their sight as icy rain dashed against the windscreen. Sissel had predicted the weather would turn. When they reached her apartment the storm was subsiding although the spiteful gusts of wind carrying the rain were still enough to chill them to the bone.

Steam billowed from the bathroom where Sissel was already running a bath. By the time she had stripped, Nathan was half submerged in its foaming water, the warmth flooding through him. Nathan held his breath at the sight of her naked body; he had been totally unprepared for this. She boldly slid into the water opposite him; Sissel had not been with a man for many years. In an instant events had thrown them together. For a brief moment a feeling of guilt swept through him, assaulting the memories he held of Lindsey and a sense of cheating on Eva, not that it was rational.

They hastily towelled the other down but the impatience of the moment prevailed and soon their damp bodies were as one. It had been so very long for Nathan. His instinct was to ignore his head. Maybe the secretive nature of their liaison made a difference, but he didn't care, he was beyond caring.

As they lay satisfied and exhausted from their exertion, Sissel whispered to him,

"I feel alive, more than I have for a long time." She drew her body up close to Nathan resting her head on his warm, bare chest. He lay perfectly still, thinking; then, restless, he rolled onto his side and noticed on her bedside table a photograph.

"Who's that?" he questioned a drowsy Sissel. "The child in the picture?"

She stretched out beneath the sheet, still reluctant to let the moment pass. She murmured, "What?"

"The photo of the young girl. She looks like a happy kid," Nathan said.

Sissel's manner immediately changed. "That's Anna." His question had unsettled her. "She's my daughter . . . have you children?" Sissel said matter-of-factly.

Nathan wondered if it was an attempt to distract him. For the first time in a very long while, Nathan felt at ease to talk about it; unknowingly Sissel had brought him to that point.

"I was married, but soon after my wife became very ill and we were unable to have children. The doctors weren't hopeful as increasingly the various treatments and drugs had no effect. She spent more and more time in hospital and we had less time together. We had been very much in love but her cancer was pulling us apart."

A silence was shared as they gathered their thoughts.

"What happened?" Sissel said.

"I lost her four years ago." Nathan paused, a moment of reflection passed. "What about you? What about Anna?"

"The first guy I ever slept with was a bum: a wild Nordic truck driver. He'd run the long hauls northward to the far reaches of Finland, Lapland and into Norway, never settling, never staying long. He wasn't the only man but somehow we'd keep finding ourselves thrown together when he passed through years later. After one trip he bought Anna and me a small cabin, something we could all call home, but he never did. I didn't think he would. She was my life, full of energy, full of fun and joy. But life can be shitty. One day coming home from school she was hit by a car; she was in a coma until she died in hospital two days later. We didn't have a chance to say goodbye. A beautiful child who had never hurt a soul. My life had fallen apart." Nathan waited believing there was more. "For a long while I looked for her in everything, but never found her. I don't know if he ever knew. I never saw him again. Like Anna, he'd gone from my life forever."

"Are you okay?" Nathan said as he turned towards her. "I'm sorry if I've upset you."

Sissel ignored his words. "You're a good man Nathan. You've made me feel like a woman again."

"It's been a long time for me too," Nathan admitted.

She looked at him pensively. "How come you've never remarried? What about the woman in Reykjavik?"

Confusion filled his head. He was unsure of his feelings. "I just don't know."

They held onto each other and for a time that put paid to any doubts he had. They made love again.

Sissel was already brewing coffee when Nathan woke. The morning light was gently casting its glow into her room. She sat on the edge of the bed, her housecoat falling open to the waist.

"It's good to love people while they're here, because tomorrow they may be gone. I need you to know something, I didn't tell you everything."

Although Nathan was far from fully awake he realised that what she had to say was important to her. He looked, inviting her to go on.

"I've got that bloody cancer too and I'm scared; I want someone with me when I die, to hold me, to look out for me and miss me, but there isn't anyone. You could die up here and no one would miss you." Her words shocked him. He couldn't think of anything to say. "Nothing is forever," she whispered, "in this lousy life."

The love they shared offered a chance to escape, be it for a fleeting moment, from reality. He wrapped his arms around her and pulled her towards him, and there they stayed for some time.

Before visiting the elderly widow on Sissel's list, Nathan needed to return to the hotel, get a change of clothes and pick up some papers. The receptionist greeted him with a message.

"A Miss Hannes phoned a couple of hours ago and needed to speak with you urgently, that was all she said."

No matter how hard he tried he couldn't figure what Eva wanted.

Her voice at the end of the line sounded distraught, "You didn't answer when I called."

"Nope," Nathan said, "do you know what time it is?"

"Yes, 10.25am."

"No, it's 6.25am. This isn't Iceland, we're four hours behind you." This fact was met with silence.

"Are you still there?" pressed an uncomfortable Nathan.

"Yes, yes, but you didn't answer."

"I was asleep. What is it, are you okay?"

"Are *you* okay?"

"Of course, what do you mean?"

"Your sister telephoned here. I don't know how she got the number, but she wanted to speak with you. We got talking and she said she was concerned about you." Nathan tried to guess what was coming next. "She went on to say that if she didn't keep an eye on you nobody would."

Eventually Nathan replied, "I'll explain when I get back."

In a meek voice Eva said, "When are you coming back?"

"Probably in a couple of days. What actually happened here is slowly becoming clear. We're off to see the wife of a veteran this morning, and I think she'll be able to throw some more light on what occurred."

"Who's we?"

"Sorry?"

"You said, we're off?"

"Oh yes, the barman at the hotel knows the locals and is proving invaluable, especially as I have so little time here." Nathan didn't want complicated questions about a barmaid, so decided being economic with the truth was the better option.

"I need to go now," Eva said. "We've a big concert next week and the conductor's putting us all under a lot of pressure, but I'll see if I can get a chance to dig anything up this end."

"Great. I'll give you a call tomorrow night," Nathan said. There was a definite sense of relief in his voice.

"Make it early, say before seven our time," said Eva. "Magnus sends his best and says make sure you keep out of danger. What danger does he mean, Nathan?"

But by then Nathan had hung up.

CHAPTER SEVENTEEN

Downstairs Sissel was waiting for him.

"It's a short walk. I said we'd be there soon after eight, then I need to get back to the hotel as I'm helping with breakfast."

Sissel had shared with Nathan the little she knew about the woman. Helga was in her late sixties, although to him her appearance belied her years. She had completed her nurse's training at Copenhagen's Rigshospitalet, coming to Thule to work in the base's Medical Infirmary in 1963. Her late husband, Joe, had been stationed here with the US Army Corps of Engineers out of Fort Hamilton, Brooklyn. Their Danish and American partnership was celebrated in 1965 when she became Mrs Helga Masini.

As the front door opened Sissel was the first to speak. "Helga, this is Nathan, the man I was telling you about."

Nathan smiled but that made little impression on this strong-willed widow.

"He doesn't look much like a journalist to me," Helga said to Sissel.

Nathan seized the initiative, "Oh, so what does a journalist look like?"

She was having none of it. "I am not sure, but not like you; anyway, you'd better come in."

He'd been trying to place her accent which seemed a contradiction to him. She spoke in a staccato, Germanic manner, with just a hint of an American drawl. In her hut was a veritable treasure of memories. Books and magazines not only filled the shelves that were straining in every nook and cranny, but piles of them competed for floor space with an excessive number of rather unattractive pieces of furniture. Pictures, mostly photographs of their families, occupied any wall that hadn't a door or window. The stove appeared to be the only flat surface that didn't benefit from an array of ornaments, models and more photographs.

Helga bid farewell to Sissel, "Off you go, he'll be safe in my hands," she said as she plumped up an armchair cushion. "Now sit yourself there. Nathan, wasn't it? So what's your real reason for being here?" she challenged before he was hardly settled. "Is it my letters?"

"No," a confused Nathan said.

"Have you come about my Joe?" she said, glancing towards a small side table.

Nathan looked hard at the table, and amongst the various photographs he had noticed earlier there was one of a smiling military man. "Your husband," Nathan acknowledged.

"Yes, dead these past twenty-seven years, but he really started to die six years before then. So what is it you want to know?" and glared at him.

Nathan looked her in the eye. "I want to find out the truth, the truth about the bomber accident and what happened afterwards."

For a minute or two Helga appeared distracted, rearranging the photographs before setting her stout frame opposite him. "After all this time you come here and want to know what happened? Why now? Who told you to come?"

"No one, but I know someone who was at Thule. He and his brother served here in the sixties. He is not a well man now, troubled by all that happened here, and by the death of his brother. He needs to know exactly what it was that killed him."

"Probably the same as killed my Joe," Helga said matter-of-factly.

"Helga, what was it like when you first came to Thule?" he asked, not wishing to sound too challenging.

Nathan saw Helga's countenance change. She relaxed. "My first recollection was stepping out of the plane and feeling as if my nose was about to turn to ice. Walking between our accommodation block and the infirmary was hard work, with snow-drifts up to ten feet deep between the buildings. I hated the cold."

"How did you and Joe first meet?"

Helga glanced again across to the photograph perched on the table, blinked once or twice, then turned to face Nathan. "It was the early summer of '64. The Coast Guard ice-breaker, *Westwind*, had been the first ship in that year and spirits were high. Joe and a crowd of engineers had headed down to the Airman's Club in a couple of jeeps. The club was a smoky, loud hang-out for servicemen. They would sit for hours around tables or at the bar, drinking, playing cards and darts and 'chewing the fat' whilst listening to the music of our radio station, KOLD. A couple of the maintenance guys had varnished the lights red and painted their idea of Playboy Bunny Girls on the walls between posters of exotic overseas places and photos of Monroe. There were few women around on the base, only us nurses and service staff along with the occasional native Greenlander or resident Dane. The absence of the opposite sex would gnaw away at the men's spirits. Our local band, *The Showman,* was backing Lauren from the Exchange Shop, singing vocals. One of the breaker crew made a grab for her. A fight broke out, but it was nothing too serious and soon over. Fights were a regular occurrence, and more often than not no one afterwards ever remembered why they had started: men just liked hitting each other if they were bored. When our boys went to leave they discovered that some of the crew, who didn't want to walk back to their ship, had taken one of the jeeps. Our boys raced down after them and this time the fight took a more serious turn. The next morning when I went into work, Joe was tucked up in one of the infirmary beds, moaning but claiming victory."

This seemingly unemotional woman let out what to Nathan sounded like a giggle.

"Against all odds our friendship blossomed and the following year I married that tall, good-looking soldier. The service in the Ice Chapel was a lovely affair and the occasion billed as a non-Breaker Boys event." Just talking about it brought a flush to Helga's face. She rummaged in the pocket of her skirt for a tissue to wipe her eyes. "Joe had become a good mate of Al, one of the 46th Engineers from Fort Polk. Al was at Thule rebuilding the ten-mile road between the air base and TUTO, the ramp up onto the ice cap. He and Joe were enthusiastic members of the Glacier Ski Club and the two boys, groom and best man, turned up for the ceremony on skis." She laughed as if picturing the scene in her mind's eye. "We were so happy, but that was before the accident."

"You mean the crash?"

"Yes," and Nathan saw sadness in her face. "The whole base shook when that bomber exploded. In trying to save the plane the crew ended up poisoning the land.

"Joe came to me that evening and said, 'Don't worry. There's a problem with one of the aircraft near the airfield, I shouldn't be long'. I hadn't seen the explosion, only the fire; the whole sky was ablaze. I can still remember the awful smell. Joe was sent with others to contain the fire, but they had only their work clothes, no protective gear. He asked the officers if it was alright not to have protective clothing and masks. All they said was that they had no other orders and assumed it was.

"I watched the clock: he was gone four hours. At that time it was hard to believe anything serious had happened. After the crash there were no alerts, no one mentioned anything about the men's safety, let alone contamination. Some of the men were hospitalised shortly afterwards suffering from the poisonous fumes; they were really ill. The doctors said they were so exhausted their bodies were starting to shut down. Radiation wasn't mentioned.

"The whole base came alive after the crash, with machines and men everywhere. We were all stopped from going out – going anywhere. Yet still nothing was said about radiation. The next day men were going around with Geiger counters. My Joe had a blood sample taken, he was told it was just a matter of routine. They took the clothes he had been wearing and said that because of the fumes it was best that they were disposed of. We later learnt that they'd been burnt.

"Within a day or so Joe started to be sick. The doctors said some of the men were okay, others, like my Joe, were not too well but they said they would continue to monitor and treat him and he needed to drink lots of milk." Helga gave Nathan a puzzled look. "Each day Joe looked like a different man, slowly I didn't recognise him.

"How I loved him – we hadn't long been married. It was as if my whole world had fallen apart. They took him away, and when they buried him it took eight soldiers to carry the coffin – the lead coffin that came from America."

Helga hardly faltered, appearing totally transported to that terrible time. For the next twenty minutes she went to great lengths relating details of the accident and the events that followed. She told of the suspicions that the sudden in-flight fire was caused by a member of the crew putting cushions over a heater's vent to warm.

"The fire filled the plane with smoke and knocked out its electrics resulting in the loss of the bomber. Usually a B-52's crew was six, but on this occasion an additional pilot, D'Amario from Wing HQ, was on board. When the Captain gave the order to bail out, co-pilot Captain Svitenko was on his rest period away from his position. All but Svitenko survived because without an ejector seat he had no chance. The plane's air gunner, Sergeant Snapp, ejected facing backwards and his helmet was torn from his head by the sheer force. Do you know, it was some nine years before it was found!

"We treated three of the crew who had minor injuries. The only other patients we had that day were men with bad lacerations from the windows in their huts which had smashed with the blast. Captain Svitenko wasn't found until much later, dead on the ground near Dundas village.

"The crash resulted in large areas of the snow and ice being contaminated with plutonium. The extent or degree of radioactive contamination wasn't established for some time. To begin with the news was kept from Denmark, fearing the back-lash. They said that an American three-star general flew in and came to one of the hangars demanding a helicopter take him to the crash site. The rotor wash when they landed and lifted off blew contaminated snow all over the place and covered the men working there. The Danish and Greenlandic workers started the clean-up without any special protection. What they were undertaking to make the place safe was, in fact, slowly going to spell the death of so many. None of us at that time realised the dangers they faced. It was a crazy state of affairs. While men were collecting the wreckage and debris from the crash to sell as souvenirs, others were boiling the snow about the site to make tea. Joe referred to them as 'dead men walking' and he was right.

"A few days after the crash the whole base took on a shroud of secrecy. Guys would half joke that there were so many planes coming in and out of Thule that it looked like JFK Airport."

Nathan continued conscientiously taking notes as Helga carried on with her account of the events. Helga was one of the few not directly involved in the panic that had overtaken the normal calm on the base. She said there was a real sense of being out in the cold, knowing that the Danes back home knew nothing of it and that's how the military wanted it. What Helga then shared she did in such a way that Nathan couldn't miss the point.

"Crews on the ice breakers anchored close to the crash site soon complained of sickness, blaming the piped water supplies from the holding tanks on the base. In the first few weeks we saw a range of skin problems, symptoms of radiation exposure – redness, burns that wouldn't heal easily, blistering and ulceration on faces, arms and hands. It wasn't long before men started vomiting and experiencing nausea, as well as a range of infections and unexplained tiredness and weakness. As time went on patients experienced falling blood counts, problems with bleeding and healing of their wounds. Lumps started to appear on their bodies for no apparent reason.

"Some did get better but it took ages. Others, who had moved on, we heard were being diagnosed with cancer – leukaemia, solid tumours in their stomachs, bladders and thyroids. Much of what we saw and learnt at that time was never discussed outside the base. The monitoring equipment we used we later discovered was wildly inaccurate, giving totally unreliable readings and a false sense of security. Men were told, 'you're going to be fine, you're well within Acceptable Levels of Exposure', but that wasn't true

"A year or so later the local Eskimo hunters began to notice deformities in the young seal population. The natives were understandably concerned what poisons were in the meat they had been eating and feeding their families. We ran a test programme looking at the concentrations of dangerous substances in the breast milk of Inuit women and found it to be seven times higher than the women of eastern Canada. Scientists warned that the dispersal of pollutants in the Arctic would take far longer than anywhere else in the world: they could persist up here for decades.

"Before he died, Joe speculated what the consequences would have been if one of the nuclear bombs on the B-52 had somehow detonated. Communication links with the air base and BMEWS network would have gone down with the US having no information to establish if it was an accident or Soviet attack on the Free World: anything could have happened. It doesn't bear thinking about."

Helga paused.

"Are you alright?" Nathan asked. She nodded.

"In the end days Joe didn't like to talk about it. In spite of being totally dedicated to his country, he would just say, 'None of us at that time thought we would have to die for it'."

A long silence rested over them both.

"The bombers no longer fly over this place," Helga explained with an air of melancholy, "so I suppose the accident did some good." The time Helga had tried so hard to forget was very much alive again for her now. "Such memories never go, only fade for a while. There is little left for me now; all that I cherished has been taken from me."

"I can't stop your pain Helga," Nathan said, his emotions overwhelming his words, "I am so sorry."

After what she had told him there was nothing more for Nathan to say. He could see the anguish in her face. He stood to leave, staring at the photograph of Joe taken before he was ill. Helga spoke to him as he reached the door,

"I thought it was about my letters and that's why you'd come."

"What letters were those?" Nathan asked, stopping in his tracks.

"The ones I wrote about the accident."

Her throw-away comment had come as a surprise and Nathan wasn't going to leave it there. "Who did you write to?"

"The Danish government, the Prime Minister and Health Secretary, but it did no good. I wrote on behalf of the workers who took part in the clean-up seeking an apology, compensation for them. When after several months I heard nothing I contacted the Danish media."

Intrigued, Nathan said, "So what happened?"

"Suddenly all hell broke loose, as they say. The Institute of Foreign Affairs contacted me, trying to shut me up but not before I had all manner of press, TV and radio stations chasing me for the story. After the fuss died down I heard nothing more, except from a radio journalist. He said he would use his pen to fight for the workers' rights."

"And now?" an expectant Nathan enquired.

"He has been in touch a couple of times, maybe more, updating me on developments, the potential US lawsuit and hearings in Denmark. There was also something about a political cover-up that he had discovered."

Nathan interrupted her. "Do you know the journalist's name?"

"Yes, I wrote it down somewhere; let me see."

"If you get it I'll contact him and find out what's happening," Nathan said, startled by the words *political cover-up.*

"Would you do that for an old woman who has little else to live for?" Helga said. "Here you are, it's Martin Poulson. He works for Danish Radio in Copenhagen. Strange that, like you, he should be so interested."

On Nathan's return to the hotel two messages were awaiting him. 'Sissel will see you tonight, she's behind the bar at eight and will be free at eleven.' The other message was strange, and would have been mysterious if it hadn't been so formal. On Air Force Space Command – Thule Air Base headed note paper, the letter which had been left by a messenger read:

We understand you are interested in the Air Force Base and Camp Century. We would be pleased to answer any questions you may have regarding our operational history. Both facilities fall under the responsibility of US Air Force Space Command and, as such, we feel addressing your inquiries directly would prove more satisfactory.

Please contact my PA to arrange a meeting at your convenience. I am available later this afternoon and would endeavour to assist you.

The letter went on to detail contact telephone numbers and was signed *Major A. T. Felker, Assistant Command – Control and Communications.*

Nathan's impression of the letter was that it was far from an offer, more of a summons, and one that he felt would be improper to refuse although he was uncertain how it would pan out.

One of the base's Terrabuses dropped him in front of the headquarters building in good time for his 4.15pm appointment. A few words with the reception officer on the front desk and Nathan was led up two flights of stairs by a young airwoman to the major's office. She knocked twice on the frosted glass of the half-glazed door and waited.

There was the sound of a cabinet being slammed, then a moment later the office door swung open to reveal a smartly uniformed officer in his thirties, wearing a grin stretching almost from one conical ear to the other, both of which stuck out below his bald shiny head.

"It's a pleasure to meet you, Professor Trent," Major Felker greeted, and beckoning him in said, "we're honoured to have such a distinguished academic visit our shores here in Greenland."

"Thank you. I was somewhat surprised to get your invitation, if indeed that is what it was."

"Please take a seat," Felker invited, gesturing towards a group of chairs set around a coffee table. "We'd heard you were asking around about Camp Century and the Air Base and considered we might be able to help. Maybe it's our Ice Core Research that particularly interests you? It's amazing what our findings are revealing. I know it's an area of work you addressed during your recent seminar at Reykjavik University."

Nathan was taken aback. How on earth did he know what had happened in Reykjavik? He had told no one in Thule about his lecture and he was equally puzzled how they knew what he had been doing whilst in Greenland. The major picked up a handset, pressed some keys on the internal phone, then started to speak. "Professor Trent is with me now, sir," Felker listened then said, "very good sir, I'll tell him. Lieutenant Colonel Roberts would very much like to meet you and is on his way down."

Nathan was lost for words. He could not understand the degree of interest shown in someone who was ostensibly merely a sightseer.

"I've got to be back to the hotel by six, I'm expecting a call."

"No problem," the major replied, "I'll get a staff car to run you back if we're tight on time."

Nathan concluded that, for whatever reason, they were determined to have their say. The office door then burst open and in walked a plump man in full regalia. Clearly introductions were considered unnecessary.

"It's good to meet you, Professor, isn't it Tom?" he said, staring at Nathan.

Nathan didn't know whether to stand, but by the time he was making for his feet Roberts grabbed and shook his hand with a firm grip.

"It's good of you to come on in, we know you're a busy man but a brief informal orientation from us will, I am sure, prove useful to avoid any misunderstandings."

Nathan returned Roberts' cursory smile and nodded.

"Grand," Roberts fired, "let's get you up to speed."

"Sure," Nathan replied, feeling there was something unnerving about Roberts' manner.

"After the Second World War Denmark owed a debt of gratitude to America. German insurgence forces frequently landed in Greenland, and whenever the Danish sledge patrols spotted them or discovered the installation of a secret Nazi weather station, they would count on us to eradicate the enemy. I'm sure you'll understand, Professor Trent, the Cold War meant Greenland was in a key strategic position, midway between the world's two superpowers. The need for us to have a presence here became abundantly apparent. We had already established a weather and radio station, Bluie West-6, jointly with the Canadians. It was decided that we would also site an airbase here which would form part of our 3,000 mile early warning shield. The vast military complex so far north was a real challenge to our engineers. What our boys created with Operation Blue Jay was a technological wonder, withstanding as it has the hostile environment and the Arctic hurricanes. They were true pioneers, I am sure you appreciate that," he said to Nathan but didn't wait for a response. "First we had to build a port to support the arrival of 125 million dollars of cargo and more than twenty thousand workers, to build the dream. It was a marvel of logistical ingenuity: convoys of up to 120 vessels landed more than 46,000 tons of steel, over 11 million feet of lumber, and so the inventory went on. Covering 625 acres, Thule Air Base was our crown jewel, as you Brits might describe it."

Roberts smirked.

"It was vital to our retaliation strategy. The World War II agreement we held with Denmark was revised and finally ratified in '51. Under NATO, it became known as the Greenland Defence Area. Thule served as a base for intercepting bomber attacks directed at Canada and the US, as well as an operational base for our long-range SAC bombers and a launch pad for our research on the Greenland ice cap.

"In only one hundred and four days we had pushed our defence line two thousand miles north, above the Arctic Circle."

Roberts paused. A cynical Nathan was unsure as to whether it was to gauge his reaction or part of the lecture, but Roberts didn't need any acknowledgement from Nathan.

"You must remember back in the 1950s communist aggression was in full flight in Indo-China and against UN forces in Korea. We estimated a Soviet transpolar attack could destroy, or injure, up to forty million Americans."

Nathan decided it was best to go along with Roberts, appear interested and patiently wait, hoping to discover what the purpose of all this was. "And the radio antennae, what was their part in all of this?" Nathan prompted.

Striding around the office, Roberts was away again. "The four giant radar antennae are part of our BMEWS defences stretching from Clear, in Alaska, to Fylingdales in your Yorkshire. They provide us with a fifteen to thirty minute advance warning of attack."

"That's not long," Nathan interjected.

"No, but within two minutes our jet squadron can be scrambled to intercept any intruder, and our armed bombers, which are on twenty-four hour airborne alert, can immediately be despatched in retaliation."

This was all very interesting Nathan thought, but hardly getting him closer to what he wanted to know. He concluded that he needed to find out just how much Roberts would tell.

"You mentioned about the around-the-clock airborne alert?"

Roberts stopped pacing and turned to look at Nathan.

Here goes, Nathan thought. "Am I right in thinking one of those airborne alert bombers actually crashed here on the ice with warheads on board?"

Roberts glanced at Felker, who was now hovering at the back of the room, then at Nathan. He dropped into a chair and edged forward on it.

"Sure, way back in '68. You know, it's so easy to misunderstand such events," Roberts advised, stroking his chin. Then, as if pre-empting Nathan's next move, "Look, you must understand the accident was totally contained."

Nathan felt uneasy, like a school boy who had just been corrected and awaited his punishment.

"The impact detonated the high explosives in the primary units of all four B28 nuclear bombs and the fuel on board, but the nuclear and thermonuclear reactions did not take place due to the PAL and fail-safe mechanisms in the weapons."

Nathan noticed Roberts' fist clenched tightly and an uneasiness descend. Nathan changed direction with his probing, at least for the moment. He offered a nod of understanding to the men.

"I was interested to see so many natives on the base," Nathan commented.

Felker eagerly took up the conversation. "At the time of the build many Inuits worked on the sites and their settlements grew up around the base. Over the years we've done a lot to support and sustain the future of the local people. The US is proud of the relationship we have cultivated with both the native Greenlanders and the Danish government. As far as our service personnel go, great importance is placed on their recreation."

Where on earth did that one come from, a confused Nathan wondered.

"The base boasts a fully equipped gymnasium, bowling alley, library, hobby shop as well as restaurants, bars and a dance hall. We organise an annual raft regatta and, for the more athletic, our Polarbear swim amongst the icebergs in the bay is a must. A golf tournament is staged on the flat top of Mount Dundas out in the bay and, having participated there myself, I can tell you there's no course more impressive."

Nathan assumed Felker's sales pitch was intended to side track him but he really wasn't listening.

"Is it true that not all the warheads were recovered from the crash and that the Danish people weren't told? Nor were they told about the plan to hide hundreds of nukes under Greenland's ice sheet?"

In a commanding voice Roberts said, "You must choose your words carefully, Mr Trent, I am sure as an academic and scientist you understand that."

Instantly Nathan appreciated how his impatience had got the better of him.

Roberts continued, addressing Nathan in a stern manner. "What you read, what you see and what you hear isn't always what happened. Not always are things what they seem. Misinterpretation can have dire consequences. There's a lot more at stake than first appears, and the situation was anything but simple. We learnt lessons from that incident.

Within days of the crash, Secretary of Defence Robert McNamara ordered the removal of nuclear weapons from airborne alert, and later the flights were suspended. It's often not healthy to look back. However, from what we've observed, that's something you seem intent on doing."

Hardly a veiled warning. Nathan had finally heard the very thing that would change everything – things are not always what they at first seem.

"The world wants to be protected from the Russians," Roberts went on, stabbing his finger on the arm of the chair. "I am certain you are aware of the Reykjavik Summit, held only a mere ten years ago now. The outcome of Reagan and Gorbachev's meeting resulted in both nations agreeing to The Intermediate-Range Nuclear Forces Treaty just a year later. Do you think that would have happened if the US hadn't proved it could be a real threat to the Soviets? You don't need to answer me – I can tell you, the answer is a categorical no. The Treaty was a crucial step in the ending of the Cold War."

Nathan could see that the end was in sight.

"Forgive me for saying, Professor, but I call it like I see it and your wisdom may not have caught up with your years in this case. I trust you'll heed the advice of friends here, for that's what we are."

The next words Nathan uttered were words of apology. "Sometimes my enthusiasm gets the better of me. Forgive me if I've overstepped the mark, I hope no harm done?"

Nathan saw a smile on the men's faces but he doubted their sincerity. All stood, and Roberts said to Nathan, "It's been good to meet with you and have a chance to clear the air so to speak, hasn't it Tom."

Nathan, however, was annoyed with himself for being taken-in by their initial enthusiasm to help.

Major Felker said, "Let me organise that car for you," but Nathan couldn't help but notice this sounded like a different man than that who had made the offer an hour or more before. Felker's parting shot caught Nathan off balance. "I expect you'll be on the scheduled flight back to Iceland in a couple of days."

This was no casual enquiry: Felker obviously presumed he would be.

"You take care of yourself Professor Trent, we wouldn't want any harm to come to you. Greenland can be a dangerous place."

AARHUS, JUTLAND – DENMARK
Monday October 13th 1986

CHAPTER EIGHTEEN

Martin Poulson stretched back in his office chair clasping both hands behind his head. He sighed, satisfied, as he scanned his news bulletin's last paragraph displayed on the word processor's screen.

'A defiant frost lingered in the air as President Reagan and Mr Gorbachev went their separate and gloomy ways following the superpowers' arms control talks at Reykjavik in Iceland, which ended today without any agreement.'

The header of Poulson's piece read, 'Star Wars Spiked Summit'. It went on, 'The two leaders had started by agreeing to halve strategic weapons and work towards a new test ban treaty. Gorbachev made the deal conditional on Reagan keeping the outer-space defence shield, "Star Wars", in the laboratory. Reagan refused.'

Content, Martin clicked on the 'send' then 'print' icons as he reflected on the extraordinary events of the past two days. Despite the talks' failure, and an historic opportunity lost, the participants and observers expressed their shock at the pace of the discussions and referred to the summit as an enormous break-through. Both sides had discovered the extent of the concessions the other side was willing to make.

As he manoeuvred the mouse, the cover of *Time Magazine* appeared on the monitor, APPOINTMENT IN ICELAND, and Martin wondered whether in the course of time Reykjavik would prove to be one of the most important summits in history.

THULE – GREENLAND
2001

CHAPTER NINETEEN

Sissel slung her arms around Nathan and kissed his cheek. Her perfume was all-pervasive, its pungency and her touch overwhelming his senses. He found old memories coming back, memories he thought he had long forgotten.

"What happened? How did it go? What did they want?"

Nathan shrugged. "I am not really sure, I think they just don't want me around."

Sissel's avalanche of questions went on. "Are you alright? Perhaps you shouldn't have gone?"

"Hey, it's okay, nothing's going to happen to me," and he kissed her. She pulled back, still worried for him. "I'll tell you what happened but first I need to shower to wash off all the bullshit I've been subjected to, and I must call someone – what's the time?" He checked his watch. "Good, I might still get her. Give me half an hour then meet me in the bar, I'll tell you everything," was Nathan's parting shot.

Sissel made no attempt to change his mind. She could see he was preoccupied and what she was desperate to tell him would have to wait.

An invigorating hot shower, a change of clothes and Nathan felt like a new man. He lifted the telephone handset and dialled Iceland.

"Kirstin, this is Nathan Trent, we met at the lecture Arni organised at the university a couple of months back, do you recall?"

"Yes, of course, how are you?"

"I am good, thanks. Look, I'm ringing on the off-chance you can help me."

"Of course, if I can. "Kirstin sounded preoccupied.

"Is it a bad time?"

"Sorry, no, not at all. I've just been putting the final edits to a piece for tonight's news, but it's done now. How can I help?"

"Some research I've been undertaking has dug-up the name of a Danish reporter. It means nothing to me but I thought you might know of him."

"Sure," Kirstin said, "who is it?"

"Martin Poulson."

Nathan took the silence on the line to be Kirstin trying to recall the chap but her next few words changed his mind.

"Yes Oskar, it's good, we can run with that, I'll be with you in fifteen. Work, Nathan, but I'm all yours again. Poulson, you said? He was with DR as I recall."

"DR?" Nathan queried.

"Denmark's National Radio and Television Service, much like your BBC. I first came across him back in 1986, when he was covering the Soviet-American Summit at the French Consulate here in Iceland. As I remember he was doing a piece on the Cold War Superpowers. I'm not sure but I think his angle was Dulles's *Taking Chances for Peace,* looking at the motives and outcomes of the talks between Gorbachev and Reagan. What is it you're researching, Nathan?"

There was a lull in their conversation.

"Are you still there?" Kirstin said.

Nathan steeled himself, wondering how to reply. "I'm looking into an incident that took place in Greenland back in '68 and I understand Poulson had contact with those that were involved or at least witnessed the occurrence."

"That doesn't sound much like glacial research to me," Kirstin noted.

"No, I'm feeling a bit out of my depth, to tell you the truth," Nathan confessed.

Kirstin, in a more positive manner, proposed he called into the station at Reykjavik and they discuss things, adding, "It would be good to meet up and it might be easier over lunch somewhere?"

"I'd love to but not for a couple of days. I'm still in Greenland."

"Greenland? Well, if you tell me a bit more about what happened up there I'll see what I can uncover in the meantime."

Over the next four or five minutes Nathan concisely outlined the incident at Thule, its subsequent fall-out and impact. He explained the line that Poulson appeared to be adopting and concluded by thanking Kirstin for any help she could offer.

"We'll meet when you get back and I'll update you then with whatever I've found out. Give me a ring on your return."

They hung up. Nathan, content that he had found an ally in Kirstin, couldn't help wonder if she could also see a story somewhere amongst this unholy mess.

The shrill ring of the telephone disturbed Nathan from his day-dreaming. Holding the handset to his ear, he rubbed his face with his other hand attempting to rejuvenate his concentration.

"Mr Trent?" The man's voice had an air of familiarity to it but Nathan couldn't immediately place it.

"Yes?"

"Major Felker at USAF Space Command HQ. I'm sorry to trouble you," Nathan was convinced he wasn't, "only our transit boys have advised us that there are irregularities concerning your entry documents."

"What entry documents?" Nathan said.

"Exactly!" Felker replied. "If you want to come in they can run over it with you but from what I've seen it looks pretty conclusive." He momentarily paused, probably for effect. "However, if you were intending to be on the next flight out of Thule, I am certain I can convince them, in this instance, to overlook it. I hope I make myself clear?" Felker asked.

"Crystal," was the extent of Nathan's response.

"I'm sorry to interrupt," the operator's voice broke in, only I have an international call holding for you, Mr Trent. Shall I tell them to call back or –"

Nathan stopped her mid-sentence. "No, I'll take it. I believe we've covered everything, Major?"

"As long as you fully understand your situation. It would be difficult for me to go back to the Colonel without news of your imminent departure. You must appreciate we're not trying to make things awkward."

Nathan didn't answer him but asked the operator to put the call through.

"Hi Nathan." Eva's voice sounded full of excitement. "How are you doing?"

"I'm okay," he replied, lacking conviction, "and you, how are things with you?"

"I've some news but you don't sound yourself, what's up?" Eva challenged.

"Oh, I've just had a bit of a run-in with the authorities on the base. They seem intent on getting me out of here. I've probably been doing too much digging for their liking."

"Some interesting stuff's come to light this end," Eva said, "and Dad wants to talk to you about it when you get back. When are you coming back?"

Nathan had an idea that's why Eva rang. "As things stand, in a few days." His reply was met with silence. "Hi, are you still there?" Nathan said, thinking she'd gone.

"You will take care won't you, only the authorities can be a law unto themselves and if anything happened . . . "

"Nothing will happen," Nathan said, attempting to bring the conversation to a close.

"When's a few days?" Eva asked.

"Soon. I must go, I've got a meeting."

"Love you," she said pathetically, but evoking no reply from him, she rang off.

The receptionist's voice over the phone made him jump. "Mr Trent, are you there?"

"Yes, I'm sorry, I'll put the phone down."

"No that's okay, Sissel asked me to call. She's waiting for you in the lobby."

"I'll be right down."

Sissel was leaning against the wall at the bottom of the staircase. Beaming, she greeted him, "Hi, I was able to get away early, are you okay?"

"Yes sure, I've just got something on my mind at the moment."

"Is it to do with the day's meeting at the base?"

"No, although that was weird enough," Nathan said.

"Anything I can help with?"

"No, not really. I need to sort a few things out when I get back to Iceland."

"Do you fancy a walk out towards the bay?" Sissel said, attempting to lift the mood.

Much to her surprise Nathan agreed and, arm in arm, they headed towards the sea, Nathan sharing the events of the afternoon with a disbelieving Sissel.

"As I said, Nathan, this is the place where people come to get away from the real world and news of what happens here rarely leaves our shores. Life here is simple and straightforward, black and white, and one thing they don't like is outsiders coming in, stirring things up."

Nathan realised this but, for whatever reason, perhaps over zealousness, he had misjudged the occasion and acted like an idiot; he was angry with himself.

"When does it get dark up here?" he said.

"What?" Sissel replied, confused.

"When does it start to get dark here?"

"It doesn't, not really until October. And as it gets darker so it gets colder."

They stood silently, looking out into the bay. A cool breeze tumbled down the nearby mountains bringing with it freshness. Patches of thin ice lay over the sea and, in the distance, small grey-blue bergs, like ships, drifted slowly into sight through the low-lying sea mist. They watched, letting time slip by, fascinated by the scene before them.

"You okay, Nathan?"

"Sure. Look at that." He nodded towards a gigantic upended slab of pack ice, the size of a small office block, gracefully floating into the bay. Translucent hues of blue reflected off the ice as it drifted on an ocean of grey-greens. The painful groans of the ice were the only disturbance to the silence.

"Isn't that unforgettable?" Nathan said.

"Mmm," she replied, her thoughts seemingly elsewhere.

Skuas wheeled high in the sky overhead.

"Just like the thousands of birds preparing to leave," Sissel said looking up, "soon you too will head south to avoid our big freeze."

Suddenly any peace was broken by a thunderous rumbling resounding in every direction. A massive ice face at the sea's edge exploded as an enormous fissure opened. Hundreds of tons of ice calved from the glacier and plunged into the depths. As quickly as it submerged from sight, it majestically rose like a surfacing submarine. The water about it churned and turned into a wild sea, and a giant wave surged before it across the bay.

Nathan turned to look at Sissel and saw in her eyes a question.

She spoke tenderly to him. "I don't want to be a complication in your life, Nathan, I truly don't, believe me. What is it you want me to do? Maybe we should forget the other night . . . Not that I regret it, far from it, but perhaps that would be for the best?"

Behind them an aircraft cargo plane taxied from the cinder apron towards the main runway. They heard the roar of its engines as it began to roll down the runway, then lift into the sky. It banked and, flying low, its twin engines strained as it climbed over the bay heading south somewhere. This unexpected interruption meant Nathan never answered the uncertainty Sissel voiced.

They made their way back to the hotel. Sissel's disquiet was still on Nathan's mind as he asked, "When you first arrived here what was it like?"

For the moment Sissel accepted his avoidance. "The base was a mess, rusting equipment, scrap and rubbish everywhere. The winter's first howling blizzard came like a squadron of angry aircraft descending from the north. The snows arrived, masking all in a thick blanket of white. Winds blowing off the ice fields, storm force two or three, froze everything in their path. It was bitterly cold, I was freezing. I don't know of anywhere more hostile on earth. Although warmth came with the start of spring, so also arrived the bugs, billions of them. The larvae hatch as soon as the temperature goes over ten Celsius, then we're plagued by them. The mosquitoes drive you crazy, eating you alive. If you're not careful you become a swollen, itching mess."

"You make it sound so appealing," Nathan said.

"Well, if you think that sounds bad, there's the bears. If the mossies don't eat you, the bears will. The males are solitary creatures, a bit like yourself," Sissel mocked.

"But I've not seen one," Nathan exclaimed.

"That doesn't mean they're not out there. In those early days we didn't run bear patrols. The bears would wander around the rubbish dump foraging for food and, when ravenous, right up to the doors of our huts. A bear can sniff out a meal from twenty miles away. They aren't just a nuisance but very dangerous. I had only been here three months when one of the soldiers dropped a bear with his rifle out by the hangers. His first shot just wounded it and it reared up then charged him."

"And wolves?" Nathan asked, attempting to get the full grim picture.

"They come in packs, often under the cover of night, and attack our dog teams on the base, baiting them, singling out the younger and weaker animals. It's not unusual for them to turn on their own, the injured in their packs. There was one terribly sad incident two winters back. Larry, a young chap who worked on the base, saw what he thought was a wolf attacking a team of our dogs. He drew his pistol and fired into the air but the wolf didn't flee. Larry fired at the skulking creature only to discover it was an Inuit child he had killed. The subsequent hearing cleared him of all responsibility but Larry was never the same. Within the month his naked body was found mauled out on the ice. He'd walked to his death. They say that wolves up here will eat right out of your hand – or your leg or your chest! Before the evacuation of the Inuits from their settlements here at Thule, their hunters would have kept the balance between man and beast, but no more.

"Despite all that, when the endless days of summer release Greenland from the icy grip of the winter and the land bursts with new life, I know why I will never leave."

When they got back to Nathan's hotel room Sissel unfastened her coat. "Do you mind if I shower, Nathan?"

"No, sure, of course," Nathan said. "I'll run the water for you."

As she unbuttoned her shirt Nathan couldn't help noticing her ample breasts showing between its folds. He watched as she stripped and stepped into the cubicle and began washing. She bent forward, letting the water run through her hair, over her back and down her long, slender legs.

CHAPTER TWENTY

Nathan watched Sissel carefully roll out of bed and, still half dazed, creep to the window, clearly not wishing to disturb him. She pulled back the heavy drapes that attempted to block the light and peered out across the dream-like landscape.

Nathan came up behind her naked body. She felt him and turned. They kissed and together watched a jeep pull out of the long shadows onto the road then drive off towards the low sun on the horizon.

"Did you sleep okay?" Sissel asked him as she climbed back into bed.

"So, so," he rubbed his eyes.

"You're not used to sharing a bed, are you? You didn't stop fighting for the covers." He could see in her face she was uneasy. They lay side by side together on the bed, staring at the ceiling. Everything was running so fast for Nathan.

His desire for Sissel was real in his mind although they'd only known each other for a short time.

"What about the woman in Iceland?" she murmured.

"I don't know," he said.

Nathan was tired. He turned onto his side and drew his legs up and Sissel snuggled in behind him, and for another hour they slept.

"Will you leave Thule?" Nathan asked Sissel when they woke.

She thought before answering him. "No, as much as I hate it at times, this is my home. You could be forgiven for thinking that this land holds little welcome, and you would be right, but for ten years I've known nothing else. And you, what do you think of the place?"

"It's not what I expected."

"How's that?" Sissel said.

Nathan considered his answer, not wishing for a thoughtless word to upset her. "The land seems to demand so much but offer so little in return . . . and anyway, contrary to what they say, there's really no green here, is there?"

They laughed. "And what will you miss when you go back?" Sissel persisted, appearing to need reassurance.

Nathan felt that there was something terribly sad about the way Sissel had come into his life and the inevitable way they would part.

"With all this cloak and dagger stuff going on, you need a hearty meal inside you," she said, changing the subject.

"Really!" Nathan said, still his mind elsewhere.

"No, not really, but I'm hungry even if you're not. How do they say – 'the condemned man's last meal'?" She squeezed her arm around his waist and laughed.

The restaurant lacked much of the finesse and sophistication Nathan was accustomed to. Nor did it boast the charm or offer the same homemade delights he so enjoyed and took for granted back in his home town in Wales. What it was, nevertheless, was the most highly regarded eating place probably this side of the Arctic Circle. The close scrutiny of the menu did little to stimulate Nathan's taste buds. Suaasat, mattak, musk ox, whale meat, eider duck, but then he spotted trout, wild salmon and halibut. Just as he was about to safely settle on one of the fish dishes Sissel interrupted his deliberations.

"You ought to try one of our local dishes. Mattak is whale skin with a thin layer of blubber; you eat it raw. It can be quite strong in flavour and needs a lot of chewing. There's also whale meat roasted with soft onions or honey-roasted eider."

"What's suaasat?"

"A soup of seal meat cooked with rice and onion."

In the end they both decided on a musk ox steak cooked with boiled potatoes and onions. Nathan was saved the problem of trying to keep down a strong seal soup as Sissel had ordered a starter dish of large tasty prawns for them to share. The steak arrived piping hot and cooked to perfection with a rolled lamb sausage on the side.

"I am sure you know seal, whale and fish are better for you. They're full of unsaturated omega 3, which helps combat cardiovascular disease in those of maturing years," and with that she laughed.

"Oh, by the way, I've got something to tell you – in fact, two things," an excited Sissel shared.

"Go ahead," Nathan answered.

"Well, firstly, the other person who witnessed the crash, Karl, has agreed to chat with you. He can see you tomorrow, is that okay?"

"Oh yes, sure, whatever, thanks."

Unimpressed, she continued, "Your Major Felker."

Now that did get Nathan's attention. "He's not my Major Felker," stating the obvious.

"Right." Sissel's patience was running thin. "Well, he arrived on base back in '98. He didn't come with a unit but just turned up all on his own. According to the lads he's not well liked, always nosing around, asking questions about things the boys say shouldn't concern him."

"So what are you saying?" Nathan blurted at her.

"Shh," Sissel said casting a cautionary eye towards the others in the restaurant. Her next words managed to attract Nathan's full and undivided attention.

"No, he's not your man, Nathan, and he's not the Army's man, nor the Navy's or the Air Force's Major Felker." Nathan was hooked. "An old boy once told me a kind of fable of how back in Newfoundland they would fish the Labrador Sea for salmon. The Americans had developed a taste for wild North Atlantic salmon. However, getting the live fish to market revealed a problem. They would ship them overland in large tanks but many died en route, and those that survived the long journey didn't taste so good, having lost their muscle tone from becoming lazy."

Nathan was struggling to see any relevance.

"Indulge me," Sissel said, aware of his waning attention.

"So, the fishermen had an idea, a simple solution to the problem. They threw into the tank of young salmon a few northern pike. Whilst a few salmon were eaten, the rest arrived toned and healthy, having spent the entire journey out-swimming their natural predator."

Nathan was now concentrating. "Well?" he said.

"Well, if you have a few hundred men involved in top secret work, several thousand miles out of the way in some isolated hell hole of a place and you are fearful they will become careless, laid back and less than diligent – throw your pike in!"

Nathan had followed her train of thought.

"Major Felker reports directly to the chiefs of staff at the Pentagon – he's CIA," Sissel revealed.

"I had another run-in with him, this time on the phone," Nathan admitted. "The man's a menace. He tells me there's some irregularity with my papers and it would be best I leave, sooner rather than later."

"When?" a stunned Sissel asked.

"On tomorrow's flight, I guess, after our morning meeting with Karl." Nathan could see the pain in her face. "I will be back, Sissel, I promise," he said, but somehow that seemed hardly enough.

* * * *

Karl's demeanour belied his seventy-eight years. Nathan noticed an air of dignity, a sharpness of intellect that still remained with this fair-skinned, bearded Dane. According to Sissel's description of the man, he had spent all but twenty-two years of his life in this most remote part of the Danish realm, in many respects living a life of a Thule Eskimo. The Second World War had seen Karl serving in the Royal Danish Navy, after which he had been recruited as a member of the elite Sirius Sledgepatrol, a special unit which patrolled the remote north and east coasts of Greenland, searching out and destroying clandestine German bases. Nathan knew Greenland was strategically important to the Germans as they needed to be able to predict the weather over Europe for their invasion and bombing campaigns. Sissel had described it as a cat and mouse game, keeping the black Swastika of Nazi Germany at bay.

Over the years Karl had travelled thousands of miles by dog sledge and boat, shadowing the country's wild and uninhabited coastline, remaining vigilant in the knowledge that should his sledge slip into the open water, the current would drag both him and his dog team under the ice to certain death.

"Tell Nathan your story Karl, just as you told it to me," Sissel encouraged.

"After the war," Karl began, "I joined the Sledgepatrol, I expect Sissel told you all about that?"

"Well, only about its work against the Germans," Nathan admitted.

"In my days Sirius was more like a police force that had to patrol a vast territory, an area as big as France and your Great Britain combined. As if that wasn't difficult enough, we were only a handful of guys, selected for the two-year posting. We worked in pairs and it wasn't unusual to be out for three months or more and not see another soul. Over time I gained an intimate knowledge of the country. You had to if you wanted to survive as compasses were of no real use up here. I guess because of that, and the fact that I was a bachelor without a family, I got the rare chance to stay on for a second tour of service."

Nathan had not come to hear about the patrols. He wanted to know about the accident but, with the telling, he realised Karl was completely absorbed in his account.

Sitting in the kitchen of his hut, Karl glanced towards the window to the weakening sun. "In a matter of days our short summer will be over and, with the disappearance of the sun, a new world is created and the sledge teams' winter drives will begin. The sounds of the howling dogs, their rattling reins, the whistle of the sledge runners as they cut through the fresh snow and my laboured breathing are still clear in my memory." Karl had no need to describe the noise of the dogs; Nathan could recall the howling and barking that had so often kept him awake since he arrived.

"Endlessly we would shout at the dogs, running ahead and guiding them, stumbling through the ice and snow in the teeth of a gale, in temperatures so low that bare skin would freeze almost immediately. Then, exhausted at the end of the day, we would try to sleep in a freezing tent. As hard as it was I loved the life, the nature and solitude."

Nathan noticed a glimmer in Karl's eyes as he spoke warmly of those times; this man who was reliving his past.

"You were here, Karl, when the bomber crashed?"

These few words were enough to bring Karl tumbling back to reality. The old boy took off his Canadian Rangers cap, ran his fingers through his wispy silver-grey hair then looked Nathan straight in the eye.

"Yes, I was there."

Nathan let him take his time.

"I ran dog teams in those days, a Greenland outfitter leading expeditions with universities and organisations like National Geographic.

"That day in January 1968 I was on the ice hunting for fox and hare. I could hear the roar of aircraft engines way off. They grew louder, closer, and I realised this was not the usual sound of a landing fighter or bomber. Then there was an almighty explosion like a crack of thunder and a huge fireball rose high into the sky, perhaps as much as several hundred feet, out in Bylot Bay. The ice I was standing on moved and then there were more blasts and tremors. The black Arctic sky was suddenly ablaze, and red and blue swirling smoke clouds were issuing from its heart, growing ever higher. Even as the inferno was blazing, men of the village had taken to sledges and were driving their teams across the pack ice towards the fire, not knowing what had happened, or of the poison that was being released, polluting our land and sea.

"For days they laboured at that place, quenching the blaze, clearing the smouldering wreckage and bombs. Then for eight months, joined by Danish and American troops, they moved some half a million gallons of contaminated ice and snow, their winter furs offering no protection against the hazard, the radiation. It's said that no one told them that the job they were doing was increasingly putting their lives at risk."

"And what of you, Karl?" Nathan chose his words carefully. "Weren't you ill?"

"No, thank God. I was far enough away and as soon as I saw that hell-fire I fled. Do you know, whilst half a million Russian and Warsaw Pact Troops were invading Czechoslovakia, the Americans were stock-piling secret nuclear weapons here. And all that time the Russians knew what was going on, broadcasting in English, telling us which runway lights were out, which aircraft had landed, and sometimes even taunting airmen by naming their wives and children.

"It seems strange to think that, within eighteen months, America had surprised the world and built a craft that could travel three-quarters of a million miles, at speeds of twenty-four thousand miles an hour and brought back two men who had walked on our moon. Our world was changing so fast, was I not wise to mistrust what lengths man would go to in the name of progress?"

Nathan had no words of consolation for him. Throughout, Sissel said nothing but sat beside Nathan, hoping that her presence would help Karl feel at ease. On his part, Karl never moved from his chair at the kitchen table and rarely did his voice or face show any emotion.

"Far below the surface of the icy sea they worked for days on end attempting to recover the bomb that had slid through the liquefied ice and become entombed beneath nine hundred feet of freezing Arctic water. Try as they might, the bomb was out of reach. A midget sub that had finally found the Palomares lost bomb back in 1966 was shipped to the Arctic Circle, but the depth of the freezing water here proved too much. And if that wasn't bad enough, it was the middle of an Arctic winter – days of total darkness, temperatures touching minus 40°C and the possibilities of Storm Three with brutal polar winds touching a 160mph or more.

"That nuclear warhead is still there," he pointed to the window, "just over there. Although the Cold War is over, nothing really goes away in life. There will never be a peace here whilst that thing is rotting in the depths of our ocean, silently spreading its death. None of us know how many more will die."

Nathan sensed that a dark shadow had descended. Karl glanced at them both.

"Man should trust man, but sometimes it's very hard to," and directing his next words to Nathan, added, "don't you agree?" Nathan nodded. No one spoke for several minutes.

"What do you do these days, Karl?" Nathan asked. Unaccustomed to such a question Karl looked vacant. He shrugged, screwed up his face into a most unnatural expression and rolled his tongue several times around his mouth before speaking.

"I still hunt, mostly for blue fox and hare, and run my team of twelve dogs. That's when the weather's fine."

"Don't you use a snowmobile?" asked Nathan.

"No, machines break down but dogs will always get you home; anyway, you can't eat your snowmobile if you're in trouble. Here has always been known as *the place to keep dogs*." He hesitated. "There is work to do on my hut, and repairs after the storms as well as to my rickety sled: it's old now and constantly needing attention. The winter months herald the coming of only moonlight. Then, if the weather is so bad I'll go on my radio, just after I did in the crash, or sit here in the kitchen watching the comings and goings of my barometer and marvel at how low the mercury will fall: just myself and my lingering memories."

Karl offered little recognition of Sissel and Nathan's departure. He just appeared to stare longingly out of the window over his cluttered sink to the world outside.

"Will he be alright?" Nathan asked Sissel as they stepped out onto the road outside Karl's house and into the crisp, clean air.

"Yes, sure," Sissel confided, "he drifts in and out of his memories and melancholy. When that's not a good place to be, like so many others, the bottle becomes his refuge, taking him to a place where he can forget everything."

After Sissel had finished her evening shift, leaving the hardened drinkers to Dylan and Johnny Cash, she and Nathan spent their last night together. Nathan realised saying goodbye wasn't going to be easy, but he hadn't appreciated just how hard it would be.

Nathan pulled her into his arms and holding her tightly he asked, "How do you feel?"

Sissel kissed him. "I feel good, better than good." Then in a whisper she said, "In another life, another place, we could have had a chance, but now we'll just break each other's hearts. Tomorrow you'll be gone."

"Come with me back to England," Nathan pleaded, not having thought any of it through.

Sissel so wanted to stay with him but knew that could never be, and what of the woman in Iceland? She would be waiting for his return.

"Life isn't that simple when you live in this place so long," she faltered. "Besides, you have your future and I have so little time left."

On her face he saw a look of anger, not with him but, he thought, at what had been stolen from her.

"You're still thinking about her aren't you?" Sissel said.

"I am truly sorry," Nathan willingly admitted, believing Sissel to be talking about Lindsey.

"You needn't be," she said. "You're a good man, even if you've forgotten it. I am sure she's still waiting for you back in Iceland."

"I feel as if I've been asleep for the past four years," Nathan shared, "and I'm just waking up."

"You know it could never be, don't you, but that doesn't mean it isn't real." As Nathan lay close beside Sissel all that she had said played upon his mind.

So much had happened in so few days and what he had learnt troubled his weary head. The cool evening sunlight relentlessly penetrated the room. Nathan lifted a pillow from the bed and laid it over his eyes. As he desperately tried to sleep, the words of Doctor Thorirsson came to him: 'There are no rules for accidents such as this. Headaches may well come and bring severe pain, then slowly fade; memories will return but it is unlikely you'll remember everything. No matter how hard you try there will always be secrets you'll keep from yourself.'

CHAPTER TWENTY-ONE

Sissel's words greeted Nathan, who was still coming to his senses after a restless night.

"The news at the airport is not good. Low pressure systems are gathering between Greenland and Iceland so we're in for some bad weather and poor visibility, risking the icing up of aircraft. If you had this weather in Europe nothing would take off. It's not uncommon here to have flight delays of two or three days: our weather is completely unpredictable." She flung open the drapes to reveal a glorious clear morning, a pale-blue cloudless sky and turning to Nathan, grinned.

"You rat," he scorned.

"Really, darling?" and Sissel's face shone as bright as an angel's.

"I care for you, you know," Nathan found himself saying.

"Yes, I know," Sissel admitted. "Will you ring me?"

"I promise," Nathan replied, with every intention of doing so.

A bright orange windsock fluttered beside the runway that looked to stretch into the sea. Beyond an ancient Sikorsky helicopter Nathan made out the scarlet livery of his Greenland Air flight.

After an emotional farewell with Sissel, the chocks were pulled away and the aircraft was soon rumbling down the runway. As they rose, the buildings vanished from sight and, for a moment, it appeared as if they were going to brush the top of the dazzling snow-capped mountains. A great plateau, an icebound wasteland, revealed itself below, bathed in stunning sunlight, a white wilderness as far as Nathan could see. Nathan was in two minds about leaving this world of so many secrets where the Inuit hunters had survived nature's wrath, but not that of man's. Once a symbol of freedom and silence where man had left little evidence of his presence, it seemed to him to be a world increasingly ruled by technology and politicians.

Its spirit and stories had awoken Nathan's imagination, a spirit that Nathan had seen nowhere else, and he feared for what the future would hold for these people. A chill came over him, a feeling of insignificance, and then he remembered Sissel and knew that soon she would lose another friend, the Arctic sun, as the darkness and cold again took hold for the winter.

He looked back passionately to the land below and felt himself physically choke.

For mile after mile bands of blue melt water fringed the ice sheet and the coast's deeply indented fjords. Icebergs spilled into the sea, these gigantic ice-castles riding the ocean currents on their journey south. They flew over vast, barren deserts of white threaded with rivers, cut deep with crevasses and blue-black lakes. Mountains rose like islands out of an empty white sea.

An uncomfortable thought came to him: he was on his way back to civilisation, and Eva. The last few years hadn't been easy. He had found it hard being on his own; fate had played him a cruel hand. Whilst Sissel was . . . Sissel, somehow he felt differently towards Eva. She had been the first woman he'd met in all this time who had convinced him that there was a reason to go on. To give him hope that he could love again. Tiredness filled him and he slept.

The plane banked. Waking, Nathan could see the orange orb of the sun's glow. An oblique shaft of bright sunlight crept up the wing surface as they banked more steeply. The dipped wing-tip kissed a thin layer of grey-white cloud and, descending, he could see through the ice-crystalled porthole the sea below. They turned again and this time lined up for the landing. A vibration accompanied a gentle groaning as the landing gear engaged. Next came the rushing sound of the air brakes, and in a matter of minutes they were down, racing along the runway, at Keflavik.

Eva was there to meet him.

"Have you been waiting long?" Nathan said. They hugged and kissed.

"It's good to see you too."

He detected a sarcastic note in her voice. Nathan had been wrong footed: it was too late to add it was good to see her. Searching for exactly what to say he'd failed to notice her new burnt-orange felt jacket. He had, however, spotted her purple silk scarf.

"Is that new? It looks good." Eva ignored his praise.

"About one and a half hours."

"One and a half hours what?"

"Waiting," she said.

"Heavens, why?" an astonished Nathan replied.

"You were very insistent in telling me your flight didn't land until half-five, so I didn't check it."

Nathan looked at his watch, "Yes, that's about right, maybe a few minutes late."

"No," Eva pronounced. "An hour late."

"In Icelandic," Eva went on, "half-five means four-thirty. Although many of us speak English, that doesn't change the meaning of our language. That hasn't changed for centuries."

Nathan tried to appease her. "I thought Greenland was bad enough with four time zones," but that didn't appear to improve things. "So what have you been doing whilst waiting for me?"

She looked embarrassed, "To tell you the truth, after checking out the arrivals boards, I got myself a coffee, sat in one of those uncomfortable plastic seats and started to count the number of floor tiles in the arrivals lounge."

"And?" Nathan said, unsure of what to expect.

"Well, it sounds easy but I kept losing where I'd counted to. All the tiles are the same. Then I forgot to count the tiles where I was sitting and, just when I thought I was on top of it, an official folded back doors to a reception lounge and the floor was covered with the self same tiles! So I gave up."

Eva laughed and looked wide-eyed at Nathan, and he knew as he pulled a quizzical face that the tension had passed.

"Sounds fun," he said.

As they made their way through the airport building heading for Eva's car, she said, "I didn't hear from you, so was it a good trip?"

"But we chatted on the phone."

"You hardly spoke," she said.

Nathan realised that the journey back to her apartment was not going to be easy.

"Yes, it was okay. I could never have imagined what that place was like, and the people I met, their stories disturbed me in a way I wouldn't have thought possible."

"What about the woman?" Eva challenged, not glancing at him, appearing to be totally focussed on the queues of traffic as they made for the highway.

"Woman?" he said, trying to deflect Eva, who was now clearly irritated with not only the traffic. "Who mentioned there was a woman?"

"You, but not in so many words. What was she called?"

So that's what it's all about, Nathan realised. Trying to sound unemotional and detached, he replied, "I stayed in the hotel. She worked in the bar there and was a great help in finding folk who witnessed the crash and were willing to talk to me."

"So she was your barmaid?" Eva persisted. "And that was it?"

The congestion had cleared and they were now cruising towards the city. Nathan's embarrassed silence told her all she didn't want to hear. She struggled to keep her emotions and disappointment under control.

The road accident back on that wet March night had had a profound effect on both their lives. The only other words uttered on that journey were by Eva, who said in a whisper, "I've come to rely on you, I don't want you to leave."

The evening wasn't easy for either of them. Eva was intent on getting to the bottom of his relationship with Sissel. "Did you fall in love with her?"

"No, not in love," Nathan mumbled.

"No, then what exactly?" Eva hadn't lost any of her determination.

"We became very close. She was good to be with . . . " He stopped there, confused as to why he was justifying himself to Eva. "Why are you asking me all these questions?"

Eva looked Nathan in the face. "You know how I feel about you?" He thought for a moment she was about to cry.

He so wanted to put a stop to this but part of him was fearful of what she might say and how it could change things. "No, how do you feel?"

Her stream of emotion wasn't what he expected. "I want us to be together always. I would do anything to make you truly happy. You need to let yourself be loved again, Nathan, before it's too late."

It was then that Nathan realised he had been right to be anxious.

The following morning Eva was like a different woman. For the moment all the questioning and doubt seemed to have gone.

Eva's phone in the apartment rang and she answered it.

"It's that woman who's on TV for you," and she offered the handset to Nathan with a look of disdain.

"Your elusive journalist in Greenland, Martin Poulson," Kirstin started to explain, "was indeed covering some sort of scandal involving the Americans. I tracked down an old colleague from my university days who is a researcher for the national broadcaster DR in Copenhagen, and she knows Poulson. If you're free I think it's best we meet. I know it's short notice but how are you fixed today?" Nathan agreed it was probably the easiest way, face to face. "What about a late lunch?" Kirstin said. "I am free for an hour or so about two, any good?"

After finalising details and restaurant, Kirstin hung up with, "'Til then."

Nathan had no need to concern himself with how he was going to explain a last minute luncheon date to Eva; she was already packing her bags ready for rehearsals.

The maître d' at the restaurant obviously knew her, greeting her as "Miss Kirstin". A window table gave them an ideal view-point on the busy outside world. It took but a few minutes to make their menu choices before settling into small talk about Britain, where Kirstin had spent two years with CNN. Nathan's memory of Kirstin had not failed him: she was as sophisticated and intelligent as he remembered.

Two plates of creamy-white sauce and fresh vegetables were put before them with a jug of iced water.

"So, how does it taste?" she asked, half smiling.

"Okay. It tastes like fish," was all Nathan could run to.

She laughed, "That's because it is fish: fresh fish."

"Can we eat then talk about Poulson after the meal?" he said, prising a bone, then a second from his mouth. Nathan's expression clearly told her he was not a man for bones!

"I'd like to help you out," Kirstin remarked, acknowledging his extractions, "but it's best you do it yourself, at least until we know each other better."

They laughed. Undoubtedly other diners heard them but pretended not to.

Following the fish course and a tangy rhubarb mousse, they got down to business over a meagre cup of espresso.

"It seems Martin Poulson originally started with radio in Jutland then, some ten or so years ago, worked as a television reporter in Āarhus. Have you been there?" she asked Nathan as an aside. He shook his head and frowned. "I have, it's Denmark's second city. The old part is a maze of picturesque medieval streets and buildings, and the new, largely unmemorable. For the past few years he has been assigned as a Foreign Correspondent based in Copenhagen, interestingly enough, specialising in UK current affairs for your BBC, amongst others."

"Really," Nathan countered, "and did your contact know anything about what he had uncovered?"

"No, he's a loner and been intent on involving no one else in his investigations. None of his news-room colleagues have been taken into his confidence, Poulson maintains a mantle of secrecy over that aspect of his work. The whole thing is an enigma and has become known at the station, somewhat frivolously, as Assignment Ellinore."

"Ellinore?" Nathan puzzled, seeking some clue.

"I don't know for certain, but I believe its meaning is *compassion,*" Kirstin explained.

From what Nathan had already discovered he considered that to be a fitting name to have chosen. "What's this Martin Poulson like?"

"Different, as I recall. He comes across as a persistent investigative journalist who tries to convey the truth simply and accurately. A professional with an insightful knowledge of international affairs. Perhaps you should meet him," was Kirstin's parting shot, "he might just talk to you."

"Do you think so?"

"Maybe." She glanced at her watch, "I really must dash, I'm on air within the hour. Thanks for lunch, perhaps we can do it again sometime when I'm not up against the clock. I'll get you the number of my contact and she'll be able to tell you more and try and make arrangements, if you want."

They stood. Kirstin, taking her leave, kissed him on the cheek. A couple on the next table seemed to recognise her and watched Nathan intently as he bid her farewell. Fumbling with her overcoat, she asked Nathan, "Oh, I should have asked, how are you after that terrible accident?"

There was just enough time for him to answer that he was okay before she had stepped out onto the pavement into the relentless September rain and was away. It was then that it dawned on him, as the maître d' looked his way and smiled, that he was left to pick up the tab.

Nathan joined his fellow shoppers scurrying about, trying to avoid a soaking and the prowling bitter wind, nearly 6,000 króna the lighter.

The phone rang in Eva's apartment. Nathan answered, expecting it to be her and wondering why she was so late.

"Nathan, is that you?" Kirstin's voice sounded breathless. "You said it was okay to call you on this number. Well, I meant to tell you that Christina said you're not the only person who's been asking about Poulson's work."

"Christina?" Nathan queried.

"She's my contact at DR. Someone else has been asking questions about him."

CHAPTER TWENTY-TWO

"Sorry I'm late." Eva's attempt to hide her annoyance was lost when she slammed the door.

"Where have you been, rehearsals? I was expecting you back an hour or more ago."

"So was I, but I had to drop by the station."

"Station?" Nathan said, still not totally concentrating.

"Police station. They wanted to check on something from my interview."

Nathan had now put to one side what he was doing and turned towards her.

"Check what?" he said sternly.

"Oh, I'll tell you sometime, but now everything is okay, I'm famished," and with that she dived off into the kitchen.

It was clear to Nathan that the whole affair was still taking its toll on Eva, both mentally and physically. He moved beside her, held her in his arms and there they stood in silence for the next few minutes. Eva was the first to speak.

"Can we get away for a bit? I haven't any work for the next three weeks, will you come with me?"

Nathan didn't need to think it over. "Yes, sure."

"When can we go?"

"I promised I'd see your father and I must do that before we go anywhere, and if we're going to be away for a while I would want to get hold of a couple of books; reading for those long, boring days." His look and joke put paid to the uneasy atmosphere and soon they were both laughing.

* * * *

Entering the bookshop Nathan heard the echoing tones of a door chime. His first instinct as he looked around was that this bore no resemblance to what he had expected and almost felt he needed to go outside and check it wasn't a music shop. Weaving between the floor to ceiling shelves stacked with dust-laden books, he finally came upon the proprietor of this emporium seated in a corner surrounded by piles of forgotten works. A musty smell hung in the air: a smell that reminded him of his father's study.

The man sat humming to music, oblivious to Nathan's entrance. At first glance Nathan put him in his mid-thirties, a plump man with dense, curly black hair framing his round unshaven face. The man beamed at Nathan.

"You're not from around here?" he greeted.

Nathan nodded, "England."

"Good, good, I am Erik," he said as he turned down the record player's volume. "Let me tell you what I have here. There are many different sections. You may be particularly interested in our Icelandic authors, perhaps their poetry, or maybe our dictionaries over there." Erik couldn't resist pointing in various directions; to Nathan it appeared almost randomly. Nathan felt he displayed a smugness which, fortunately, was quickly dispelled as soon as he spoke again. "No, seriously, what can I help you with?"

Nathan said, "Greenland. Have you any books on Greenland and the Cold War?"

Erik looked amused as he headed to an arrangement of shelves at the end of an aisle where, facing them, were some four or five hundred books of all colours and sizes. A call came from deep within the bowels of the store, a woman's voice. Erik responded excitedly in what Nathan assumed to be Icelandic, and shortly after, a woman wearing a woollen hat and a pink raincoat appeared carrying two books which she duly paid for. They exchanged pleasantries in hushed voices then, once again, he addressed Nathan.

"This is where you will find books about Greenland and the Arctic and the settlement of its first people, and over there by the wooden chair is a section on the Cold War period. Any books in English will be amongst those. If you're struggling to find what you're looking for give me a shout: they call me the Book-hunter." Above the wooden chair hung a framed, signed poster of Bobby Fischer. "He came here when he was competing in the World Chess Championships back in 1972," Erik announced. "A nice guy that Bobby, odd, but nice enough for an American. The competition was billed as the 'Cold War Confrontation', which is why I hung his poster with the Cold War books." Erik grinned, then went back to his reading.

It was a few minutes before Nathan discovered a title in English. Stepping back into better light so he could peruse the pages, he nudged a small stack of volumes initiating a mass avalanche of books. Erik's voice boomed out from somewhere behind the racks. "Don't worry, it happens all the time. Leave them and I'll sort it later."

Nathan was already bent over the sprawling titles, trying to bring some degree of order and clear an exit for himself. The dust that had been taking refuge amongst their bindings must have taken exception to being disturbed, and Nathan was beginning to experience an irritation in his nose. He sneezed loudly twice.

"I am always sneezing," Nathan heard Erik reassure him. "It's a hazard of the job."

Within the hour Nathan had stumbled upon five books and was now standing in front of Erik, seated at his desk which had been styled more from books than wood.

"What are you reading?" Nathan asked, trying to find a place to set down his new-found treasures.

"*A Song of Ice and Fire*, by the American novelist, George R R Martin, do you know it?" Erik showed him the sleeve. Nathan admitted he didn't. "It's an epic fantasy trilogy and this first volume was four years in the writing."

"So, it's fantasy you're into?"

"No. I love poetry. Poetry inspires me. I am reading a collection of Stefán Grimsson's work; he is regarded as one of our modernists. Such writing creates within a new consciousness, a new self image; it is part of who we are." Erik paused, probably expecting Nathan to ask some learned question. "But I mostly read *Tintin*," Erik confessed with a twinkle in his eye. "Now what have we here?"

Nathan had considered his tactic for haggling the price down but, in light of Erik's jovial manner, he had second thoughts. Anyway, such an approach was totally unnecessary. "I make it 2150 Króna, Erik said, let's call it 1700 for the lot, how does that sound? They're not the easiest of books to come by, but they are also physically difficult to get to in here, and if it wasn't for you they wouldn't be going anywhere for ages, if at all."

Nathan left wondering what secrets, if any, they would reveal.

* * * *

Many months earlier Magnus had posted a notice on a US military veterans' website which had resulted in a handful of responses from servicemen who had been stationed at Thule during the late fifties, early sixties. He had all but forgotten about his appeal for information when he received an email from a Jack Marshall of Green Bay, Wisconsin. Jack's tour had initially meant he was stationed at Century, which he described like 'a sunken ship out in the middle of a frozen sea'. He was an ice-cutter. Gangs of men with chain saws would slice back the encroaching ice that threatened to crush the buildings. Jack headed up the teams and, as a structural engineer, had been instrumental in evaluating the viability of sustaining structures beneath the ever-moving ice cap. He had been based at Thule at the time of the B-52 Broken Arrow incident and had been horrified by how ill-prepared they were for the fall-out from the crash. Jack's replies to Magnus' emails had intimated that there was more he could say, but either they should meet or, if that was impossible, call each other in future.

Magnus' initial telephone call had revealed that, like him, Jack had remained uneasy with much that had happened at Thule. Jack was unaware of the significant impact that the incident had made on the health of so many, nor was he fully au fait with the secrecy surrounding the presence of nuclear weapons on Danish territory. He hadn't deliberately avoided the truth, he just didn't know, explaining that news came slowly to Green Bay, if it came at all. What Jack revealed to Magnus he found hard to believe, for he had never before heard of the

Iceworm Project, yet he and Ernst had been stationed in the very place where the notion was being explored. Magnus had never considered the possibility of the US adopting a different response to the crash of the bomber. As soon as Jack spelt out the likely scenarios Magnus was aghast, terrified at the consequences. He knew full well the Soviets continually monitored all communications within the Polar Theatre of Operations, patrolling both the waters and sky about the northern hemisphere. He was blown away by the idea that the perceived bringing down of an American nuclear armed bomber by a hostile force could precipitate the US taking immediate retaliatory action which, in turn, could lead to the mobilisation of Soviet strike forces. Magnus appreciated that these occurrences could develop at such a pace that in no time at all, the chain of events would prove impossible to stop.

Magnus was expecting Nathan, and having ushered him into his flat wasted no time in pleasantries. "Do you know about Iceworm?"

Nathan was thrown by Magnus' question and his answer was equally direct, "Yes."

After comparing notes and explaining about Jack Marshall, all that Magnus could manage to say was, "I had no idea. Is there no end to which the US would go? Did you know in 1961 the Russians had tested their one-hundred megaton Czar bomb? Its destruction stretched over three hundred miles. Jack told me the Americans would estimate their death or injury figures on the basis of roughly one million deaths per megaton; can you imagine that, Nathan? The world was on a catastrophic path to mutual destruction and the days of conventional weapons were long gone. I know it sounds melodramatic, but, that's how it was."

Nathan eased himself back into his chair and raised his eyebrows.

"I am forgetting myself, my dear boy. You should have put a stop to my ramblings. How did it go in Greenland? What did you think of the place?"

Nathan frowned, "You need to be a particular type of individual to cope with life up there. It's so dramatically different from anywhere else I have ever been. The reclusive natives are a dying breed and as things change something fundamental is being lost: trust. And I don't believe it will ever return while things remain as they are."

Magnus appeared lost, Nathan assumed he was probably thinking back to the time when he and Ernst had first set foot on Greenland. "Of course we had very little contact with the Inuit people. They had been moved out long before we arrived." Then, breaking his chain of thought, he said, "I've got my television set-up in the lounge, have you seen any archive footage of Century and Thule?"

"No," Nathan said, welcoming the interruption. "Where did you get it?"

"From the States, Jack sent it over. It's a film he made whilst up there. When he heard of my interest he got me a copy."

"What's it like?" Nathan enquired as he settled in front of the screen.

"Not bad when you consider his original was probably 8mm film which he must have projected onto a wall, then re-filmed with a camcorder. I have got his tape in my old camera and hooked it up to the TV. It works okay but the quality isn't great, but I guess the original wasn't much better."

For twenty minutes not a word passed between them, only the occasional glance as they watched.

"What do you think?" said Magnus switching off the camera and TV. Nathan was lost in contemplation, palms pressed together, his index finger resting against his mouth. Following a moment of reflection he spoke.

"I've heard people's first-hand accounts and, like you Magnus, studied the documents and reports, but I never realised how bad things were."

Magnus' reply came in a hushed voice. "None of us knew when death would come, but we knew there was no escaping it."

Although the images Jack had recorded were far from sharp and steady, there was no getting away from the significance of the movie. The blazing bomber appeared as a distant orange and yellow fireball reflected in the ice. The magnitude of the inferno had shocked Nathan. A sequence of shots showed Inuits with their dog teams illuminated by the blaze, some joining military personnel appearing to search the area for survivors. The scenes that proved to have the greatest impact on Nathan were those of the clean-up: scores of men, protected by little more than yellow boiler suits over their winter gear, shovelling snow and debris polluted with plutonium. What was deeply harrowing was seeing the band of men looking as though they were enjoying the challenge, ignorant of what they were really doing.

Magnus spoke, "Having watched it, it feels as if the bomb is exploding all over again."

The film concluded by showing tank-like vessels, not unlike massive open-topped shipping containers, being filled with snow, then loaded onto low trailers to be put on board ships heading for the US. One container slipped on its strops and tipped some of its contaminated load onto the workmen below. A shiver ran down Nathan's spine as he exclaimed, "My God."

"Someone's been trying to contact Jack about what he knows," Magnus said, "that's why he was cautious in talking with me. His suspicions were raised by the fellow's persistent questioning."

"A reporter?" Nathan asked.

"No, he didn't think so. From what he said, more like someone on the inside, he thought a military man."

CHAPTER TWENTY-THREE

Over the ensuing days Eva became increasingly conscious of Nathan's almost fixation with the Thule affair. She knew her old father had the ability to draw others into his schemes, recognising he could be like a tenacious terrier once he got his teeth into something. Eva thought Magnus had probably harboured a degree of guilt in not having pursued the matter years earlier, but now he had seen in Nathan an ally, one who was young and fit enough to take it on for him.

Eva decided she needed to distract Nathan from his all-consuming quest, if for no other reason than his sanity.

"Fancy some music tonight?"

"You said you hadn't a concert," Nathan managed.

"No, not until next month, when our winter programme begins. I was thinking of one of the downtown dive bars." Nathan looked puzzled. "A music bar – the Gaukar ā Stöng. It'll be fun."

"If you want," Nathan said.

"Can't you show a bit more enthusiasm when a woman asks you out?"

"Oh, I'm sorry, my mind was on something else," Nathan said pathetically.

"Yes, I know," Eva replied, concerned.

The moodily lit bar was adorned with glistening chrome fittings, dark woodwork and gaudy paintings. It wasn't that easy to get a feel for its true character because the place was so packed and already Nathan was doubting the soundness of the idea.

"You can't move. Is it always like this midweek?"

"I know, fab isn't it?" Eva said as she bumped into a crowd she knew. Someone proposed they get some drinks and find a quiet corner.

"You're looking good Eva," one of the men volunteered. She turned to him then smiled. Nathan also turned to him but didn't smile. The fellow's words were enough to gain Nathan's full attention.

"How do you know him?" Nathan said, scanning the half dozen strangers.

"He plays here in the bands. Why?" Nathan didn't answer, gulped his gold beer and looked far from easy.

"Is it okay?" Eva asked, meaning the beer.

"Sure. It's pretty hoppy, Carlsberg?" Nathan said, uncertain.

"No, Thule beer," and she laughed.

"This is Nathan," Eva announced to all, "the man I almost killed." That went down well, attracting plenty of attention that Nathan was clearly uncomfortable with.

"Hi," was the extent of his reply.

"Don't worry," one of them said to him, "she doesn't normally make a habit of it," and slapped Nathan on the back. Two stood and, explaining they needed to get ready for the session, took their leave.

"Relax," Eva encouraged Nathan, "you'll love it, wait and see."

As the six guys came out onto the platform, the crowd quietened and a few minutes later Far North struck up.

"They're really good," a surprised Nathan said to Eva. "What sort of music is it?"

"I said you'd like it. It's a kind of cross-over between electric folk and rock. But you just wait."

For thirty minutes the crowd was gripped by the haunting, ethereal sound. Some were dancing as best they could, crammed like rush-hour commuters, others swayed en masse. After applause for the first set, the man who had admired Eva earlier put down his guitar and came to the mic. "We've someone in the crowd tonight who I know is desperate to bring a bit of classical class to proceedings, someone who is no stranger to you all. Please welcome our old friend, Eva Hannes."

Nathan hadn't seen that coming and by the time he had turned to say something to her, she was looking back at him and smiling as she made her way to the stage. One of the band offered her his electric violin and following a few bars of introduction, she struck out, sending the audience wild.

"Was that cool or what?" Eva asked him on her return, "I told you it would be fun."

"Sure, but I thought you only played classical," Nathan said, still reeling.

"There you go, there's more to me than meets the eye." To that Nathan could only agree. This gentle, quiet woman had surprised him. He had underestimated her and he wouldn't do that again he decided.

Eva was aware that Nathan had found the night rowdy and anything but relaxing, finally getting him up onto his feet for a dance. She also realised he'd seen a different side to her, one which appeared to shock him. They got back to her apartment around 2am, exhausted.

The next morning, over their late breakfast, Eva saw an opportunity to tackle Nathan on the subject of Thule. She knew that sooner or later he would expect her to say something.

"Why are you helping Father dig up all those old memories?"

"I'm not," Nathan said, buttering some bread, "he is more than aware of his memories."

"But don't you think what you are doing could be dangerous? What about your run-in at the base?"

He looked her squarely in the face, "Yes, I suppose so, but if I don't follow it through, who will? Someone's got to and it certainly won't be Magnus, will it? When you see things are so wrong, you have to do something."

Eva couldn't disagree. "You're an idiot," and as soon as she had said it she regretted her words.

"What do you mean?" Nathan challenged with more than a hint of annoyance in his voice.

"The answers you are seeking strike to the very core of the American government, their military and the Danish government. They are secrets which they have kept all these years and they're simply not going to let them go. I fear, Nathan, that if you carry on you'll end up risking your life for this . . . Please don't do that."

Over the months Eva had grown close to Nathan. In many ways it was unnatural: he had given her little encouragement, and he was still a relative stranger to her. Her brief conversation with his sister, Jane, had only fired Eva's interest in him the more; his family life, his wife, the woman he had spent so little time with. She could hardly imagine what it must be like to lose someone so early that you love. She was only too aware that there were those who thought her foolish, acting silly, chasing a nearly fifty-year-old man, but Eva didn't care. She didn't see it that way.

"Do you have to get back to England and to the university?" she said not really wanting him to go.

"To be honest, after losing Lindsey I found it hard to go back full-time to my work and lectures. The university was supportive and understood the pressures and, in the short term, agreed that I would take on a consultancy role. This has been a god-send and allowed me space to think about my future. I sold our home; I could never have lived there without Lindsey. So you see, there's no need to rush back. Anyway, everything will be fine, I promise you."

There was something either about the way he had said it, or the way he looked, that caused Eva to feel uneasy.

"You asked me why I'm helping your father. I suppose, if I'm honest, it's out of selfishness on my part. For years my father talked me down, telling me I'd never come to anything. What little self-esteem I had he took away. As far as he was concerned if I wasn't going to make it in the military, then I wasn't going to make it at all. Having destroyed my mother he set about us children. Thankfully Jane escaped but he wasn't about to let me out of his clutches. In spite of his bullying, or maybe because of it, there was something inside that made me want to fight back, to become stronger, more determined. I'd like to think it was part of his plan but I don't think for one moment that was the case: he was never subtle enough for that.

"For the past year or so I have searched for something; a cause which will give me a purpose and take my mind off my loss. And, if I'm completely honest, I want to prove to myself that my father was wrong. You see, Eva, that is the cause: this is something I have to take a chance on, but I'm not sure you understand."

Eva held him, placing her hands on his arms. She slid her hands lightly up and down before softly kissing him. He tried to embrace her but she gently pushed him away.

*   *   *   *

September brought shorter days and falling temperatures, heralding the impending start of Iceland's winter. At least winter in Reykjavik wouldn't be as severe as that of Thule, Nathan thought. The rain, which seemed to him more intense than ever, would soon give way to fierce onshore winds, fog and falls of driving snow which would linger for months on end. The green rolling fields of southern England and the dense rustic-orange woodlands seemed a world away to him. Eva had tried to console him by explaining that because of the geothermal activity in the city it stayed noticeably warmer than in the countryside. It's all relative, Nathan cynically concluded. Once again his thoughts turned to the bitter barrenness that was Thule, and, inevitably, Sissel.

Across the room Eva's PC bleeped and the monitor reverted to her screen saver, a photo of the impressive waterfalls of Gullfoss. Nathan had intended to use his time that morning to settle down to some concerted research on the web. Eva was out so he reckoned he wouldn't be disturbed, but he was finding it hard to concentrate. There were moments when his mind wandered and this was proving to be one of them.

The apartment door burst open.

"Have you heard the news?" Eva said, pushing in with her bags and not bothering to close it behind her. "Isn't it dreadful?" she said dumping her bags and coat.

Meanwhile Nathan had made it to the door and closed it. "What?" he said.

"Don't tell me you haven't heard?" she said indignantly while switching on the TV.

Immediately the screen showed a burning tower block with dense clouds of black smoke belching upwards into the sky. For a minute he didn't know where it was or what had happened, then a caption rolled across the bottom of the picture – 'CNN Breaking News: WORLD TRADE CENTRE DISASTER – one of the Twin Towers is on fire.'

"I just caught the headline on the car radio, it sounds horrendous," she said sitting on the couch beside him.

Two reporters started to discuss the tragedy as the scene unfolded, their voices uncertain and hesitant.

"This is just in – unconfirmed reports this morning state that a plane has crashed into the World Trade Centre at the south end of the Island of Manhattan. It looks as if it could be the North Tower. We're seeing a devastating scene before us.

"For those joining us these are live pictures of the World Trade Centre Tower." There was a moment of silence as the broadcast switched between two different viewpoints of the Tower. Clouds of black smoke poured from the building, engulfing its upper floors and darkening the sky.

Nathan and Eva sat riveted to the screen, not saying a word, stunned at the sight before their eyes.

The news anchor spoke:

"As we're watching it appears the second tower is on fire, there is smoke coming from the South Tower."

"That's staggering, what do you think has happened Nathan?" Eva was clearly finding it hard to understand the horror unfolding.

Before Nathan had the chance to say anything, Jim, the news anchor spoke. He was loud and disbelieving.

"We are just hearing right now of another explosion – it's taken place at the . . . the Pentagon's on fire. Huge plumes of smoke 200 yards across are rising from the west side of the Pentagon. Reports on the news network are saying that it was hit by an aircraft at 9.37 and both the US Capital Building and the White House in Washington DC have been evacuated as they are believed to be targets."

Without a word Eva got up and took herself off into the kitchen closing the door behind her. Nathan followed.

"Are you okay?"

"Sure, I can't watch anymore, it's so terrible that anyone would want to do that."

Tearful, she began busying herself preparing food and keeping out of the way. Nathan decided it was best to leave her to it and returned to the television. For nearly an hour Nathan continued to watch as the frightening events of 9/11 unfolded.

Eva came back into the lounge. Nathan looked up, "The Twin Towers have collapsed and they've just reported five storeys of the Pentagon have also collapsed due to fire."

Eva shook her head. "How many people have lost their lives, it must be an enormous number."

Nathan was unsure if Eva was asking or sharing her concern. "They say many, many thousands are dead and the injured could be ten thousand or more."

With a look of despair in her face Eva said in a faltering voice, "The world's a hideous place."

Nathan added, in a considered tone, "The Cold War was the Third World War that never happened, but terrorism, that's the real Third World War, it's the horror and violence so few can inflict on so many.

CHAPTER TWENTY-FOUR

Eva spent a restless night still very unsure about Nathan, still uncertain how he felt towards her. Pleading with him, demanding an answer, even anger she was certain would do no good. Maybe, she considered, he didn't find relationships with women easy, or perhaps it was just with her.

Over breakfast she decided to tackle him, endeavouring to be as non - confrontational as possible – she didn't want a scene, not so soon after his return.

"What happened up there in Greenland?"

"I told you. I met some people that witnessed the crash."

"Sure, but what was it like?

"There was nothing but wilderness, an emptiness, even in the sky," he said, suddenly appearing lost in his own thoughts. "I travelled hundreds of miles to the top of the world to discover its secrets, and what I found was a spirited people, hardened by their harsh way of life which they were trying desperately to hold onto, along with their fading memories. I thought I would understand that place but I couldn't have been so wrong." Nathan stared through Eva.

"Tell me about the woman." Her words seemed to bring him crashing back to reality.

"The woman?" he muttered. "What about the woman?"

"How did you meet her? What was she like?" Eva promptly added. The silence that followed Eva left uninterrupted, allowing Nathan to consider his response. She needed to know.

"I told you, she worked in the hotel where I stayed." There was an air of aggression, or maybe annoyance in his voice.

"Oh yes," Eva acknowledged, hoping for more. She looked at him, expectant. A considerate Nathan obliged her curiosity,

"I don't really know how I'd best describe her. Despite the harshness of that place she was still an attractive woman. Things were challenging enough for her, having lost a young daughter and her man, so she started a new life way up north. Without her I would have found it impossible to have got to the truth of those days in '68. She had a way that endeared her to those we met; they trusted her and would speak to me, a stranger. I heard many different voices while I was there but they all said the same. The crash had turned their lives upside down, and for many there had been no place to hide from the wind of death." Nathan paused, "The justice they deserved, they never got."

Eva so wanted to know more about the woman herself. She couldn't help but suspect their relationship had been more involved than he implied and thought it strange he never used her name. She decided against pressing him right now.

"Why did you get so tangled up in the whole affair and go to Greenland on what many would see as a wild goose chase?"

She didn't want to risk questioning his judgement again but still didn't fully understand. The answer she got was of no surprise.

"As I've said before, Magnus, of course. Your father convinced me that the truth was out there, and, if revealed, could make such a difference to the lives of so many people who were struggling to come to terms with the consequences of the disaster. It was clear he was in no fit state to undertake the journey himself, yet without someone going the truth would probably have remained a secret. Even after thirty odd years those that were responsible have remained silent. I can't help but think that finally their moment has come."

"Surely that's not something you can do by yourself?" Eva cautiously remarked. "That sounds like a monumental task, not to say a dangerous one."

"Sure," Nathan said, sounding distant, "that's why I need to go to Denmark."

This came completely out of the blue to Eva. "Why, what's in Denmark?"

"No, who," Nathan explained. "Martin Poulson. He's an investigative journalist for their national broadcaster based in Copenhagen, and for the past fifteen years has been looking into the affair. I need to meet him."

"Does he know what you've been doing?"

"Yes, well, kind of. I sent a message via a contact here in Reykjavik. It seems he's happy to meet up."

Eva was sure her concern for Nathan's safety was evident in her face. "Will you come with me?" he said.

"Yes. When are you planning on going?" This was all coming too fast for her.

"I haven't booked a flight but he's expecting me out there soon. I know winter in Copenhagen doesn't sound too much like fun."

"Okay," Eva confirmed not wishing to appear over-eager, although she couldn't think of anything else she would rather do . . . But then, "Oh, I can't." Her head was in a spin, his unexpected words had thrown her.

"Why not? Don't tell me it's the orchestra?" he instantly replied.

"I am playing at Airwaves."

"So what's Airwaves?" he said.

"The biggest music party in the Northern Hemisphere when Iceland showcases its music to the world. All Reykjavik's pubs, clubs and gig venues go wild for a week in October. We're billing for three nights along with other foreign bands, I can't let them down."

"Who's 'them'?" Nathan said.

"The guys, Far North," she replied.

"Never mind," Nathan said, "I'm sure you would have been bored."

Thinking fast, Eva said, "Could we get sometime away before you have to go?"

To her surprise Nathan offered no resistance to the idea.

Their road trip began on a crisp, bright September morning. The early milky light had little warmth as yet.

"It's going to be over a four-hour run so we'll make a stop," Eva said negotiating Route 1 south-east out of the city. With the movement of the car Nathan was soon drifting in and out of sleep. The sparsely populated expanse of treeless meadowland passed largely unnoticed.

He woke with a start. "We're not there yet are we?"

"No," Eva said grabbing her coat from the back seat, "about halfway. This is Vik." A fresh sea breeze accompanied her opening of the car door. "Are you coming? Do you fancy a hot drink?"

"Sure. It feels bitter out there." The warmth of the car had ill-prepared him for what Iceland's autumn had in store. Nathan's lungs filled with the fresh air. He shivered.

"I hope you've packed some warm clothes," Eva called, heading across the car park, and, disappearing into the coffee shop, left Nathan to take in the dramatic panorama. Atlantic rollers driven by a ferocious wind were crashing across the wide-reaching beach of black lava sand which stretched below the settlement.

"Is it always as harsh as this here?" Nathan asked Eva as he settled opposite her, taking comfort from his hot chocolate.

"Pretty much this time of year. It's the most southerly village in Iceland; there's nothing but ocean between here and Antarctica."

"No wonder it's so bloody cold," he muttered.

Driving east they headed inland, leaving behind the towering cliffs of Vik and its pretty white church that stood on a hill as if guarding the village. The car clattered across the single-track steel bridges that spanned river tentacles which weaved their way to the sea. The flat featureless landscape extended south as far as the eye could see, the coast now lost from sight. Fine black ash edged the road, broken only by boulders of lava covered in a velvet mat of vegetation which shimmered light-green in the weak afternoon sun. Car headlights glowed dimly in the distance, and lingered for what seemed far too long before a vehicle rattled past sending a shower of gravel in its wake. For mile after mile the road, hemmed in by mountains to the north, skirted the barren highlands and alluvium plains, the only colour provided by the red and white banded marker poles erected along the roadside.

"It's hard to imagine, but in the spring and summer this whole area is ablaze with the vibrant purple of lupins," Eva shared in an attempt to break the monotony. "After the winter, when the glacial dam breaks or there is an eruption under the ice sheet, roaring torrents of massive icebergs, water and debris surge across these lowlands to the sea. Each year stretches of the road that are washed away by the ice have to be rebuilt."

The afternoon was wearing on and the weak sunlight that remained would soon fade. Second-guessing what Nathan was thinking Eva said, "We'll soon be there. I have booked a guesthouse on the edge of the glacier, I hope it's okay."

Fifteen minutes later they pulled up outside a substantial timber lodge. They registered with a rosy-faced woman of ample charm who appeared to chuckle as she fastidiously completed the paperwork. Parting to their rooms for a shower and a change of clothes, they agreed to meet downstairs for a drink. Following dinner they relaxed in the lounge pondering the changing evening sky. The cold orange halo that kissed the distant horizon had now given way to a ghostly grey light. Winds drove across the plain whipping up clouds of ash dust before it.

"What do we do tomorrow?" Nathan asked sipping his whisky.

"A short thirty mile run onto Jökulsárlón which sits on the coastal edge of the Vatnajökull, Europe's largest ice sheet, but then you probably knew that, didn't you?"

For once he didn't answer her and she was left unsure if he had heard her final remark or was preoccupied thinking about something else. "Tell me about your wife," she said, looking awkwardly at him. "What memories do you hold of her?" She could hear the anxiety in her own voice.

After a long silence he spoke. "It's funny," he confessed, "I can still smell her and, at times, I almost sense her near me, and sometimes when others speak it's as though it's her words I'm hearing. I so want to remember Lindsey as things were, as she was, beautiful and wonderful. I miss her every single day. In the beginning things couldn't have been better, we couldn't have been happier. We didn't know then that our time together would be so brief. I think she knew she was going to die but not how she would die. I told her it would be alright, I said it would, but I knew it wouldn't – but then so I think did she."

"I'm worried about you," Eva said. "Lindsey was your life, and now you are on your own. You are going to need to find another reason to get on with your life, another person to believe in."

Nathan brushed his eyes with his fingers: eyes that, to Eva, appeared haunted by loneliness and vulnerability. "There were times when I would dearly have gone with her. My world fell in on top of me. Her last words to me were to tell me how much she loved me and how now I was free to love again." Nathan, looking at her smiled a cold and lost smile. "You know, Eva, there's nothing worse than when you don't feel as though you belong to anyone."

Eva just sat, she didn't move, she didn't answer, trying hard to contain her emotions. All that Nathan had told her made her more certain that, as badly as he needed someone, so did she.

"You will find love again," she said, trying to sound convinced.

"I don't know anymore. After all that's happened I'm not sure."

His words left her with a strange feeling, an ache. She had so hoped. "Keep believing," she replied in a whisper.

"Being with you these past weeks has helped," he said. The strain on his face had gone, his whole countenance had lifted, "Thanks."

Eva wanted to say so many things but . . .

The groaning of a generator starting up interrupted their chain of thought.

"Hell, life goes on," Nathan proclaimed, "and you must be exhausted after the drive, I know I am even though I slept a good bit of the way."

Eva conceded she was ready for bed. Any doubt about sleeping arrangements was short-lived. As Nathan stood, offering a hand to help her up, he said, "Sleep well, I'll catch you over breakfast, say nine? Is that okay?"

"Yes sure," she heard herself saying. He leant forward and kissed her on the cheek, "I hope you don't mind," he added as an afterthought.

A sort of queasiness overcame her, and in an instant she felt differently towards him.

"No," she said. Perhaps there was hope after all.

* * * *

The frigid glacial lagoon stretched out before them. They stared upon a mass of pale-blue icebergs, freshly broken off the ancient glacier, floating in the turquoise water. Behind loomed the massive Vatnajökull ice cap like an advancing giant. The air felt crisp and clean, alive with negative ions.

"It's magnificent, isn't it?" Eva said. "It's like a surreal painting . . . no, a sculpture."

"Yes, truly spectacular," Nathan admitted.

As they spoke bergs creaked, slowly rolling in the lagoon disturbing the deep freezing waters.

"The chilling silence always feels weird to me, as if nature had imposed the silence. There's something sinister about this place, almost alien," she said. "There was an eruption of the volcano beneath the ice cap only three years back, it was a hellish sight to see."

"It's not really surprising," he said. "The ice cap sits directly over the Mid Atlantic Ridge as well as above a hot-spot, a kind of fiery underworld."

"Of course," Eva said, "you know all about this, don't you?"

"Well, I'm supposed to," he said, smiling.

"So you'll know why the glacier looks blue?"

Nathan decided a simple approach might be the best. "As sunlight travels into the ice, light at the red end of the spectrum is absorbed by the ice, showing only the blue end of the spectrum."

"Oh," she exclaimed. "And how is it such an enormous mass of snow like a glacier can move?"

Before he realised what he was saying Nathan heard himself launch into a lecture. "As the surface snow on the glacier melts, so the water drains through fissures and great gashes in the ice from enormous lakes and flows down to the bedrock. This lubricates the glacier, helping millions of tons of ice to slide down the mountain. Some can move over forty yards a day."

"Yards?" she echoed.

"As much as thirty-six metres. I visited Norway's and Continental Europe's largest glacier a few years back," he continued. "There, twenty-five years earlier, a light aircraft had crash-landed and then disappeared like a phantom: the glacier had swallowed the aircraft. For years it had been expected that the glacier would give up its secret, but as yet the aircraft and pilot remain in their frozen tomb, gradually moving to where the ice will release them and spew them out."

"Wow," Eva instantly responded.

"What?" he said, looking about.

"For a moment I thought I was in one of your seminars!"

"Sorry, old habits."

"No, you're good. You must be because I understood what you were saying."

A pair of rigid inflatables, each with a dozen or so tourists in bright orange life-jackets, motored across the lagoon, icy sludge gurgling in their wake as they weaved between the bergs. In the distance, a great rumbling resounded and a berg up-ended, rolled, submerged then rose towering out of the water. The whole sequence played out as if in slow motion.

"Do you fancy a trip across the lagoon?" Eva asked.

"Yes sure. On one of those RIBs?"

"No, I've got something else in mind," she said heading along the water's edge towards a group of buildings.

Parked behind the Visitors' Centre were two formidable amphibious boats with wheels. They looked like sleek modern landing craft decked out with a dazzling yellow hull and white superstructure. Nathan and Eva joined a queue of expectant tourists, back-packers and locals who were anything but orderly as they put on life vests while jostling to clamber up the boarding steps. Forty or more squeezed aboard. The growl of the diesel engines completely drowned out their excited chatter before the vehicle rolled down the slipway and slid into the glacial waters. The craft negotiated the maze of icebergs, cruising right up to the glacier's face. A pod of seals lazily avoided the agile RIBs which slowly circled the bergs, checking ahead of the crafts.

Eva could tell Nathan was impressed, he was smiling. "What do you think?" she said.

"Fantastic, it certainly raises the experience a few notches. What an amazing machine. It's a first for me, I've never seen anything quite like this before."

"Really?"

"Yes, I think there's little call for these in North Wales."

"So you're not a movie fan?" she said, and added, "Lara Croft?"

"Who?" he said.

"Tomb Raider."

"Tomb Raider?" For Nathan this clearly made no sense.

"I am sure you've heard of Angelina Jolie?" Eva said.

"Yes, of course, why?"

"Well, they filmed part of the movie Tomb Raider here on the lagoon in these land boats last year, or maybe the year before. The film came out this summer."

"Right, I do recall now. In fact I think Jane took the boys to see it. So what were you going to say?"

"That's it," Eva replied, "but I didn't expect it to be so involved," and laughed.

After comments along the lines of, "No, this one's bigger," "I think this is the most amazing shape and colour," "That's a beauty," interspersed with the clicking of cameras as people barged to the side rail to get a better view, the craft stopped in the middle of the lagoon. With that the guide gave a brief talk followed by a chance for all to taste 1,000-year-old ice, then headed back before too many complained about being cold.

As they landed ashore and joined the hordes coming and going Eva said, "Do you want to get away somewhere quiet for dinner? Can you cope with a half-hour run?"

Agreeing, they made it back to the car and headed west, shadowing the coastline much of the way until they reached the fjords that opened up each side of the peninsular of Höfn. Eva drove the back road down to the working port, then onto Restaurant Humarhöfnin.

"I sure hope you fancy fish," she said as they perused the menu, "there's lamb, but fish is their speciality."

"That's fine," he said.

"Good; the langoustine's straight from the boats, the Arctic Char off our south coast – grilled or smoked. Their salt fish fillets and herring are caught and processed at the local fish factory."

Nathan looked bemused. "No horse burgers?"

"No, but the real treat is lobster, local lobster; Höfn's known as the lobster capital of the north."

"Right, well, lobster it is," and with that he closed the menu putting it to one side. A handful of locals looking cosy in a variety of traditional hand knitted sweaters, each with their own distinctive herringbone and scalloped pattern, were crowded about a small table upon which bowls of prawns and bottles of beer were arranged. Their talk was loud and raucous. Two other tables were occupied with what Eva took to be tourists.

"Sorry, it's noisier than when I was here last."

"That's okay," Nathan said, "they say you can't keep a good Viking down."

"What will you do with what you've learnt in Greenland?" she said, hoping he wouldn't think her question was crass. She sensed that sooner or later he would realise that she would want to know, and thought now was as good a time as any.

Nathan lolled back in his chair, "I learnt that in Greenland nothing is what it seems. Beneath its beauty and magic there's an ugliness. I went to find out—"

"What?" she interrupted.

He raised his hand to stop her, "I didn't know, but what I found out was more than I had bargained for. Thule is a place shrouded in secrets of power and cover-ups. I've learnt a lot but still not all that needs to be told: not the whole story of how that day changed the life of so many. That's why I need to go to Copenhagen. Magnus had only suspicions, he didn't have any firm evidence, but that evidence exists; it's out there and people need to see it." His voice rasped so he sipped some water. "My father should have been my rock, the very one I should have been able to rely on and look up to, but he became a stranger to me with principles that were alien to me, that I couldn't respect. He told everyone I was a disappointment to him – I am determined not to disappoint your father and, without sounding over-dramatic, the many who have placed their hope in me." He took a handkerchief from his pocket, stood, and coughing once wiped his mouth, breaking the tension of the moment. "Are the toilets out the back?"

"Err, yes, left of the counter," and she pointed.

A small piece of paper had fallen to the floor when Nathan had got out his handkerchief. The folded slip lay across the white and black glazed floor tiles, waiting to be retrieved. Opening it her heart sank. The name 'Ellinore' was scribbled in biro and beside the woman's name a telephone number with what she recognised as a Danish International dialling code: she was sure, Copenhagen.

"Well, that was good and not expensive," he said glancing at the bill before sliding it into his pocket as he returned. "Shall we go?"

On the quayside men were shifting stacks of orange plastic fish boxes from their boats as Arctic terns circled, shrieking overhead. A young lad sat hunched on a crate, casting his rod into the fjord. She didn't hear the 'bloop' as the lure hit the water; she couldn't get Ellinore out of her mind.

CHAPTER TWENTY-FIVE

Eva was late down to breakfast. She made no attempt to disguise the fact that she had been crying.

"What is it, what's wrong?" Nathan asked.

"It's Magnus."

"What about Magnus?"

"I have just had a call from his neighbour. He was ill in the night and has been taken off to hospital."

"Who's taken him?"

"The neighbour called an ambulance; they were concerned when he didn't pop by this morning like usual before work."

"What's wrong with him?"

"She doesn't know."

"Okay, but what does the hospital say?"

Eva burst into tears.

"I'm sorry, I didn't mean to be so thoughtless," Nathan said.

"I don't know, I can't get through, my mobile signal keeps fading."

"You must use the phone here," he said instantly.

Five minutes later a more composed Eva rejoined Nathan.

"I've got you a coffee," he said. "Tell me what's the latest, in your own good time."

She settled at the table and savoured her strong coffee. "He had a fall in the night getting out to the toilet. It would seem he spent most of the night on the floor and is suffering from mild hypothermia. They say he's comfortable and stable, thank God, and they're going to continue to monitor him. They don't think he's broken anything but he shouldn't be on his own." After a moment of thought she added, "I've told him he must keep the heating on but he's too mean."

"Eva, there isn't anyone more determined and obstinately independent than your father. I can't see Magnus willingly going into a home. And as for moving in with you . . . well, I suppose anything's possible but I'm really not sure how long that would last before you both went mad."

"I know," she said. "You're right, but what do I do?"

"The first thing we need to do is to pack and get back to Reykjavik as soon as we can and see him."

"Do you mind?"

"No, of course not," he said.

"It rather ruins our break."

"That's not important. You're his only family and you need to be with him," he said attempting to reassure her. "Don't worry, he'll be alright, the old boy's a fighter."

A broad beam filled her face. "I know, and that at times makes it doubly difficult."

* * * *

Eva came in and slumped in a chair. She kicked off her shoes and declared she needed a drink. As Nathan poured her some wine he enquired how things had gone at the hospital.

"Oh fine, I suppose. When the paramedics got there they found him on the floor, confused and shivering. His breathing was shallow and it wasn't possible to accurately say how long he had been like it. Much longer in their view could have resulted in further complications. They immediately endeavoured to bring his core temperature up with heat pads while monitoring his heart rate. Once in the hospital they administered warmed fluids intravenously and continued to monitor him, and they dressed his leg where he'd cut himself when he fell. They say it may take some time for the wound to heal, but that's normal for older people.

"He's no longer drowsy, nor is his speech slurred as it seems it was, and he is stable. They told me they will discharge him tomorrow, but only after they asked whether he ate regularly and about his alcohol consumption. You know what he's like with his whisky. And they wanted to know whether there was someone who will keep an eye on him." Distressed, Eva began to cry tears of despair. "I don't know what I should do."

"What does Magnus have to say?"

"As you can imagine, it wasn't his fault," she said indignantly. "He blames the woman who cleans. He says she must have moved a table or not put it back where it should be and he accused her of turning the heating down. When I mentioned about him maybe moving into a home, for a period of respite just while his leg healed, he went berserk. He raved on about being perfectly fine and there was no way I'd get him into a home, even for a day. He's a stubborn old sod. I don't know anyone more awkward and unreasonable. He's impossible."

Nathan let Eva bemoan the old boy as he was fairly sure that to interrupt would be a big mistake. "It sounds to me as though you don't have too many options," he said. "Perhaps you'll have to pop in more often, just until he's back on his feet. Couldn't the neighbour keep an eye on him without him realising?"

"Back on his feet?" she scoffed. "The old bugger's already walking and complaining that his leg hurts. I could ask her, I suppose. I know she'd be only too happy to, and for some reason he seems to take it from her." She shook her head, "I'm quite certain my old father is getting worse."

"Mmm," he mused. "Maybe something that awaits all of us sooner or later."

"But my father has a real talent for it," she sighed, and then, looking at Nathan, said, "What's the matter?"

"Well, my timing may not be great but I feel I need to go back to England. Jane and the boys will be on their own, I've never missed a Christmas at theirs, and the university will be giving me up for dead, if they haven't already."

Almost before he had finished explaining, Eva spoke. He noticed a faint quiver in her voice.

"You'll come back?" Nathan didn't need to be holding her, he could feel her tension.

"Yes, of course," he said.

"When? What about Copenhagen, will you still go?"

"I can't not, not now. I am committed to seeing this through whatever it takes, for everyone's sake including mine and Magnus'."

"Do you see yourself as some sort of lone hero, fighting for good?" she said, frustrated.

"No. You watch too many movies," he replied sharply. "I just see the faces of hundreds of lost people."

CHAPTER TWENTY-SIX

For nearly a week the sleepy city of Reykjavik exploded with the most enormous party. Eva had said it was going to be a massive event but Nathan never imagined just how big.

"It's one of the rare chances for our small country to punch well above our musical weight," she said.

Billed as the hippiest international music festival in the northern hemisphere, bursting with the best of avant-garde, nostalgia and novelty, 'Iceland Airwaves' definitely leaned towards the unconventional as far as Nathan could see. It didn't take him long to realise how sheltered his upbringing had been. Thousands flocked to this isolated capital, 'the smallest big city in the world', to experience dozens of weird and wonderful acts.

"We're starting to get festival goers from around the world," Eva said, "just like the acts, but there's no end of cool new Icelandic bands I've never heard before. It's amazing."

Nathan was feeling well out of his comfort zone. "What about you guys?"

"We're playing twice over the five days and we've got some off-venue gigs."

"That sounds mad," he said.

"No, not really. If there's someone you want to see, make sure you're there at least a couple of hours before. If you leave it to the last minute you'll never get in."

Nathan perused the festival programme: Egil Sacbjorrison, Klappir – Jutting Rock, Oddi, Emiliana Torrini and Ađeins i nótt. The schedule appeared endless, concluding with the footnote, 'Iceland Airwaves – where genres mix and morph naturally until meaningless'. He was none the wiser.

By the end of the two days Nathan was exhausted; the crowds were overwhelming, the noise overbearing and, to say the whole event was accompanied by a degree of immodesty, was a gross understatement. He was far too old for this kind of northern party and for the rest of the week took refuge in Eva's apartment on the city's quiet outskirts. In an attempt to break the monotony of these four walls, he headed across the city to see Magnus.

Magnus was delighted to see him; agitated, but nevertheless, delighted.

"How are you doing?" Nathan greeted.

"Come in, my boy, I'm alright it's everyone else. They fuss over me like clucking hens; never get old, it's not worth it."

"I don't think I have a choice, none of us do."

"Of course," Magnus said with an air of indifference. "Sit yourself down and I'll pour you a drink." There was a clink of glasses from his kitchenette as he called out, "Not at the festival then?"

"No, not my scene," Nathan admitted.

"Nor mine," Magnus added as he refreshed his own whisky glass, "I don't need any more excitement."

"I guess you've had enough of that lately, what with hospital and resurrecting this Greenland thing."

Magnus appeared disturbed. "Hmm, you're right, I never realised how harrowing reliving that time would prove."

"You've held on to this all these years and now you must let others take on the fight. Does that whole explosive event still haunt you?" Nathan asked.

Magnus stood and, walking to the window, peered into the darkness. He turned and stared at Nathan, then said, "I know you're right. I know I should let go, but what about you?"

"What do you mean?" Nathan said.

Magnus' manner changed. "Think of where you've come from." Nathan was confused. "How have you moved on since your wife's death?" It then dawned on Nathan what he was getting at. Magnus added, "Is your silence because you are thinking or because you don't want to say?"

"No, I suppose I've never considered that before."

"Unless I'm not mistaken, you still haven't let go, have you? I've learnt grief serves no purpose, it's worthless. For an old man like me the future means very little, but for you, just as the past means so much, the future means everything so don't give up on it. You came here lecturing me with advice, I know it's your profession, but to be honest I see no reason why I shouldn't have a go as well!"

Nathan laughed but deep down Magnus' words had unsettled him.

"I know what it's like. One builds one's life around a person and when they are gone you are on your own. You have to start again. Come on, let me top you up," Magnus said, reaching for Nathan's glass.

* * * *

The peace of Eva's apartment was shattered; she burst in full of . . . everything.

"How did it go?" Nathan said.

"Amazing, the gigs were brill, folks loved us and the bar's booked us for regular spots through the winter. There were some fantastic acts, and the bands, apart from one or two duff sets, unbelievable. You should have come. So what have you got up to?"

Nathan could see the woman was on a high and he didn't know whether to let her come down on her own gently, or help her. He settled on the latter.

"I saw Magnus."

She raised her eyebrows. "Oh, so what's the problem with him now?" she asked, turning to look at him.

"No problem. We had a good chat and came to some decisions."

"Anything I should concern myself with or just some more of the boys' stuff?" Eva said.

In the same way as Nathan had decided it was best not to trouble Magnus with Martin Poulson's latest disturbing suspicions about being spied on, so he equally kept the news from Eva. "No, you're alright, everything's okay."

After a thirty-five minute run-down of the festival, Nathan was beginning to feel exhausted and glad he gave it a miss.

"Have you eaten?" he interrupted.

"Well no, have you?"

"No, but I don't fancy battling it with all the crowds."

"Me neither, I'll fix us something," she said.

Nathan could clearly see Eva was still on a high, totally wrapped up in the happenings of the past few days.

"Great," he said following her into the kitchen. "You've never really told me about your music, the orchestra?"

"No, but I could at the risk of boring you," she said, messing with some vegetables on the stove.

"Give it a try," he responded.

"Well, I'm not from a musical family. It doesn't take much to realise that, you have met Magnus." Nathan acknowledged her assertion. "Nobody sang or played an instrument, all we had was an old record player. At school you could play an instrument if you wanted and I fancied the violin. It's odd but I loved it. There was only one spare violin in the school, the scruffiest, grottiest instrument I had ever seen. A string was missing and the case was battered; it was a violin, but not what I had in mind. At the age of seven I started off trying to play all sorts of tunes, from simple kids' songs to bits of classics. I drove Mum and Dad, and myself, mad with 'Tea for Two'. Do you know that?"

Nathan nodded.

"I spent weeks secretly practising a piece by Tchaikovsky. When my teacher heard it she was astonished and told Mum and Dad I needed to go to music school. Joke, we had no money. I won a part scholarship to the Conservatoire where my teacher was a prickly German chap. You simply didn't get past the second note unless everything was absolutely perfect: your posture, bow control and pressure and, most of all, intonation. But I learnt. I stuck at it and was glad in the end that I did, because if I hadn't I wouldn't be half the player I am now. After endless practise, lots of trials and auditions and more than my fair share of luck, I finally got into the orchestra. My first concert piece with them was Mahler's Tenth, his final and uncompleted work before his death. The first movement is regarded as a reflection of the inner turmoil he was suffering, knowing he had a failing heart and an unfaithful wife.

Arguably one of his most discordant works, it's a nightmare, every bar has a different time signature. In those early days I would easily get bow shakes.

"After saving up, getting some money from Dad and a scary bank loan, I was able to buy my own violin. I now have an Italian Brandini from around the mid-seventeen hundreds. It sounds a world away from my early violin, but then it should since it cost me over twelve million Króna. There are many more different colours to its sound, and its deep lush tone is beyond what I could ever have imagined. It has an amazing power and quality. My old violin possessed nothing of the subtleties or variety.

"Being principal second violinist is not the most glamorous role. We're generally regarded as not having the same technical strengths as firsts, but while the more prima donna firsts are dashing around playing the tune, we keep the music going and the orchestra motoring on. We are the solid, competent types although not adverse to a bit of giggling when something silly happens, or to playing jokes on each other, clowning around. We have a fun time, not like the miserable-looking viola and 'cello players."

Seeing his chance Nathan said, "Do you all get on? You must spend a lot of time together."

"Yes, in the main. There's always someone having a fling with another member, often they are one-night stands, especially when we are on tour, or last no more than a month or two. It's a funny old world."

"Hmm?" Nathan said, inviting more.

"I had a brief relationship with a conductor once. He led us with such flair and imagination." Eva said coyly. "I think, in hindsight, it was more of a father figure thing: he was a lot older than me."

"Are you saying you have a thing for older men?" Nathan teased.

"Well, maybe some," she said playfully.

Before he had a chance to react, Eva said, "So you've tricked me into revealing my home truths, it's your turn now. Tell me, who's the woman in Copenhagen?"

CHAPTER TWENTY-SEVEN

The following three weeks were busy. The winter concert season was well underway and, while Eva was involved with the orchestra, Nathan took the opportunity to bring some logical order to his research. He knew that Christmas and the beginning of the New Year looked pretty hectic, what with his planned trip home to England, two weeks at least he thought, and then spending however long was needed back at the university in Wales. Soon after that he needed to be heading out to Denmark to meet up with Martin Poulson to share his findings. Although research was Nathan's business, this was not his field and he imagined that being an investigative journalist, Martin would approach the task rigorously, thoroughly ordering his findings and evidence.

"Would you come to our Christmas concert?" Eva said.

"Yes, sure, when is it?" Nathan replied.

"Two weeks Saturday and you'll know the conductor."

"I doubt it, I am not that up on the classics," he said.

"Ashkenazy," Eva announced.

"Wow, oh yes I've heard of him. He's big isn't he? How come he is conducting?"

"He has been involved with us over the years and talk is that he is to become our new Conductor Laureate. On Wednesday we have our final rehearsal for a recording session with Osmo Vänskä conducting, do you fancy coming? Chandos Records are laying down a recording of Prokofiev's ballet *Romeo and Juliet*, I think you will find it interesting."

Having no reason to refuse, and with Eva having gone on ahead, Nathan made his way to the university campus. The Háskólabió Cultural Centre appeared like a series of interconnected, unimaginative block buildings, skirted by parking, roads and roundabouts. The large entrance hall proved equally uninspiring, lacking any atmosphere and, as the concierge purposefully approached him, Nathan couldn't help but think gate-crashing rehearsals was not going to be straightforward. After offering his name, the man's indifferent attitude changed and he became positively helpful.

"Eva said about you, will you follow me please and we'll squeeze you in at the back." The chap's idea of 'back' caught Nathan off-guard. He was seated to one side and behind the conductor's rostrum, facing the assembling orchestra. However, it was interesting to see no one took any notice of his intrusion. The hall walls were hung with black floor-to-ceiling drapes and lights were deployed to cast sufficient illumination to allow the musicians to read their music without uplifting the otherwise sombre mode. A handful of guys frantically busied themselves repositioning microphones and cables while checking sound levels with some lanky fellow in jeans and tee-shirt bent over the largest mixing desk Nathan had ever seen. All the time, casually dressed orchestra members were taking their appropriate places, fiddling with their instruments and chatting. He had never studied an orchestra before and was absorbed with how the instruments were arranged. Strings appeared to swamp the whole front of the stage with violins to the left and 'cellos to the right. He spotted who he thought was Sabina, turned out in Levis and a baggy grey sweatshirt, 'cello gripped between her legs. A tall, curly-haired bespectacled man, dressed in black, took to the rostrum. He spoke in English to the assembled musicians,

"We will put the finishing touches to Prokofiev's work so we can do him justice before we record." He gestured to the lanky fellow, "And Bjarni will perfect the balances in readiness for the recording."

He tapped his baton on his music stand and the orchestra, as one, sat up. "Remember," he addressed, "this is Romeo and Juliet, people are dying." The conductor then counted, "One and two, one and two . . . " and the music commenced.

The sound took Nathan's breath away. The whole hall was filled with the slow, deep melodic voice of the orchestra and a sense of peace came over him. Soon the brass and percussion sections were playing and there, in the middle of the orchestra, was Eva, completely transfixed and in another world. With every movement of her bow her whole body rocked back and forth. The deep sounding timpani resounded as the string section countered each other with the haunting theme.

The conductor interrupted, "Number thirty-six. Everybody play softer, thank you." They played and Nathan could now hear the two harps, the piano and the violins building and fading, like night stars. The theme returned with more vigour than before, interspersed with more restful interludes. The conductor called out, "Fifty-two." The orchestra stumbled. "No, it should be E flat, four flats . . . play." They started yet again, he called, "Faster," beckoning the violins.

Then, unexpectedly the music ended. Nathan felt exhausted, as if all the energy from within him was drained.

"We will go back to the beginning. Could it be my heart is broken?" the conductor said and gestured, putting his hands over his heart. "But first we will take a break, be back prompt in fifteen."

He had hardly finished speaking before five or six musicians had escaped to the edge of the hall and were on their mobiles.

"Tell me, what did you think?" an exuberant Eva enthused, breaking Nathan's concentration.

"As I said, I'm not up on classical music but I found it moving, maybe even more so for the conductor's interpretation. I can see how you can become totally engrossed, in love with the music."

"So will you still come and hear our performance?"

"Sure."

* * * *

Nathan didn't recognise Háskólabió's elaborately presented foyer. Vibrant seasonal decorations decked the walls and a wonderful Christmas tree shone with an extravagance of light and colour to mark the occasion.

Eva had done him proud with a seat at the front of the raised section, as near to the middle as you could get, an excellent position for viewing soloists, she had said. He made himself comfortable, hopeful that he would be spared a bustling concert goer in the adjacent seat breathing down his neck or stealing his leg-room. No such luck. But once the little old dear had pointed out the Mayor, explaining that she attended all the concerts, the woman settled down and he hardly noticed her.

Overhead arrays of spotlights created a magical atmosphere. A single spot highlighted the conductor's waiting rostrum. The orchestra looked so different from when he had seen them in rehearsal as they began to assemble, immaculately turned out in black gowns and suits. According to Eva there would be nearly one hundred musicians for this special occasion, The Northern Lights Concert – A Celebration of Christmas, and he could just make her out to the left of the rostrum.

The orchestra looked almost complete. A violinist stood near centre stage, turned to the woodwind section from where an oboist played a sustained note following which a cacophony of sound was produced. The house lights dimmed and a diminutive elderly man, violin in hand, proudly strode across the platform to take his place as leader of the orchestra. There was a polite ripple of applause and recognition. Almost immediately Vladimir Ashkenazy stepped into the spotlight, mounted the rostrum and gave a slow, low bow. Nathan was surprised by his reception. It seemed as if everyone appreciated he was a great man.

Nathan quickly scanned his programme, *'In 1961 Ashkenazy married an Icelandic-born woman. He left the USSR taking residence in London and from there they moved to Iceland in 1968 where subsequently he became an Icelandic citizen.'*

As Nathan studied the orchestra he couldn't get out of his mind 1968, the year Ashkenazy moved to Iceland and the Americans were hunting for a lost nuclear bomb that could have been destined for the conductor's homeland.

The music began, stirring music that Nathan recognised – Holst's *The Planets*, and Jupiter with all its bold energy had been chosen to open the concert. In a marked contrast Venus followed and he was struck by the coolness and purity of the woodwind and strings. There was something magical about the music. Sibelius' *Karelia Suite Opus 11* was next, described in the programme as part of his orchestral tone poem. The conductor's gestures appeared to orchestrate every flow and shape of the piece. The remaining piece marked a departure from the classical. A young lady stepped out from the violinists and took her position left of the conductor. She nodded to him and the piano led the orchestra in the theme from *Cinema Paradiso*. Her dreamlike violin almost took Nathan's breath away, its mournful cry totally immersing him in the sound. He sensed that, like him, the audience was transfixed, captivated by every melodic note. Absolutely no one made a noise, the soloist stood completely still. Then a voice shouted, "Bravo!" and as a delighted audience showed their appreciation, the old woman next to him got up.

"I have to stretch my legs after sitting so long and need to find the ladies room." She beamed, shrugged and was gone.

Dvořák's *Largo* opened the second half. Nathan found this piece immensely sad and intensely nostalgic with its haunting melody of clarinets set against the strings, whereas the *Scherzo* came across as vibrant and full of life: a wonderful contrast. He had already scanned the introduction to the next piece, *Peer Gynt* and, as he listened, he could see the romantic story unfold in his mind's eye; the vivid sound-picture of the countryside.

Next was a hymn of *'deepest spirituality and amazing beauty',* Karl Jenkins' *Benedictus*. The principal 'cellist, Johannes Svelberg, introduced the theme, then a chorus of voices joined the orchestra as the tempo built to its triumphant conclusion. Ashkenazy gestured for the soloist and orchestra to stand and bow. Cheers and applause rang out, and soon most in the hall were on their feet waving their arms and calling for more.

After several minutes of adulation, Ashkenazy quietened the audience and said, "We bid you all a Happy Christmas with one final piece of music."

A deathly hush filled the hall. Lines of children, perhaps fifty or more, silently appeared walking in single file down the aisles towards the platform. The orchestra introduced the simple melody and the children started to sing the enchanting theme from *The Snowman*.

Rapturous applause, cheering and stamping greeted the end of the concert, one that Nathan would remember for a very long while.

Making his way against the crowd Nathan slid through a side door which Eva had pointed out to him, and joined the melee of musicians grabbing their belongings from the rows of lockers.

An excited Eva caught his arm. "Well?"

"I loved it. I found it a moving and an emotional journey, unusual for me," Nathan said.

Eva laughed.

"What?" Nathan asked.

"You said it," she scorned.

She led him out alongside the lake towards the harbour. The thin skin of ice that had covered the lake since first thing in the morning remained unmelted, glistening in the moonlight. "Aren't we going back?" Nathan said.

"Yes, but I want to show you something first."

As they neared the square Nathan noticed it was getting busier, then turning the corner a massive Christmas tree stood before them, garlanded with twinkling fairy lights, the many colours reflecting in the crisp covering of snow.

"Hey," Nathan said, "that looks bigger than the one in Trafalgar Square."

"Each year a tree arrives as a gift from the people of Oslo which the Norwegian ambassador presents to the city. It's great, isn't it," Eva said to the amazed Nathan. "When we get back I must search out my old decorations then we can jolly-up the apartment."

"I don't think I can cope with anymore excitement tonight," he said.

"Nothing had been further from my thoughts," she teased.

*   *   *   *

The following evening, as they made their way to the orchestra's Christmas party, Nathan asked, "Do you mind the darkness?"

"No, not really, you get used to it."

"I am sure the monotony of the endless gloom would drive me mad."

She giggled, "It's funny but I feel somehow protected in the darkness. For a while when the sun returns, it feels really weird, then it's daylight nearly all the time; it's as if the mountains reappear just as you remember them."

They both plodded on in the snow. "How deep does this get up here?" he asked.

"It's often up to your knees but it's cleared quickly."

"London would grind to a standstill with this much snow."

"Many Icelanders live for the winter, everything is transformed. Sometimes the snow is like a wispy dust hanging on the air, but another time it's thick, swirling and blowing everywhere, the flakes so hard and brittle they crackle like steel. Drifts can be deep, covering cars, re-shaping buildings and piling against doorways and our windows get decorated with fern-like patterns of ice. The whole city is softened in a white cushion, its harshness is lost and nature takes hold. Women in long winter coats, men in fur-lined parkas struggle through the wind-driven drifts. Children slide and sledge to school while cars crawl along the slippery streets. Away from the noise of vehicles there is an uncanny silence. The moon's silver light casts a magical peace over the city and stars flicker in the crystal clear sky. I love every minute of it, I feel at one with my land. In the quietness I can play in my head all those beautiful melodies I know and nothing interrupts them. It's fantastic, except, that is, for my numbing nose and fingers."

The wind picked up and a crisp chill bit their faces. "Sometimes in the winter during the storms, my whole apartment creaks and I lay in bed wondering if I'll be blown away," Eva said wistfully.

The blast of a horn brought them up short. They stepped back out of the way of a monstrous snow plough spewing forth clouds of snow and ice, filling the air with whirling crystals glimmering in its headlights.

"We're nearly there," Eva said.

An elderly man, dressed in a sharply-pressed blue pinstripe suit and standing at one end of the hall, coughed as he stepped out from the crowd. He struck an imposing figure as he spoke to the assembled crowd in a deep husky voice.

"Dobrodošli – welcome! As chair of the trustees it's a pleasure to welcome you all to the annual Christmas festivities in celebration of another successful year for our National Symphony Orchestra. This year we are proud to also celebrate the fiftieth anniversary of our prestigious orchestra, introducing new and exciting works along with the traditional classics to the people of Iceland and, through our recordings and touring programme, to the world. Please join me in recognition of the orchestra's great accomplishments." The room erupted with applause and cheers.

"Most visitors come here for our scenery, Mr. Trent, to see our magnificent waterfalls, volcanoes and geysers, or to be inspired by the open wilderness and wild rugged coast, so what is it for you?"

Eva had introduced this middle-aged benefactor of the orchestra as Rune Pedersen, a tycoon of sorts. On his arm was a thirty-something brunette wearing a vibrant red strapless evening dress which plunged at both the back and front.

"Did Eva say you were an academic?" Rune persisted.

"Yes, I'm a glaciologist, and what about you, Rune?"

"I have a corporation called Geothermic. We're spearheading the harnessing of renewable energy from Iceland's natural environment and creating a means by which we can export it through a 'supergrid' to the more lucrative markets in Europe. After all, there's no reason why our massive natural thermo resource should only supply Iceland. But Nathan, don't let me bore you, that's enough about me Tell me, what's a glaciologist doing at our orchestra's Christmas bash, and who was the young woman with you?"

Nathan replied, "She plays in the orchestra, the violin."

"She looks a sweetie, doesn't she Petra?"

Petra tugged his arm. "Rune, can you get me a drink?" she said petulantly.

"Would you be kind enough to amuse Petra for me while I grab her another Chablis? Can I get you a top-up Mr Trent?"

Nathan held up his full glass and dubiously added to a departing Rune, "It will be my pleasure."

"Don't mind his comment about your friend, Mr Trent, Rune's appetite for business is only matched by his appetite for beautiful women."

"I can see that," Nathan heard himself saying, and quickly added, "I'm sorry, I shouldn't have said that."

"Oh, should I understand you don't think I am beautiful?" she said in a sweet, girlish voice, raising her eyebrows. Any embarrassment had tactfully been shifted; she was playing with him. This woman was not as dumb as Nathan had first assumed.

"How have you got on?" Rune said on his return, holding their drinks.

"Fine," Petra said, "he's avoided making any advances."

Rune ignored her, "I'd be keen to talk later, Mr Trent."

"Please, it's Nathan."

"Well, it would be good to get your thoughts on the exploitation of sub-glacial volcanic geothermal energy, but until then you will need to excuse us. Bjorn Hansen, the former chief economist of Seōlabanki wants to introduce me to Iceland's Minister of Industry."

No sooner had they headed across the room to join an official looking group of suits and gowns than Nathan was taken by surprise.

"How are you doing?"

Turning, he looked on a beaming Eva. "I want to introduce you to Rafael, our conductor. He's keen to meet you."

Nathan had never met a conductor, a maestro, before and Rafael was all the things he had not expected: young, upright, slim build, professional and personable with an engaging charm so apparent in his Bohemian character.

"Eva speaks of you warmly, Nathan. I don't know where our second violins would be without her leadership," and as he spoke Rafael glanced towards her. Eva's eyes twinkled.

Avoiding the unfamiliar territory of classical music, Nathan opted for, "It's an impressive gathering, Rafael."

"Yes, we continue to be encouraged by the generous support and sponsorship without which we couldn't sustain our challenging programme. I hope you have found a warm welcome here in our country."

Eva laughed at his words and Rafael grinned. "Of course, that is with the exception of the day you arrived, I understand. When I came out here two or three years ago my first impression was of a people forged by their land: a bit cold and rough. Over time they revealed themselves to be a kind and sensitive people, poetic, loyal and warm hearted; isn't that so, Eva?"

She acknowledged with what Nathan took as a degree of embarrassment.

"Where is home for you, Rafael?"

"Bavaria, although to be honest, I tend to regard Iceland now as my new-found home. And you?"

"England, but for several years my university seat has been based in Wales from where my studies have taken me all over the world, however, I must say never to Iceland before, or Bavaria for that matter."

"And what of England do you miss most?"

"Other than my family, my sister and her boys, then probably trees."

With that Rafael smiled, "Me too."

Out of the corner of his eye Nathan spotted a woman making her way towards them. She might have been a model by the way she crossed the room.

"This is Sabina, Nathan," Eva said.

He was lost for words. Could this really be the woman that Eva had told him about?

"Hi, Rafael, great party," Sabina said. Then, in an affected voice, looking at Nathan she said, "We don't know each other, do we?"

"No," was all he managed.

"You appear almost speechless," she challenged, raising her eyebrows.

"I'm sorry. It's good to meet you, I've heard so much about you."

"Really," she said as she twisted a large sparkling ring on her finger. Rafael made a funny noise, like a quiet laugh, and explained he needed to circulate, to which a seemingly disgruntled Eva said she would join him.

For several minutes a few words passed between Nathan and Sabina. He could see that his blatant rejection of Sabina's every advance cut her cold, like the thrust of a knife. She smiled appealingly at him but beneath he sensed anger, annoyance, realising that she'd never be a threat to Eva as far as he was concerned. He turned in Eva's direction. She was busy talking to a tall spider of a woman wearing a long black dress and they appeared to be enjoying a joke together. Sabina dropped her wine glass. It smashed into hundreds of shards, spilling the red wine across the white-glazed ceramic floor. Eva caught his eye and a look of horror filled her face. She hurried across and grabbed his arm as Sabina shared an apology.

"How clumsy of me, Nathan."

He shrugged, "Not to worry, I don't think others even noticed."

A look of defiance contorted her face: a face as cold as glacial waters.

Nathan and Eva left to join the 'black widow' who was now laughing, struggling to contain her delight at Sabina's obvious lack of success. An infuriated Sabina stormed off.

Eva whispered to Nathan, "She does that. What on earth did you say to her?"

"I'm not sure."

"Well, whatever it was it did the trick," Eva said as they watched Sabina prowling through the throng, as if a panther in search of its next victim.

"You did well to escape from her wilful clutches and entanglement," Eva said.

"I could say the same about you," Nathan replied.

"Hi, I am Frida."

"Sorry," Eva said, realising she'd completely ignored the spider woman.

"Frida, my name's Nathan."

"I know."

"Frida is a writer and turns-out pieces on our orchestra," Eva said.

"Turns-out, darling?" Frida said tauntingly. "And what is it you do, Nathan?"

"I am a glaciologist, but I don't suppose that helps much," Nathan added.

"Mmm. No, what does that mean?"

"I watch and measure and ponder glaciers." Nathan's answer was briefer than even he expected.

"Fascinating. Is it exciting?

Nathan was unsure if this woman was being sarcastic or in fact just teasing him. "No, not really. Well, it was once."

"What exactly do you ponder?"

He thought a moment. "Essentially if it will be a hundred or a thousand years hence when the ice will return and cover our earth."

By now Eva had excused herself, muttering something about needing to visit the powder room.

"And now, Nathan, you've come to discover Iceland, our land that was once known as Thule."

"That's weird, I had no idea. I visited Thule in Greenland back in August."

"Really?" she said. "Then you're following in the footsteps of the great explorers. It is said that one of Iceland's most famous sons, Leifur Eiríksson, when sailing to Greenland discovered North America. Did you know his Norse father, Eric the Red, named it Greenland to make it seem attractive to settlers?"

"To me life there felt like one of drudgery in a lost land too hostile to ever consider settling in. Who is it you write for?"

"No one in particular, I'm freelance so I write for whoever: magazines, publishers, PR companies and occasionally the university here want me to translate their study programmes."

"Interesting," he said.

"Yes and no."

"So do you know anything about Rune Pedersen and Geothermic? I met him earlier," Nathan said.

"He operates in the international energy market with his headquarters in Norway, where they are exploiting hydro and wave power, as I recall."

"So why is he involved in Iceland?"

"He's here to tap our vast, lucrative geothermal resources, I believe, and is even in discussions over the building of a hydroelectric dam on the east coast. Why do you ask?"

"Eva introduced me to him and his wife, Petra. When he discovered I was a glaciologist he said he wanted to talk with me later; maybe he has plans to capture the heat from freezing ice, I don't know."

"No, neither do I," she returned. "One thing I do know is that Petra is not his wife, she's his daughter."

A confused Nathan repeated, "His daughter?"

"Yes, and be careful. He's a ruthless man and very protective of her." Frida looked at him in a way he found unsettling, then spoke, "Women often misjudge a man's affection for love. I know of you, Nathan, but I don't know you. Forgive an old woman for asking, but which is worse: spending the rest of your life alone mourning the loss of your wife, or finding a new life with someone who loves you? Sometimes one has to let go."

It was as if she was reading his mind but he didn't want to face it, not now.

"Frida, have you heard of a reporter called Martin Poulson, he's Danish?"

"No, I can't say I have. What does he write about?"

"I believe he's an investigative journalist and covers foreign affairs. He was here for the Reagan and Gorbachev summit."

"I'm afraid that's way outside my field, Nathan, but you could try the ICIJ. I am sure if he is anyone of significance in that line of work they would know him."

"ICIJ?"

"International Consortium of Investigative Journalists. Oh, and by the way, may I congratulate you?" Frida remarked.

"What for?" Nathan said, not following her reasoning.

"You completely changed the subject as soon as it got uncomfortable, but you didn't fool old Frida," and she gave him an all-knowing look. It was odd, but in a strange way he didn't find her words threatening.

CHAPTER TWENTY-EIGHT

Nathan stared ahead to the gentle Hertfordshire countryside, shading his eyes from the late afternoon sun. The translucent purity of the winter sky cast a magical half-light upon the tall evergreens which skirted the undulating green fields. With the slow passing of clouds teasing the sun, long shadows shed their creeping gloom and the landscape's mood was changed.

Nathan loved England, the sheer extravagance and beauty of its seasons. He loved the rich countryside, the ever-changing colours of the trees and hedgerows, their radiant autumn hues, its native wildlife and the dawning bird song. Iceland and Greenland seemed far away, a million miles away.

His sister's house was modest in every respect, but the one redeeming factor that sold the property to Jane was its position. The small back garden opened onto the most spectacular farmland that this part of England had to offer. The garden gate was hardly ever closed and for the boys was a door into their own secret adventure land. Nathan was surprised how much they'd grown and matured. It had only been ten months since he last saw them but at this age they were changing fast. One thing he noticed hadn't changed was the amount of clutter they seemed to accumulate. With the Christmas tree and a teetering stack of presents there was hardly room, as the boys would proudly say, to swing Mum's cat.

Jane loved this time of year. A chance for a well-earned break from her work at the nursing home, as well as a time of over-indulgence with the boys, maybe watching some old re-runs on the telly. To have Nathan to stay was the icing on the cake, as she put it. "The boys never get tired of their uncle's stories," she warned, "and still welcome the odd bundle now they stand a real chance of beating you."

"Wouldn't it be great to get some snow this Christmas? There's never too much snow and ice for you, Uncle Nathan," they would taunt.

"Don't you believe it, lads, I've seen enough to last me ages."

"Tell us again, Uncle, what was Greenland really like?" would be their plea each evening before bedtime.

Nathan found it hard to truly recall his first impressions of that land, sitting as he was in front of a coal fire in a comfy armchair drinking hot chocolate.

"Think of the very worst winter weather you can imagine then multiply it tenfold. The place is a barren wilderness, hundreds upon hundreds of square miles of ice and snow, a freezing inhospitable land. Little grows and survival is a constant battle. In the summer the sun never leaves, the day never ends, whereas in the winter, the day and night are like one in darkness, and that's when the big chill strikes, squeezing even harder. Vicious freezing polar winds bring with them vast amounts of snow forming endless unbroken drifts making prisoners of all in their path. In the biting blizzard you can see nothing, maybe only white. Temperatures plummet to a trembling minus 50°C and if any of your body is left unprotected for more than a few minutes, your flesh freezes and begins to die on you. All that you think of here as normal, your usual way of life, has no place up there. To get by you have to think differently if you don't want the land to take you."

The boys were totally mesmerised by Nathan's account, the horrific picture he was painting, but Jane, who had entered and caught his last few words, exclaimed, "What on earth are you filling their heads with? They'll never get off to sleep at this rate. Upstairs the two of you and say goodnight to your uncle."

Objections aside, Nathan privately promised them there would be plenty more days for stories.

The week running up to Christmas was hectic. The school play marked the end of term and the start of the boys being at home more. They were smart; they'd try and stay up late, lie on in the morning and be happy to play computer games all day. Occasionally Nathan was able to persuade them to dress up in their thick sweaters, overcoats, hats and boots and venture outside with him. He relished the brisk walks on frosty mornings when the air was crisp. When the boys joined him it was more a wild, rowdy scamper through the woods to see just how muddy they could all get.

Two nights before Christmas Eve they drove into town in Jane's old car to see the lights and decorations and fight through the last-minute shoppers.

Much to the boys' delight Christmas Eve saw the first fall of snow.

"It's going to be a white Christmas after all, Uncle," the boys declared with great delight.

The great day arrived and with it a buzz of excitement. The traditional roast turkey with all the trimmings was accompanied with carols on the radio and followed by presents. It seemed to Nathan a long while since he had sat down to such a tasty roast. After ripping open their gifts both boys took to their room to play and a rare peace returned. Nathan had been in a dilemma with what to buy his sister, but clearly following the shop assistant's advice in the department store had proved successful. He reassured her that if it was the wrong size, colour or if she didn't like it, she could change it.

"No, it's lovely, how thoughtful of you," and gave him a hug. With the surprise of a new cardigan, just in case Nathan was heading north again, as Jane put it, the exchange of gifts was complete. "And these are for you," she said passing him four envelopes. "I'll tell you now that the big cards are from the boys, they each wanted to send you one."

Having opened Jane's card, he assumed the fourth was from the university in Wales.

Nathan's shock was clearly evident.

"What is it?" Jane said, half suspecting.

"It's a card from someone I met in Iceland," he paused to read again her message. "How on earth did she get the address?"

"I gave it to her," Jane confessed.

"When?"

"When I telephoned the university in Iceland to find out if they had any contact details for you, they gave me a telephone number and a woman answered. I phoned because I was concerned about having not heard you'd arrived safely in Iceland, and that's when she told me about the car accident. I asked her, Eva isn't it, to keep in touch and gave her my telephone number and address. She's been keeping me up to date since; it was no good relying on you." Preoccupied with his thoughts, Nathan missed Jane's comment, "She sounds nice on the phone."

"Sorry?"

"Eva sounds nice when I've spoken to her and she obviously cares about you."

"Yes, I daresay she does."

"Come on, you can do better than that, Nathan, I'm your sister. What did happen up there?"

For the next hour Nathan attempted to explain to Jane about the air crash and the lost warhead, the secrecy and illnesses amongst the workers. The way none of the authorities wanted to admit to what happened and his discovery of the Danish reporter who was attempting to reveal the truth. He shared with Jane almost everything: everything, that is, except about Sissel.

"It doesn't sound like your usual line of work? Where does Eva fit in?"

He told her about Magnus and Ernst and their part in the clean-up. "Something's driving me to get to the bottom of it all."

"Does she love you?"

"Wow!" he exclaimed. "Where did that come from?"

"Call it female intuition, if you like. Well?"

He hesitated. "I think so."

"And you, what do you feel for her?"

"I really don't know. I like her, she's good to be with but . . ."

"You have doubts. You don't know if you love her?"

"No, I don't," he said. "You know better than anyone what happened, it's hard to put that behind me."

Jane looked at him in an impassioned way, "It's good to have doubts, but it's not always possible to be certain. We must at times take chances."

"I know you want me to let go," he said.

"No," her comment then surprised him, "but who was like a sister to Lindsey? Who spent the last weeks constantly by her side? Who knew her nearly as well as you? Me. And what I know for certain is that she would have wanted you to move on."

*   *   *   *

Once the boys had gone back to school and Jane returned to her nine to five job, Nathan had time to be alone and think things over, meditating on all that had happened. A visit to Lindsey's grave brought back a flood of memories, some sad but many good.

January slipped by effortlessly. There was the occasional dinner party with the wealthy Hertfordshire set. Personally he couldn't see what Jane saw in them but there again, they had been there for her when things got tough. His sanctuary came when he would strike out for long walks by himself, and the evening chats with Jane, once the boys were in bed, were like old times. But Nathan had to admit to himself that he missed Eva and longed to be with her again.

"Are you going back to the Eskimos, Uncle?"

"Yes, eventually, boys. But they don't like being called Eskimos, they are Inuits, it means 'the real people'. First, though, I need to visit my university. I expect they wonder what's happened to me, maybe even if I'm still alive!"

The farewells were far from easy. "Travel safely," Jane said as they shared one last hug.

"Don't get caught in a blizzard," one of the boys shouted as Nathan got into the hire car.

"No," he replied, "no chance of that, spring will soon be on its way. Look after your mum."

The winding Hertfordshire lanes, awash with slush and ice, soon gave way to main roads. Gritters had obviously been out the night before as he could hear the stones pinging off the underside of the car. Would Britain again grind to a standstill with the next light fall of snow, he pondered. He drove on, heading west towards the soft winter sun, deep into the heart of Wales.

"It's good to see you back, old boy," a haughty, middle-aged academic greeted Nathan.

"Yes," mustered Nathan, "it's good to be back."

But in truth, it wasn't. He was weary of all that was the university, it felt so strange now. The man's mobile rang, its irritating ringing tone played one of Queen's hits which Nathan couldn't quite place. As he raised it to his ear Nathan tried to remember if Gareth had a crew-cut last time he saw him; he didn't recall his head being so egg-shaped.

"The Vice Chancellor wants me, probably to save her bacon again. Catch you later, over a drink," and he was gone.

It took Nathan only another hour and three more conversations to realise nothing had truly changed. When he considered all that had happened to him over the past few months, the place seemed to be locked in some kind of time warp.

"Your old study is free, Professor Trent, and I don't believe anyone's touched your things, except to clean," Mr Jones, the porter, said. "We hadn't realised you would be on sabbatical for so long. I'll sort things out, sir. Have you any idea how long you'll be with us?" Jones politely waited as the silence lengthened. "Well, let me know, sir, so I can instruct housekeeping, and please tell me if there's anything you need. It's good to have you back."

"Did it go well?" Devan asked.

Devan Williams had been his closest friend and confidante in the faculty and Nathan had no hesitation in apprising him of the situation. "If I was you, my old lad, I'd stop around for a couple of weeks or so, get yourself seen. I know you're not sure of your intentions long-term but there are some big changes on the horizon, a possible take-over of Mach College to establish a new environmental campus. None of us know the full implications but, as the saying goes, 'out of sight, out of mind'. Best they still think you are here and have a part in any future developments. Have you caught up with the departmental secretariat yet, and Pauline?"

For the next few days Nathan followed Devan's advice and circulated. Pauline was highly delighted to see him and proceeded to plough through his outstanding mail although, as usual, all but a handful she had dealt with. Academic research papers awaited his final approval as joint collaborator and, much to her relief, they were soon checked and signed off. It was apparent that some colleagues hadn't missed him at all, while others assumed he was working overseas and nearly all of them wanted to know if he had the inside line on the expansion. One advantage of not having a lecture timetable was that the graduates didn't notice his absence, and he guessed that whilst management were embroiled in negotiations they probably had enough to occupy them.

Nathan took advantage of the university facilities over the following weeks to continue background research concerning matters around Thule. It was also a chance to liaise and to begin to cultivate a relationship with Martin Poulson over in Denmark. He considered that, by adopting the university as a point of contact, Martin might initially feel more confident that Nathan's interest was genuine.

A plan was beginning to take shape in Nathan's mind. He judged another week would be enough to tie up any loose ends at the university and then he would head back to Iceland. It was time he finally squared things with Eva. Martin Poulson had shared some surprising news about potential legal actions and it was crucial he told Eva. She would then understand why he needed to get to Copenhagen by April, when Martin was available and willing to meet up. He considered that maybe he'd been foolish to admit to Martin that he'd come this far and wasn't about to give up – only time would tell.

* * * *

The night flight for Nathan, on Icelandair from London, was uneventful.

A stewardess's commanding voice over the intercom accompanied the seatbelt sign illuminated on the panel above his head. He peered through the black porthole trying to glimpse the world outside to gain a sense of the weather. The darkness hid all from his gaze but for the torrential rain. The half-empty Boeing 757 effortlessly touched down at Keflavik International Airport. It slowed then taxied to its stand beside the terminal building.

Clearing passport control he boarded the last shuttle bus of the day heading for the city. A dozen or more tough independent types bundled their rucksacks and boots into the overhead luggage racks and settled at the front of the bus. Lone travellers, probably homeward bound, disappeared into the back, and an elderly couple, confused as to where to sit, finally took refuge across the aisle from him. The forty-minute road trip to Reykjavik passed without him uttering a single word, lost in his own world. Nathan's impression of being half asleep proved enough to stall the old boy opposite from making any conversation. Heading northward on the West Coast Highway wind and rain buffeted relentlessly against the bus, causing it at times to noticeably roll, while passing vehicle headlights bathed the road in light, casting weird patterns on the wet tarmac. Nature's forces were telling him he was back in Iceland.

Disembarking at the City Bus Terminal he couldn't help but think he'd never seen such rain. He shivered, and a chill ran down his spine as he remembered that he had experienced something like this before. Cursing, he pulled up the collar of his tweed overcoat, wondering how much more the heavens had in store.

"It's been much like this all the time you've been away," Eva said, irritated, "this infernal weather. Get in before you get soaked."

He needed no encouragement and within a minute they were heading for her apartment.

The spring concert season was well underway, and while Eva was tied up with rehearsals Nathan took the opportunity to find out more about Martin Poulson, sharing with her what he had learnt.

"The first thing I discovered about Poulson was that back in 1997 he was awarded The Cavling Prize for his revelations about how the people of Greenland and Denmark were duped regarding the presence of nuclear weapons at Thule Air Base, despite Denmark's official non-nuclear policy. Poulson had begun to reveal the part the governments of America and Denmark had played in the whole Thule affair.

"Born in 1953, Poulson started his career working with DR in Aarhus for the regional station East Jutland Radio. In 1991 he moved to Copenhagen and TV news where he was assigned to the foreign editor's office, focusing on the UK. His crucial break came in 1986 when he visited a worker who had helped clean up the plutonium-contaminated snow after the crash, and was claiming many fellow-workers were suffering with mysterious skin problems, or had died. Following Martin's appeal on air for workers to come forward, the radio station's switchboard was inundated with calls for several days."

"That's amazing, what happened then?" Eva said.

"The story was born, and it is evident from the various articles on the internet that the Danish people were getting behind the cause. So much so that in 1987 two hundred former workers took legal action against the United States. The action resulted in the release of a mountain of hitherto classified documents, and in 1995 the Danish government paid a so-called ex-gratia payment of 50,000 Kroner to 1,700 workers, reportedly to buy their silence."

Nathan was only too aware that fifteen years later Poulson was still on the case, delving into the Land Steal and Denmark's exploitation of Greenland and its innocent people.

Nathan had successfully captured Eva's attention. "In the summer of 1995 Poulson himself had published confidential documents relating to the former Prime Minister and the storage of nuclear weapons. Six months later he was reported to the police authorities for violation of the Archives and Data Protection Act by the national archivist of the Danish Ministry of Culture, as well as the Foreign Ministry who, in turn, had been contacted by the US State Department. After nearly a year of considering the evidence, the Public Prosecutor closed the case as Martin Poulson couldn't be found guilty of any criminal offence. Poulson had survived."

To Nathan's mind it seemed as though the hunter had now become the hunted.

* * * *

On an evening, which to Nathan looked like any other, Eva announced, "We should go," and with that she added, "the night is right for it."

"Go where?" Nathan asked.

"Out of the city, just trust me."

They drove for over thirty minutes, away from the houses and beyond the city's glare to the hills. She pulled off the byroad and parked.

"And now we must wait and watch," she insisted expectantly.

"Watch what?"

"Wait and see," was all she said.

The sky was moonless, clear and black but for the shining stars, with no clouds to hide their presence, nor to blanket the warm earth. A chill lingered in the fresh-smelling air, and as they watched to the north, the sky's countenance changed. Silently a faint greenish glow, a luminescence, appeared over the horizon. Then moments later streaks shot across the blackness like psychedelic curtains billowing as silk in a whirling wind. Spectacular multi-coloured patterns were being painted high in the Arctic sky, dying briefly only to reappear again and again.

"I was only eight when my father brought me out here one December," Eva shared. "We stood ankle deep in numbing snow, and then the heavens opened. Teal-like strands of light emerged eerily from the black, and within minutes the sky was full of colours, like rainbows that magically bounced off the snow. It seemed as if the snow had fallen to deliberately reflect the light. There are some that say the appearance of the aurora heralds the coming of war."

CHAPTER TWENTY-NINE

Magnus' flat was cosy, and sparsely furnished to say the least. It incorporated a cupboard-sized shower-come-loo, and a kitchenette which he always described as quite adequate for his needs.

His bed was set alongside and under a window. On this particular night, readying himself to retire, he part-drew the curtains across his half-open bedroom window. Then, settling beneath the heavy blankets and gathering the bed clothes snugly round him, he listened to the ghostly howl of the wind outside. He found there was something deeply satisfying and comforting, wrapped as he was, in his cocoon. Tonight though, unlike other nights when he would toss and turn fitfully while trying to sleep, Magnus' journey into unconsciousness was swifter, more peaceful than usual, and oblivion came to him in a way it hadn't before. Tonight was going to be very different.

The storm strengthened, lifting the curtains from the sill and causing gloomy shadows created by his dim bedside lamp to dance about the room. Normally, if Magnus woke he would stretch and be reassured by the lamp's warm glow that all was safe. But not tonight, nor any other night: for Magnus there would be no other nights.

The funeral service was a painful experience for Eva. Nathan attempted to console her as best he could, as did a few of Magnus' old and close friends. Even his elderly neighbour made an effort. The priest's words of comfort highlighted, as also did his short address, the man's lack of knowledge of the deceased. However, what continued to play on Eva's mind most was the pencil note Magnus had left for her on his bedside table, trapped under his half-empty whisky glass.

Magnus' words of love and gratitude for his daughter's devotion and tolerance of an irascible old father broke her heart. A deep sense of regret overwhelmed her when she thought of all the things she had said and what she could have said. The arguments and disagreements played on her mind and she felt wretched. Deep down she knew she would miss him so. For years he had been the sole focus of her love.

CHAPTER THIRTY

For nearly an hour Nathan's airport bus wound its way along the main road between downtown Reykjavik and Keflavik Airport. On both sides eerie, black volcanic rocks skirted the road, and in the distance the Atlantic Ocean stirred.

The three-hour flight to Denmark passed quickly with Nathan amusing himself browsing the in-flight magazine. Its piece on Iceland's music scene, extolling the rise of ethereal music in advertising and TV soundtracks, proved less than riveting. He wasn't too sure why he was reading it but thought he ought to so he could hold his own with Eva if the subject ever cropped up. What interested him was the article on Iceland's Golden Circle, the wild waterfalls of Gullfoss, the Great Geysir and the picturesque valley of Thingvellir.

In no time his fellow passengers were straining to see the landscape spread out below, and from his window he viewed the flooded marginal land stretching towards Kastrup Airport on the outskirts of Copenhagen. As the aircraft touched down, its engines roaring, Nathan felt his seat belt squeeze his chest as he was violently thrust forward.

The inside of the terminal building looked much like any other small provincial airport, hardly worthy of a capital city. The route along the corridors to passport control was tedious and long. Purchasing a ticket in the main airport concourse he descended to the railway platform where he boarded the half-empty S-Train en route for Copenhagen Central Station. The carriage was clinical and clean, the fourteen-minute journey quiet and smooth, so very different from the tube or trains in London. As he neared the suburbs, cold bleak buildings bordered each side of the track, grey concrete lumps marring the skyline, projecting high above the yellowed grass cutting.

Hotel Danmark was located on Vester Voldgade, literally two roads across from Central Station past the Tivoli Gardens. Its front appeared to possess all the charms of a 1950's characterless office block. The pleasant member of staff in reception directed Nathan to his first floor room. He assumed that the bedroom at one time had looked smart, but that was long ago. The dusky-blue carpet, showing signs of wear, bore evidence of a long, demanding existence. Striped floor-to-ceiling drapes were bunched each side of the two secondary-glazed windows, which, as well as offering ventilation, provided a means of silencing the traffic. An indescribable musty smell lingered, one which reminded him of his old gran's house shortly before she died. A tall mahogany wardrobe offered space behind an ill-fitting door for nothing more than half a dozen garments. In spite of these failed attempts at luxury, Nathan found the room clean, the double mattress sound and firm with crisp, freshly-laundered bed linen offering, he hoped, a good night's sleep. On the bedside table, of less than generous proportions, perched an unattractive lamp which was equipped with a less than impressive low wattage bulb. Two prints, one of a soldier in scarlet uniform, the other an uninspiring landscape, hung in heavy gilt frames. A dark patch of wallpaper of similar size probably marked the one-time position of a third picture. A plastic Carlsberg waste bin appeared almost as homeless as he felt, and the accommodation was supplemented with a compact shower room. This was to be his home for the next few weeks.

Nathan found Copenhagen strange. He had been so used to the desolate white of Greenland, and the murky rain-soaked landscape of Iceland, that Copenhagen came as somewhat of a surprise. It still felt very much like a Nordic capital, fostering a certain degree of gloominess, but was smaller, more compact than he anticipated. However, the trading port of Nyhavn he found particularly attractive. Eighteenth-century merchant houses, some of which had been converted into cafes, bars and restaurants, lined the canal side where yachts and barges were berthed. Nathan thought it looked like one of those rare scenes re-created by a movie director.

He contemplated that probably the reason he felt so different about this city was because of what he knew. A feeling of unease came upon him as he considered the deceit that lay beneath its mediaeval exterior. That evening he decided to wander the city and soak up its atmosphere. Brightly lit shop fronts, displaying all that was trendy and fashionable, lined the broad pedestrian precincts. Cosmopolitan crowds ambled from window to window chatting about the cold and whether to join the queues waiting to purchase a hot dog. In the dim light of street cafes youngsters of all ages huddled in drab-coloured shawls and blankets around tables on flimsy garden chairs, warmed by patio heaters. Their excited talk echoed over the sound of passers-by. A small band of lonely vagrants trolleying their worldly possessions moved from bin to bin, while old women in overcoats lay propped up in shop doorways taking refuge from the wind.

With Martin Poulson tied up for the next couple of days, Nathan took the opportunity to explore the city. A short walk from the hotel brought him to Castle Island and the Neo-Baroque Palace of Christiansborg, home to the Danish government. Strolling along the waterfront he came upon a small garden which, on entering, led him into a cobbled square whereupon he witnessed the noon-day ceremony of the changing of the guards.

Passing through one of its colonnades he soon came upon the old pentagram-shaped fortress, The Kastellet Barracks – The Citadel, with its grassy ramparts and surrounding moat. Maybe Denmark's answer to the Pentagon, he wondered. A little further on and close to the water's edge, a group of tourists, mostly Japanese equipped with their Nikons and Canons, were pre-occupied photographing and posing on the rocks with the city's iconic statue of The Little Mermaid. The bronze figure, sitting all alone on a rock at the water's edge, was smaller than he had imagined and possessed an air of sadness, a forlorn feeling to it.

The next day, following the back lanes, he came upon the Round Tower from the top of which he observed the full extent of the city. He lunched at the nearby Food Hall and then made his way to the Botanical Gardens where brigades of noisy magpies in their butler's uniforms were frantically scouring the lawns. The impressive glass Palm House stretched high above the lake; ferns, rubber plants and other giant specimens from the tropics flourished in the high temperature and humidity, which was more than he did. Retreating, the coolness of the air outside came as a welcome relief.

As he walked the city's back alleyways Nathan wondered what to expect of this man, Martin Poulson. He anticipated that he might be faced with a sharp-tongued, piercing-eyed intense individual, probably unshaven with wild wiry hair. It mattered little the picture Nathan had created in his head, what was important was the reality for which he would only need to wait until tomorrow. The resounding ring of bicycle bells jolted him back to the real world. Hordes of these machines that had earlier been racked outside offices and shops, chained to every inch of railing, were now on the move, courageously being navigated in formations, like some chaotic Tour de France, along the busy highways as evening fell.

That night he was unable to sleep and found himself lying on the bed mulling things over. Flashbacks to his accident overcame him and for an hour or more he tossed restlessly, reliving those moments. As he thought of the many troubles that had recently plagued him, considering how they might well pale into insignificance compared to what the future had in store, exhausted, he eventually drifted asleep.

* * * *

Next door to Hotel Danmark, on the corner of Stormgade, was Tivoli Hallen, a cosy old-fashioned restaurant just a step or two down from the pavement where Martin had said one could savour genuine Danish food. The place was almost empty but for one couple enjoying their meal, and Martin Poulson, who was seated at a small table at the far end of the restaurant, busy scanning his diary.

"Sit yourself down. It's great to finally meet up with you and amazing that you've come all this way," and repeating himself Martin said, "I am truly delighted you came."

Nathan instantly liked him. He seemed warm, far from threatening, and there was little evidence of the deep guttural pronunciation most Danes possessed. Years involved in overseas politics had resulted in his eloquent mastery of English. Martin's manner conveyed an impression of someone who was quietly self-confident. Evident in his face was inquisitiveness and, at times, as they talked, Nathan was unsure whether his wide eyes weren't on the verge of revealing a smile or two. There was little remarkable about his appearance: short black hair, smart casual attire, average height and build. But from what Nathan already knew of the man that was as far as average went. Here before Nathan was an advocate for truth: someone who was using his writing to expose the injustices committed by powerful people.

As they spent time with each other, Nathan saw little sign of the ego that one might expect from a renowned journalist of Poulson's calibre. In conversation he was generous with praise for his fellow reporters and colleagues at DR, most notably for his editor. If it wasn't for her wisdom and guidance Martin was adamant he would have got into more scrapes and tight corners than he did. As Martin went about championing causes it would be conceivable, Nathan thought, some might view him as obsessive, a fanatic perhaps, and one who might attract the attention of the establishment, the guardians of public opinion. A willingness to sacrifice much to secure the truth was evident from his words, "One has to find the truth and share it if one is going to remain human."

The more Nathan talked with Martin the more he felt that, in many ways, he was pretty conventional. He spoke warmly of his wife and daughter but Nathan sensed that was his private life which he would have to wait to be invited into. Martin told of how, over the years, he had asked a lot of questions and made a lot of people nervous. He wouldn't say he had made enemies but perhaps, through his investigations, he hadn't always made close friendships.

"You must think me rude," Martin said.

"No, why is that?"

"I have not asked if your hotel is alright."

"Yes, it's fine, thank you. It's not the smartest," Nathan confessed, "but the staff are helpful and the food is good."

Martin appeared satisfied. "We should order, what will you have?"

"I'll be guided by you," Nathan said, "I'm up for anything."

After a mere ten minutes the waitress delivered a fish dish of marinated herrings.

"I've chosen a traditional meal for us, I hope that's okay?" Martin explained. The main course that followed was a smørrebrød, an open beef sandwich with grated horseradish, fried onion, lettuce and salted fat. More fat accompanied the rye bread. All was washed down with a dark beer brewed on a nearby island and a small glass of limoncino spiked with . . . Nathan wasn't sure.

"This is one of the 'must experience restaurants' in Denmark," Martin pointed out, "especially if you're hungry. It's often packed here. Here is one of the few places where both politicians and news people dine, rubbing shoulders and ignoring one another. They say more decisions are made and headlines dreamt up here than anywhere else in the city. This was where we first got wind of the collapse of our biotech industry, Medicon Valley, and the burst of the IT and financial bubbles post 9/11. It's amazing what truths and lies have been shared within these walls."

They talked over coffee for another hour or more, sharing what they had learnt of the Thule incident, the 'Death Zone' as Martin referred to it, and discussed their next move. Martin knew nothing of Project Iceworm: he hadn't appreciated quite how extensive the clean-up operation was and how many it involved. Nathan shared with him how dramatically the life of the Inuit had changed with the coming of the Americans, and the knowledge that the dead had been whisked away to some foreign and unknown place shocked Martin.

"Maybe, Nathan, you'll get lucky with your enquiries. They're fed up with me chasing them all the time but you're a stranger, and they don't know you." Nathan realised Martin was under increasing pressure as he shared the words of his editor, "I need this domestic story to have a significant impact internationally." Nathan quickly appreciated the insightfulness and professionalism of this man; his stubborn persistence, enthusiasm and exceptional commitment was hard not to notice.

"Much of my own time over the past years has been devoted to this case, sadly to the detriment of my family."

"In the beginning what made you believe those people coming forward?" Nathan said. "They could have been wrong or deceiving you, taking you for a ride in an attempt to gain compensation?"

"You are right, of course, and at first I was sceptical, doubting the stories I was hearing, but as I came across more people struggling with similar disorders, and wives speaking of their dead husbands, it was hard not to believe something was dramatically wrong. At that time few knew about Thule and as I asked questions and got so few answers, new questions arose. The scientists at the Risø National Institute of Radiation

Protection had vehemently claimed that the cause of the high death rate amongst workers was alcoholism brought about by the isolated environment. A wholly unconvincing view that no one truly believed. Many found this claim just as polluted as the snow they removed. I needed to find out the truth for myself so I took a drive north to Roskilde, to the Radiation Protection Centre at Risø. There, sprawling over a huge part of the coast, the Danish Ministry operates eight research departments on the site. This was where they undertook the initial health tests of the Thule workers and the monitoring and analysis of samples from the crash site."

"What did you find out?" an anxious Nathan enquired.

"That was the peculiar thing: nothing. Well, not at that time. I had made an appointment to meet with the lead scientist who had been involved in the work, but on my arrival was told he could no longer meet me. I assumed that at the last minute he'd been called away or something but the reception put me through to his extension and he answered. He explained he was sorry for my wasted journey but really was unable to help me; there was nothing he could do. But then something weird happened. I was about to pull out of the car park when some half insane guy in a white lab coat started banging on the window of my passenger door. The chap was bumbling on about how we needed to talk and threw a scrap of paper in through my open car window, then disappeared."

"Weird," Nathan agreed. "What was on the paper?"

"His name, Roald, and a telephone number."

"What did you think?" Nathan said.

"To tell you the truth I thought I'd struck lucky and found someone who had a conscience."

"So what happened?"

"I called him that evening and we chatted for nearly an hour."

"And?"

"He told me that the results were flawed, that the workers were not regularly monitored. The analysis of the snow samples from the crash site was conducted in far from ideal conditions, utilising primitive and inadequate methods and equipment. He had no faith in the 'No radiation danger' conclusion. He told me he would try and send me copies of correspondence from the Danish Atomic Energy Commission and others."

"Did you believe him?"

"I wasn't sure, but within a week an envelope arrived. In it was a letter dated April 1974, from the DAEC informing the US government of the planned visit of Danish scientists to Thule, for the purpose of gathering information on what had happened to the plutonium deriving from the Thule accident. What's particularly interesting is the reference it made to previous investigations in 1968, and again in 1970."

"And he sent correspondence from others as well?" Nathan asked, now intent on knowing the answer.

"Yes, copies of several letters from a number of professionals. A chief physician at one of the hospitals in Denmark named a number of Thule workers with possible radiation injuries, while a British expert strongly disagreed with Risø's final conclusion that the plutonium at the bottom of the sea did not pose a human risk. There was also a letter from a senior administrator working at a local hospital and responsible for patient records expressing concern, stating that following a renewed interest in the Thule case, a large number of files had mysteriously disappeared."

"It seems time and again facts have a habit of disappearing when folks start digging around for sensitive information," Nathan said.

"Lastly," Martin added, "a letter from a statistician claimed that the published figures relating to incidence of deaths from cancer amongst the workers were wrong. In his view, calculations showed a very different picture: a three-fold higher than normal rate of deaths."

"Do you think the incorrect figures were deliberate?" Nathan asked.

"I don't know for certain, but what do you think?"

Nathan frowned, "What do the authorities say about the instances of cancer?"

"As you might imagine," Martin said, "they insist those involved were closely monitored, whatever that means. Since the latest revelations there have been calls for a systematic study to be carried out and the Danish Health Department has been talking about investigating all 1,016 Danes who were employed at Thule at that time. Many say it's too late and that the longer they procrastinate, the fewer will still be alive. I can understand people's frustration: after all, many of the doctors who originally said everything was okay were in the pay of the American and Danish governments."

"The whole thing is far more complicated than I first thought, shrouded in subterfuge. There's a lot going on out there, more than I ever imagined," Nathan admitted. "Why did you get involved and stir up all this dirt?"

"I don't know," Martin said.

"Yes, you do," Nathan dismissed.

"In many ways it's a journalist's dream: secret documents and hidden agreements between Denmark and the US. Ministers being economical with the truth, national betrayal, enforced evictions sanctioned by our government, poisoning and pollution, and innocent people caught up in the politics of denial. There are many influential people in powerful positions who are feeling more than uncomfortable and would go to great lengths to see this disappear."

"One thing is certain, Martin, you will leave a valuable legacy behind you."

Martin looked indifferent to the idea. "I have been astonished at the number of people who have contacted me, thinking I can make a difference for them." Martin then appeared to do a double take having looked at his watch. "I need to get back to the office, so can I leave you with some of my findings?" And with that he passed Nathan a stack of papers. He quickly explained that there were files from the Peace Movement, as well as a report from Greenpeace, which related to the pollution and impact on wildlife. Amongst the papers were facts and figures regarding the health of workers, and, lastly, there was a collection of documents from the law firms representing the settlers in Thule.

"I have taken the liberty of including some of my notes on radiation and the nuclear warhead, knowing you are a scientist. I hope you won't be offended?"

"Not at all," Nathan said.

"Good, now I really must go but we'll meet again soon. Is tomorrow good for you?"

"Sure," Nathan replied eagerly, "it's been great to finally meet you Martin," and with that each went their separate ways.

Over the ensuing days Nathan grew to know better the true Martin Poulson. In many respects their ideology and beliefs were much the same. He developed a fondness for Martin's enduring ways, an admiration for his insightful determination and dedication. Above all Nathan would discover the private man, his moments of humour and the love he held for his family, the family he fought so hard to protect.

CHAPTER THIRTY-ONE

Arriving at Sophie's Diner Nathan settled at an empty table facing the door. The cafe was buzzing with shoppers coming and going and business-men totting up their expenses. The place reminded him of a quick food joint that was trying hard to be more up-market. He studied the clock; he was early by ten minutes. Better that than late, he thought. Nathan amused himself by speculating which of the staff might be Sophie. By the time a waitress had served his coffee, Nathan had looked at the clock twice – Martin was late. Maybe delayed in the office or held up in traffic, he'd give him another twenty minutes. The waitress returned, this time with a note.

"A young lad asked me to deliver this to you. I assume you're Nathan Trent? He pointed you out."

Thrown, Nathan took the envelope and acknowledged the waitress with a smile, "Yes, that's me, thank you." Nathan glanced towards the door, and the waitress, noticing his interest said, "Oh, he's long gone."

Inside Martin's words read, *'I had a problem in the office and it was impossible to get away. Please be at the station in front of the main Arrivals and Departures board at 5.00pm this afternoon. I will explain then. Martin'*

What Nathan took to be a straight-forward meeting had suddenly taken on a more mysterious nature. It had elements of the thrillers he had read in his student days, resembling those clandestine liaisons, the secret communiqués. As with the reading of those stories Nathan wondered what would happen next. Convincing himself that his over-active imagination had got the better of him, he paid the bill and left.

At fifteen minutes before the designated hour Nathan arrived at Central Station and, unconsciously recalling some of the basic techniques of spy-craft, found himself taking up a position which, although almost totally obscured from general view by a pillar, allowed him a clear view of the Arrivals and Departures board. He saw Martin arrive a few minutes before five looking out of breath and anxious. Nathan made his way eagerly across the station concourse towards him, scanning fellow travellers, although he wasn't sure for what.

"Sorry to mess you around, only I got stuck in meetings and I couldn't get away," Martin said, appearing flushed.

"Is that all?" Nathan said, disappointed by the anti-climax.

"What do you mean?"

"Oh nothing, just my wild imagination, forget it. Do you want to grab a coffee?"

The coffees were ordered and the men wasted no time in updating each other on developments. Even as the cups were slid across before them they didn't falter from their exchange.

Martin addressed Nathan. "Your part has been invaluable in securing the factual accounts that help make this a case, one that the public will understand and pledge their allegiance to in the fight to find the truth."

"That sounds a bit melodramatic," Nathan said.

"Not really, but there is no escaping this for me. However, you should get out, Nathan, before it gets too nasty, as it undoubtedly will."

"I can't walk away from it now," Nathan said. "I've no choice, I must finish what so many started and invested their lives in. They are relying on me . . . on us."

A warm grin filled Martin's face. "You and I are more similar than you perhaps realise." The grin then disappeared. "Well, as long as you understand there will be times when you'll feel afraid, that's inevitable, but if you ever feel unsafe then you've gone too far. That's when it's no longer worth it, trust me."

Nathan found it easy to trust Martin, but if he was honest and it came to the crunch, he doubted he would take Martin's advice.

"I've been lucky," Nathan said. "I've got a meeting at the Ministry of Foreign Affairs set for the morning."

"Be careful," Martin said, "and be clear who you are dealing with. You are not just taking on the Danish government but, in essence, the Americans as well."

"I hear what you say but I don't feel anxious," Nathan said.

Martin looked him up and down. "If you were smart, you would. They have wanted to end this thing quietly and won't take kindly to you going around stirring things up. It's hard to trust those that insist on secrecy in the name of national security."

* * * *

Nathan couldn't help but be impressed by the Ministry building as he was ushered through its corridors.

"I appreciate you sparing me the time," Nathan said, trying hard to mask the feeling of being out of his depth.

The office was large, impersonal and plain except for a grand oak desk; Nathan took up the offer and sat across from the man. He was only too aware that to get a meeting with the Ministry's Permanent Under-Secretary was unusual in itself, and doubly so for a non-national. Lars Nielsen rocked back and forth in his generous tan leather chair, appearing to gain pleasure from its motion. Nathan watched him toy with a fat cigar which he rolled between his fingers. Then, twisting its red and gold foil band, he raised the Colorado to his nose, savouring its leaf. Taking a cutter from his desk top he clipped one end, then, with a match, lit it and inhaled deeply. Heavy blue-white halos of smoke gracefully lifted from the brown stub anchored in the corner of his mouth. A thick mellow aroma began to fill the room. Nathan couldn't help himself. He coughed.

"You don't mind, do you?" Nielsen said, making no effort to stop his pleasure. "I am pleased to help you in any way I can, Mr Trent, but you must realise, my time is short."

"Yes of course," Nathan said, far from convinced.

"Good. Now my PA tells me you wanted to ask about our territory of Greenland, for an academic publication, I imagine. Your interest in our foreign affairs is commendable and, whenever we can, the Ministry likes to help. What is it you want to know?"

It seemed apparent that the politician had no idea of Nathan's real motive for the meeting, so maybe this would be the opportunity to get to the truth. Nathan summoned his courage.

"What did the government of the day know about the Americans' nuclear activity in Greenland during the 1960s?"

He could feel his heart thumping in his ears. The politician spun around in his chair to face Nathan directly.

"You are not with our or the Americans' media, are you?"

"No," Nathan said, thinking fast.

"So might I ask, who the hell are you then . . . Mr Trent?" Nielsen pressed, drawing hard on his cigar. Nathan's mind went blank. "Excuse my bluntness but I understood you wanted to discuss foreign developments on the west coast of Greenland."

He tapped his cigar over a heavy glass ashtray and half an inch of ash fell.

"For my academic paper," Nathan blundered, "I need to get some context to the American presence, their activities and how that has clearly impacted on developments in that region."

"Your paper?" delved Nielsen, his caution now evident. "And who or what is the piece for?"

"I am sorry," Nathan said. "I obviously failed to fully apprise your staff. I hold a professorship within the department of Earth Sciences and Overseas Development in the University of Aberyswyth." Nathan had come to the conclusion that a deviation from the truth was both necessary and worth the risk. "We are studying how international collaborations and agreements have helped to benefit the more remote land areas of our planet. My remit is to focus on the Polar regions. You are undoubtedly aware of Antarctica's unique status in this respect, as a continent owned by no one nation but shared by many who work together for the greater good, putting the territory outside any war or political crisis."

Nathan realised he had been somewhat naive not to have fully rehearsed his back story. He was certain that if his explanation was checked, it would hold up. After all, no one really knew what he was up to these days and he could always get Pauline at the university to cover for him if need be.

Nielsen eased himself back into his padded chair, noticeably relaxing. The aggression in his voice had gone, replaced with more conciliatory tones.

"My apologies, I had no idea, a failing on our part. Will you forgive my less than accommodating manner? I am sure you will understand but I am continually being harassed by all sorts of fanatics and activists with their mad campaigns and quests, as well as the less scrupulous section of the media, journalists wishing to create some wild stories out of thin air."

"I understand," Nathan said, grateful that he hadn't been rumbled, and wondering which of these labels would eventually be pinned on him.

The internal phone rang once. Discarding his cigar to the ashtray Lars lifted the handset and waited . . .

"Tell them that's okay, we'll reschedule for next week. Agnes, fix us two coffees would you, thanks."

"Perhaps it would be better if I arranged another time that was more convenient, or should I contact the Secretariat to speak with another department?" Nathan offered, attempting not to sound enthusiastic at the idea.

"No, you are alright, my three o'clock has had to reschedule. It was somebody here in Trade and Investment so that's no problem. Now, what was I saying . . . Ahh yes. In 1947 we requested an end to the '41 agreement which allowed the Americans the right to build and operate airfields, as well as other military and meteorological installations in Greenland, and a new joint defence area was formed."

"Was that the basis for the construction of the air base at Thule?" Nathan asked.

"Amongst others things. It also proved the foundation for collaboration with NATO," Nielsen added.

"May I ask how that impacted on the region for the better?" Nathan said.

"Employment for one," the politician came back instantly. "Take Thule as a typical example. While clearly many specialist and highly skilled professionals had to be shipped in, the nature of the project necessitated the need for large numbers of semi-skilled and unskilled workers, valuable opportunities for the Greenlanders."

Treading carefully, and avoiding the term *strategically expelled,* Nathan said, "Would these be the Inuit who had to be relocated north of Thule because of the building of the US military base?"

"The Inuhuit people," Nielsen said, correcting Nathan, "moved of their own free will and were successfully re-housed in the village of Qaanaaq, along with vital facilities, provisions, equipment and, of course, healthcare. They benefitted from new hunting grounds. Old Thule had never been a good hunting area."

"Right," Nathan acknowledged, only half believing the explanation. "Is there not some controversy over their move?" he went on, knowing full well a case was currently resting with the Danish Supreme Court.

"There's always controversy over everything in our country, no matter what," Lars dismissed, staring into the air, letting his words hang for a while in the emptiness. "You must understand how crucial the American presence was, not only for Europe but for the world at large. The Cold War could have so easily been a precursor to nuclear annihilation. The alliance Denmark formed with the US brought about a new relationship, one where our nation was suddenly sitting at the top table in NATO's First Division, so to speak. For the first time we had direct access to the President of the United States and his key security advisors; we had become part of the strategic solution. We may be small but we are an important ally nevertheless, a net security provider who, by being smart, are able to punch well above our weight alongside other major contributors. It is true to some extent that our nation is beset by the dilemma of political ambition set against our limited resource capability, but what's new? As one of NATO's *musterknabes – wonder boys* – we contributed to the US-led coalition against Iraq, as well as in missions in Croatia and Bosnia when NATO decided to attack Yugoslavia. But then came 9/11 and that changed everything. We moved from being involved in traditional peace-making operations to counter-insurgency and regular warfare, while further strengthening our ties with the US."

Nathan had not anticipated an exposition but could see Nielsen was well in his stride.

"We still exercise sovereign control over Greenland's foreign and security policies, but are supporting the country's move to self-governance."

"What of the American's legacy?" Nathan interjected.

"What do you mean?"

"You spoke of providing healthcare for the Inuhuit." Nathan stumbled over the unfamiliar pronunciation. "I guess that was vital after the accident?"

"Accident?" Nielsen queried.

"Yes, the crash of the nuclear armed bomber in 1968. Weren't hundreds of Inuhuit and Danish personnel affected, along with Americans?"

"In what way do you mean, affected?" Nielsen said robustly.

Nathan put an end to the to-ing and fro-ing of questions. "I was referring to the deaths and incidents of cancer amongst the workers and service personnel. As I understand, high occurrences of a rare lymphatic cancer which can be attributed to radioactivity." He was aware Nielsen was about to interrupt but ignored him. "Moreover, doctors concluded symptoms pointed in many to a weakening of their body's defence systems and I believe your Institute of Social Medicine, here in Copenhagen, even spoke of an AIDs-like phenomenon among some of the workers."

That proved more than enough for Nielsen. "Where on earth, Mr Trent, did you get that idea from? You obviously have a scientific mind but you have no medical training, am I right?"

"Well, no," Nathan confessed.

"Just as I thought. Such ill-founded accusations can get one into deep water."

But Nathan was having none of it. "I understand that, which is why I have undertaken thorough research and listened to people who were involved."

"People," Nielsen retorted. "And tell me, how many of these people can be trusted to be totally honest? At best folk can become confused, especially after such a long time, and some will have hidden agendas, ulterior motives to distort the truth, perhaps for selfish reasons or just to discredit others." He paused, and Nathan noticed what he took to be a realisation in Nielsen's face, "You've been to Thule, am I right?"

Nathan nodded and smiled, looking Nielsen squarely in the face, demonstrating a defiance which the politician was clearly not used to.

"Did you feel at home up there?" Nielsen said, attempting to humour him.

"No," Nathan said. "It's a place where even the Inuhuit no longer feel at home and your government has known all along about what happened up there and how so many have suffered, totally unaware of the risks they were exposing themselves to."

Up until now Nielsen's approach had been condescending but a natural arrogance, typical of his position, was immediately evident in his reply.

"People will tell you what they think you want to hear and it takes a special person to distinguish between truth and fiction. Many think they can do that but few can, believe me. Life is not black and white in the way that you see it, Mr Trent. There are many things about what happened in Thule that you cannot begin to understand. You believe that workers were poisoned by a mythical, lost bomb because it suits you to hold onto that idea."

"It doesn't matter what I believe, it only matters what is true," Nathan said.

"We have found no compelling evidence that the Thule workers have been exposed to radiation. There is no missing bomb, there never was. We, along with the Americans, took measures to stand against the evil of the Soviet's nuclear threat. In your eyes that makes us evil, does it? Our action could have prevented a full nuclear war. Perhaps your judgement would be different if that threat had materialised. I can't tolerate those who take a holier-than-thou attitude to our actions without fully understanding." And in a moment he came again. "Do tell me, what would you have done?"

Nathan was too wise to be taken in by Nielsen's blustering and bullying. Here was a man who possessed the invaluable quality as a politician to avoid making a clear and unambiguous statement, to dance all around the issue and commit to nothing. Nathan thought to himself that to say, *'There is no missing bomb',* could mean that what has been lost has been accounted for but it doesn't mean it's actually been recovered. He judged Nielsen to be a diplomat who would probably put duty above honesty when circumstances dictated.

Nathan challenged, "Why was the news of the accident withheld?" Nielsen didn't speak. Nathan persisted, "Danes weren't made aware of the possible risks or the presence of nuclear weapons."

Still no reply; Nielsen was now fidgeting in his chair.

"The Americans had for years stockpiled nuclear warheads on Danish soil, totally violating Denmark's non-nuclear policy, and the people didn't know: it was kept from them. You kept it from them!" Nathan thought that any moment Nielsen would reply, even if only to say, 'no comment'.

Nielsen responded but not as Nathan expected. "Not all of us knew, not at first." Nathan sat back. It had worked, the politician was talking. "And when they did know they realised that, had it got out, it would have stalled the impending elections and caused mayhem amongst our people. Regardless, many were far from happy. They wanted to tell the people but knew it was vital the election was clean, free of any complications."

"But even when the news did finally come out, it wasn't the truth, was it?" Nathan challenged.

Stealing a moment to reflect, Nielsen eventually replied, "No, you're right, but we didn't know that at the time. We were led to believe the bomber was not on a routine mission over Greenland but diverted due to an emergency and had to make a forced landing. Had we known at the time that was a lie, and the real truth had been suppressed to avoid an international incident, many would have . . ."

"Would have what?" persisted Nathan, who wasn't giving up.

"I don't know," Nielsen said wearily. "Maybe they would have gone to the Minister, perhaps the press."

"And if that didn't work?"

"I really don't know. All along they wanted to carefully manage the breaking of the news, at first after the vote, then after the Queen had formed a new government and ministers and the cabinet had been installed. All the time the PM and government knew about the warheads, but a pact had been struck with the Americans to keep it secret." Nielsen's voice changed. He sounded less vulnerable, more threatening. "Why are you doing this, Mr Trent, digging up the past? What good will it do?"

"You really don't know what's going on, do you?" Nathan said in an understanding manner and, giving no opportunity to reply, continued. "Don't you know what happened to those people who had to clean up the mess?"

Nielsen appeared lost, out of his depth.

"This isn't a game; lives have been ruined." Nathan asserted. "You must have seen some of the media coverage about the appalling deaths and illnesses that have plagued so many."

"Yes," Nielsen replied, "but I believed it to be scare-mongering by compensation opportunists."

"Well, I can assure you, Mr Nielsen, it is true. I've seen it for myself."

Nielsen's eyes narrowed and in them was a look of fear: a fear that maybe what he was about to hear would make him realise that all along he had been wrong. Nathan chose his words carefully, wishing to stay focussed on the facts and avoid any over-dramatisation. What he shared caused the politician's face to pale. His lips pursed, his eyes appeared to become tighter, sinking into pools of darkness. His motionless body conveyed no hint of what was going on in his head.

"Those secrets must be driving you crazy," Nathan said. After what he judged to be an appropriate time, he spoke again, "You had no idea what actually happened, had you?"

"No," a sombre Nielsen admitted. He rose from behind his desk and, without offering his hand, concluded, "I don't expect we'll be seeing each other again. Good day, Mr Trent."

The April air was unseasonably chilly. Heading for his hotel, Nathan stopped, turned and looked back towards the austere, grey Ministry building. He shivered, a spiteful sea wind biting his face as he strolled over Knippelsbro Bridge, before threading his way through the city. Try as he might he couldn't recall exactly what he said in response to Nielsen's repeated probing about Nathan's contacts here in Denmark. He didn't think he had mentioned Martin's name, but he wasn't sure.

THE DANISH PARLIAMENT, COPENHAGEN – DENMARK 2002

CHAPTER THIRTY-TWO

At five-fifteen the following afternoon, Greta Klausen, Head of Public Relations for the Danish government, was seated in a room on the top floor of The Castle, addressing a select group of four ministerial officials. The reason for the meeting was a matter of some urgency. It was to discuss a subject which she knew all would wish they had heard the last of. The Permanent Under-Secretary to the Ministry of Foreign Affairs, Lars Nielsen, had received a visitor yesterday, someone attempting to resurrect the Thule affair. The English academic was collaborating with Martin Poulson, an investigative journalist who needed no introduction to the group. Greta glanced at Georg, who audibly sighed, then to Erin, and was indignant that both their Defence and Health Ministries needed to be on board with this one.

Erin was the first to speak and explained things were far from easy now that a hearing in the Supreme Court concerning the health issues looked almost inevitable. With that Erin shuddered. She cautioned that any review of decisions on the health monitoring of local people and workers would be seriously bad news at this time: it would be the last thing the Ministry of Health needed. Greta added swiftly that none of them needed that.

Attention was then steered to Defence and Georg, who was clear that further accusations of negligence regarding the handling of the clean-up operation, substantiated or otherwise, would undoubtedly make things difficult. He went on to explain that friends at the Pentagon were concerned. They were banking on the nuke's presence and the overflying issue, as well as the 'lost bomb' scenario, having long ago been put to bed and the matter closed.

Greta needed to know where Environment and Oluf were on this one. They had stood firm concerning the lack of long-term pollution in the area and had no desire to re-visit their methods or results: such a resurrection would be, as one would say, opening a *kan af orme!* At that Greta concluded they were all of the same mind, and having already consulted with a senior adviser in the Prime Minister's office, it was established that the embarrassment regarding the whole affair, not to mention the public revelation of the tacit agreement of 1957 between the Prime Minister of the day and the Americans concerning the deployment of nuclear weapons on Danish soil, would prove highly undesirable.

Then Greta gestured towards Mikkel, who had patiently sat silent, listening. Somehow they needed to find out what these two men, the journalist and the academic, knew. She was unclear how they were going to do that, but in essence they needed a sympathetic eye and ear inside DR. There were those key persons within that propaganda fortress that she regarded as red wing sympathisers and they, for everyone's good, needed to be watched. Greta looked again at Mikkel searching for some acknowledgement on his part. He asked if she wanted Poulson's calls traced and recorded, and whether he should be tailed. She told him to fix the phones so they could go live at a moment's notice. Regarding tailing, the answer was no, not as yet. Greta needed to know what the two had in mind first and she didn't want them scared off. How it was done she didn't care, she just wanted it done, and she asked Mikkel if that was clear. Understandably he didn't regard Greta's words as a question. She charged him to tell her the moment he learnt anything, absolutely anything, as it was crucial to know what they intended to do with the intelligence they were digging up.

She emphasised it was vital they got someone close to them, and fast, and it had to be someone they could trust who was entirely believable and would not be suspected. Mikkel considered before replying that he had someone in mind. The individual worked for him within the Defence Intelligence Service based at the Citadel and currently operated as an Army Liaison Officer in DR Broadcasting. Greta expressed great satisfaction with this and instructed him to keep her updated on their progress. Then, addressing the gathering, she cautioned that none of what had been discussed should go outside the conference room. Checking all understood she added that there was too much at stake, citing the last thing they needed was for this to break all over DR, or for that matter, becoming headlines on BBC news bulletins.

* * * *

By the end of the next day telecoms technicians had visited DR Radiohuset Skyriser offices at Rosenørns Allé, and carried out the necessary work. No one in the office saw anything unusual in this as the phone system was regularly troubled with faults, so engineers tinkering with the system were regarded almost as routine. Only one person there knew otherwise.

Mikkel updated Greta, who was heartened to hear that Poulson's line was tapped and he wouldn't be able to breathe without them knowing. The call monitoring could go live at any time on her word. For the first time since Nielsen's call three days earlier, a clearly relieved Greta acknowledged Mikkel's endeavours. Again she appealed to Mikkel to understand that this must never get out.

Attempting to put her at ease, Mikkel explained that the insider had always exercised the height of discretion and he was certain there would be no problems. Greta told him that if it was absolutely necessary, as a last resort, they could slap a notice on DR stopping them publishing on the grounds of national security, although she admitted she wanted to avoid that at all costs. She then stressed that they needed to be prepared to attack Poulson and the Englishman's credibility. They had to be in a position to persuade the Danish people to disbelieve them, even before they opened their mouths and spoke out. Being crystal clear for Mikkel's benefit, she told him her belief that conspiracy theories were not the sole domain of the paranoid. She emphasised people's need to make meaning out of the meaningless, and explaining the inexplicable often led them down some strange and dark alleyways and it wasn't to be underestimated what damage could be inflicted if that occurred.

DR HEADQUARTERS – COPENHAGEN

CHAPTER THIRTY-THREE

The six-storey offices of DR Radiohuset rose like some monolithic watch-tower, and the huge letters 'DR' illuminated in red on the front of the block, shone as a beacon over the north west suburbs of Copenhagen.

Martin Poulson arrived at the offices on this bitter morning as his colleague, Sig Søvensen, was just greeting the over-coated doorman who had paused from stamping his feet and slapping his broad thighs in order to welcome them both.

Sig Søvensen had graduated from the Copenhagen Business School, and with honours from The Royal Danish Military Academy. That grounding had stood him in good stead to take on a role as an analysis and logistics officer within Army Operational Command and here he had excelled. His expertise both in domestic operations as well as overseas theatres was quickly rewarded with promotion to Senior Training Officer – Intel – within the Military Academy. His technical knowledge and experience in communications and coordination had made him an ideal candidate to operate as Military Liaison Officer within DR. The army had embedded him within the national broadcaster to provide face-to-face collaboration; an insider to help protect the military from any collateral damage and achieve a mutual understanding between two very different worlds which had little in common.

Sig's three years of operating within DR's Editorial Department had ensured he was not now considered an outsider, but seen as one of the boys, albeit one who kept himself very much to himself: a lone wolf – Mikkel's lone wolf. His work over the past five or so months had been routine and mundane. There had been little of any consequence to refer back to Operations, little to tax him. This new assignment was different. Sig could see the scope to utilise his significant skills and make a vital contribution. He relished the challenge.

The two men weaved their way through the open-plan office, between the partitioned vacant work stations and voiceless phones. When they reached the news office the atmosphere was rather subdued; not surprising as Brigitte had called an 8am meeting, far too early for the majority who had struggled in. She had failed to convey any details or reason for the early start, but just insisted that everyone was in. The pungent aroma of freshly percolated coffee was beginning to stimulate life back into the tired bodies of those who had arranged themselves around the conference table.

Brigitte coolly addressed the group. "I've been looking more closely at Martin's work." Martin moved uncomfortably in his chair. "It's an excellent piece of investigative journalism, a bit dull and lacking the tension to grip our audience, but I am certain you guys can do something about that." Everyone very much respected Martin's work but knew it fell well short when it came to making an impact. "There's something here and I want to get to the bottom of it, and quick. Martin's been doing pieces on this for ten years and no one's taken much notice. It's time we got it together and told it as it is; what do you say, Martin?"

Martin was somewhat thrown; this wasn't what he expected when he was summoned. "I've worked hard to find out what really happened, that's my job, that's what I'm good at, and I won't stop until I find the truth and tell the world."

He watched Brigitte scan each in turn around the table.

"I know there's a story here," she said. "I am bloody sure we've a story and I want each of you all over it, whatever it takes. I want something we can run with."

"A conspiracy?" someone piped up.

"Maybe," Brigitte admitted, "it wouldn't be the first."

"I wouldn't define it as that," Sig remarked.

"How would you define it?" Brigitte came back.

Sig appeared to let the pressure of the moment get the better of him and addressed his outburst to Brigitte. "You're over-reacting, it's just a misunderstanding, a lot of fuss about nothing." He looked her in the eye, "You're making a big mistake," he snapped.

She glared at him. The others stared on, surprised he should take such a hard line. Martin sat unperturbed: finally he could see the pieces of the puzzle beginning to fall into place.

"If we've a story, Martin, we'll go with it. I want to see you, so would you wait outside a minute for me?" He smiled, "Good," she acknowledged.

As the throng left, Brigitte addressed Sig, "Not you." Martin couldn't help notice in her voice a sense of abhorrence towards the man. She yelled at Sig, "Don't think that because there was something between us once you can contradict me in that way in front of my team."

Sig had over-stepped the mark and Martin, who was waiting outside, looked about to see if he was the only one who had overheard. As she left the meeting room, following a sheepish Sig, Martin could see in her face the realisation of what he had just overheard.

Sig had revealed his true colours and Martin wondered if this would be the last time he would make such a mistake.

DAGENS – *TODAY* NEWSPAPER OFFICES – COPENHAGEN

CHAPTER THIRTY-FOUR

Across the city in the offices of a daily broadsheet, the editor-in-chief had called a meeting with his managing editor along with the news and chief assignment editors.

"Our source says there are rumblings in the Foreign Office. Some Englishman has been kicking up the dust on the old Poulson story and they say rumours abound that the government, along with the Americans, are preparing to deny any conspiracy existed over a land-grab and nuclear weapons storage in Greenland at that time. Word is that even Greta Klausen in The Castle is on it. As we know, the government's like a sieve, full of holes."

"Fortunately for us," piped up the managing editor as he cracked his knuckles.

"The Castle will inevitably be extremely uncomfortable about the situation and put all sorts of spin on the decisions and actions taken back then," one of the others said.

"We need a lead story," the chief admitted. "For the past four months our readership has been falling, we're losing ground to the internet. We need a story which can pull us up the ratings." He turned to Gudrun, his news editor, "Put together a small seasoned team, say three, and see what they can find, what's been concealed from the public. Get back to our source and other contacts, and see what you can squeeze out of them. Give me a heads-up in forty-eight hours. We've got to be discreet in case there is anything in this: I don't want it breaking before we're ready, is that clear?" She nodded. He caught the eye of the sub, "If it looks like it's going to be big we'll want legal on board. I don't need to tell you it's imperative we've hard facts as the backbone to the story. There are questions, such as what part the Danish government played and how heavily influenced they were by the Americans."

"We may be looking into the biggest political scandal for years," Gudrun threw in.

"Just what we need," the chief concluded, appearing to hold little regard for the country's recently elected coalition government.

* * * *

Two days later the group reconvened.

"So tell me Gudrun, what have we got?" the editor-in-chief's steely words cut to the core.

Gudrun took the floor. "Following the declassification a few years back, details of US nuclear weapons deployment during the Cold War have become more accessible." Two of the men shifted in their seats, obviously considering it was going to be a long session. She continued, "Much has been in the public domain even though theoretically classified. It is interesting that although Greenland was one of the most thoroughly documented cases of US overseas deployment, many references to it have been deleted.

"In 1993 declassified USAF records disclosed that SAC bombers routinely overflew Greenland during the 1960s."

Gudrun added, "Our bomber crashed on the ice at Thule Air Base in January 1968."

"Our Broken Arrow," interjected the chief.

"Accusations from the Russians cited that Denmark had violated her own nuclear ban, in spite of our government insisting that it had been an emergency landing. The declassified documents revealed that not only this aircraft, but others, routinely overflew Greenland armed with nuclear weapons as part of a top secret mission, Hard Head, to protect the Thule Air Base and BMEWS radar installations against a Soviet nuclear strike. The Danish government knew nothing of these B-52 overflights, which the US considered fell under the 1951 Greenland Defence Agreement."

The managing editor interrupted her flow. "Give us the base headlines, Gudrun."

"Okay, I'll try to be brief," Gudrun said. "Illness amongst former Thule personnel prompted the Danish government to conduct an internal record review. The review, presented to the government in 1995, confirmed violation of our non-nuclear policy. Blame was attributed to the late Danish PM, H C Hansen, for not making the policy clear during a meeting with the US ambassador in 1957. The US had deployed nuclear weapons in Greenland. However, subsequent to the report's release, US Defence Secretary, William Perry, met with Danish Foreign Minister, Niels Helveg Petersen, and assured the press that no nuclear weapons had been deployed on the ground. Within a few days the Danish government had received a letter from the US government contradicting that assurance, stating that weapons had been so deployed. Embarrassed by the scandal, the Danish government went public but not before the details of deployment were leaked and then released in 1996. As far back as 1958 weapons were introduced at Thule, with weapons remaining in place up until summer 1965. In '67 the US deployed on Danish soil the Airborne Alert Program, maintaining up to a dozen nuclear armed bombers airborne twenty-four hours a day, of which two overflew Greenland daily for nearly a decade. The Pentagon feared a possible Soviet surprise attack could destroy large portions of the US bomber force on the ground."

"Shit. I don't even remember half of this coming out," one of the assignment boys exclaimed.

"It didn't at the time. Go on . . ." the chief said.

"The nuclear armed programme continued, code named Head Start, Round Robin and Chrome Dome, up to the day of the crash. The US Air Force told the joint chiefs of staff that there appeared no restrictions on flights over Greenland with nuclear weapons. As it happened the catastrophic crash of the bomber occurred less than forty-eight hours before a national election in Denmark. The day after the crash the Pentagon ordered removal of the nukes on the aircraft and the US Embassy warned the State Department to stress that the crashed plane was diverted to Thule, not on a routine flight, and that became the official line. However, for eight years prior, four to eight nuclear bombs had been almost continuously present in Greenland airspace." She paused waiting to gauge the reaction.

"There's plenty here for us, good work, Gudrun," the chief said. "I want you to look into the human story – what Poulson was chasing regarding the health of the ex-Thule personnel, there must be something in that." He addressed the chief sub-editor, "Use your contacts, get to the bottom of our government's response and any cover-ups. We need a break if this is going front page. At the time the media was filled with speculation, but let's get to the truth; find it for me. We've got the Americans and the Pentagon, the Soviets and the indigenous native Inuits, NATO and the Danish government – what more could we want? Let's hope it's not a good conspiracy, for a good conspiracy is unprovable."

He hesitated briefly.

"Gudrun?" She looked up. "We'll run with it under the banner of 'Thulegate', that seems to sum it up."

"Thulegate," she repeated, and smiled. How appropriate, she thought to herself, since after all, the recent scandal of 'Watergate' had successfully gripped the world.

CHAPTER THIRTY-FIVE

She picked up the phone on its third ring. "Hello."

"Eva?"

"Yes."

"It's Nathan."

"I know. How are things going?" Eva's voice was uneasy.

"Okay, but the weather's no brighter here than in Reykjavik. Are you alright, you sound different?" Nathan said.

Eva sighed, "No, I'm fine, I've just been worried about you." Her tone changed, "It's good to hear from you, it seems ages." A sense of relief swept through her.

"Yes, I suppose so, I've lost track of time," he admitted.

"How are you getting on with Poulson, is he as you expected?"

"I guess so – I think you'd find him a bit straight-laced."

"Straight-laced?"

"Dull and a bit boring, but he's totally committed to get to the truth."

"It's over thirty years ago and, from what you have said, the truth seems the last thing many of those in power want."

"I know," Nathan said," that's becoming increasingly evident."

"You will take care, won't you? I wish I could be with you," she said pensively.

"What are you up to?" Nathan asked.

"You know, the usual run of concerts and little else. When are you back?"

"Soon, maybe a couple more weeks."

"Then will it be over?" she asked hopefully.

"No, as things stand I'll need to come back later in the year." His words were greeted with silence. "Are you there?"

Her meek voice came back, "Yes. Can I go with you?"

"Sure." Nathan's reply was instant. Then, "What about the orchestra?"

"I'll get time off," she said, unable to tell if he was pleased.

"But what about your career, music is your life?"

Eva decided she would be direct, "Yes, but what about us?" emphasising 'us' deliberately. It was impossible – she couldn't see him, see his face and what he was thinking. She waited, and then she understood: he didn't know how to reply. "I don't believe Lindsey would want you to be alone."

"It wasn't what I wanted either," he said coldly.

"I realise that," she asserted, "so you must let others in, others who can help ease your pain."

I may not know all about you but I know enough to love you, she thought to herself.

"I didn't think I could live without her but you've shown me I can." She could only imagine what he was thinking.

Eva interrupted the awkwardness of the moment. "I meant to tell you, Rune has been trying to contact you," Eva said, attempting to control her emotions.

"Rune?" Nathan replied, sounding puzzled.

"Rune Pedersen. Isn't he Geothermic's chairman, its CEO or something? You met him at the orchestra's Christmas party, don't you remember?"

"Oh yes, he was the guy who came on heavy about thermal energy generation."

"And his daughter's been at the concert hall trying to get your number," she interrupted.

"Right," and without thinking, he went on, "that's the last thing I need, getting mixed up in some holy mess between father and daughter, no matter how attractive she is."

"What?" Eva snapped indignantly.

"Well, why is he chasing me?" Nathan sounded irritated.

He was obviously uptight but she saw no reason why he should take it out on her. "The message was," she spelt it out calmly, "that he wants to talk to you about harnessing the power from waterfalls in Iceland, and in particular Gullfoss."

"And how does he think I can be of any help?" a partly relieved Nathan asked. "Did he say?"

"Yes, in fact he did," Eva impatiently countered. "Basically you know about glaciers, and glaciers feed waterfalls. That was it, I think." She was trying to make it clear she'd had enough of this.

"The guy's full of wild ideas."

"He told me you might initially be sceptical, so you needed to know someone tried it in 1920 and it's now time to try again." Surely there was no more to be said on that matter. "Honestly, how are you?" Something disturbed her about how he sounded.

"As I said, I'm fine . . . why?"

"You don't sound yourself." She waited, unsure as to what response she would get.

"To tell you the truth I feel as though I am sinking. I never realised how stressful this whole thing would get, I don't know how Martin has survived all these years."

So finally she got the truth. "Are you keeping well?"

"Yes, I think so. Why do you ask?"

"Jane phoned me. She wanted to know if you'd had any more dizzy spells and when I asked her what she meant, she told me you almost fainted when you were with them at Christmas."

"Oh that, that was probably too much drink." His reply was too quick to be believable.

"Really, so you've not had any dizzy spells since?" His hesitation said it all. "And was Christmas the first time?"

"No," he admitted, "not the first, but the first for ages."

"Have you been to the doctor?" she asked but it was pointless: she knew the answer. Then a dreadful fear came over her, "Did you have the spells before the accident?"

Her doorbell rang, twice.

"I'll be with you," she called out to whoever it was.

"Well, Nathan, did you?"

The bell rang again. It was hard for her to concentrate, but she needed to know.

"Hi, are you ready?" came the woman's voice from the other side of the door.

"It sounds as if you'd better go," Nathan said. She sensed relief in his voice.

"I'll call you back Nathan, we must talk this through."

"Mmm," was all Eva heard before the line went dead. It then occurred to her that Nathan hadn't asked about Jane and the boys, which was odd and completely out of character.

CHAPTER THIRTY-SIX

Nathan attempted to take the opportunity over the following few days to explore the city. He visited some of the many galleries and museums, parks and gardens, cruised the inner harbour and canals, and walked the back lanes and alleyways of Christianshavn, stumbling across the different world that is Christiania. Nathan stayed out most of the day, returning to his hotel around six.

Early on the evening of the third day Nathan was in his room when the phone rang.

"Hi, I wasn't sure whether I would get you," Martin sounded pleased. "What have you planned for tomorrow night?"

"Nothing, why?" Nathan said.

"Well, I've just come out of a meeting with my editor and, amongst other things, we discussed a possible spot on Channel One for a live interview panel about the whole Thule thing."

"That's great," Nathan said, unperturbed at such a thought. "It is good, isn't it?"

"Yes and no, but I'll tell you more tomorrow evening.

"You want to meet up?"

"Not exactly. Brigitte, my editor at DR, would like to meet you and has invited us both to a media event hosted at the US Embassy. It's short notice, I know."

"How does your editor know about me?" Nathan said.

"I'll explain tomorrow, you can't say no," Martin protested. "Oh and it's a tie do. Don't worry if you haven't a suit, a jacket will be fine."

The evening of the function turned out to be bright and balmy, unusual for May, Nathan supposed, and certainly not typical of the past few days. The Embassy was across the city and located a short distance from the Citadel. Martin had arranged to meet on the steps of the National Gallery, and as they made their way he took the opportunity to update Nathan.

"I'm certain my calls are being monitored by someone in the office. I have adopted a scatter-gun approach when searching on the internet, carrying out wide trawls, looking as if I'm stumbling across bits of information along with irrelevant data, but I suspect it's too late for that. I'm led to believe it's possible to remotely identify what I am searching for. I told Brigitte that I think someone has accessed my appointments. It's ridiculous, because who would be bothered with me? Am I being paranoid?"

"What did she say?" Nathan asked, deliberately ignoring his question.

"That maybe I was imagining it but she would look into it. Last week my wife said she got back from the shops to find a chap wandering around the front of the house. When she challenged him he came up with some story about being from the water board or something, undertaking a survey of properties in the road, and he started to ask her questions about how many occupants there were and their patterns of usage."

"Did he look suspicious?" Nathan asked.

"Not particularly, but the funny thing was that when he left he didn't visit any other houses so Mia asked the neighbours if he had called on them. Although they had been in all day no one else had seen him. It makes me wonder."

The three-storey building was most unimpressive. Nathan considered it had all the hallmarks of an uninspiring council office, with the exception, that is, of the Stars and Stripes fluttering high on a white flagpole. He adjusted his tie in the cloakroom mirror, ran a comb through his hair then ventured out and, together with Martin, joined the throng. Sipping his glass of chilled champagne he circulated and quickly concluded that apart from a wise old hack, a young researcher and a woman smoking a cigar, all the rest were probably dull and boring.

Nathan had naively anticipated the evening would prove entertaining, filled with stimulating conversation and wit, but instead folks were occupying themselves in salacious gossip and plenty of alcohol. The scene around the lavish buffet was quickly deteriorating into blatant self-indulgence. Martin saved the day and introduced him to Brigitte.

The woman was both charming and smart and her enthusiastic reaction to meeting Nathan came across as genuine.

Nathan opened, "Martin tells me you are responsible for DR's news output and topical current affairs programmes."

"For my sins," and she seemed to blush.

"And Brigitte is also involved in our online news presence," Martin threw in.

"We go back a long way together," she said warmly, looking to Martin, "way back to those early days at the School of Journalism in Aarhus."

"Where she is Chair of the Board," Martin added.

"You may be aware we very much want Martin to present a live debate with politicians and those involved in the health and land scandal. Up until now there has been little public interest in it and no great appetite from the powers that be to give it air time."

"Who is 'we'?" Nathan said.

She smiled. "Our editor-in-chief and myself. We hear from Martin that you have played a significant part in adding to his research, visiting our Foreign Office and not least those witnesses up in Greenland, isn't that so, Martin?"

While Nathan wanted to side-step the compliment Martin had no hesitation in agreeing.

In a conciliatory tone Brigitte addressed Martin. "On that matter you raised with me I've looked deeper and, while having no conclusive evidence, I have my suspicions."

Martin's interest was self-evident and as he met her gaze she glanced towards a fellow across the room chatting to a woman.

"Are you serious?" he said.

"We'll discuss it back in the office. This is neither the time and certainly not the place," she noted.

Nathan traced their focus of attention and observed an immaculately dressed, silver-haired and suited gentleman talking to a couple of guests.

The woman particularly appeared to relish the attention, putting her arm around her male companion.

"Who's the older gentleman?" Nathan asked.

Brigitte wasted no time. "He is our host. Allow me to introduce you to him."

"And what of the withering chap with the woman?" Nathan continued as they made their way towards the group.

"He works with us at the station," Martin said with little enthusiasm.

While Brigitte was tackling the formalities of introductions, Nathan tried hard to stay engaged, finding himself distracted by the woman. There was something crude and unsubtle about her manner, and when she opened her mouth to speak she seemed dramatically out of place.

After five minutes or so of small talk, with everyone politely accommodating the woman's continual prattle, Brigitte took her leave to 'show her face', as she put it, and the couple moved on as did the ambassador. The experience had been for all, bar one, grossly embarrassing. It was like watching someone who had turned up at the wrong party but didn't realise it. Martin was now Nathan's only refuge of normality and together, having endured ninety minutes, they took their leave, convinced no one would notice their absence.

Agreeing they would meet the following evening for a drink at Hviids Vinstue, off Kongens Nytorv Square, they said their good nights and went separate ways.

*   *   *   *

The steps from the pedestrian walk led Nathan down into the warm cosy bar that was Hviids Vinstue. The walls of dark oak panelling were covered in caricatures, lithos and old photographs all dimly lit by antique lamps and light fittings suspended from the low ceiling. A bald-headed man in collar and tie was serving behind the bar. An ancient silver cash till sat beside a credit card machine, while behind him stacks of wooden crates were loaded with bottles. Martin was seated on a red leather bench beneath a portrait of an armed Royal Guard standing in the doorway of the bar with two men.

"That's one of the owners and the other a regular," Martin volunteered, nodding towards the picture. "I've ordered you a Grimbergen, a double amber beer, okay?"

"Thanks," Nathan said. "How old is this place?"

"Three hundred years or more."

The waiter's clicking shoes on the flagstone floor preceded the arrival of two beers and a menu. Five minutes later plates of sandwiches were laid on the oak table before them.

Martin's mobile phone rang from his inside pocket. Nathan thought the burst of jazz reminded him of Dave Brubeck – perhaps Take Five. As Martin fumbled to retrieve the handset it jammed in his pocket. His annoyance was heightened when he read the text message that appeared on the screen. It took just a minute or two to view it and the attachment, then he slid it across the table to Nathan.

'I am sure you wouldn't want this attached photo released to the press. People regard you as an honest reporter, a man of integrity. It would be so sad if all of that changed and you couldn't be there for them in the future. We all make mistakes but it's best for everyone's sake if they are forgotten.'

Nathan viewed the attachment. A rather blurred photograph appeared on the screen of a young woman and a man who vaguely looked like Martin. Both were naked, pictured in what seemed to be a poorly lit hotel bedroom. Nathan looked up at Martin, who was now confused and tired, his face ravaged by overwork.

"What do you think?" Martin said with a trace of bitterness in his voice.

Nathan was clear, "It's not you, I know that, but those who want to ruin you will find any way they can to discredit you. Your future is no longer in your hands, it's in theirs."

"This fight is costing me everything," Martin sounded weary. "The woman in the picture, I think it's Hilkka, the one who was chatting with the ambassador at the reception."

Hilkka's hour-glass figure had caught Nathan's eye at the party, along with every other red-blooded man's. She had worn hugging Levis, a black leather bomber jacket and, complete with perfect white teeth, an encouraging smile. Her jet-black hair touched her shoulders, and as she moved her head, a single silver earring glistened. When he spoke with her she was making a bad job of inhaling a foul-smelling cigar, one of those Café Crèmes, Nathan thought. It kept going out so, G and T in hand, she was continually approaching different men for a light.

Nathan said, "What are you going to do?" as he slid the phone back to him.

"I don't know," Martin replied. "I dread to think how Mia will take it if this breaks. She'll know it's not true but . . . it will be hard for her."

"You need to prove the photo's a fake. Is there someone you know who can help, an expert who will be convincing?"

"Even those working alongside me I can no longer trust," Martin said, sounding lost.

Without switching on the light on entering his hotel room Nathan opened one of the casement windows. The air that greeted him was cold and dank. Opposite, just beyond a car parked on the pavement, stood the lonely figure of a man, illuminated in the half-light from the street lamps. He appeared to be looking up at Nathan's window. From the man's sudden movement it was evident that he must have spotted him and instinctively Nathan edged away from the window. Moments later he returned to catch a glimpse of this unknown observer, but the figure had gone: he was nowhere to be seen. Nathan waited at the window to see if he would return, confused as he attempted to explain away the recent occurrence. A feeling of vulnerability swept through him. It took a few minutes before he realised how irrational his reaction had been. Why would anyone be interested in him? However, that was before he noticed the large brown envelope which had been slid under the door of his hotel room.

By noon the following day Nathan had managed to get Martin on his mobile. Martin told him that a copy of the photo had turned up in his morning mail. A colleague, who Martin judged to be the soul of discretion, worked as a senior picture researcher and had agreed to give it the once-over, off the record. Taking the photograph he had enhanced it and worked on the two subjects. Martin had seen the scanned photograph enlarged on a computer screen, and what on the photo had seemed slightly peculiar on the screen looked positively odd. There was an unevenness in the background lighting surrounding the man's and woman's heads. The technician continued working at the keyboard, changing the contrast and sharpening the image. Martin said at times the photograph became just a blur, a jumble of countless dots filling the screen, so nothing was clear, and then a face began to emerge.

"I was looking at myself," Martin admitted.

All this time Nathan had listened patiently. "And?" he said.

"And, as they say, you could see the join," Martin revealed. "According to my colleague this was not the work of amateurs, although the program that had been used to manipulate the image was hardly state-of-the-art, certainly not up to DR's capability."

"So what now?" Nathan said.

"I don't know," Martin sounded exasperated.

Nathan asked, "Where does Hilkka live?"

After a pause, Martin replied, "I'm not sure. Why?"

"I just thought I'd call on her and show her the photo, maybe she's not seen it," Nathan said.

"But you haven't got the photograph."

"I have. Someone kindly slid a copy under my door last night, probably wanting to shut me up as well."

"All I know is that she's got a flat over Albertslund, near Route 21 and the railway. Sig mentioned she had got some sort of clerical job in the Ministry," Martin said.

"What's her last name, and who is Sig?" Nathan asked.

"Sig's the guy who was with her at the party, he works at DR, and it's Hilkka Loft."

"Grand," Nathan said. "I'll give you a call if I have any joy," and he hung up.

Nathan had little problem in tracking Hilkka down; it was almost as though she wanted people to find her. To the side of the door, below the doorbell, was her name printed in solid black capitals. He pressed the button. The door opened, half ajar, revealing a wreck of a woman in a pale yellow housecoat whose hair was wild and wayward. Nathan detected a faint but definite smell of Indian food coming from inside her flat. She stood paralysed, seemingly frightened at Nathan's presence, a shadow of the woman he met at the party. An image of a butterfly in purple, emerald and blues, no bigger than a krone piece, adorned the bare flesh of her cleavage. Nathan considered how incongruous was the woman's appearance, and even her bright red toe nails peeping from white flip flops did little to persuade him of her natural elegance. He stood facing her, wondering who she really was. Nathan considered that such attempts to discredit individuals no longer shocked journalists like Martin, who had undoubtedly seen far worse, but Nathan was truly surprised. Without make-up this woman's face looked remarkably different, however, he could see that she was the one who had flaunted herself at the party and appeared in the doctored picture.

Nathan spoke, "I have no desire to do you harm, I just want to talk with you."

To which Hilkka remained impassionate, almost lost in another world. Nathan hadn't expected that. He thought she would be uncomfortable, maybe scared, feeling guilty at the sight of him. Maybe she hadn't recognised him.

"What do you want?" she managed.

"The photograph. Why?" he said.

"Oh that. Why not? I needed the money and anyway, it was a bit of fun, I like being photographed."

"There must have been more to it than that," Nathan exclaimed.

"Must there?"

To think that he was going to get an apology, some sort of bearable excuse, was clearly misguided. Her indifference and lack of emotion shocked him.

"So what if I told you I wasn't taking my foot out of your doorway until you agree that the photo is a fake, what would you say?" Nathan challenged.

"Give it here," she finally said reluctantly, and scrawled on the back of the picture with Nathan's biro more or less the words he dictated.

"Sign it and add your name," Nathan demanded.

"It's not a great likeness of your friend, and my arse is never that big. Still, no harm done," she said handing it back. "Now you're here, you might as well come in for a drink," Hilkka said, stretching the front of her housecoat tightly over her body. "You'll have to excuse me, I've only just got out of the bath. I thought you were maybe someone else."

With that she allowed the housecoat to reveal a hint of her naked breast. Nathan knew that would be just what this cunning and deceitful bitch wanted: a chance to compromise someone else in or out of her bed.

It took him but a second to reply, "No, that's one offer too many."

She glared at him, trembling with anger and incomprehension. "You don't know what you're missing."

But he could imagine and that was enough. He left the woman standing at the door, certain this excursion into coercion and blackmail would not be her last, and wondered who was behind it.

"Tell them not to waste their time with this snap," he called back to her but she had already slammed the door.

CHAPTER THIRTY-SEVEN

Awaiting Nathan on his return to the hotel was a brief message neatly typed out on the hotel's headed notepaper addressed to him personally. As he read it, he realised things would never be the same again. *'Please contact Dr Niels Petersen as a matter of urgency, he wishes to talk with you regarding one of his patients.'* The name of the hospital preceded a telephone number. Nathan's stomach tensed, and an overwhelming sense of dread consumed him as he dialled the number in Greenland. The news was what he feared, and he felt helpless knowing that whatever he did couldn't change things.

Nathan immediately telephoned Martin, made him aware of what had transpired following his meeting with Hilkka and was grateful to hear an audible sense of relief in Martin's voice. He explained his reason for having to return to Greenland but promised he would get back to Copenhagen as soon as he could.

* * * *

The twin-engine Airbus 330 climbed steeply. His seat belt strained against him as the plane fiercely banked, passing high over Copenhagen. Nathan had been fortunate to get a late seat on the monthly direct flight to Thule. In spite of his worst fears for Sissel's health he found himself drifting in and out of sleep during the five-hour flight. Disconnected voices of fellow passengers, fragmented conversations of strangers came and went.

The aircraft descended into a thick blanket of fog rolling in from the ocean, obliterating all from view.

"Wonderful, isn't it?" a fellow in the adjacent seat proposed.

"Sure," a sleepy Nathan replied, not thinking about what he was saying.

They bounced and yawed, rumbling down the runway and there before his eyes was the bleak desolation of Greenland again.

"Sissel specifically asked for you, and we don't believe there is anyone else." Dr Petersen said. "She has little time left and there is nothing more we can do other than make her comfortable."

Nathan steeled himself. "Is she in much pain?"

"No, not with the drugs she's on. Are you aware of her history and what she has been through?" Nathan confessed he wasn't, not fully. "Following the initial discovery of her breast cancer, Sissel was operated on to remove the tumour and underwent a short course of chemo. You must realise, Mr Trent, this was before she had settled here in Greenland, long before we had the drugs we have today. The world was a very different place then. After a period of remission we discovered the cancer had spread to her lungs and, fearing the worst, we realised there was nothing else that could be done for her at that time."

While the doctor was explaining, endless horrific memories began to fill Nathan's head: memories of Lindsey and what she went through in her last days. Memories he had been fighting hard to forget. Now for Sissel there was no escaping the inevitable. Lindsey had been surrounded by her loving family, but there was no family, no Anna here for Sissel. He could hardly imagine what it must be like to think you are going to die and have no one who cares. Words came to him, words that had been shared with him at Lindsey's funeral. *'We die twice, once when our body dies and once when the memory of us dies.'* Who, he asked himself, would remember Sissel? He knew her so briefly but in that time they'd shared so much. Maybe he would be the only one who would remember her.

"You can see her, but try not to over-tire her, she is very weak." The doctor's words dragged him back into reality. He wondered if she would recognise him and what she would be like. He recalled how in the final months Lindsey had changed as the awful disease took hold. At first her body altered gradually then it showed the pain. Its failure became increasingly apparent, not only to him but more so to others who were not with her day after day.

The room where Sissel lay was in half-light and long, chilled shadows cast their gloom. He heard her before he fully saw her, and she gasped a sigh at the sight of him. Her frail form was slumped back on pillows. She looked exhausted. Her pale face was barely recognisable and her eyes had lost the sparkle he remembered. Although he had prepared himself for the worst he was not ready for this; she was so, so different. She spoke, her voice quiet and weak, her words faltering.

"Thank you."

She had no need to say any more, those two words said it all. Nathan sensed she knew why he had come and he felt a coldness run through his body as he tried to swallow back the bitterness which filled his mouth. The full realisation that she was dying hit him.

"Can you prop me up so I can see you better?"

He took hold of her as he had many times before and gently drew her fragile body close to him and kissed her. There was so little of her. A single tear ran down each of her ashen cheeks.

"I'm sorry, did I hurt you?" Nathan said.

"No, it's not that, it's just a while since anyone kissed me," Sissel managed a half smile. "Could I have some water?"

Nathan passed the beaker and watched as her pale mottled hand reached out. She put the straw to her pinched lips and weakly sipped.

Taking the beaker from her, he eased her into his arms. "Doesn't it scare you?"

"No," she said, "I've had enough, I have no more to give."

For the next two hours he held her, listening to her shallow breathing as she drifted in and out of sleep. He was aware of her slowly withdrawing, and for him it seemed an eternity as he relived those end hours with Lindsey.

A soft but shrill alarm began to sound. Nathan whispered, "Sissel?" He gently pulled her closer towards him. She breathed a long slow sigh. Her eyes were open, staring sightlessly and then she was still. Sissel had no more fight left in her, she was no longer there and he felt terribly alone. As he lovingly laid her down, he thought of her being with her dear daughter Anna once again, and somehow he managed a smile.

*   *   *   *

Nathan stayed on in Thule for Sissel's funeral; he couldn't consider doing anything else. The service was short and impersonal, and had it not been for a dozen or so colleagues from the hotel, the chapel would have been almost empty.

"You miss her?"

"Yes, of course," Nathan said indignantly turning to face his questioner. The imposing figure of an Inuit puffing on his pipe stood facing him.

"That was rude of me, we have not been introduced. My name is Qigiq. I knew her not well yet she spoke warmly of you, Englishman." The native was dressed in a colourful tunic made of seal skin, as were his trousers which were tucked into whale skin boots. His face was rough, heavily wrinkled by the unforgiving sun and wind, and Nathan saw before him a determined man, one who he considered would not be ignored. To Nathan it felt like the meeting of two totally different cultures, from different times, linked only by this place and a woman.

"Do you feel empty with her loss?" Qigiq went on.

"Yes, I guess so, and guilty," Nathan replied.

"Why guilty, it was not of your fault?"

"I wasn't there for her."

"But does she not still live in your memories?"

"Sure," Nathan smiled.

"Then, you are still there for her."

"But it's not the same."

Qigiq looked him up and down, "It can never be the same, of course it will be different, it must be, but that doesn't mean you think less of her. Sissel's still important to you, she lives on because of you when maybe without you she would be truly dead and forgotten. She told how you helped her forget sad times. You have a choice Englishman: you should be happy, for that is what she would have wanted – I know." Nathan found it hard to reply. "Had you not come asking about the crash she would never have known you."

Nathan frowned. "What made you mention the crash?"

"You were asking about it, weren't you? So the good woman Helga tells," the Inuit said, holding Nathan with a penetrating look. Nathan waited, expecting more but no more came.

"Asking?" repeated Nathan.

Qigiq's haggard face changed with what Nathan took to be disdain, maybe even hatred. "About those that betrayed my people. When they came as a mighty wind of destruction blowing across our land, everything changed."

"Who?" Nathan asked, knowing full well who.

"The Americans, putting an end to the only life we had ever known. Our ancestors came ten centuries before to this place from the west at the breaking of the ice floes, travelling for many days across treacherous seas. They dragged their open oak boats up onto this land and, praising their gods for their deliverance, named it Thule. This place is inhabited with our memories. You came here by plane in a day. You sense nothing of this place, smelling, seeing and hearing little that is Greenland."

His voice was guttural, from the dry depths of his throat, there forming strange sounds as he spoke in a staccato fashion, yet Nathan understood him. Nathan felt awkward, uncomfortable as he recognised the truth in Qigiq's words.

Qigiq went on in a warmer manner. "I believe you to be a wise man, holding many secrets, yet here there are many more."

Aside of their great differences Nathan sensed a feeling of mutual respect and understanding between them.

"Tell me," he implored, "tell me what secrets I should know?"

Qigiq spoke. "My brothers no longer stand motionless hour after hour over seal holes as their fathers did. Our women fished, our men hunted – life was hard but it was our life, the life of our forefathers. All has changed. We have been stripped of our spiritual heritage, traditions and culture by money, bureaucracy and kindness. We are hurtling at great speed into a new age, like your spacemen. Many families lived here at Thule, but the coming of the massive American Air Base forced us to leave our homes and sacred gathering place to settle north, leaving the only life we had known. Our crude turf huts, lit by blubber lamps, were abandoned; we were put in wooden boxes, houses from Denmark with paraffin stoves and lit by electricity. Thule was the cradle of our souls, a monastery to the endurance of our hope and faith, and the survival of our human spirit. It was upon our mountain at Dundas that we buried our dead." He hesitated, disturbed. "We are no more the indigenous people of Thule."

Nathan sensed the hostility in his voice was not towards himself.

"The US fortress rose like a monster from the ground," the native's anger was now apparent. "Their coming was relentless. Submarines moved below us, living in secret under the ice. We never chose to be a frontier but that's what we were, between two mighty warring nations, crouching, waiting with their nuclear holocaust. The idea of war is something beyond our imagination. Time and again we show courage and fortitude as we struggle against the elements, or when confronting bears, yet we are unable to understand such violence for we have no word for 'war'. Our old ways weakened as the new capitalist ways brought a different life-style and money. We knew nothing of this life, and what we valued and clung to was being taken from us. The world is moving faster than many of us can bear. Our children wear Levis and Nikes and drink Coca Cola standing beside their grandmothers clad in seal skin. In two generations many have made a leap from hunting to a society relying on technology. Our boats are no longer covered in walrus skins but plastic."

"Along with that though comes education for your children, medical care for your sick and elderly, communications and trade, aren't these things important?" challenged Nathan.

"They have not been our ways. It is too late for us," Qigiq replied. He looked at Nathan, no emotion evident in his face, and ended with these words. "It is told that the children of Israel wandered for forty years in the wilderness before they returned to their homeland. Our children will never go back to Thule."

Nathan believed he was hearing about the end of an era, a life that hadn't changed for hundreds of years.

"What is it you want of me?" he asked Qigiq.

Qigiq's response was forthright and unequivocal. "To understand. I want you to see with your own eyes."

Nathan was confused, "To see what?"

The reply was quick and certain, "You asked of the crash and what happened. Come see for yourself."

*　*　*　*

Within an hour of leaving Thule Air Base the Bell helicopter had travelled the sixty-odd miles due north to Qaanaaq. A boundless wilderness of brown earth and grey-blue sea was before them, the desolation broken only by brightly painted huts, perhaps two hundred, scattered near the water's edge, and the striking white drifting ice floes in the fjord. Somehow the emptiness surpassed what Nathan had already seen here in Greenland.

"Temperatures in winter reach minus 50°C and most of the land remains frozen solid, except for the top that thaws in summer," Qigiq shared. Nathan found himself inwardly groaning at the thought, trying to imagine what it must be like living so cut-off from the rest of the world in such conditions.

As they circled the village Qigiq pointed to a mountain slope outside the settlement. "There rest our dead now, their bodies permanently frozen deep in the ground. Those that were not taken by the cold, the bear or their years, but died from sickness within from the radiation, they are not buried there. They were taken from us, taken by the soldiers. Where they lay is unknown to us. Our prayers for them drift out on the wind across every part of this land."

As the helicopter lined up then settled on a gravel pad, Qigiq turned to Nathan and said, "Welcome to Qaanaaq, the most northerly settlement in the world, known as Ultima Thule – the most distant and remote land."

"It feels good to be down," Nathan said, looking about at the Spartan scene before him.

"Yes," Qigiq said, "we've lost three helicopters already on this flight, that's more than enough."

Within minutes they were climbing the slatted steps to Qigiq's green hut perched on stilts above the permafrost, which he described as his *Scandinavian kit house*, not his home. With the opening of its door Nathan's nostrils were assaulted by a pungent and overwhelming smell of fish. Qigiq kicked off his boots and dragged Nathan, still tightly grasping his holdall, to where a woman was bent over a stove beside which were two plastic buckets overflowing with raw seal meat. Qigiq spoke to the woman who turned to Nathan and, as she did, Qigiq touched Nathan's breast and said, "Ikinngut – friend." He then looked to the primus stove where a pot was issuing clouds of steam as it bubbled away on the heat. They sat on benches around the crude table in the meagre room. Bowls of hot broth were slid before them. Qigiq explained, "Reindeer broth, its good."

Much to Nathan's surprise it was, and as it cooled he dipped chunks of heavy, dense bread into the salty broth. With every sip the rising steam clouded and moistened Nathan's face. They ate in silence, the only sound a sighing wind outside.

Qigiq was first to break the silence. "This is my arnaq," he glanced to the woman, "she is called Nirliq, which is Snow Goose in your language." Nathan noticed a glimmer in Qigiq's eyes as he glanced towards her.

The old lady looked up showing plump cheeks veined and red on her deeply wrinkled face, and stopping only a moment from eating, she grinned, revealing a row of worn-down yellow teeth with two missing. Soon her fat sausage-like fingers were again pushing chunks of soaked bread into her mouth. She never eased her gaze from him, fixing Nathan with her inquisitive eyes.

"Some of our ice cream?" Qigiq appealed. "It's cloudberries, ice and blubber." Nathan pretended to think it over, masking a feeling of nausea, "No thank you."

"Then I want you to come with me, you need to see something," Qigiq insisted.

Up until now Nathan had gone along with this native's wishes, trusting this relative stranger, but he was beginning to doubt the significance of what he would learn here.

They ventured out and started to climb steeply up a dirt track away from the settlement. A limpid sun hung over the clear Arctic horizon.

"Many believe our world is a different world, cut off from all else, but that is not true. Now we too have shops and hotels, but our life few know, and fewer could survive. Living here is hard, the hunting not easy, the climate harsh and for many, the weeks of endless darkness difficult to bear. Yet look about, what do you see?"

The landscape that unfolded before Nathan resonated with a brutal beauty and a sense of freedom; a landscape the like of which he'd never seen before. There was something about it that thrilled him and something that scared him.

In front of them, in an isolated spot over-looking the fjord, were arranged sixty or more simple white crosses and before a few lay flowering garlands splashing summer colour upon what would otherwise be naked earth. Some graves were bordered by low, white wooden picket fencing, marking the precise place of the burial. Words of unknown meaning to him were cut into the crosses themselves or scribed on plaques at their foot. Nathan sensed Qigiq's mood had changed. He waited for his friend to speak.

"Here amongst my people, my brothers and sisters, should rest the many who died before their time; those who died agonising and hideous deaths, an end unbefitting of proud hunters."

Nathan saw sadness in the native's face.

"When the Americans came to our land in the 1950s to build their eight-hundred-million-dollar fortress, our people were forced here from their homes in Thule. Moved from the hunting grounds we knew, moved from our roots that like a tree held us firm for so long. The Americans said that because the noise from the airplanes frightened away the polar bear and walrus, we Inuit chose to move north, but that is not the truth. They needed men to help with the building work and many of my brothers stayed, labouring to keep their families. On that dreadful January day in 1968, the day of the crash, everything changed for them. My brothers were first to the burning site on their dog sleighs but they did not know how dangerous it was. They helped the Americans, veterans from Vietnam, collect the wreckage of the bombs and aircraft. What happened to them and when we do not know, but we do know that no brothers of that time are alive today."

The wind sharpened, filling the air with its voice. Nathan stepped back, nearly treading on a neatly tended grave which looked recent; saxifrage, cotton tuft and poppies were set about with dried moss. The name Puja was all that denoted that place.

"Who was Puja, was it one of the men of Thule?" Nathan said.

Qigiq replied, head bowed, "No, she was a teenage girl of our village who killed herself this past winter."

"Why?" Nathan asked.

"It was said the long dark days and the relentless cruel weather were more than she could endure . . . everything is fine until it is not." He gestured to Nathan to take their leave. "If you stay at this place too long you will hear yourself talking to the wind and, in time, listening for its soulful reply and that of the mountain spirits."

That evening they sat close to the stove and, over coffee, Qigiq spoke of earlier times. Nathan listened enthralled by the sagas of how he and his brothers pulled up their nets through the ice laden with seal, the winter drives in dog sleighs to where the lone bear roam, the discovery of two female reindeer carcasses, their antlers entangled, having died of starvation, the trips by boat and kayak stalking prey, then the kill and returning with fish and whale blubber for everyone. Finally, Qigiq told Nathan a story that he explained had become part of the history of his people of Ultima Thule.

"There was a rich master,
This master wished to colonise the world's far flung places so,
defying the wild oceans, he travelled to find a brave new world.
He sailed to this land that he knew not and there he settled.
He was a most powerful master,
So powerful was he that none other than the master was allowed
  to prosper where he settled.
There the master and his sons prospered and all others were
  forced to leave that land,
And, like lonely ghosts without a home,
 they forever wandered."

A restless night awaited Nathan. Light flooded through the small pane of dew-covered glass into the room where he lay. Here in the Arctic, light played by different rules. The pages torn from newspapers and magazines that papered the walls were almost irritatingly legible in the partial light. He could shut out the far-off noise of the baying and howling of the hungry tethered dogs, but not the things he had learnt which haunted him until tiredness and dreams finally overcame him.

The following morning Qigiq insisted that before Nathan returned to Thule he should visit the settlement's tiny museum and learn something of the memories it harboured. They walked out along the water front.

There a group of Inuit stood, their deep rhythmic chatter flowing like a slow, tuneless, tone song. Beside them a flotilla of battered kayaks were moored and one old man was fiddling with a Japanese outboard. "Nothing is useless here, hoarding is in our blood!" Qigiq explained. Further along the beach Nathan watched a group of young children playfully teasing a puppy with strips of walrus hide, then hitting it with sticks as it bounded over the hulls of beached boats and through the fish drying racks. One young boy, perhaps five years old, gathered the fluffy white mutt to him, then grabbing it by the scruff of the neck threw it into the water. Nathan watched but it didn't move in the water. Older folk stood seemingly oblivious, drinking and smoking.

"Our men have become dependent on the gifts your Scottish whale hunters and the American polar expeditions brought to our shores, but now many are alcoholics," Qigiq said in resignation. He looked to the sky, "The south wind will come and bring with it a late summer storm. It is good you go soon."

They entered the old white house, the one-time trading post and bank of the explorer Knud Rasmussen. "This represents the heritage of my people, our cultural past."

Pictures of turf and stone-walled dwellings illustrated the old way of life along with many scenes of hunting for seals and walruses, whales, foxes and birds. A series of black and white photos recorded the stories of families being evicted from Thule and their move here, showing the months they spent living in tents along with portraits of old folk who had died from the fierce cold.

A traditional sledge was displayed with skins, stone-bladed knives and walrus ivory harpoon heads.

"The early sledges used whalebone runners, and as a boy I spat water on them to hasten my father's journey across the ice when he hunted. The dogs would slavishly pull for mile after mile, hour after hour, Father not uttering a single word. For years we believed that everyone who came here journeyed by dog sled but then we also thought the whole world was made of ice!"

A grotesque collection of images faced Nathan. Contorted, ruptured and brightly coloured fish.

"Many of the fish caught look odd," Qigiq explained, "as if they have been bitten, but they are not bites. Some say it's nothing to worry about but they have a reason to tell us that."

Photos of pop-eyed seals with no hair, musk oxen with deformed hooves and whales with their bodies covered in sores and calluses were all on display. "It's the pollution from the base after the crash; the plutonium on our seabed."

Nathan replied in bewilderment, "I had no idea."

The degree of respect these people had for this land, for the animals they hunted and their culture was something Nathan had never before witnessed.

Beneath a label entitled 'Inughuit' were arranged coloured photos of Inuit in traditional dress. A young Greenland woman wore a beautiful costume. Her smile was broad and her black hair, drawn back from her face, was gathered in a shoulder-length plait.

Qigiq, noting Nathan's interest, explained, "Inuit means 'the people'; Inughuit refers to us, the Greenlandic people who live in the polar north of our country – Arctic Highlanders. To the Americans we are a poor people, with little or no hope for the future, but that doesn't mean that we do not dream big dreams, and we don't wish for higher things."

In spite of Qigiq's fears, to Nathan it felt as if time had largely passed Qaanaaq and its remarkable people by. In his mind Nathan pictured time, frozen and resting deep below the ice and, as the warmth came, it suddenly surged forth, like the release of a tightly coiled spring, much like a time bomb.

Before Nathan boarded the helicopter for the flight to Thule Air Base, Qigiq thrust an object into his hand.

"This is for your memory."

In Nathan's palm was a crude carving of a whale, a narwhal perhaps, no bigger than a penknife, but intricately worked. "What is it made from?"

"Walrus tusk, I made it, it is a gift," and with that Qigiq's broad flat face beamed. "Very soon the snow and ice that has surrounded us all summer will once again come down from the peaks, engulfing our lives, our world. You will soon forget us and this place but I ask you not to forget those that died – remember their voices, their cries. Few hear their cries from the frozen north and fewer remember."

There was nothing Nathan could manage to say. He grasped Qigiq's hand, then put his arms about his new friend. Nathan climbed aboard and buckled himself into his seat between a young lad, who had his arm in a sling, and piles of rancid smelling skins.

Qigiq shouted, "Inuulluarit . . . farewell," as the rotor blades began turning, and Nathan couldn't help think that Qaanaaq looked a very lonely place.

CHAPTER THIRTY-EIGHT

The pulsating noise in the chopper was almost deafening as they lifted off and swiftly rose into the air. The helicopter's nose dipped as it turned and headed out across the fjord following the coastline south. Below, the floes appeared like wedges of ice cream floating across an azure sea. Nathan spied a pod of giant whales surfacing, their dorsal fins cutting through the water like knife blades then, as swiftly as they appeared, they were gone. A sense of timelessness seemed to inhabit this world that he had briefly stepped into. A world where the elements reigned supreme and its people lived where others would find it impossible to survive.

Within the hour Thule's giant twelve-hundred-foot radio tower was in sight as if signalling man's technological achievement in a very different world. Approaching the Air Force Base, the runway and Thule *city* came into view. They landed with a bump onto the helipad and, with the engines still running, the passengers disembarked, bent low scurrying under its beating blades. Once again the monstrous sign, 'Air Force Space Command's 12th Space Warning Squadron' welcomed Nathan.

Stepping out from the shadows of the terminal building, the bald-headed Major Felker greeted him as he walked from the helicopter.

"We thought you had left us, Mr Trent, to go back to Iceland or the UK." Nathan was beginning to find the major's interest in his movements annoying. He could feel his chest tighten, enraged at Felker's audacity. "You see, Mr Trent, it would appear, unless you tell me to the contrary, you have no permit to travel through Thule Air Base. You don't have one do you, Mr Trent?"

Nathan was quite clear, "I enquired before I left Iceland and was told that I didn't need a visa for Greenland."

"Not a visa but a special permit. You need entry approval to travel through Thule north to Qaanaaq, approval you would obtain from the Danish Ministry of Foreign Affairs or through one of their embassies. As such, Mr Trent, you have illegally entered the base."

Nathan was bewildered. "There would be no reason why I wouldn't have applied and got the permit, Major," Nathan insisted, "had I known."

"You're not a spy then?" Felker said and smirked. "Perhaps just a bit of a boy scout?" His tone changed, "The fact remains you should have been refused transit." His next words were deliberate and forceful. "When are you leaving, Mr Trent?"

"In the next day or so, as soon as I can get a flight," Nathan said, hopeful that it would end this game.

"That's good," came Felker's reply, "only you'd be amazed how inhospitable it can get up here, especially if you don't take care of yourself."

Nathan could hear his heart thumping in his ears. "Thanks for the advice," he said, holding back his disdain for the guy.

"Just concerned for you, Mr Trent," was Felker's parting shot, "we wouldn't want anything to happen, or for you to be arrested when you leave us. You must trust we only have your best interest at heart."

I don't have to trust anything, Nathan thought.

Nathan's return flight to Keflavik proved largely uneventful. When he enquired of the cabin attendant regarding the flying conditions she curtly replied that she was glad it wasn't winter yet.

"Why, what's it like in winter?" Nathan asked.

"We can be thrown around in the sky like a paper glider in a gale, and the landings, well, I hold my breath with every bounce before we finally stay on the ground."

"I notice some of the rear seats have made way for an orange crate, what's that?" he said.

"That's the polar pack: extra survival equipment should we need to make a forced landing on the ice cap."

"And have you ever used it?" Nathan asked with more than a casual interest.

"Oh yes. I wasn't on duty, but the stewardess that was threatened she'd never fly this route again in the winter." Whatever happened to the cabinet trolleying down the aircraft filled with sandwiches, snacks and drink, or the First Officer's rundown on the route, pointing out landmarks they would fly over, Nathan wondered. Unsurprisingly, the full extent of the in-flight entertainment on this trip was limited to the explanation of the polar pack and an announcement to adjust one's watch to Icelandic time upon their arrival at Keflavik Airport.

Leaving the airport building, Nathan glimpsed Eva waiting outside. The evening light cast a mellow glow, highlighting her hair and, as she turned, her scarf unravelled in the breeze. Nathan took hold it, and wrapping it back around her neck, he pulled her towards him and kissed her.

As they drove into the city massive storm clouds darkened the evening's sky. For the past few days Nathan had hardly missed the soaking drizzle, the noise of congested traffic nor the hordes of people milling about the streets and bars. He had, however, missed the refuge provided by Eva's apartment, and her.

CHAPTER THIRTY-NINE

Nathan didn't even bother to take his coat off but just slumped in the armchair, washed-out and with an expression as black as sin. Eva couldn't help think he painted a sorry picture. She hadn't seen him looking like this before, so mournful, lost in his own dark, desolate world. Only the clinking of the ice cubes as they swirled around his whisky glass broke the silence.

"What's wrong? What are you thinking?" Eva ventured.

"Oh, nothing," was as far as it went.

"Is it something I've done?" she tried.

"Hell no, not you."

"Then what?" Eva waited but there was no reply. "Was it awful?" she said.

"Bloody awful. I thought I would be able to cope with it okay but I couldn't have been so wrong. Her life was a bloody tragedy." After a moment, he said, "I'll never forget how in the end I let Lindsey down. Unlike Sissel, she had the best private medical care, as well as the latest medicines and treatment available, but over time this began haemorrhaging the little money we had saved. I stepped up to the financial responsibility, but as a husband I shrank back. I couldn't bear to see her in such a state. Needing to meet the fees I immersed myself into my career and my work became my salvation. Of course I visited her but when it came to the final moment I wasn't there. I wasn't there for her. She died surrounded by strangers. I hadn't planned it that way, it's just how it worked out."

Eva interrupted Nathan's thoughts. "Many people are not with their loved ones in their final hours, but that doesn't mean they love them any less."

"I realise that," Nathan said in reflection. "I couldn't bear to let the same happen to Sissel."

Eva's heart ached to see Nathan in such a state. "There really wasn't anything else you could have done." He appeared to recognise that but she wasn't certain. "You have some good memories to cling to, don't you?"

For the first time he looked at her and she could have sworn he smiled. "After you lose loved ones, it's hard to rely and trust others again. I feel as though I am trapped."

Eva's intuition told her she should tread carefully. "You're so good with telling others what they should do, but hopeless with yourself."

"That's not fair," he rebuffed.

"It may not be fair but it's true. Why do anything different? While you keep wallowing in your misery nothing will change, it'll just be more of the same. Is that what you want?" It was then that she wondered if she'd over-stepped the mark. She decided to say no more and put on the record player. The music filled the room. Eva stood transfixed as she listened to one of her favourite pieces. A couple of minutes in as the music lightened and took on a refreshing jollity, Nathan asked, "What is it?"

"Do you like it?"

"Yes." She could see his whole countenance had lifted.

"Borodin's *Nocturne for Strings*, you may know it better as *This is My Beloved*, and I love it," she said in a soft voice and, without really thinking, she went on, "was your home in England filled with music?"

"No," Nathan replied immediately, sounding disenchanted. "Mother loved music but to her eternal disappointment Father had no time for it. I eventually escaped Father's pig-headedness and overbearing ways, but Mother had no chance. Only death would be her way out."

"He sounds like an old fashioned father set in his military ways," Eva observed.

"He wasn't so very different in age from Magnus."

"But perhaps he was of a different time, a different world," she reasoned.

"I don't think I ever really loved him, maybe because he never loved me. The only ones I have loved I have lost," a forlorn Nathan said.

"But life doesn't have to end with your loss. Surely love is still worth pursuing, isn't it?" she pleaded. "Well, I think so," she added bluntly.

Clearly enough was enough and Nathan took himself away to shower, perhaps to try and wash away some of the unjustified recrimination he was bearing, Eva thought. After a few minutes she heard him cry out.

"Are you alright?" an anxious Eva called.

"Yes, I'd forgotten how foul-smelling your hot water is."

Eva grinned, "I don't notice it but they say it is like bad eggs."

"They're right," Nathan came back.

Clean clothes, hair washed and groomed, Nathan looked a lot brighter.

"Are you sure you're alright?"

"Sure," he replied and smiled.

"You haven't had any more dizzy spells, have you?" she asked.

He frowned, "Why do you ask?"

"Well, when I heard you call out I thought . . . "

"No, it was the water."

"I know that now, but have you had any spells?" She couldn't help but notice how he hesitated over answering.

"I had a turn on the flight back from Greenland, but it was probably because I stood up too quickly. It was nothing really."

"Do you think it might have been a touch of vertigo?" she asked, trying hard not to sound as though she'd been reading up on the web. It was evident her interrogation was unwelcome so she quickly changed the subject. "While you were in the shower I was checking my computer, some orchestra stuff," she said, lying, "and I found an email to you from Martin Poulson. He sent it last night."

"What did it say?" Nathan's calmness had gone.

"Not much. He was wondering how things had gone up north and if you had any idea when you were coming back out, because the TV programme is scheduled for three weeks' time."

"What do you think?" he said, gazing at her intently, seeming anxious as to her reply. "Will you come with me?"

"Whenever you want. I've warned the office that I may not be around for a bit and they've lined up a freelance to cover the last concert of the season, so my time is my own. I'm in your hands, as they say." Eva saw a wave of surprise and relief fill Nathan's face. "I'll book the flight if you like," she offered.

Tired, Eva could stay up no longer and, leaving Nathan alone, went to bed. She hoped he wouldn't keep churning things over and drink himself into oblivion.

THE *TODAY* NEWSPAPER OFFICES – COPENHAGEN

CHAPTER FORTY

"Talk to me people, what have we got?"

Everyone attending the afternoon briefing knew from Gudrun's strident tone she meant business.

"I need angles, facts, if 'Thulegate' is going to run," Gudrun demanded, "so start talking."

A young researcher in her mid-twenties spoke first. To the rest of the team she only had to open her mouth to demonstrate her lack of experience and judgement. Gudrun kept her on because the girl was keen and full of energy, if at times misguided. She also saw something of her early self in the young woman.

"There's the Thule Society," the girl announced, perhaps expecting some degree of recognition, but none was forthcoming. The girl took a deep draw on her cigarette and as she inhaled, coughed and spluttered.

"Go on," Gudrun insisted. A cone of cigarette smoke stretched upward to the ceiling. She inhaled again, and coughed again. Gudrun nodded to the old boy seated next to the girl and, acknowledging, he took the cigarette from her and stubbed it out in the ash tray. A moment of realisation dawned before the girl nervously continued.

"I am not clear if it has any relevance but it's a society that goes back to the Nazis, paving the way for Hitler himself. One theory is of its involvement in the creation of weapons of mass destruction and terrorist organisations.

"Well, Ultima Thule was a lost ancient landmass in the extreme north of Greenland, supposedly the centre of a lost, high level civilisation. Not all the secrets of that civilisation had been completely wiped out and those that remained were guarded by highly intelligent beings. Membership is by invitation only and it's rare to find a member who isn't stinking rich and hugely influential, such as writers, professors, military officers, politicians and business leaders. Historically they've been involved in secret operations all over the world, including Antarctica, linking with other secret groups to increase their knowledge and power. It would appear the society is not beyond performing criminal acts to get what they want in furthering their cause; the end justifies the means, so to speak."

They had all sat listening patiently.

"Oh, and it's reported that many of the members of the inner circle own publishing concerns and have a powerful media presence."

With that laughter broke out, uncomfortable laughter, but laughter nonetheless.

"What else have we got?" Gudrun said, avoiding any response and putting a stop to the outburst. "What about the eviction story?"

A middle-aged woman edged forward in her chair and, resting her arms on the conference table, spoke. "Originally twenty-seven Inuit families that made up the community were told to leave. Most were given only forty-eight hours to resettle one hundred miles north, making way for the American base. When they arrived at the new settlement they discovered the houses they had been promised had not been built and the 150 homeless Inuits had to live in tents. Their case has now been taken up by Danish human rights lawyers who claim that for decades the government lied, stating that they moved voluntarily and were not forcibly evicted. They are fighting for the Americans to clean up Thule and give them their homeland back. In August 1999 the Qaanaaq pressure group won an historic victory in the High Court. They argued that under the UN convention on the rights of indigenous and tribal peoples, and under the Danish constitution they had been unlawfully moved. While the victory was hugely symbolic they were each only granted under ten thousand kroner in compensation."

"I want you to keep on that, Astrid," Gudrun directed. "Talk more to the lawyers about the court judgement and the paltry settlement. Work on the angle of the smallest, most remote community on earth, battling against one of the world's largest and most powerful nations." She turned to the old boy, "Rasmus, give me something juicy?"

"What about spies?"

Gudrun knew him to be a shrewd and wise old reporter, but also a man of few words, "What about them?" she said.

"My contacts in DR tell me that over the past months Poulson has been under increased pressure to if not entirely drop his investigations, then to at least ease off the government."

"I knew in the early days DR wasn't on board with Poulson's own research, but I thought they were now thinking of running with it," a confused Gudrun shared.

"They are," he confirmed. "There's word of a live TV debate about the whole affair."

"So where's the pressure coming from?"

"From within, so I understand. There are strong suspicions that someone close to him, a colleague, has been trying to persuade him to cool off on what's an old story. My source in The Castle says the Foreign Office is on fire with rumours and that an MP from the Left-Green Alliance is tabling a question to the Minister of Defence, asking them to confirm or deny that they have one or more associates inside DR. It's expected that the Ministry will make no comment but allegations are starting to fly; it sure makes for interesting times," Rasmus concluded.

"When the issue goes public I want to know and we'll run a piece on it. All along they've been banking on the malleability of the Danish. I need you, Rasmus, to stay on top of your sources in The Castle and DR. As the news breaks and the public find out, officials will all start to desperately reposition themselves, passing blame on to others. Find out what DR have planned to debate and, importantly, when. We need to know who the insider is and who they work for."

Gudrun then turned her attention to the group, "Have we got anything new on Poulson . . . anything."

A sprightly-looking college lad interrupted her, "I've nosed around, followed his movements – dropping his daughter off at school, shopping, family meals out and meetings with the Englishman. Little out of the ordinary other than this Trent fellow keeps popping up. The same chap who had the run-in with Nielsen at the Foreign Office. There's nothing new on Poulson other than it would seem that, while many in high places had turned against him, he has the ears of an ever-increasing number of influential people. As for Mr Trent," he said, second-guessing Gudrun's next question, "he's no journalist. He's an academic who, it is said, has busied himself nosing around the Thule back story. The two have met at least three times and, as we know, together attended the American Embassy bash. One thing I did dig up on the Englishman was the run-ins he had with the authorities during his student union days but there's nothing to say he was a militant activist. It's probably harmless but I have a friend in the police trying to find any background."

"Maybe he was a young Red, perhaps KGB. They were successful in recruiting many English academics." Everyone around the table looked on in disbelief while Gudrun, out of respect for her senior colleague, let Rasmus have his say. "They're into intelligence gathering, seemingly unimportant people appearing to go about their ordinary everyday jobs. Look at Jørgen Dragsdahl, the Danish journalist and a one-time correspondent for DR, with a watching brief on American security policy and a violent anti-nuker. He was recently accused of being an agent for the KGB."

"Accused, but that's all, according to the High Court," Gudrun said. "Are you serious, Rasmus?"

"No," he said, "but what a story!"

The group stirred, mumbling to one another.

"Where's Trent now?" Gudrun asked the lad, not wanting to waste any more time.

"He's just flown back to Greenland." The comments became more audible.

Addressing the lad, Gudrun asked, "Have you any photos we can use? Check the library and archives but I doubt we'll have anything on Trent."

"I was able to snap them during their meetings; they never saw me."

"Well done!" Gudrun congratulated. "I want you both," and she turned to the young girl, "to stay close to them, and also we'll see if we can turn up anything on the explosion and the lost bomb front from an environmental angle. Try Greenpeace, they're bound to have a view on how the so-called accident spread destruction and pollution. I don't know what you'll find but scratch at a few sores. Crimes against wildlife and our environment, that's the slant. The authorities and scientists will be wanting us to believe everything is, and has been, okay: assume it is not.

"Astrid, I need you to get underneath the health scene. Hundreds of workers, natives and military personnel riddled with disease and dying; after all, that's how Poulson first got involved. Concentrate on the human tragedy behind the accident. I've got the okay for our health correspondent to work alongside you on this one. We'll need some inside track on the stats because they'll use them to try and deceive us."

Astrid beamed and was already scribbling like mad. Gudrun was relishing the moment, her chance to bring in the big story.

"Rasmus." He looked intently towards her. "You and me, we'll pull it together, but I also need you to work up a scenario for me." His face showed no emotion. "I want to play out the worst case scenario so people understand what the implications might have been if it had gone wrong. For example, if the bomb's safety features had failed resulting in a nuclear explosion, and if no one had immediately claimed responsibility for that explosion. What if the base's communication systems had gone down and an American retaliation strike had been initiated and couldn't have been rescinded, and the Russians responded by attacking the US, Greenland and here, Denmark? It may have been over thirty years ago but if we present it in that way the reader will get on board, engaging as if it were only yesterday. Have you got the idea?"

She was pleased with herself – the briefing had gone well. Gudrun knew now for certain that she was sitting on a story of international importance and suspected Rasmus was already mapping out in his mind the exact sequence of horrific events.

CHAPTER FORTY-ONE

Copenhagen was nothing like Eva had imagined. Unlike home, it lacked any impressive views but she had yet to discover the city's true attributes: its spacious squares, wide avenues, vast parks, lakes and water fronts. The city was bustling and full of noise, with bikes, like agitated flies, weaving about everywhere. While it had a vitality to it, she wasn't sure how much she liked the place and was certain she could never feel at home here.

The hotel was just as Nathan described and her room much the same as his. She appreciated that if they were going to be here for some time it was important to have found accommodation within their budget.

She had never seen so many shops: trendy designer outlets, chic boutiques, up-market department stores, galleries and an endless choice of restaurants and cafes. They settled on an eating place up a narrow cobbled alley and tucked into scrambled eggs with chopped bacon, chives and potatoes all washed down with a glass of *husets vin*.

"Will you do me a favour?" Eva asked across the table.

"What is it?" he replied, savouring the bacon.

"Can we be honest with each other and not say what we think the other wants to hear?"

He stopped and looked gravely at her, "I thought we did."

A defiant Eva persisted, "No we don't. You know we don't but will you from now on in?"

A watchful Eva saw his expression change. "Okay," he said. She half wondered if he was sincere and, being conscious of her doubt, he added,

"I promise, now do you believe me? I'm not just saying that because you want me to, I mean it," relishing his own joke.

She instantly came back. "Maybe sometime soon we could talk about us."

By the end of the afternoon, with what seemed like many miles of walking behind them and Eva's shoes about to create a blister, they made their way back to the hotel, stopping only for Eva to buy a new pair. That evening Martin phoned and Nathan was embroiled in conversation with him for what seemed to Eva to be hours.

"Martin wants to meet," Nathan announced the next morning.

"And good morning to you too," she cut him short. She knew it was important but that was no excuse. "When does he want to meet you?"

"No, he suggested we go over to his place tomorrow, meet his family and chat over dinner."

"And you said?" she asked, showing no reaction.

"I said fine, is that okay?" She could see he was unsure.

"We're being honest with each other, aren't we?" she goaded.

"Yes." He looked really worried.

"That sounds good to me," and smiled, conscious of his relief.

The morning was taken up browsing the many Danish and international works of art housed in the National Gallery. Not being a gallery-goer Eva was certain it would all be too high brow, but to her great surprise she thoroughly enjoyed the paintings.

The following day Nathan wanted her to experience something completely different, a stroll through the free city of Christiania. Nestled amid high-class canal-side apartments, with their own luxury yachts and cruisers, was the gateway to another world. Eva had never seen anything like it before. A large sign greeted them: 'No photos. No cannabis. No chasing and causing panic. All welcome – except tax government officials'. A hippie commune of a thousand folk offering alternative lifestyles to a range of middle-aged dropouts; well, that's how Nathan described it, this colony that rocked with the sound of Bob Marley and John Lennon. Two women were busy painting a psychedelic mural on a workshop wall. Eva wondered if it was going to have a political message or be about drugs. Scruffy dogs lazily scavenged around cafe tables and unfamiliar smells drifted on the air, emanating from kitchens and smokers alike. Meanwhile, young men dressed all in black with scarves over their mouths patrolled the site as amused sightseers mingled with the residents.

Having seen enough, Eva and Nathan headed alongside the river, making for their hotel and a chance to freshen up before their evening dinner date.

Martin's home was not what Eva had been expecting. However, she couldn't help but think the modest decoration and furnishings reflected well this man she had heard so much about. Welcoming them in, Martin was clearly pleased to see them both. No sooner had they stepped into the hall than a young girl came bounding down the stairs and made a beeline for Eva. Martin stopped the young lady's advance.

"Hey, hold on, I haven't welcomed Eva yet," and he duly kissed her on her cheek. "Right, now you can say hello to our guests, Eva and Nathan."

"I am Katja," she pronounced it Kaht-jah, "but you can call me Kat," this boisterous youngster said to Eva.

"And I am Eva. I hope that's short enough as it is," she said much to Kat's amusement.

Before Nathan had a chance to introduce himself, the precocious youngster said, "And you are Mr Trent."

He shook her hand and added, "Nathan," which was greeted with a broad grin.

"Can you get Mummy?" Martin instructed. Turning to Nathan and Eva he said, "She's slaving over a hot stove."

"If she's busy don't disturb her," Eva suggested, but no sooner had she spoken than Martin's wife emerged from the kitchen.

"Don't take any notice of him, the meal is ready, we can eat any time." She handed her apron to Kat. "Hang that up for Mummy please, sweetie." Then, offering her hand she said, "You must be Eva, and this is the man I've heard so much about." Eva saw Nathan look at her, suitably embarrassed for once. "We're delighted you both could come. I am Mia."

For the briefest of moments Eva's heart sank. She had so hoped Martin's wife was Ellinore, as that would have solved the puzzle of the scribbled note she had found that Nathan had dropped when they were in the restaurant in Iceland, but it was not to be. They were invited to sit, and while Kat and Mia carried in the dishes Martin poured the wine.

"Kalvebryst i frikeseé," Mia announced. "We hope you eat veal?"

Eva rarely did but smiled, "That smells good."

The veal, boiled with vegetables and served in a creamy white sauce with peas and carrots, was delicious and Eva found herself accepting seconds.

Martin's news that it was time for Kat to go to bed was received with marked disappointment. "You've school tomorrow so say goodnight to our guests, and Mum and I will pop up to settle you in a minute."

Eva proposed that, if it was okay with Martin, she would love it if Kat could take her up and quickly show her her bedroom.

The two men retired to the lounge and had started to talk over developments as the women joined them.

"What a delightful young lady," Eva said, to which Mia added,

"Yes, and she's on her best behaviour for you today. Tomorrow her talent for misbehaving will undoubtedly return," and she cast Eva a mischievous glance, one which Eva thought closely resembled the glance Kat had given her earlier.

Acknowledging why the two men wanted to meet, Eva said, "What's the latest with your television show, Martin?"

"It's coming together better than I expected. So far we've been successful in lining up three speakers. The Ministry of Health have agreed to put forward a spokesperson, we don't know who yet, so we have to wait and see if it will be a politician or a medical expert. The Ministry of Defence will have someone who can also speak on behalf of the DDIS." Noticing Eva's confusion Martin added, "The Danish Defence Intelligence Service."

"What about the Foreign Ministry?" Nathan asked, recalling his run-in.

"We're not certain but it could well be they'll front your old friend, Lars Nielsen," Martin said mischievously, to which an indignant Nathan responded, "He's not my old friend?"

"Don't be so touchy," Eva pronounced.

"I'm not really, I just find it amusing. What of the Americans?" Nathan asked.

"As things stand they are sending a statement and it appears any questions of a general nature will be fielded by our own Foreign Office representative."

"And you," Eva chose her words carefully, "what's your role, Martin?"

"Well, I am chairing the debate and questioning each individual representative. There will undoubtedly also be questions from the invited guests and I sincerely hope that you will be one of them, Nathan?"

"I wouldn't miss it."

"And would you be happy to say something, if the opportunity arises?"

"Sure, if you think it would be helpful."

"Hearing about the massive amount of research you've been doing I am certain it would be," Mia remarked.

"How, Martin, have you managed for all these years to maintain a degree of secrecy around your work?" Eva asked.

"When I started fourteen odd years ago it was just me, no one else was involved. Our spare room here became my study."

"And still is, if you can get in there for all the piles of papers and books," Mia provoked.

Desperate to find out more, Eva hoped Martin wouldn't be irritated by her questions. "And how did you cope with such vast quantities of data, and keeping it to yourself?"

"It wasn't much of a problem in the early days because the information came through a little at a time and no one else was interested in what I was doing. But, as the years went on, I became aware this story wasn't going to go away and it was bigger than I ever imagined. To begin with it didn't seem like a criminal story, a conspiracy. I thought initially it was a few guys who'd had a raw deal in the military trying for compensation." Eva realised she was the only one pressing Martin, but thought the others probably knew the answers.

"What changed your mind?" she said.

"I started to find many who had no contact with each other displaying the same symptoms – radiation sickness. When my research led me to key ministerial figures in the Danish government, their scientific research establishment as well as the US Department of Defence, I knew

I had a story, and my instinct has proved right. I began to see collusion and deceit everywhere. My files at the office went missing so, for the sake of the people on whose behalf I was working, I needed to protect my sources and the material I had gathered. All the sensitive data I encrypted and protected with multiple passwords and I stored it on my home computer, which isn't connected to the internet. I never spoke to anyone openly about this aspect of my work, even over the telephone. That's why I was hesitant when I got Nathan's call," Martin divulged, looking towards Nathan, who clearly understood. "I didn't share it with any other person. I think I may have gone over the top, but I didn't trust a soul. I now know what it feels like to be one of your English foxes, Nathan, trying hard to evade the hunt!"

"I always thought of you as a lone wolf, dear," Mia said.

Martin nodded, "Yes, maybe that."

"Did you ever feel under threat?" Eva asked, and went on to add, "My own father constantly complained that someone was watching his every move, didn't he, Nathan? And if that wasn't enough, the chap he had contact with in the States was certain that someone in the US military was pursuing him."

"To tell you the truth, no." As Martin spoke Eva couldn't help notice his look of unease towards Nathan.

It had been a good evening and an opportunity to get to know the real Martin Poulson. Eva admired his singlemindedness, his brilliance and his ability year after year to remain totally focussed, committed to the task, when few knew what he was doing and still fewer believed in him. For the very first time Eva could fully understand why, for Nathan, this journey to discover the truth had been so very important. It was not easy for her to admit but she also finally realised her father had been right all along.

The early evening sun, which had warmed Eva and Nathan during their stroll across the city to Martin's, had long gone and the night was now brewing something far less pleasant. Dashing back to the hotel, Eva huddled up close to Nathan, trying to keep out of the worst of the downpour. She shivered.

"We need to get dry and warm," Nathan said, climbing the stairs. He unlocked his hotel room door and helped her inside. "Get undressed while I run you a hot bath."

Taking off all but her underwear, Eva stood cold and speechless. Through the gap in the doorway she could see Nathan hang his sodden jacket on the towel rail.

"It won't be long before you can get in," he said as he took her in his arms.

A strange feeling ran through her body, wondering what he was going to do next. He rubbed his hands up and down her back and sides until she pulled a face. "You'll soon be warm," he said.

She held on to him as he guided her to the bathroom. The steam hit her like some exhilarating sauna. She slid beneath the warming water and let it lap over her, enjoying the feeling of life returning to her tired limbs.

Eva called to him, "Are you alright? I'm sorry, I didn't mean to lean on you so," and with that Nathan peered around the door.

He stood wearing only his briefs, rubbing his hair with a white bath towel. "I didn't realise just how cold I was."

"You need to get in the bath," Eva said.

He dropped his towel and briefs and eased himself in opposite her. Eva didn't know whether to be embarrassed or to laugh; then she laughed.

"What is it?" Nathan asked.

"I didn't mean for you to get in with me."

"Oh," he said with a strained look on his face and attempted to ease himself out.

"No, you're okay," Eva replied in an instant, regretting her earlier prudishness.

He settled again, effortlessly positioning his legs either side of her slim body. Eva watched as Nathan tried in vain not to stare at her breasts.

"What?" she said.

Casting another eye over her, he said, "I was just thinking you'd make a wonderful dancer."

"Dancer?" she said, trying to sound offended.

"You know, in one of those clubs."

She didn't know what came over her but with that she pushed out her chest. It was strange. Before she had always felt awkward about her nakedness but for some reason not now. As she rubbed the soapy face cloth over her body she could feel Nathan staring.

"Forgive me," he said apologetically, and with that he pushed himself up out of the bath. Wrapping a towel about his waist, he held a towel for her to step into, "The water's getting cool."

Obliging, Eva stood. The firmness of his caress thrilled her. They dried each other and that night proved to be the most exhilarating Eva had ever experienced.

DR HEADQUARTERS – COPENHAGEN

CHAPTER FORTY-TWO

"I thought, Martin, we ought to meet and run through last-minute arrangements for the show since it's only two days away." Brigitte's commanding manner was typical of the woman.

"That's fine by me," Martin said, "it will be good to clarify a few things."

"I've invited John Beck, the producer, to join us. Do you know him?"

"Yes, I've worked with him on a couple of current affairs programmes, he's a good man."

And as if benefitting from some sixth sense John Beck knocked and entered Brigitte's office.

"Great to see you again Martin, it must be eighteen months since we worked on 'Headline'. I've been hearing a lot about you."

Martin side-stepped John Beck's last comment saying, "Nearer three years, and they were good times."

"Enough of this reminiscing, let's get down to business." Brigitte didn't wait for John to get seated. "We've got a seventy-five-minute slot running immediately after the 9.00pm news summary and, being a Sunday, I would expect to get an audience of around half a million plus, but it's hard to tell: there's also the online audience. Our tech guys are organising the web-casting of the debate and creating a feedback forum as well as a media centre, hosting it from our main news site. We'll also post a transcript of the debate on the website; there will be no cameras or electronic devices allowed into the studio. What about on the day itself, John?" Brigitte asked.

"We're staging the event in Studio Six, it's a medium size production facility. It takes care of all the logistical problems created by outside broadcasts, but limits the number of guests. That's why, as I specified to you, we can only accommodate seventy studio guests, seventy-six at a push. There will be terraced seating and a raised platform with four separate lounge seats for you, Martin, and the speakers. We want you all to feel relaxed. I'll have a camera on the group, one on you and a couple of rovers. We'll need an additional camera panning on the guests and mics for the question time." John looked at Brigitte, "What's the latest on the guests?"

She shuffled some papers and laid out three sheets of close type, "Fifty-nine guests have accepted – health professionals, academics, defence consultants, relatives and civic group members, a couple of lawyers, students and the press. We await twelve replies. Being an exclusively ticketed occasion we don't anticipate problems, but security will be tight; we don't need any uncontrolled outbursts on air. A bit of fire's good for the ratings but nothing that looks as though we've orchestrated it."

"Can you go through the speakers for me," Martin requested.

"The Ministry of the Interior and Health is represented by Olivia Bach; I believe her title is Head of Public Relations. Hugo Olsen is something in the Defence Ministry, and the Foreign Ministry have fielded one of the permanent secretaries, Lars Nielsen. Regarding the Americans, their statement is in your file but I understand Defence and the Foreign Office will field as best they can."

John piped up, "I know of Olsen, he appears to relish the rough and tumble of a political debate. As for Nielsen, he's an intellectual who worries a lot."

"Ingrid's included the profiles of the speakers in your file," and Brigitte pointed to beige folders in the centre of the table. "She has also added the guest list, as we have it, and seating plan. Ingrid has attempted to group guests with similar interests and views to make life easier for you, Martin, when managing the question time. There will be some strong views amongst them but we don't anticipate any heckling. Have you considered how you're going to apportion the time?"

"I've given it a lot of thought. Seventy-five minutes, right? Opening and introductions, five minutes tops. About eight questions from the guests in the audience, half a minute a question, two minutes for the answer. They'll need to understand I will only accept questions at the end and they must be on-topic and kept short; time taken up with guests' reactions is time taken from the speakers' response. That allows nearly forty minutes for the speakers and myself to have our say. I'll cut short anyone who waffles. For my closing remarks I've allowed four minutes along with the rolling credits. "What do you think?"

"That's a demanding schedule but if you can keep to it . . ." Brigitte said.

"I am determined to. There's a range of aspects to cover, and unless we watch the clock we'll run the risk of losing our audience."

"I'll be in the control room, and if it looks as though the timing is slipping we'll relay to you through the floor manager," Brigitte stated.

"What do you think about using stark black and white archive stills of the accident projected on the backdrop during your introduction?" John Beck proposed. "Nothing that can be accused of being too controversial, but it would be a good way to thrust viewers into the heart of the incident from the outset?"

"I'd go with that," Martin said, with Brigitte agreeing. "What's the top floor's stance on our approach, Brigitte?" he asked.

"They recognise that this is an old story which many, especially the younger generation, won't know much about. They believe, with the growing coverage in the press, and the current legal hearings here and in the European Parliament, it is news-worthy and we need to take a strong stand on this one. It's imperative that our contribution is factually based and the programme represents sound, thought-provoking, compelling television. Pressure has been applied on the station at a high level to suppress the story, to step back from it, citing misleading reporting and issues of confidentiality threatening national security. As you both know DR has been criticized in the past for being politically biased, so it's crucial you present an even-handed approach to the debate, Martin, especially as you manage the question time and our political delegates. It mustn't escalate into a verbal brawl. We undoubtedly will get some political kick-back, but that's not a problem if our legal department can put up a strong case." She paused. The two looked on expectantly.

"Having right on our side and believing we are doing what our conscience tells us needs to be done may be virtuous, but isn't in itself enough. Being too tenacious, challenging and provocative will not get us to the heart of what actually happened. We don't need the old nightmare of mushroom clouds, so trumpeting an ideology will do little to reveal the hidden truths, the dark mysteries of Thule." She looked at Martin. "The faces will always be in the back of your mind but if you are going to do the best for them you must shut them out. I am certain you can pull it off."

Martin contemplated Brigitte's advice.

"Before you and I review the questions for the speakers," she said, looking at Martin, "there's one more thing we need to discuss – your concern regarding an insider. Are you okay for John to be in on this?"

John Beck spoke out, "I'm happy to call it a day. There's more than enough to occupy me on the production side," and with that he took his leave saying he'd catch up with them on Sunday.

"Do you have a distrusting character, Martin?" she asked.

"No, it's a character I assume when it suits."

"Well, on this occasion you were right to. Sig looks to be our mole. Looking back over the time he has been with us as a liaison officer it's not difficult to see how he has influenced the direction of some of our reporting. More than that, it is evident he has slowed down some of the critical journalistic work within DR. Beneath his professional facade he has a manipulative streak."

As she was talking Martin wondered how much of her assessment was based on her own personal experience.

"We discovered recordings of your private telephone conversations and copies of some of the early confidential Thule files hidden away in his desk and cabinet. The person who has been intent on disrupting your investigations is now history, as far as I am concerned. Sig Søvensen is on extended leave until HR decide how to best handle the situation."

"Stirring things up, that's my business. I've never fought shy of the risks or even the dangers of my work."

"I know that, Martin, you refuse to lay down and die and that's what makes you the reporter you are. But you need to be aware that while what you are about to do will win you many friends, it will also see some powerful individuals become antagonistic towards you. It's taken you years, against all odds, to get to this moment in our country's history, but remember that any fall-out will not only impact on Denmark but on the huge, unstoppable USA." Brigitte eased back in her chair, "Enough of that, let's review the questions."

*   *   *   *

The phone rang for the fourth time before Martin picked up.

"Martin Poulson," he said abruptly, fumbling to turn the television volume down with the remote.

"Martin, it's Nathan, I wanted to catch you before the show tomorrow to see how the briefing went."

"Hi, sorry if I sounded off-hand only I was in the middle of the football, but it's half-time so you're alright," and he laughed. "It went well. Did you get your invites okay?"

"Yes, thanks," Nathan confirmed.

"So what have you been doing with yourselves?"

Nathan explained that he and Eva had spent the day before in Tivoli Gardens. He had never been one for fairground rides but they'd really enjoyed themselves and had a meal in one of the restaurants before taking in a concert. "We couldn't get over the illuminations."

Martin said, "Did you have a go on the rollercoaster?"

"I'm afraid so." Martin was certain he could hear the pain in Nathan's voice.

"Eva loved the ride but I hated every minute. Tomorrow . . ." Nathan started.

"What about it?" Martin said.

"It is the chance to put all the deceit to one side and get to the truth. You know I'm fully behind you, Martin, we want the same thing. Without your courage and determination it would never have come to this."

"That's as maybe but at the moment it looks a bloody mess," Martin shared.

Nathan hesitated before attempting to encourage him. "Eva says that after tomorrow we will all be able to start afresh."

"I hope so. I can't remember what a decent night's sleep is like." Martin's mood changed. "Why aren't you watching the big match?"

"I am. As you said, it's half-time. Not being a football fan I am enduring England's defeat of Denmark as an act of loyalty to my country, and anyway, it's one of the few things on television where a non-English commentary is hardly a problem."

"The way you're scoring you'll be through to the quarter finals of the cup."

"Have all the preparations gone well?" Nathan asked. "What happened in the end about the Americans?"

"Now that's a funny thing. I told you they declined the chance to have a seat at the table, saying no one was available and sending a statement instead. Well, I decided to try a direct approach. I rang the States direct and got put through to one of the Air Force's Press Liaison Officers."

"Good for you," congratulated Nathan.

"I told him I was after some information for a piece on the Cold War and the US Air Force activity in the northern hemisphere. He sounded up-beat and only too pleased to help. I asked him if I would be right in thinking that B-52 bombers on Operation Hard Hat would have been on full twenty-four hour alert overflying Greenland. He told me I would be right. And would they be armed with nuclear weapons, I put to him, and he agreed they would have been. He was still sounding at ease with my questions so I carried on: clearly this was a press guy who hadn't been fully briefed. I told him I didn't want to get my facts wrong but was I correct in understanding that over the past thirty odd years the design and safety features of the H-bombs they carried had been dramatically improved. He said that was outside his terms of reference and offered to give me the name and number of someone who could help me with that. I thanked him, dialled the contact and, referring to the press guy, asked the same question, and guess what?"

"What?" Nathan obliged.

"He couldn't stop talking."

"Who was he?" Nathan asked.

"I am pretty sure he was an engineer involved in the bomb's design. As I had a service telephone number I didn't know if I was talking to someone at Sandia or Los Alamos; I didn't like to ask at the risk of losing my credibility. What he said staggered me. It seems that following the loss of that B-52 bomber loaded with hydrogen bombs in southern Spain and then two years later, almost to the day, the accident in Thule, the engineers were put under pressure to improve the efficiency of the bomb's fail safe devices and safety of the conventional explosives. He explained at great length how improvements have further ensured the integrity of the device. Following his comments I asked him if earlier devices could have been considered less safe and, for the first time, he hesitated and implied that the later refinements and design changes certainly improved its safety. I sensed my good luck was running thin so I thanked him profusely and ended the call, wondering why it was that the day after the Thule accident the bombers were no longer armed with H-bombs?"

DR STUDIO SIX – COPENHAGEN

CHAPTER FORTY-THREE

"Fifteen minutes everyone," the floor manager announced, directing one of the cameramen to reposition his camera.

The last guests in the audience were taking their seats and the instruction to close the doors on Studio Six had already been given. Martin had been on set some forty minutes, ensuring everything was in place and familiarising himself with the sea of expectant faces staring from the terraced seating. He raised his hand in acknowledgement and a number in the crowd turned to see Nathan and Eva wave back. A dozen or more crew were busy checking and putting the final touches as the guests were brought in. A nervous Martin broke away from what he was doing. Before every shoot the pressure of the moment always got the better of him, but he knew well that once underway he would be fine. A young girl in make-up powdered Martin's face and wished him good luck.

The floor manager stepped up and, along with Martin, welcomed the speakers. He briefed them on the basic cues he would be using, reminding them of the run order, and left Martin to settle them in their seats on the platform as he in turn addressed the audience. Touching his earpiece he spoke into his headset, then holding up four fingers he called, "Four minutes please."

Martin checked his tie knot and, positioning himself before the camera, waited. The on-camera teleprompter burst into life and Martin scanned the opening words. The floor manager indicated thirty seconds, then holding one palm up signalled stand-by and the camera went live.

"Good evening, this is Martin Poulson welcoming you to 'Outlook', a debate special, live from DR's Broadcasting Centre here in Copenhagen. On 21st January 1968 an American aircraft crashed within the Arctic Circle, but this was no straightforward accident that could be relegated to the history books. The aircraft was armed with four nuclear bombs and although it crashed thousands of miles from Denmark, the Broken Arrow incident, involving the loss of nuclear weapons, occurred on Danish soil in Greenland."

As he spoke, shaky black and white movie images of the crash, the massive fireball and trail of flaming debris were projected on the back drop behind the speakers.

"Only now are the implications of such an event being fully realised, the secrets surrounding the aircraft's movements and US nuclear weapon displacement revealed. Thirty-four years on and the ripples of the disaster are still being felt.

"Tonight we will try and answer the many questions that still shroud the Thule incident. Was it true that one of the 1.1 megaton bombs onboard the B-52 bomber was never fully recovered and the decontamination of radioactive material from the site, which took nearly two thousand workers nine months, put hundreds of Danes and Inuit at risk? Why was it necessary to forcibly evict hundreds of Inuit, days before they became Danish citizens, from their home of a thousand years? And what was the purpose of the American sub-ice city of Camp Century?"

As Martin spoke, a movie sequence of the US Star Three, two-man submersible searching beneath the ice led into shots of workers clearing snow, some in protective clothing, others in their everyday work gear. A frightening scene showed an Inuit kneeling in the snow retching, spewing up the contents of his stomach as fellow workers looked on.

"To help me I am grateful to my fellow guests: Olivia Bach, Head of Public Relations for the Ministry of the Interior and Health, Hugo Olsen, Ministry of Defence, and Lars Nielsen, Permanent Under-Secretary at the Foreign Ministry. Thank you for joining us tonight."

The audience spontaneously applauded as the speakers fidgeted, appearing a trifle uneasy in their seats.

"I'd like to start by asking Hugo Olsen about the accident." Hugo's face gave nothing away, showing no signs of nerves or, for that matter, compassion. "Would it be wrong to describe the explosion that erupted on that January day as heralding one of the worst nuclear accidents in our history? After all, each of the four bombs on board the B-52 was some seventy times more powerful than the bomb dropped on Hiroshima."

"It's important to acknowledge, Martin, that there was no nuclear explosion."

"That's true," Martin conceded, "but the aircraft crashed perilously close to the Thule Air Base where hi-tech military hardware and warheads were stock-piled. And, am I not right that bombs being unarmed should not be confused with bombs being incapable of nuclear detonation?"

Hugo reluctantly nodded.

"If we, for a moment, turn our attention to Camp Century, the top secret American city buried under the ice cap, what precisely was its purpose, do you know?" Martin waited on his reply.

"It was an installation for carrying out research in this hostile environment. Both Century and Thule were critical in the event of a Soviet surprise attack on the West."

"Thank you for clarifying that for our audience," Martin expressed to a rather confused Hugo Olsen.

Then he ventured, "I would like to bring in Olivia Bach to talk us through the health implications of the accident and clean-up."

She immediately pronounced, "I must state there was categorically no health risk to the workers involved in the clean-up at Thule. Any radioactive dose was well under the acceptable level."

"And you know this? How?" Martin responded, not wishing to sound too threatening.

"We monitored each and every one."

"Each and every one? That's quite an undertaking. How and when did you monitor for radiation?"

Bach, referring to notes, read, "Each worker was subjected to external and internal testing – that would include urine tests and nasal smears. These would indicate any dosage."

"I see," Martin said. "And when exactly did this monitoring begin? Let's be clear for the viewers that this testing was for radiation?"

She again scanned her briefing notes, turning pages. Trying to maintain an authoritative air she spoke quietly, "I don't have the exact date but it would have been soon after the incident."

"Would I be right to say that the Americans began decontaminating and monitoring their service personnel immediately, but the fifteen hundred or so Danish and Greenlandic nationals involved were not monitored for some time and then not all of them, and with testing methods and equipment that could not be relied on to work accurately at such low temperatures? Well, that's what a number of witnesses have sworn to be the case. They have also stated that while the Americans were equipped with full protective clothing and face masks it was many days before even rudimentary protection was provided for them."

Bach looked positively uncomfortable: she was well out of her depth. "I couldn't possibly agree with that."

Martin decided to change tack. "Could we turn to the health outcomes for so many of those involved?"

Bach only acknowledged the question and it was impossible not to notice the unease of the other two speakers.

"I understand from official records that since the clean-up hundreds have died, half from cancer related illnesses. Perhaps you can share with us the Ministry's view?"

"What do you mean?" she replied.

"Allow me to quote: *'We believe the Thule workers' health problems must be as a result of the rowdy alcohol and tobacco-laced lifestyle, typical of Arctic military bases and construction sites'*."

Bach re-joined the debate. "I believe it's unfair to judge the Ministry's response by a one-off unscientific reaction, a seemingly off-the-cuff remark. You must appreciate the Danish workers were not engaged in the more exposed tasks: that was left to the American service personnel."

"So we understand," Martin noted. "They were, nevertheless, manually filling barrels with debris and exposed to the same airborne particles, a powerful poison if ingested. So what was the result of the radiological examination of the surviving workers commissioned by the Prime Minister of the day?"

He waited on her answer.

"The report concluded that the death rate among the workers involved was higher than other workers at the base, but it did not conclude that radiation exposure was to blame. Just because two things are associated does not necessarily mean that one causes the other."

"Even with cancer being evident in nearly a third of workers and cases being more than fifty percent higher than what we might expect here in Copenhagen? We know plutonium can cause severe damage to the kidney and liver, and uncontrolled growth in cancer cells." Martin believed the point was clear for all to see.

She didn't respond.

"Miss Bach, there has been much speculation as to the precise nature of the explosion and the associated risks and fall-out. Can you tell us, was the Ministry fully au fait with what we were dealing with? The nature and size of the threat and what exactly was retrieved and neutralised?"

An obviously somewhat embarrassed public relations officer stated that the Danish government, concerned with the impeding melting of the contaminated ice in the summer, insisted on its removal from Greenland. With that Olivia Bach admitted she was unable to be more precise, and Martin, thanking her for her frankness, turned again to the man who had taken on the mantle of representing the Danish Ministry of Defence and the interest of the USA.

"What, Hugo Olsen, did we know with absolute certainty about the bombs?"

The white-haired official, wearing a tired expression, gestured dismissively with his hand. "I am not sure what I can add to the statement the United States Air Force issued to you." He slouched back in his chair contentedly and appeared to smirk.

"You're right," Martin said, humouring him. "They have indeed, in response to our invitation to join us around this table, declined the offer but issued a statement instead. In essence it emphasises that the B-52 developed a fire on board necessitating its emergency landing near Thule, resulting only in a small conventional explosion. They add that the incident was quickly contained and subsequent investigations have established no long-term threat exists. It concludes with a vote of thanks to those that worked diligently to ensure the safety of both the local population and the environment. Would you say, Mr Olsen, that this is a fair representation of their statement?"

The old boy brushed his hand over his knee as if trying to sharpen the appearance of his creased suit and managed, "Mmm."

"Maybe you could fill in some details for us: the radioactive materials present at the accident site, the scale of the impact area, and what remnants are left as a legacy of this major incident?"

Olsen glared at Martin. This wily old official had been brought to task, and on live television. Martin was unsure if his wavering over a response was tactical or due to uncertainty; he plumped for the former.

"Please allow me to help you. What was the area impacted by the accident?"

That appeared to regain Olsen's attention. "The crash site was relatively small, stretching no more than a few hundred metres."

"But we know parts of the aircraft were found two miles from the point of impact. So what about the fall-out area?" Martin persisted. "It must have been huge to require tens of thousands of tons of snow to be removed – some say as much as two hundred thousand tons?"

"I couldn't comment on that, but yes, probably eight square kilometres of snow was removed," Olsen voiced.

Martin was not letting go that easily. "My understanding from eyewitness accounts is that the fire burnt for six hours and reached around eight hundred and fifty metres in height. Both meteorological and radar observations suggest the smoke was driven south and southeast, and that winds blew from the north at an altitude of one thousand metres and above that from the west. One could expect airborne contamination to have extended to the settlement of Narsaarsuk eight kilometres south, and again, only a few days later during the Arctic storms of January 24th and 29th, carried west towards Saunders Island. Yet did these thousands of square kilometres not fall beyond the boundary of the clean-up?"

An audible gasp could be heard from the audience.

"I couldn't say," was all Olsen could offer.

"Well, maybe you could say where the Danish nationals that became ill after the clean-up and died were taken and are now buried. If indeed they are buried?" Martin added, as if an afterthought.

"What are you talking about?" Olsen bit back.

"I have a list of people," Martin explained, holding up several sheets of typed paper. "These are the names of workers whose families have no knowledge of what happened to them after they became ill and died." Martin handed Olsen the list.

"I know nothing of this," Olsen said. Then looking at the top sheet, and reading the first name, he remarked, "Who's this Joe Masini?"

"Now that's interesting," Martin said. "I know someone in the audience who can tell you all about him and some of the others on the list." And looking towards Nathan, Martin said, "My friend Professor Nathan Trent, who has just returned from Greenland. Could you tell us briefly something about Joe Masini and how he died?"

Nathan stood and for a minute or two highlighted Joe's involvement in the clean-up and the hideous illness that haunted him, leading to his death. He shared Helga's memories of the way Joe's body was taken from her in a special coffin, lined with lead. Nathan sat. The studio was silent. Olsen had nothing to say.

Martin spoke, "This isn't about recrimination, but in getting to the truth." He waited, allowing what he'd said to strike home "Did we ever fully know what materials were present in the bomb?" he asked Olsen.

"No, not fully." Martin could see the irritation on Olsen's face as he answered. "We, perhaps naively, asked the Americans for details of the components and construction of the bombs, but it only resulted in a polite say-nothing reply. They were not about to reveal classified elements of their nuclear warhead."

"Allow me to share with our viewers what we understand about the bomb – a B28 F1, maybe Mod 1, 1.1 megaton thermonuclear weapon. The package is believed to consist of plutonium 239, 240 and 241, lithium-6-deutride, uranium 234, 235 and 238, americium 241 and tritium, as well as the highly toxic metal beryllium. It's imperative to understand that you can't just sweep up the radiation, or expect it to dissolve. For example, the half-life for plutonium is up to 24,000 years and for uranium, extending from 250,000 to 4.5 billion years."

As a murmur and disturbance broke out in the crowd, a frustrated Olsen contended, "It is dangerous to speculate. The media is good at that and in sensationalising events."

"I appreciate that," Martin confessed, "and I am not a physicist, but I don't think it takes a scientist to comprehend the dangers."

A belligerent Olsen came back, "They were turbulent times. We were balancing on the knife-edge of war, endeavouring to face our ministerial responsibility."

"But it's not about your responsibility, it's about the responsibilities and fate of all of us. Surely, hosting these deadly missile assets was high risk? Such provocation could have brought us to the brink of a missile crisis."

"You must remember, only the President or his successor could authorise the use of nuclear weapons," Olsen asserted.

Martin said, "My understanding is to the contrary, that such authorisation rests with a number of specified air defence commanders in the case of an emergency. Equally, there is always the risk of a computer malfunction signalling a Soviet attack—"

"I don't think that's feasible," Olsen held.

"I was about to add, as occurred at Thule in October 1960 and NORAD HQ Colorado on June 3rd and 6th 1980."

Martin was not surprised that Olsen didn't respond.

Throughout the exchange with Olsen, Martin had noticed both Olivia's and Lars' faces becoming increasingly riddled with doubt and Lars' note-taking had reached a level that no one could fail but notice: maybe now he was beginning to realise the full implications of these events.

"Perhaps I could call upon Mr Nielsen to clarify two or three points for us," Martin encouraged, "from a Foreign Office perspective." Lars looked up, fidgeting in his seat. "Am I right that the news of the accident was kept from the Danish people by the then government and the Prime Minister, who failed to make our Danish non-nuclear policy clear to the US?"

"Not exactly," Lars remarked, "they were told."

Martin noticed the floor manager put his hand to his ear. "So when were they told? And can I ask you to speak up, please? What you have to say is really important to all of us."

"A few days later," Lars admitted.

"A few days later. Is that because we were on the brink of a national election? In fact, only two days away and the government wanted to avoid any repercussions in light of our non-nuclear policy?"

"I couldn't say," Lars professed.

"No, of course. Forgive me, it was a long while ago and I guess that's politics," Martin baited. "Let us turn to the issue of the native Greenlanders who were evicted from their homeland to make way for the Americans."

Lars spoke out, "They were not evicted, they were resettled, relocated to a newly constructed, modern village – Qaanaaq."

"To make way for the US base," Martin shared. "But surely the United States abandoned its territorial claims to the area in 1917, am I right?"

All that Lars could muster was, "The Danish High Court subsequently upheld the Danish – US agreement and agreed that the base had been legally established."

"I see," Martin coaxed. "It would seem to me that the native Greenlanders had become mere spectators to their own future, would you agree?"

By now it was evident that the speakers seated around the table were becoming increasingly agitated.

"Is it true, Mr Nielsen, that at the time of the accident the US Air Force had awarded Danish companies contracts to maintain the Thule Air Base to a value of 268 million dollars? That's an awful lot of money even today, yet back in the 1960s, well—"

"I believe contracts were awarded in 1966 for the following five years," Lars admitted.

"And did any of those contracts include work on Camp Century, the experimental city under the ice cap?"

"I couldn't possibly say," Lars said.

"You couldn't say. So you wouldn't know if any of the contracts involved working on Project Iceworm?" Martin presumed.

"Project Iceworm?" Lars repeated.

"Yes. A project to test the feasibility of boring deep vertical shafts – silos – hundreds of them, across Greenland to conceal a vast array of nuclear missiles zeroed in on the Soviets," Martin said. "That was the terrifying technology of Project Iceworm."

At this point it proved impossible for Hugo Olsen to remain silent.

"Of course it never happened," he said.

"But what a thought if it had," Martin surmised. "Perhaps I can ask you all: what of the lost fourth bomb, bomb number 78252, which currently sits on the seabed?"

Again Olsen jumped in, "The Americans have always maintained the four bombs have been accounted for."

"Accounted for," Martin asserted, "but the Pentagon would not categorically confirm what was 'retrieved' in the quarter-of-a-billion gallons of ice and debris collected when we asked them. If 'there was never a lost bomb' turns out to be a lie, then it's a mighty big lie, but there again, folks say it is easier to sell a big lie than a little one."

"I've watched you, Mr Poulson," a flushed Olsen challenged, "making your moves, influencing the audience. You speak far too freely."

Martin, at a loss to fathom his sudden aggression, cut him short. "I never speak freely, as you put it," he insisted. "I use my eyes and ears, I ask questions and I listen. I am not involved in the way others are. My only weapon is my word processor." He waited just enough time for it to sink in. "I think it's time we heard the questions that other people want answers to."

Questions came fast and furious and Martin needed his wits to manage the exchange. One elderly veteran likened his role in the clean-up to that of a canary, there to determine the extent of the danger. Olivia Bach attempted to dismiss his concern, unsuccessfully.

A woman asked the panel if they had seen someone die from exposure to radiation, then graphically explained how she had nursed her husband through his last horrific days.

Someone, sounding remarkably like a scientist, addressed Lars Nielsen and Hugo Olsen asking that, if the clean-up had been successful, why was plutonium now being detected in the bay's shellfish at up to one thousand times higher than pre-crash levels.

A young student wanted to know how the government was going to respond to the UN, demanding for the return of the Inuit's ancestral land, and a woman calling herself an eco-warrior claimed that Greenpeace had evidence that the Americans were still blatantly polluting the land around their air base.

Questions kept coming. The floor manager signalled for Martin to begin to wrap up. In stepping up to the camera, Martin thanked his guests, adding that none of this was of their making but equally, none of us are completely free of blame. He began to summarise with his closing remarks.

"The doubts surrounding what exactly happened on that day in 1968 still remain. The Americans are not alone in polluting the Arctic; it is believed the Soviets have despatched no less than sixteen reactors to a watery grave in Arctic waters. Many feel there is no place for nuclear weapons and nuclear energy. Some may be of the opinion that the lie regarding Denmark being nuclear-free kept the enemy away. Meanwhile there are those in Greenland who fear that by making Thule this 'strange unworldly place', as Edgar Allan Poe described it, part of the missile shield would ensure it became a target in any future conflict. Of course had there been a nuclear explosion, maybe a full-scale attack would have been the result, but we will never know. We do know that US Secretary of Defence, Robert Strange McNamara, following the crash put an immediate suspension to the routine carriage of nuclear weapons over Greenland. We also know that B-52 bombers are still flying. Today the majority of the armada of B-52s are at the 3,000 acre Preservation Farm in Arizona, waiting to be scrapped. Their destruction is regularly observed by Soviet satellites, and twice a year the Russians come to call, just to check.

"The Cold War was a confrontation between two giants. Military tension along with the possibility of an all-out nuclear war and mutual destruction proved enough to ensure no shot was fired. That doesn't mean that it came without a cost.

"It would seem we learn little from our past: we have seen that past but can only imagine the future. We should resist undermining our country and our leaders, but equally they must live up to the trust we have placed in them. Every society has to face difficult decisions and we all face the responsibility history has placed upon us. Our country becomes a dangerous place when you can no longer trust it, when our leaders no longer strive for truth. It's easy for men to do bad things when good men do nothing. If we turn our backs on that which is wrong, we do so at our peril. Our decisions define who we are and what we believe in and live by.

"Perhaps the deafening silence has gone on long enough?"

He waited as a film sequence of the bomb exploding was projected onto the back screen accompanied by the sound of an enormous explosion which shook the studio.

"This is Martin Poulson, grateful for your company and wishing you all a peaceful goodnight."

THE *TODAY* NEWSPAPER OFFICES – COPENHAGEN

CHAPTER FORTY-FOUR

It is said that *the sharper the storm, the sooner it is over,* but this storm had been rumbling on for years and there seemed no prospect that it was soon to end.

Gudrun's extension rang on her desk. She answered, "News editor." It was her boss.

"I need you in my office, now!"

She could hear the displeasure in his voice. What the hell had she done now, she thought, as she hurried up to the fourth floor. What was the old man going to lay on her this time? Gudrun knocked twice on the editor-in-chief's door.

"Don't stand out there," came the cry.

She was taken aback when she saw how grave he looked. Then it dawned on her, he'd seen the headlines in today's *Xpress* newspaper: *Scandal at DR. Allegations of government insider subverting investigations into political conspiracies.*

"Jurgen Norgaard called me," he shouted.

Here it comes, she anticipated, the boys at the *Metro Xpress* have beaten us to the leader.

"We should have run with what we had, I can see that now," Gudrun pronounced.

"Although their scoop is our loss, that's not why I called you in. No, Norgaard heard from his source inside The Castle that there's talk of a high level enquiry. It appears Poulson has really kicked things off this time with his TV show. We've all known Poulson was hungry for the truth and would stop at nothing to get to the bottom of what went on back in the fifties and sixties, to find out who was responsible, so the government's reaction is hardly surprising as they face history finally catching up on them. I told Norgaard to get us the facts: the who and the what. The time's passed for speculation, we can do without unsubstantiated hearsay. Norgaard needs to get to his source and, if necessary, talk to Poulson himself and get back to me, like yesterday. The last thing we want is a restraint order slapped on us."

Gudrun understood now: this was their break, their chance to get the real story.

The chief's phone rang. "Good, put him right through, Nina. Norgaard, you're on speaker, Gudrun's with me. What have you found?"

"You'll never guess what's happened," Norgaard exclaimed.

"No, we won't if you don't tell us," the chief said harshly, fast losing the little patience he had left.

"My source confirmed that something big is going down. No one at The Castle would talk to me, not even the Press Secretary. The place was as tight shut as a snake's arse. So I tried Poulson and . . ." Norgaard's voice wavered.

"Yes?" the chief said. "What did he have to say?" The line sounded dead. "Come on, man, we haven't got all day, we've got a paper to write."

"I couldn't get hold of him, no one knew where he was," Norgaard finally admitted. "So I rang his home. His wife answered. After I said who I was she told me she couldn't talk. I thought she was probably expecting a call from someone else, perhaps Poulson. She sounded in a terrible state." Gudrun doubted if this account was going anywhere, but even her wildest imagination hadn't prepared her for what she heard next. "Poulson may be dead!"

"What the hell are you saying?" the old man boomed.

"It seems there was an accident. He just collapsed." It was obvious Norgaard knew little more.

"Hold on the line," the chief demanded, and turned to Gudrun. "Dig up everything you can on this one. Get what you can on the family: did he have any kids, their school, what his wife does, any good causes etc, you know the stuff. Norgaard," he commanded.

"Yes?" came Norgaard's reply.

"We need to get on top of this and fast," the old man insisted. "Use your contacts in the police, find out what happened and the cause of death, if indeed he is dead. Someone there must know. I want you to work with Neils Holm on this one. We need a piece within the next couple of hours, denying or confirming the reports. I have to trust you on this one to find something meaty. We need Neils to clear copy ready to roll for tomorrow's edition. Ring in as soon as you've got anything, we'll all re-convene at two in my office."

"What have we got?"

Norgaard looked across at Gudrun, then at the old man and sighed.

"Well?" the old man again challenged.

Norgaard spoke. "It's confirmed, Poulson is dead. He was dead on arrival at the hospital. Early reports put it down as death attributed to unknown causes. He was down by the harbour when he collapsed and paramedics were called. I've a meeting with a police contact to get the latest."

"Does it look like foul play?" Gudrun asked.

"It's too soon to say, I'll know more later," he said.

"The word from my political source is that the governmental cover-up has spread everywhere. Poulson had got to the heart of the deceit and realised there were few at that time who hadn't been involved. As soon as they knew what he'd got they became paranoid. Although it was thirty-odd years ago many still hold respected positions within public life and posts of significant control and power in the private sector. Vital information that could ruin them and destroy the government's credibility was destroyed, corrupted or taken off-line. They slurred his character amongst his colleagues and generally screwed things up for him. They knew that if the word got out the political fall-out would have been horrendous for them."

The old man chipped in, "Is your source reliable?"

"I'd stake my life on them . . ." Then Norgaard hesitated as he fully realised the implications of what he was saying.

"Will they name names? We have got to attribute these statements if this is going to stand up; I don't want any kick-back on this. If we get this one wrong we'll all be looking for a job. Go as deep as you can. I want every sordid little detail. We'll make Poulson the hero he deserved to be and show the politicians for the *rotturs* they are."

Gudrun flicked through her spiral-bound notepad. "Poulson's assignment was largely a personal one, investigating the deaths and illnesses of ex-Danish service personnel and civilians returning from Greenland. Much of his research he undertook at the National Library at Slotsholmen and I'm chasing up details of the material he referenced."

"Right, so was he doing this all on his own?" the old man puzzled.

"Well, that's the funny thing," Gudrun said. "One of the librarians remembers him regularly coming in with another man over the last two or three months."

"A reporter?"

"No, that's what's strange," Gudrun continued. "He was an Englishman, and checking with the records it was," and she browsed her notepad, "one Nathan Trent, the woman thought an academic. I've checked at the university but they have no record of him."

"Find out who he is," the old man insisted. "The wife will know, but with her recent loss you'll need to be tactful. Send a bouquet and a message of sympathy, then contact her and see what she can tell you."

Gudrun dialled Poulson's home number, knowing she couldn't afford to leave it any more than a day before she tried to make contact. Mia Poulson answered.

"Hello, Mrs Poulson?"

"Yes?"

Gudrun recognised a feebleness in the woman's voice. "I am so sorry to hear the news, it must be a distressing time for you."

"Thank you. Did you know my husband?"

"Not personally, but we respected his work tremendously and held him in high regard."

"We?" she said.

"Yes, I hope you will have received our message of sympathy and the flowers. I am Gudrun Lund."

"Ah yes, thank you."

"I was wondering if you could help us? It's essential I talk with Mr Trent who worked closely with your husband," she avoided using Martin's name, "here in the Black Diamond Building of the National Library. I was asked to call him urgently and, whilst we have a number, we get unobtainable. I think we must have got one of the numbers wrong, so could I quickly check it with you please?"

"Hold on, I've got his hotel number here." Gudrun could tell the woman was understandably preoccupied.

Having carefully copied the number down Gudrun thanked her profusely, assuring her that if there was anything she could do, her contact number was on the card of condolence that came with the flowers.

"That's very kind," and Mia Poulson hung up.

Gudrun realised there was only one man now who could tell them what really happened at Thule.

CHAPTER FORTY-FIVE

"I've nearly finished in the bathroom," Nathan called out to Eva.

"No rush," she replied. "The news has just come on."

The presenter was running through the headlines and Eva was only half listening, then she heard it. *'In the last few minutes a spokesman for the network has confirmed that DR reporter, Martin Poulson, was found dead here in Copenhagen yesterday. Initial reports are that he collapsed while out jogging. We will bring you more details on this breaking story later in our bulletin.'* Eva sat there shocked by the revelation, trying to convince herself it couldn't possibly be true.

"It's free," Nathan announced.

"No, you must come in here; it's terrible, I can't believe it."

A dishevelled Nathan appeared from the bathroom wearing a bath robe. "What is?"

"It can't be, it's impossible," was all she could say, glued to the screen. He sat beside her on the bed alarmed by her outburst. Nathan put his arm around her but she shunned him.

"Are you alright?"

"No. Watch." He looked at the set and, confused, saw what appeared to be a group of workers with banners protesting outside a hospital building. And then: *'At around 10.45 yesterday morning police were called to attend a body found on Larsens Plads, across the water from the new opera house site. It has been confirmed as forty-nine year old Martin Poulson, a reporter from DR here in Copenhagen. Police have advised it is too early to know the exact cause of his death but it appears he was taking exercise by himself. At this stage they are pursuing their enquiries believing the fatal accident may have been health-related. Hans Dahl, deputy political editor at DR said, "Martin Poulson will be sadly missed. His recent televised debate affirmed his standing as a committed investigative journalist, highly respected by colleagues throughout the media world. Martin's death represents a severe blow for journalistic integrity. At this tragic time our thoughts are with his family."'*

The news of Martin's death came like a bolt of lightning to Nathan, completely devastating him. Despair washed through every part of his being. Only a few days before he had been at the studio, congratulating him on the phenomenal impact of the televised debate. Even before the end of the broadcast DR's switchboard was jammed with callers sharing information, wanting to know how they could get involved in fighting for justice, or needing advice on where to turn in supporting a sick elderly relative who had been one of those serving in Thule.

And now Martin was dead! Eva could see in Nathan's eyes bewilderment, the look of total loss. In this short time, Eva had witnessed a change in Nathan as he spent more time with Martin. She had seen a growing admiration and respect for this Dane's selflessness and singular endeavour as he drove on with his investigations. There had been people who believed that this quest could only end with the death of Martin Poulson, and in some ways they had been proved right, but she was convinced what Martin had courageously started was now so important to so many that the people would decide when it would end. It was only now that the real truth was being revealed.

To Eva, as she watched Nathan, it felt as though his world had fallen apart. "Are you okay?" she said softly.

He waited before answering, "I don't know. I just never expected it."

"I know," she said. For so long Nathan had been a driven man, someone with a purpose, but now she saw doubt casting its shadow over him. She could see the pain in his eyes.

"I need to speak with Mia," he said, "but not today. I'll call her tomorrow."

They changed their plans, eating in the hotel that night. Anxious for Nathan, Eva thought it vital she stayed close to him for the next few days.

Eva scanned the newspaper over the breakfast table before Nathan had come down. A piece halfway down page two, was entitled *'Reporter's Sudden and Suspicious Death'.* She read, *'DR reporter Martin Poulson, only 49 years old, died mysteriously on Wednesday while jogging near to the harbour here in Copenhagen. Martin Poulson was involved in uncovering the Inuit dispute over seizure of their traditional lands in Greenland which took place in the 1960s, and the compensation case of hundreds of serving personnel involved in the clean-up operation after the nuclear accident at the US Air Base at Thule, NW Greenland.'* It went on to describe in some detail the discovery of a high level international cover-up regarding US nuclear weapon deployment in Greenland, and Denmark's collusion with the Americans. The article continued in a more general tone: *'The DR Press Office stated Martin Poulson never ceased his campaign in search for the truth no matter what, even in the face of grave personal risk. He will never see the outcome of his endeavours, but we the people will, and we owe it to him to find out the truth about his death. Martin Poulson leaves behind a wife, Mia, and a daughter, Katja Poulson.'*

By the time Nathan had joined her she had placed the paper to one side. He was considering the breakfast menu when the receptionist came to their table.

"A Jurgen Norgaard is on the phone asking for you. Will you take the call or shall I get his number?"

"Who's Jurgen Norgaard?" Eva asked as Nathan stood up.

He shrugged and said, "I don't know."

Eva found it hard to think about breakfast, wondering why Nathan was so long.

He returned nearly fifteen minutes later and poured himself a cup of now lukewarm tea. "He wanted to talk about Martin, he's from the Press."

"What did he want to know?" she said.

"He told me he was sorry to hear of Martin's sudden death and somehow he knew I had collaborated with him. I told him he sounded a bit melodramatic and explained that I hadn't collaborated, but he insisted he understood I had been involved of late in fighting for the same issues. When I asked him how he knew that he dropped this bombshell. According to this Norgaard fellow, that's how the authorities are describing what I have been doing. They are saying that Poulson was misled, manipulated albeit unwittingly, and that both his and my endeavours were misguided, falsely trying to convince the Danish people there was a case for the government to answer. They're calling him a flawed character, a malcontent, trying to make a name for himself, angling for any opportunity to raise his profile and reputation. They deny that Martin has been the subject of either official monitoring or surveillance and claim that the police believe there is nothing suspicious about his death."

Eva looked puzzled, "What did you say to him?"

"I told him what I thought and asked him why he had contacted me."

"And?" Eva said.

"And he said he wanted to talk with me because they didn't believe it. When I asked him who 'they' were, he said 'me and my editors', adding that in their opinion the government would adopt any means to reduce future hostility and defiance towards the establishment." Nathan pushed his cold tea cup away and, getting up again, said, "I must ring Mia and see how they both are."

Eva smiled, "Send her my love."

Eva waited what she considered a reasonable time, certainly enough for him to telephone Mia. He wasn't at reception so she went on up to their room. The door was unlocked. Nathan was sitting in a chair, bent forward his head in his hands.

"How is she?" Eva said.

He looked up, "Mia wants to see me. She wants us to go over later."

"Do you think that's a good idea, so soon?" she ventured.

"Yes, I think so," he replied, almost sounding convinced. "Anyway, that's what she wants."

Mia opened the door; her face was colourless but for her red eyes.

"Come in, it's good of you both to come," she uttered.

Eva embraced her.

Mia took three mugs from a stack on the kitchen drainer and made them all tea, seemingly glad to be occupied, and Eva's feeling of awkwardness passed.

"Are you sure we're not intruding?" Nathan said as he glanced at the array of mugs. "It looks as though you've been busy?"

"Yes, the police have been here most of the morning."

They retreated to the lounge. Mia moved a coat from the sofa and they made themselves comfortable.

"What did they want?" Nathan asked.

"They asked me lots of questions. They wanted to know about Martin's health and if he had seemed worried or disturbed lately. The officer was terribly apologetic but explained it was important that they learnt as much as they could, and as quickly as possible. He asked about Martin's home life and our relationship. I told him we had our disagreements like any other married couple but nothing more than that, and things were fine between us. He then wanted to know if they could take a look in his study for anything that might help in their investigations, maybe a note or a letter."

With that Nathan almost erupted, "Surely they're not suggesting Martin—" Eva stared at him, her penetrating glare sufficient to stop Nathan mid-sentence. His changed his tack, "Did they take anything?"

"No, I don't think so, although they found Martin's staff pass at the scene. They . . ." she stumbled, "need me to formally identify the body."

"Do you want us to go with you?" Eva suggested.

"Would you? Oh, but there's Katja."

"How is she taking it?" Nathan said.

"I don't think she fully understands what's happened; I don't really know."

"Where is she now?" he asked.

"Up in her room, I thought it was best she stayed out of the way when the police were here." Mia directed a glance to Eva, "Would you stay with her? I know she would feel safe with you."

"Of course." Eva needed to say no more for a look of relief to fill Mia's face.

"This is just the beginning," Mia said. "Martin had always warned me that, if this day came, the authorities wouldn't leave me alone until the story was dead."

CHAPTER FORTY-SIX

"We had offered for an officer to accompany Mrs Poulson so that she could identify her late husband, however, she said that wasn't necessary. Thank you, Professor Trent, for coming with her, it's been a huge shock to her." The police detective gestured to Nathan to sit. "I'd like to ask you a few questions, purely as a matter of routine, about Mr Poulson."

With that the door of his office opened and a young officer breezed in clearly wanting to speak. "Mrs Poulson?" the detective asked.

The young officer replied, "She's having a rest after the ID and one of our female support officers has made her a coffee and is sitting with her."

The detective spoke, addressing Nathan. "It is our understanding that over the past few months you have spent a lot of time with Mr Poulson, is that correct?"

"Yes, we have seen something of both him and his wife and daughter."

"We?" the officer responded.

"An acquaintance who is here in Copenhagen with me."

"Would that be one Eva Hannes, a resident of Reykjavik?"

"Yes," a surprised Nathan answered, assuming Mia must have told them.

"How have you found Mr Poulson's demeanour over your last few meetings with him?" The detective looked at him intently. "After all, only a week earlier he had the run-in in front of the nation with some pretty powerful public figures. That must have been stressful?"

Nathan thought to himself, I can see where this is going. "Suicide, is that what you think? Who the hell goes out on a jog to commit suicide?"

The young officer shifted, the older said, "I guess no one in their right mind." Before Nathan had an opportunity to reply, he went on, "No, we don't think he committed suicide and we know he wasn't drunk or had taken drugs, but please appreciate we have to consider all possibilities."

The detective nodded to his young colleague who then left the room.

"We know from his wife that he regularly cycled and ran along that walkway, but do you know if he had arranged to meet anyone, perhaps in the days before? Perhaps a lawyer?"

Nathan was clear. "Not to my knowledge, he never spoke of such."

The young man returned, this time with Mia. The detective addressed them both, "I want you to understand I am sincerely sorry, he was a good man. Too few do the right thing for others as your husband did, Mrs Poulson." He coughed, clearing his throat. "I am sure you are aware that the Justice Department has announced that they will carry out an investigation into the events leading up to what the press are calling, 'Thulegate'. We have briefed the media and asked that they act responsibly and sensitively in this instance, concentrating only on the facts. . . I am afraid not everyone in the media world respects the facts, some create them."

"May I speak freely?" Nathan said, looking to Mia, then across to the detective. "Do you know what happened?"

"No, not exactly," he came straight back. "It is too early. I will obviously discuss the doctor's conclusion with you, Mrs Poulson, when we have his report. Initial findings and witness reports would appear to support your observations, that he was suffering with extreme physical and mental fatigue. You said, Mrs Poulson, that over the past four or more months he had been experiencing chronic insomnia, frequent headaches, sore throats and pain in his muscles and joints. I believe he wouldn't see his doctor at the time, putting it down to stress. We are exploring whether this alone was the cause of your husband's death or a contributing factor, maybe combined with some viral infection."

"You mentioned a witness, if I'm not mistaken," Nathan said.

"No, you're not, but there's a problem."

"How's that?" Nathan pursued.

"It's a child. His mother was in the park at Amelia-haven reading while her seven-year-old son was peering through the railings towards the water. He says he saw what happened but it's hard to know exactly where truth and imagination meet; for many youngsters we know it's one and the same thing. We have a special counsellor working with him and his mother and I'll let you know as soon as we have anything concrete."

Taking their leave Nathan allowed Mia to go ahead and, turning to the detective, said, "Is there any chance anyone else was involved?"

The officer, noting Nathan's surreptitious approach, spoke quietly, "Unfortunately there are no cameras near the location where we found him. We have no hard evidence currently of foul play or to think it was anything other than a freak accident involving a man, who was, perhaps, far from well."

Katja came running down the stairs to greet her mother.

"Hey, are you alright?" Mia said entering the hall.

Eva was close on her heels and, as Mia with Katja headed off to the kitchen, she asked, "How did it go, Nathan?"

"As well as you might expect, I suppose. Mia seems easier since talking with the police, and now she's with Katja she's a different woman. Thankfully the detective was quite understanding and spoke highly of Martin."

Mia interrupted as she came back in. "I really must thank you Eva for looking after Katja. She's so full of your time together, it's a blessing, and Nathan, it was very kind of you to go with me."

"That was the very least I could do."

"No, it means a lot." She went on, "To be honest I wasn't sure who else I could turn to."

"Is there anything else you need me to do?" he said.

Mia looked at him, and he could see she was reluctant to say.

"Please let me help," he encouraged.

"Find out what happened to Martin for me," she pleaded.

Nathan left the two women chatting and took himself away to Martin's office. Immediately it was evident that the police had taken his computer. Filing cabinets overflowed with papers, documents were arranged in orderly piles on the floor and folders, clearly marked with headings, were propped against the wall. He took a deep breath: where to start?

Nathan returned to the living room twenty minutes later with a stack of files and correspondence in his hands.

"I'd like to take these away with me, if that's okay? I'll return them, I promise, but I need more time to go through them. Do these numbers in Martin's notebook mean anything to you, Mia?"

She peered over his shoulder, "No, I don't think so. I feel as if I've fallen into the unknown, unsure and uncertain of everything about what he was up to." Mia again appealed to Nathan, "The truth was everything to Martin. Please find out what happened."

Then, perhaps out of a feeling of loss, she hugged him.

On Eva and Nathan's return to the hotel a message awaited him. A woman had phoned only a few minutes earlier and wanted him to call her back. The receptionist was sure the code was an Icelandic number and said the woman made it sound as if it was urgent. Using the reception telephone Nathan dialled the TV Station in Reykjavik.

"Kirstin, it's Nathan."

"Hi, thanks for calling back. Did I have a job tracking you down!"

Nathan was curious. "How did you?"

"I remembered you mentioned a close friend called Eva in the orchestra and, using a contact on their management team, I found out she was on leave. I'm afraid I lied and said I needed to speak with her about a mutual friend who was seriously ill. When they explained she was on vacation in Copenhagen I guessed she was with you."

"Quite the detective," Nathan congratulated her, "but why the charade? Not that it's not good to talk to you," he said, masking his impatience.

"Word's just come over the wire that the reporter you were asking about, Martin Poulson, is dead. I assume the reason you went to Copenhagen was to meet him. Were you with him when he died?"

"No, I wasn't, but I had seen him three days before. We'd been working together for the past weeks on this Danish and American scandal."

He thought Kirstin's long silence was totally out of character.

In a deliberately slow and clear voice she finally said, "Have you looked on the internet?"

"No."

"Well, you should."

"At what?"

"Just type in 'Martin Poulson'."

"And?"

"And you'll see it's alive with theories of why, and how, he was murdered. Conspiracy theories about poisoning."

"Who would believe that?" he said.

"Look," she said, "and you will see many do. A whistle blower in a law firm has divulged that Poulson was about to hand over confidential documents relating to the case. That in itself would seem reason enough for his life to be in jeopardy." The lull in conversation heralded her question, "Are you still there, Nathan?"

He was totally staggered by what she was telling him. "Yes."

"You need to look out for yourself, Nathan. Be careful who you talk to and what you say. As much as the media can be a forceful ally, so it can be a powerful enemy."

Kirstin concluded the conversation by reminding him she was only at the end of the phone if there was anything she could do.

"Is everything alright?" Eva said, knowing it wasn't.

"Yes. What have you been doing?" he asked.

"To tell you the truth, I've been thinking about Katja and how what's happened over the past few days has turned that young life upside down."

"I think she'll get through it," Nathan said, his mind still occupied with what he had heard only moments earlier.

"Both her and Mia," Eva added.

"Yes, her and Mia," Nathan said, noticing the sadness in Eva's face.

"Will the cover-ups ever end?" she asked.

* * * *

Somehow Nathan managed to sleep soundly late into the morning. The opening of the bedroom door disturbed him from his sleep.

"Morning," Eva said, and tossed a newspaper onto the bed beside him.

Nathan yawned. She looked intently at him, "What did you say to that newspaper guy?"

"Why?" he asked, shuffling the pages of the broadsheet. She folded the paper revealing the article. Nathan noticed the headline, *'Reporter's death may be an attempted cover-up.'* He read on, *'A close friend of Martin Poulson has claimed his recent death may not have been an accident.'* Nathan sat up. He hadn't realised his suspicions would appear in print and presented in such a forthright manner. *'There are those that believe Mr Poulson was silenced to avoid further public humiliation and risk of historic legal action against figures in public office.'* Nathan looked again to the headline, below which was the reporter's name, Jurgen Norgaard. The article continued in the same vein. *'Following my enquiries I can confirm that only months before his death Mr Poulson had taken out a life policy. We have been advised that prior to the commencement of the cover he underwent an extensive medical examination and that he would have had to be regarded as in A1 health to be offered such cover, as the policy was without any conditions or exclusions. Official sources have informed our staff reporter that Mr Poulson's insurer has requested full details of the cause of death from the authorities. Dependant on the pathologist's findings, the insurance company may request they be allowed to carry out a toxicological examination of the deceased. Speculation runs high surrounding Mr Poulson's death and it would seem this story has a long way yet to run.'*

Nathan opened his laptop and, accessing the internet, typed in Martin's name in the search box.

"Look at this," he said to Eva.

"Aren't you getting up?"

"Yes, but take a look, I've just searched for Martin."

They both looked on astonished: 1,543 results. As he moved down the pages, time and again the entries referred to foul play, cover-ups, poisonings and endless theories about why he had died. There were photos of him, and Nathan recognised one of the family.

"Who's Professor Sólveig Brandt?" Eva asked, pointing to the television which she'd just switched on.

The screen showed a woman talking. Brandt and Poulson's names were repeated in the rolling caption bar below the picture.

"Take it off mute," Nathan said.

'.....and during their press conference the police stated it will be critical to establish Mr Poulson's precise movements prior to his death and the details of his final meal. The University of Copenhagen's Professor Sólveig Brandt, an eminent plant expert at the Botanical Gardens in Copenhagen, has been asked to examine the body. She stated she would conduct a thorough investigation to eliminate the possibility of poisoning and, should it be a case of poisoning then tell-tale traces of substances will be present, not only in the body fluids but also in the organs and tissues of the victim as well as the nervous and respiratory systems. Professor Brandt had stated it was vital a rigorous investigation be carried out as some poisonous plants such as Gelsemium are exceedingly hard to trace in the body, adding, however, that a range of specialist techniques are available to help discover such toxins, including Microcrystalline Testing and Spectrometry. She went on to say that it is imperative such tests are undertaken immediately to avoid any loss of critical evidence.'

Nathan keyed in Gelsemium on the laptop and learned it was 'a highly toxic compound related to strychnine, causing paralysis of the spinal cord, leading to almost complete loss of muscular power and asphyxia'.

Forgoing breakfast Nathan started to pore through the pile of papers he had retrieved from Martin's office at home. As he studied Martin's journal he understood more about the man himself and the impenetrable bureaucracy he had faced. During one of their meetings Martin had told Nathan that he hid the more sensitive and controversial papers in one of his shoe boxes in the wardrobe. *"If you want to hide your secrets ensure they are in plain sight,"* Martin had advocated, and obviously it had worked. The police had completely overlooked them and now Nathan was able to delve into the documents and discover something of the political intrigue that had so consumed Martin in his final days. He began to appreciate why he had found it necessary to keep so much detail from Mia, to protect her and Katja.

Totally engrossed in examining the papers, Nathan failed to notice Eva peering over his shoulder,

"What's that written on that file?"

Nathan sat up with a start, "I didn't hear you come in."

"Sorry, but what's that file called?" She could see for herself but couldn't believe it.

"It's the name Martin gave to the Thule case – 'Ellinore'. I believe it means 'compassion', why?"

"Oh, no reason, only I think I've seen it somewhere before," Eva uttered, smiling to herself.

THE *TODAY* NEWSPAPER OFFICES – COPENHAGEN

CHAPTER FORTY-SEVEN

"So run past me what we know so far," Gudrun addressed Jurgen Norgaard. "What are the authorities saying? It's been over a week now, we must know something."

"Not a great deal," he said. "In cases which involve a sudden unexpected death, the first step is to conduct an independent autopsy, and as soon as we get our hands on the report we'll call one of our friendly forensic pathologists and ask for a lay version; something we can use to go to print. But . . ." he stalled.

"But what?" Gudrun probed.

"Well, in Poulson's case the preliminary determination is 'pending'."

"Remind me, Norgaard, what precisely does that mean?" Gudrun said.

"Basically, the pathologist has examined Poulson's body but is unable to determine the precise cause of death."

"Should we be concerned by that?" a frustrated Gudrun remarked. "We need the story to run, not only for our readers but to get to the truth. We owe it to Martin's family," she added ruefully. "Where do we go from here?"

"There will be further tests carried out, reviews of the police reports and Poulson's medical records. They will take account of any witness reports, any expert opinions and then, potentially, we could start to move further away from the truth as political and bureaucratic pressure is brought to bear."

"And I think we know where that's going to take us," Gudrun said dismissively.

"How long?" the chief asked Gudrun.

"We don't know. Norgaard says it could be weeks rather than days."

"So tell me our options. How are we going to keep this one running? What about the widow?"

"I really don't know. I've spoken with her and while she's determined to see the truth out she doesn't want to be seen to be directly involved, and I think I can understand that," said Gudrun sympathetically. "Our only hope is this Professor Trent fellow. He worked closely with Poulson, he has gained Mia Poulson's confidence and, it would seem, is intent on seeing this through to the end. What do you think?"

"I don't," the chief said, "I just suffer the consequences, I pay you to think. But it would appear we have little alternative."

"What can I offer him?" Gudrun asked.

"Whatever it takes," the chief announced after barely a moment of consideration. "This story has caught the people's imaginations; we need him. You've got carte blanche on this one, Gudrun. Check and double check every detail: the last thing we need is accusations of fabricating or manipulating the facts to sell papers." He paused, then, in a manner she couldn't fail but understand, said, "I hold you personally responsible, is that clear?"

Gudrun didn't need to, but she nevertheless nodded and left his office.

* * * *

"Professor Trent, this is Gudrun Lund. I'm with the *Today* newspaper here in Copenhagen." She was going to explain that she was the news editor but Nathan didn't give her the opportunity.

"You're the . . . You turned out that piece about me stating Martin's death may not have been an accident."

Gudrun hadn't anticipated Nathan's aggression: she'd made a mistake. "We never revealed you as the source of that comment," she countered. "My reporter, Jurgen Norgaard, would have only repeated you verbatim; is that not what you said?" She waited what she considered long enough to make her point. "We'd like to chat to you about the whole Thule affair."

"So you can twist my words in the name of honest journalism?"

"No," she fired back. "We're after the whole picture, the truth that Martin Poulson fought so hard to reveal. Won't you at least meet with us?"

CHAPTER FORTY-EIGHT

The weather had turned. What had started as a passable summer's day was now anything but. The land and sky had melted into one offering the same pale hue. There was no wind to stir the human spirit. For Nathan, this would be one of the darkest days of his life.

Walking on the soft turf between the orderly rows of gravestones, they drew near to where a modest gathering of mourners was assembling for the private burial. The grave diggers had opened the ground and Nathan was aware of the smell of damp earth. Mia sat on a chair at the graveside, dressed all in black, a large-brimmed hat shading her forlorn face. Beside her stood Katja, confused and lost, clasping her mother's hand, her only assurance.

When the priest finished speaking, the coffin was gradually lowered, the ground swallowing it up. Nathan knew there was nobody in the coffin but that didn't stop his soul from quivering as Mia and Katja each dropped a garland into the pit. The silence was all-consuming, beyond anything Nathan had experienced for a very long while.

"None of us know when we will die," Nathan uttered to Eva. Tears rolled down her cheeks.

As the close friends and colleagues of Martin spoke to Mia before departing, Nathan overheard many of their words of comfort.

"At yesterday's meeting of Danmark's Radio News Team, I was asked to tell you of their great sadness on hearing about Martin and offer our sincere condolences. Should there be anything we can do please speak with me," some smartly-dressed executive shared, passing Mia a card.

Another spoke of the sudden shock and how they had held a minute's silence out of respect for Martin.

An elderly couple approached Nathan. "We were so moved by the priest's words," the woman confessed. "Time after time Martin would come into our home, on our screen, to share the latest news from somewhere."

An old boy addressed Eva and Nathan directly. "You knew him well?" Then, waiting only for Nathan's nod, he said, "There's rarely been a month over the last seven years when he and I haven't spoken over the phone. He always made time to ask after my health. In many ways he was like the brother I didn't have," he said with tears in his voice.

Mia, no longer occupied trying to be pleasant and grateful towards the guests, caught Nathan's eye. As Nathan and Eva walked across to greet her, a lone press photographer continued to surreptitiously record the event.

"Thank you both for coming."

Katja wriggled on Mia's arm. Eva suggested she take the young one for a stroll around the gardens and a relieved Mia accepted.

"He had a great passion for others, you know. He always tried to find the best in everybody," Mia said.

"I know," Nathan comforted her.

"Martin had a very close relationship with his father," Mia revealed, "and the shock of his death last year continued to haunt him, he never got over it." She cast her eyes on Nathan, "Do you know, it's strange but I feel as though he's still here. I think that's how he'd want me to feel." She stared up into the empty sky. "He was my best friend and the love of my life, I'll miss him so terribly."

"We seldom get what we expect and are rarely prepared for what we do get," Nathan shared, fully understanding her loss.

A confounded look filled her face. "I will need to be strong for the sake of Katja." She breathed in deeply. "What will you do now, Nathan?"

He looked at her, "Just because the world isn't perfect doesn't mean we should stop trying to change it. Martin didn't."

Returning with a tired-looking Katja, Eva said, "I think, Mia, they are waiting with your car," and pointed back towards the access road.

Mia thanked them both and made them promise to keep in touch. Katja waved to Eva as the two lonely figures walked along the tree-lined avenue towards a black chauffeur-driven limousine.

"Would I be right in believing I am addressing Professor Trent?"

"Yes," Nathan said, instantly turning to face the stranger. "And you are?"

"I am unimportant," the heavy-set, silver-haired man in a black raincoat replied. "And your young lady?" The man gave Eva a half smile.

"My friend from Iceland."

"Ah yes," he said, "and together we have buried my friend."

From behind his spectacles he cast his eyes down to where two men were busy shovelling earth on top of the coffin. Seemingly oblivious to the confusion he had created in Nathan, the stranger carried on, lowering his voice, "Poulson was lucky, in a way."

"Lucky?" Eva broke in.

"Yes, my dear, they think Poulson didn't suffer any pain."

Nathan couldn't help wonder how this stranger knew him and noticed that this *friend* of Martin referred to him as Poulson. "Have we met?" Nathan asked.

"Oh no, dear boy, but Poulson asked me to keep an eye out for you and see you were alright. Poulson was one of a kind, an original, someone who never ran with the pack; do you understand my meaning?"

"I think so," Nathan said, sensing that the stranger probably realised his presence was making them uneasy.

The stranger dropped his voice so only Nathan could hear, "Poulson died on Wednesday morning but by noon the *Today* newspaper online edition had already published the entire history of this relatively unknown man, complete with photographs of him and his family, an intimate biography, and a transcript of the earlier television debate. Don't you think that sounds odd within a matter of a few hours of discovering the body? Almost as if they had suspected or anticipated his death. And doesn't it occur to you as strange that such a healthy man should suddenly die so young with no real medical explanation?"

"I've only just realised how much the establishment felt threatened by Martin," Nathan said.

The stranger spoke, "Maybe it began with them thinking he would give up, just go away, but it didn't take long before they realised how wrong they were. I can only imagine how the shock-waves resounded around The Castle. Many are of the opinion that the police have been totally incompetent in tracking down the official Poulson met with."

The man's gruff, almost inaudible voice paused as he cast a glance to beyond the graves to where a man stood beneath a tree. Nathan looked hard and was taken aback when he realised it was the detective who had interviewed him about Martin's death.

"Poulson spent much of his life seeking the truth, fighting for the victims and, in the end, perhaps, he was the victim. He told me he felt scared for the first time, really scared."

"You never told me your name," Nathan put to the stranger.

"No, I didn't," and reaching into his inside coat pocket he took out a packet. Flicking a lighter, the end of a cigarette glimmered, then glowed and a cone of exhaled smoke stretched upward before being whisked away by a light breeze. "You don't know of the meeting I refer to Professor Trent, do you? No, of course not, but now is not the time to talk of it. Ring me," he said and gave him a scrap of paper on which was scrawled a telephone number. "We are each half-open doors, and until entered what lies on the other side remains a secret."

Nathan had always thought there was something wrong about the way Martin had died. Something that, up to now, the police hadn't told them.

With the parting of the stranger, Eva said, "Are you okay? Some say I have an overactive imagination, but was that weird or what?"

An hour or so later, when Nathan came off the phone, Eva asked, "What did he have to say?" Nathan could detect the concern in her voice and anxiety was evident in her face.

"Immediately before his death Martin had delivered a tranche of documents to officials of the Danish Court and Ministry of Justice. The evidence he provided included secret American documents and correspondence leaked to him from within Denmark's Ministry of Defence and the Danish Ministry of the Environment and Energy. It would seem this action had put him in jeopardy.

"The stranger believes that the subsequent disappearance of the lawyer, who had brokered Martin's meeting with the justice officials, was one coincidence too many. He was adamant that the man needed to be found. It seems that the morning following the believed meeting with the lawyer, Martin complained to Mia of feeling unwell with stomach pains, diarrhoea and a persistent headache."

"But Mia never said?" Eva shared, trying to take it all in.

"No, not exactly, she wouldn't, not to us, but seemingly, it was in her statement to the police. They have been wanting to find the so-called lawyer to establish exactly what happened, and if the meeting did in fact take place. The stranger explained that he telephoned Martin that evening after the meeting and was concerned; Martin sounded disturbed and worried but wouldn't discuss it. He said he didn't want to drag the man into the mess. That was the last time he spoke to Martin."

"So, is he convinced that Martin's death is suspicious?" a stunned Eva challenged.

"Yes," Nathan confirmed, "and he completely rejects the authorities' explanation that Martin died of sudden adult death syndrome, whatever that is. He wants me to meet him."

"What?" Eva exclaimed in disbelief.

"He said he won't give up trying to find out what really happened to Poulson, no matter what it takes. If I am willing to talk and share what I know, he believes that might help him get nearer the truth."

"And are you? You don't really know the fellow. As you say, he's a stranger," a wide-eyed Eva said.

"But I vowed to complete Martin's work. That's exactly what Martin would have done; he would have tried everything to get to the truth."

CHAPTER FORTY-NINE

In the brief time Eva had known Nathan her life had dramatically changed. Before she had envisaged life would remain simple and uncomplicated; how wrong she had been. And here she was, sitting in some Copenhagen hotel room worrying about a man she had known only some eighteen months. A man she was very much in love with and who had, before breakfast, gone out to meet a perfect stranger.

The ring of the room's telephone disturbed her train of thought; she answered.

"It's reception here, could I speak to Professor Trent please?"

"No, I'm afraid he's not here," Eva said.

She over-heard the receptionist pass the message on.

"Could you pop down to reception, only there are two men here who wish to speak to him."

Eva thought little of it and, picking up the room key, went down the two flights of stairs to see what they wanted.

A sharp-featured man with half-moon glasses spoke first with an American drawl. "Mrs Trent?"

"No, afraid not," Eva replied, "just a friend." She wasn't sure how else to describe herself. "And you are?"

"Hoping to speak with him," the same man said.

"We're representatives from the American Embassy here in Copenhagen," the other enlightened her.

"Do you know when you'll expect him?" the bespectacled guy asked with an air of indifference.

"No, not really," Eva said. "Can I give him a message?"

They looked at one another. "Sure," he took his glasses off and rubbed his eyes. "We understand he collected some files from a Mr Poulson's house and we need to clarify some details with him."

The other added, "Nothing to worry about." But she couldn't help thinking it was as they handed her a business card.

"I'll tell him," Eva said.

She watched them step out onto the pavement and into the rain, share a few words then walk off purposefully in opposite directions.

"Where's Cafe Bjørgs?" Eva enquired.

The young receptionist opened a map on the counter top and, taking a pencil, highlighted its location, "Straight up the road we are on, Vester Voldgade, on the right side."

Eva knew where Nathan had gone as it was on the note he had left her, but little else.

Returning to their room to collect her coat she was taken aback by a weird noise as she entered, a beating or flapping sound. Between the drapes and a half-open window a small, brown bird, perhaps a sparrow, was frantically trying to escape. It could see the open sky and was desperately hitting the glass, pounding its fragile frame again and again against the glass pane unable to see the opening in the window. Eva lifted the stay, threw open the window wide and the frightened bird flew off into the distance. A bad omen, she thought, then dismissed the idea as being ridiculous.

Pausing in the lobby to put on her coat, the receptionist called to her, "It's only five or so minutes' walk, ten at the most. They say the rain could get heavier," and smiled before returning to her desk.

Setting out to meet Nathan her mind began to play tricks on her. When this was all over, maybe then she would get back the man she knew and loved. After all, love didn't have to be only for the young, she consoled herself. She wouldn't even mind living in London if that's what he wanted; she could think of no one else she would rather spend the rest of her life with. Nathan had found it so very hard to trust anyone again, even himself, yet she was certain he could learn to trust her. Thinking back on what had gone between them she realised how dreadful she had been, not supporting him when he needed her alongside him, much in the same way as she had treated Magnus. Her old father had always said she didn't know when to stop.

A nervousness overcame her and she shivered. Eva looked up to the rain-laden heavens and was surprised how quickly the sky had taken on such a menacing nature.

Nearing the cafe she could see folk who had been sitting outside, beneath its awning, gathering their things and taking refuge inside. She wasn't certain, but thought Nathan and the stranger were still outside the cafe at a small table near the entrance. A blinding flash of light startled her. The shower had become a deluge and was quickly turning the pavement into a flowing river. A rumble of thunder filled the air. Eva turned up her coat collar and, pulling a scarf from its pocket, draped it over her head. She was now almost running to get to shelter and Nathan.

Through the downpour Eva made out a lonely cyclist hurtling around the corner beyond the cafe, battling to keep the bike upright on the slippery road. She saw him rise from the saddle as he tried to maintain his balance. The handlebars twisted and the cycle frame slid effortlessly from under him. Her pulse quickened. She stood completely still, taking in the scene and shivered. As a lone figure in a rain cape rushed over to help, images flooded Eva's mind: yellow pools of blinding light, a dark figure in a rain cape and hat crouched over a crumpled body, swirling weird patterns of rain and blood disappearing into the ground. It appeared to her as if time had been re-wound. She felt sick and her head was swimming. A solitary voice spoke to her. Nathan grabbed hold of her.

"Are you alright?"

"What?" a confused Eva uttered.

"Were you looking for me?" Nathan persisted, registering her unexpected presence.

"Yes," she said, slowly coming to her senses.

"Well, you've found me."

"You saw him?" a troubled Eva asked.

"Yes." He paused. "What made you come looking for me?"

"Two Americans came to the hotel asking for you, something about documents, Martin's papers that you took."

Nathan didn't appear totally surprised at the news. He stood in thought for a moment before replying, "I realise now this was never a game and from all that I've seen and heard I can appreciate what Martin was up against. The odds were never in his favour."

"Why, what did the man say?"

Nathan didn't hold back. "He said Pandora's Box has now been opened and questions are being asked about me by officials in The Castle. It seems they have in their minds that I could go public with Martin's papers and name individuals. They even fear I might write a book. He told me the Americans were beginning to show an unhealthy interest in me, regarding me as secretive and a threat. They're convinced I've got his computer and am able to access all his secure files." Nathan paused as if assimilating what he had learnt. He looked at Eva, "Magnus was right about those dangerous days of the Cold War."

"And I was so wrong," she said. "I doubted him and, although I've known him all my life, I began to think I had no idea who he was." Her eyes filled with tears.

CHAPTER FIFTY

"What do you intend to do now?" Eva asked.

"I'm really not sure," Nathan replied. "I'm too far in and there are too many people relying on me for me not to see it through; but where I go from here . . . ?" And he shrugged.

The parting words that the stranger had shared were playing on Nathan's mind, unsettling him.

"I can't let so many down: Helga, Qigiq and Mia, as well as all the others. And then there's your father and Martin, I owe it to them both. Did I tell you I spoke with Martin's old editor at DR, Brigitte? She called me."

"No, so what did she say?"

"She was still greatly shocked by Martin's death, that much was clear at the cemetery, but she sounded different – lost, angry." Eva's look of surprise prompted him. "But not with me. She'd been pulled off the Thule story to cover developments with the US and Russian nuclear arms agreement, and it seems there are rumours of a North Korean nuclear arms programme. She's seriously concerned how long DR will run with the Thule affair. She couldn't stop apologising to me, explaining that this decision was none of her making and how she felt powerless to go against it." He sighed deeply. "For the first time I feel out on a limb. To tell you the truth, I don't know if I can do this."

Eva reached out to him, squeezed his hand and in a calm, confident voice said slowly, "I know you can."

"They want me to work with them to see this thing through."

"Who?" Eva exclaimed. "You said DR are holding back on it."

"The press," he said.

She looked puzzled.

"The *Today* newspaper. The ones who first broke the news of Martin's death." Nathan said.

"The ones who misquoted you . . .?"

But Nathan stopped her. "They didn't attribute it to me, and even if they had it wouldn't have been misquoted. They want to meet and discuss things; to explore the possibilities of collaborating."

"And what do you want?"

"I can't let all that Martin achieved come to nothing just because he's dead," Nathan asserted.

An uncomfortable feeling lingered between them over his involvement with the paper.

"I phoned Mia to see how she was doing," Eva admitted.

"And?" Nathan said.

"And she wants me to call over. She's greatly concerned for Katja who's understandably finding it hard to come to terms with her father's death."

* * * *

Having entered the newspaper offices, an anxious Nathan was greeted by Gudrun, who chatted enthusiastically throughout their journey up in the lift to the top floor and the editor's office. Acknowledging them both, the PA ushered them in and, as she did, the chief wheeled his chair back from his desk, rose and stepped out to greet Nathan. He took his hand and rested his other on Nathan's shoulder.

"It's good of you to come, Professor Trent."

Nathan was struck by the stuffiness of the office. It felt airless and a veil of gloom engulfed it. The man appeared to Nathan just as a newspaper editor might look.

"Coffee?" the old man announced as a tray was slid onto the desk. "Please make yourself comfortable. As I see it, Professor, we only have one chance to see this thing through. We can speculate on the cause and impact of Martin's death, but one thing is certain: the man who led this fight is no longer here today to take the battle forward. That's why we need you."

"Why me?" Nathan said.

"If you really need to know then I need to tell you, but you already know the answer, don't you?"

Nathan was going to argue with him but what he saw in the old man's eyes told him not to bother.

"Look at what he did and how things have changed, but also consider what is still to be done," the old man said. "I don't want a third party narrative written by some staff reporter. I want a story that no one can ignore, that everyone will believe. I need the inside story, the fundamental truth. We want the reader to think that if something equally hideous happened to them, would this be how such a crime would be handled?"

The proposal was more than Nathan had imagined, and far too much for him to instantly take in. For a while he rested in his confusion undecided how he should respond, but the newspaper boss wasn't having that.

"Wanting something to be true doesn't make it true, that's not enough in itself. Martin can no longer fight for the truth, but you can."

A deathly silence rested upon the room. Gudrun nervously glanced from Nathan to the chief.

"Professor Trent? Professor Trent, did you hear me? Did I make myself clear?" the old man said.

"Forgive me," Nathan spoke up, "I was thinking about what you said."

"And?" the chief ventured.

Nathan couldn't help notice a look of pain etched deep in the face of this newspaper man: a man who, he imagined, was accustomed to getting his way.

"Otherwise what do you imagine will happen to Martin's work?" The old man looked grave, then, changing tack, said, "I met him, you know. Just the once when he was awarded The Cavling Prize for investigative journalism. There was something about him, I could tell he was different, special. How well did you get inside the man, Professor?"

"I had the privilege to work closely with him over the past few months. I guess I got to know something of what motivated him, his ideals and belief in mankind and truth. Before that I had only dabbled in the mystery, playing around the edges, but after meeting Martin that all changed. One couldn't fail to be influenced by his drive, determination and methodical approach: his endless energy and humility."

"And now?" Gudrun said.

Nathan turned to her, "I'm really not sure that I can come up with what you are looking for."

Without a second breath the chief interrupted, "Allow us to be the judge of that. Trust me, Professor, I'll give you my word, we will honour Martin's memory and that of the hundreds he tried to save. What do you say?"

Nathan was again lost in thought.

"May I call you Nathan?"

"Yes, of course."

"Good," the chief said, casting a smile to Gudrun. "Can I ask you what made you take this on in the first place, Nathan?"

Nathan searched for an answer that he considered would sound convincing. He then heard himself say, "I had no choice."

The old man smiled, "This is a story that's still being written. The power of the press is one thing and, speaking plainly, I have no appetite in bringing The Castle down, but that's nothing compared to the power of the government. When our politicians and the Americans attack what we print, ask yourself why. There will be consequences but that's not for you to worry yourself with, that's for me to deal with."

Some unspoken message passed between the old man and Gudrun, following which she said, "I'll run through our initial ideas with Professor Trent anyway, to—"

"Please call me Nathan," interrupted Nathan.

"Yes, Nathan," she corrected, "to see what together we can come up with. Is that okay?"

Nathan agreed.

"Thank you," the old man said taking Nathan's hand.

Opting for the stairs Gudrun confessed to Nathan, "Rarely does he smile."

"Who?" Nathan said.

"The chief, didn't you notice?"

"I took it as the norm."

"No, far from it," she explained, "there's no norm when it comes to him. This way," she said, entering a vast open-plan office.

They weaved between endless rows of desks resting beneath banks of fluorescents which bathed all in their stark white light. Amongst the babble of voices men and women were busy and appeared not to notice them.

"This is me," she said opening an office door. "Make yourself at home. Would you like tea?" and switched on the kettle. "Are you planning on being in Copenhagen for a while?" she asked.

With everything that had happened he hadn't given it much thought. He hadn't even discussed it with Eva.

"I guess at least for another week or so. We've commitments back in Iceland and I've a hospital appointment." A look of concern crossed Gudrun's face. "A routine check-up," he said as an aside.

"Ah," Gudrun acknowledged, whilst retrieving a pile of files from a cabinet. "I hope everything's okay." And without waiting for a reply she said, "Oh, by the way, the stranger that you asked about earlier, the one at the cemetery," she glanced back at him, "he doesn't work on the paper. Any ideas as to who he is, Professor?" She caught his glance, "Sorry, Nathan?"

He shook his head.

CHAPTER FIFTY-ONE

Eva headed across the city, the yellow taxi negotiating the morning rush-hour traffic. As they made their way into the quieter suburbs the car pulled up outside a florist's. Entering the shop Eva was greeted by the sweet perfume emanating from the profusion of colourful blooms and bouquets. What to choose?

The taxi stopped outside Mia's house, and before Eva had got out she could see Katja's face peering from between the curtains of the ground floor bay window.

"It is good to see you," Mia welcomed. "Come on in, I've just put the percolator on."

Katja's excitement was evident, bouncing into the hallway and chanting, "Eva's come Mummy!" and, pointing to the flowers, "Are they for you, Mummy?"

"You go and arrange them in a vase, Mia," Eva said, "and I'll spend some time with Katja."

Mia needed no more encouragement and half an hour later Eva found her in the lounge, dozing in an armchair. Eva's entrance disturbed her.

"It's okay, Katja's reading in her room, I think she's very tired. Give it a few minutes and I wouldn't be surprised if she's gone to bed."

"I'm really grateful, Eva, the last few days haven't been easy. Kat's slept in my bed with me but I've found it hard to settle, conscious of her every move."

Some ten minutes later Mia checked on Kat and found her fast asleep. For the next hour the two women talked over coffee, and as they chatted something Mia shared began to play on Eva's mind.

"People have been so very kind. Rarely does a day go by when I don't get a call from a well-wisher offering condolences or support. In fact, before you arrived this morning a man phoned, I'm pretty sure he's called before. When I heard the telephone I thought maybe it was you. He said he knew my husband and wanted to know if there was anything I needed."

"Who was he?" Eva said.

"He didn't say, even though I asked him, and, what was odd, he continually referred to Martin as Poulson; no one does that!"

"That's strange. You'd think if he'd known him he would have called him Martin."

"I know, that's what I thought," said Mia. "An operator had connected the call. She never said who was calling so before the line disconnected I asked her. She said she didn't know, but all she could tell me was it was someone in the Ministry of the Interior. Surprised, I asked her where she was calling from. The woman worked as an operator on the switchboard of The Castle. How weird is that?"

Eva could tell that the telephone conversation had caught Mia completely off-guard, clearly troubling her. Controlling her voice so as not to betray her concern, Eva told Mia about Nathan's contact with the press, hoping such news would serve as a sufficient distraction, dispelling any lingering worries she might have over the caller. As for Eva, she had already decided that she couldn't leave it there. She needed to know more about this mystery man.

"Kat's still sleeping."

"Then I'll not disturb her," Eva said. "Tell her goodbye from me and, if it's okay, I'll try and call by again in the next few days but I'll telephone first."

"I'd like that," Mia said, a smile filling her face.

Eva thought to herself, I don't suppose you smile much these days. "Will you both be okay?"

"I'm sure Kat will learn to cope over time, but I'm not sure I ever will," Mia said. They kissed and Eva waved before climbing into a waiting taxi.

"Where to, lady?" He had started to pull away before Eva replied.

"The Castle, please."

Crossing the bridge onto Castle Island the taxi driver asked, "Do you want the museum, or perhaps the Royal Stables?"

"No, the parliament buildings," Eva said.

He swung the taxi into the service road and stopped. "It's an impressive building isn't it, Neo-Baroque style I think, late 1920s or thereabouts. They like to think of it as the country's power-house, we all know it as Borgen." He pointed to some steps leading to an imposing entrance. "Reception's through there, I believe." Eva settled the fare, thanked him and made her way into this unknown world.

"It's very unusual for someone to ask to speak with our switchboard operators. Can you tell me what it's about?" the stylishly-dressed, twenty-something receptionist asked.

"Yes," Eva volunteered, "one of them spoke to my friend this morning but we don't know the woman's name." Eva could see this austere guardian was anticipating, no, expecting more. "The operator was interrupted mid-call, you see. It was an important call."

"So why didn't she, your friend, telephone us?" the girl pursued.

"She was going to but she thought it might get complicated, and anyway, I was passing by."

"I see, and your friend's name?"

"Mia Poulson."

"Please wait, I'll see what I can do. There's a seat over there," the girl said as she prodded into thin air.

Minutes later, to the click of high-heeled shoes, a middle-aged woman entered reception. Her hair was fair as was her complexion. "You're the woman about your friend's call?" Eva nodded. "I remember the call well. I recognised your friend's name from the news – is it the same . . .?"

"Yes," Eva replied, to save any difficulty. "Can you remember anything about the caller? I think you said the Interior Ministry."

"At the time," the woman said, "I didn't know who it was. It was only afterwards, after your friend had rung off, that I remembered him: he has a very distinctive voice, you see. From time to time he visits for meetings, but he's no longer based at The Castle. I've worked here since leaving school and that's when he was here; back in the 1970s."

Eva stared at her, patiently waiting.

"Oh," she said, "I'm sure he was in the government then, one of the ministerial officials I think."

"And now?" Eva asked.

"I believe he sits on various committees, but I'm not sure what." And as an afterthought, she added, "I suppose he might still be in the building."

Thanking the woman, Eva asked, "Can you tell me the man's name and where exactly the Ministry of the Interior offices are located?"

The woman pointed out the offices on a wall plan and wished Eva the best of luck.

"What sort of day have you had?" Eva asked Nathan.

He explained about his meeting at the *Today* newspaper. How, initially, he had been reticent to get involved, but having spent an hour or two with their news editor, together they were able to work up the bones of a feature piece to go in the Saturday edition.

"There were many facts they were not aware of and information that I only discovered having gone through Martin's papers. I was impressed with Gudrun's integrity as we set about the writing the article."

"Isn't there a bit of a risk in getting involved?"

"No, I don't think so. They've a political writer on board and are conscious it's a dangerous story which they can't afford to get wrong. The chief editor seems to be prepared to go all the way with it; well, as long as it doesn't put their publication licence in jeopardy. To be honest, I've heard so many lies, the sooner I can help put a stop to that the better." Nathan appeared to be gathering his thoughts, "But enough of me, what about you and how was Mia?"

"I really don't know. She seems to be putting up a brave face but there again . . . There's no question she's worried about Katja."

"I'm sure she was pleased to see you though?" Nathan said.

"Yes. She seemed grateful to have some company. We had a good time together, and then I visited The Castle."

Eva couldn't fail to notice Nathan's surprise at the news.

"Why?" he said.

It only took a few minutes to explain about Mia's mystery caller and the outcome of her visit.

"And what was his name?" he said.

"The woman on the switchboard couldn't remember much. . . Gunnar something, but realised that wasn't very helpful as Gunnar was such a common name. She could picture his face but not recall his full name."

"So a wasted journey," Nathan surmised.

"No, not exactly." Eva was delighted to see his growing curiosity.

"While the woman's directions seemed straight-forward at the time, I wasn't exactly certain where the offices were, nor did I realise how many corridors and rooms there were."

"So, did you eventually find him?"

"No, I think he found me."

Nathan looked puzzled.

"While searching along one of the second-floor corridors someone brushed passed me, intently studying his papers as he walked. I thought maybe he could help me with directions but he didn't notice me, then he stopped, turned and apologised profusely. And as I cast my eyes upon the heavy-set, silver-haired man I couldn't help but think I'd seen him somewhere before. Suddenly it struck me, I had: he had been the one in the graveyard, the stranger at Martin's funeral, the man you met in the cafe, and a small voice told me this was the stranger who had telephoned Mia. This was the man who referred to Martin as Poulson."

Nathan was speechless.

"Do you understand?" she said. "He worked in The Castle, he was in the government back then."

Nathan still didn't answer.

"What is it you don't follow? What's wrong with you?" Eva implored.

"Perhaps I shouldn't tell you this, I don't want you to worry, but he phoned me today and wants me to meet with him on Sunday."

CHAPTER FIFTY-TWO

"I'm grateful, Professor Trent, you were able to meet with me," greeted the stranger, waiting by the bronze lions that guarded the entrance to Rosenborg Castle.

Nathan had heeded Eva's pleading that he arrange to meet in a public place, her other wish being that he be careful. As the two men strolled through the Royal Gardens talking, Nathan quickly sensed this was to be no casual encounter.

"You need to listen carefully to what I am about to say, it's important," the stranger insisted, his voice sounding edgy. "If you don't listen closely you may well miss something: something that I believe is vital you should know," and he gave a conspiratorial smile. "The findings regarding Poulson's death will be announced as 'inconclusive' – a wholly unsatisfactory outcome but one, nevertheless, the authorities have finalised on." Nathan stopped and, looking at the stranger, was about to speak. "Don't ask me how I know," the stranger said, "let it be enough that I just do."

"Who are you?" Nathan asked. "Why are you telling me this?"

"When you first meet a man you judge him by his appearance. When you leave him you judge him by his heart. That's why I'm telling you, Professor Trent." The stranger walked on, his every step grinding the loose gravel under-foot. "Newspapers are there to sell copies, sometimes at whatever cost, but your story in yesterday's *Today* newspaper was about the truth of what happened and is still happening. Poulson was a guardian of the truth. He had a special gift – the gift of hope that the truth would finally win through. Forgive me, Professor Trent, but that is now down to you: you must carry on exposing the deceit and lies. But do not delude yourself, you have embarked on a dangerous journey. To many it may seem that you are hell-bent on sabotaging our government."

The stranger's silence allowed Nathan's confused mind to make some sense of what he had been told.

"Many now feel trapped by the lies that were told back then and want to be free of them. They will not take kindly to you resurrecting the whole sordid mess."

"Was I naive to think that our leaders, our politicians, were basically good and honest, or was I stupid?" Nathan said.

"That is for you to decide," the stranger asserted. "Government is riddled with conspiracy theories, so much so it's hard to see where truth ends and lies begin. Truth comes at a price, but its absence threatens our democracy and everything that many of us believe in and stand for." The stranger looked Nathan in the eye. "I believe it's best you return to Iceland for your own safety, but you can still stay involved. The fire Poulson lit is such a blaze now, it's too big to be put out but will need fuelling and you can do that from afar."

"What of you?" Nathan asked. "What was your part?"

The stranger said nothing.

"Are you not involved in the government?"

The stranger cast his face to the ground and purposefully strode on. "So she did recognise me, your young lady?"

"Eva thought she saw you at The Castle and wondered if it was you who telephoned Martin's wife?"

"Indeed. Where does a guilty politician hide, hoping not to be recognised? Amongst the others, in The Castle. It would have been so much easier if I had never been involved in the affair. I never wanted to be wrapped up in the deadly game, in all the deceit, but clearly not badly enough. The last years have been hell trying to live with this knowledge, and that's why I spoke with Poulson, taking him into my confidence, trying to broker a meeting between him and the Justice Department." Nathan noticed beads of perspiration glistening like jewels on the stranger's brow. "However, Poulson found it hard to believe anything would change." He hesitated before speaking, "I have failed and not served my country as I should have."

"So why now?" Nathan said.

"I have been in the darkness for too long, I need to come out into the light."

Nathan looked upon this tormented and lonely man.

The stranger took Nathan's hand. "Don't judge me, my friend, no one can – I am beyond judgement now. Follow the truth, the declassified documents and the hearings. I will try and send you what I can, but I can't promise."

With that he gave a half smile and was gone, heading deeper into the gardens alone.

Nathan had failed to notice earlier the children playing or the dog walkers taking their weekend constitutional. Nor had he appreciated the brilliance of the morning sun that now warmed and offered him some degree of reassurance.

CHAPTER FIFTY-THREE

Eva was concerned. She paced the hotel room repeatedly, returning to the window hoping to be able to catch a glimpse of Nathan. He had been gone several hours, longer than she thought was necessary. The misgivings she had about his meeting with the stranger she prayed were ill founded. They knew so little about the man, only that he, in some way, had been involved. She tried to convince herself that he was nothing more than a harmless enigma.

Again she went to the window. In the street below the cars and pedestrians went about their Sunday afternoon journeys; no pattern, no rhythm, each to their own. Above, the pale-coloured sky offered not even the merest hint of comfort. It looked cold out there, she thought.

On hearing the door open she turned, and much to her relief Nathan entered. He looked tired and, she considered, somewhat lost.

"You're back, I'm so relieved," she said, embracing him. As she did she could see his expression change, a warm smile filled his face. "I was so worried, are you alright? What happened?"

He edged away from her. "I'll tell you but I need a cup of tea first."

Eva wondered if this was what it must be like to be married, always wanting to hold and protect someone. Sitting beside him, she resisted her natural inquisitiveness and said nothing while they drank their tea.

"It's not like you," Nathan said.

"What isn't?" she said, looking disturbed.

"Not to want to shower me with questions."

"Don't worry," Eva replied, "I will. And if you like, now!"

Nathan went to great lengths to repeat the stranger's words and share his own thoughts: there was no need for Eva to prompt him, he was intent on explaining everything.

"The man made one thing very clear. He believes we should leave Denmark. After my article in yesterday's paper he's certain that exposing publicly for the first time much of the political background, as I did, will convince the authorities and, not least, the Americans, that I hold some of Martin's secret files. Files they want and information they wish suppressed." Nathan put his arm around Eva, "There's nothing to keep us here now. I can continue the fight from anywhere, and anyway the orchestra must be wondering what's happened to their star violinist."

Eva had expected this and was prepared. "Yes," and consumed by a great longing said, "and what about us? What does our future hold? We have spent nearly all our time together and care for each other, don't we?" A mischievous grin passed across Nathan's face. "Well, don't we?" she insisted. "And we share the same bed. Why are you laughing at me?"

"I'm not, honestly."

"But . . ?" she began.

"Hold on," he said. "I intended to give you this earlier but when I went out you were still asleep." He handed her a small, black velvet covered box. Eva hadn't expected that, and the wind had been taken out of her sails. A gift, a peace offering, earrings, she thought, but opening the box she was speechless.

"It's a ring."

"Yes, I know, I bought it," Nathan said smugly.

"It looks like an . . ."

"An engagement ring," he said. "Is it really such a surprise?"

"Yes, it bloody well is," Eva exclaimed, her amazement getting the better of her.

"I love you, you know," he said. "You must believe that, even though at times my insensitivity may mean I have a strange way of showing my feelings towards you. For a long while I was lost, and that couldn't have been easy for you to deal with. I've found it difficult to change but you have patiently waited. The more time we have spent together, the more I realise just how much I love you. It's weird, but I don't feel lost anymore. The times when you may have thought I was pulling away from you, I wasn't: I was being pulled to something else. Foolishly I never appreciated how much Thule would take over my life. I never wanted to hurt you although I fear at times I did."

Eva's eyes sparkled with pleasure. "You tell yourself what you want to hear, you know, time after time, daring to believe that one day it will be true, but there is always that doubt that nags away. There are few things in life I believe are worth fighting for, and, Nathan, you are one of them."

"So," Nathan said, "do you accept my offer? I should make it clear there is one condition."

"And what's that?" Eva said, her head still reeling.

"That even when we have our disagreements you won't try to kill me again!"

"I think I can manage that. It may not be easy but I'll give it a try," she teased. "I accept, of course I accept," and she flung her arms around him. They kissed. "When?" she said excitedly.

"When what?"

"When will we marry?"

"Hold on, let's get back to Iceland, then we can make the arrangements."

Content with the suggestion, Eva then remembered Mia's call earlier that morning.

"While you were out Mia rang for you. She's alright but wants you to call her back. It's urgent, so I said you'd call her today."

"Do you know what it's about?" Nathan asked.

"Yes, but I think it's best she tells you."

"Is everything okay?"

"Just call her."

Nathan's mood had changed, Eva's news had seen to that. She hadn't intended it to be that way, it just happened. Sliding the ring onto her finger Eva proposed she'd go downstairs to the bar and get a bottle of wine to celebrate, leaving Nathan dialling Mia's number.

Over a glass of wine Nathan shared his conversation with Mia. Much of this Eva already knew but she wasn't about to interrupt him.

"Mia's been invited to attend a Press Association Ceremony here in Copenhagen next week to receive an award they wish to make in recognition of Martin's work. She realises it's short notice but needs us to accompany her. I told her we were intending to head back to Iceland, at least for a time, while things calm down, but she was having none of it. She said it was vital we go and couldn't we delay our return a few days? I honestly didn't think I could let her down, it's obviously important to her. I hope you understand?"

"That's absolutely fine," Eva said, "I would have done the same under the circumstances."

Unlike Nathan, she rested in the knowledge of why Mia was so insistent but decided it was best not to tell him.

* * * *

The Admiral Hotel, situated on the waterfront, had, once again, opened its doors to the Danish Press Association's Annual Award Ceremony. Eva and Nathan entered its impressive lobby which was alive with activity. Signage directed them towards the Function Hall where, joining a short queue, a young man was checking invitations and directing guests to their seats.

"Professor Trent and Eva Hannes," he referred to his list. "Welcome. We are pleased you could join us. I see you are the guests of Mia Poulson." Pointing them to the front of the room, he explained, "You will find your reserved seats on one of the front row tables to the side of the hall. I hope you enjoy the evening."

Eva could see Nathan was taken aback, not only by the welcome but also that they were sitting at the very front. It was clearly apparent that their arrival delighted Mia, who up until that moment had felt a bit out of her depth and had been trying hard to avoid anything other than small talk.

Nathan complimented Mia on her appearance and, after a prompt from Eva, agreed that she looked special too!

Elegantly attired guests continued to make their way to tables where, greeted by excited chatter, they finally settled.

With the dimming of the lights, a small, smartly dressed group made their way onto the platform. A formidable-looking middle-aged man stepped up to the microphone. Mia leant across to Eva and in a whisper said, "That's the gentleman who came and saw me last week."

Eva smiled.

"It is my great pleasure," the man began, "to welcome you all to this, our Annual Press Awards. The distinguished guests joining me on the platform tonight will need no introduction," and he half turned to them, clapped and the audience applauded. Nathan looked at Eva, bemused. "Without further ado," the speaker continued, "we are here to celebrate all that is commendable in Danish journalism today. To honour those individuals who have taken our profession to new heights, while maintaining truth and integrity. So, if you will join me and welcome our Chair, Lisa Andersen, to the microphone, we will reveal our award winners for 2002." Again, with one accord the audience clapped as the woman took the microphone.

After some fifteen minutes the top three awards had been presented and culminated in a brief acceptance speech by the winner, who was obviously greatly moved by the proceedings.

The host stepped forward once again and spoke. "This year we are breaking with tradition and, following a unanimous decision by our board, combined with the enthusiastic support of The National Press Club of Denmark, we are introducing a special award in recognition of the work of one individual who has made an outstanding contribution over the years to journalism, both nationally and internationally. It is a privilege to be able to welcome Mia Poulson who will collect this award on behalf of her late husband, Martin. There are few who would strive for the truth, year after year after year, seeking no recognition, no glory, just the reward of knowing that what they were doing was right. A truly honourable man and one we wish to honour tonight."

Lisa Andersen, looking towards Mia, spoke. "Mia Poulson, would you please join us here on the platform and we would be pleased if Professor Trent, who worked tirelessly alongside your husband, would accompany you."

Eva couldn't help but notice the look of amazement in Nathan's face, something she had rarely seen before as he accompanied Mia onto the platform. Her heart warmed to see Mia receive the most spectacular crystal glass bowl. As she held it forward under the spotlights, shafts of brilliance fired in all directions. And for Nathan, a warm hand-shake and the presentation of an inscribed Royal Danmark pen in recognition of the part he had played. Eva felt so proud of him. Mia had told her what was to happen but nothing had prepared her for this.

The audience were triumphant, their standing ovation continuing for nearly five minutes.

With Mia and Nathan returning to their table, Eva flung her arms around Mia and hugged her. Overwhelmed by the occasion, Mia was in tears and couldn't stop thanking people for being so kind. From the corner of her eye Eva could see that a burly old man, dressed in a baggy, blue pin-striped suit, was about to approach them, along with a finely dressed woman at his side.

Nathan stepped up to undertake introductions. "This is the chief editor of *Today*," and, as if an afterthought, said, "I don't think I've ever known you by anything other than the chief. And this is Gudrun, my co-writer who heads up the news for the paper."

The chief approached Mia and, turning his impressive figure to face her, said, "The chief, I'm only known as the chief." He took her hand, "It's indeed a privilege to meet you. I met your husband and have long held his work in high regard. I am delighted that his important contribution to ethical journalism has finally been acknowledged. It's just recognition. I know Gudrun," and he turned to her, "has spoken with you. Please be assured that if there is anything we can do, you must not hesitate to ask."

Mia gratefully thanked him.

"And so this is Eva, Nathan's secret. And what of this news I hear?" he fixed Nathan with a piercing look.

Eva was surprised by his question. They had agreed to tell no one of their engagement, believing that to do so at such a time would be insensitive.

"I hear you're leaving us," the chief said, in a gruff voice, sounding disappointed.

Nathan nodded and Eva relaxed.

"It won't make any difference to our working together, will it?" Gudrun claimed, glancing across to Nathan.

"No," he said confidently. "I'll be able to file online and, if needs be, I'm not a million miles away. Anyway, we still intend to keep up with Mia."

She beamed.

"Was it a sudden decision?" the chief asked.

"Yes, I suppose so. Increasingly I'm aware that too many people here have an interest in me for my own good."

"And he did it for me," Eva interrupted, "to bring back some normality to our lives."

"Eva plays in the Icelandic Symphony Orchestra," Nathan explained, but other than looks of acknowledgement nothing more was said on that.

The chief's manner appeared to warm as he complimented Nathan on his weekend revelations regarding the plutonium levels at Thule. "Highlighting Risø's recent report proving that far more plutonium was released than scientists originally estimated, substantially increasing the risks, was an excellent and masterful piece of writing, wasn't it, Gudrun?"

She enthusiastically agreed, smiling at Nathan.

The old man addressed the group. "Unless I am very much mistaken, what we are doing now marks the beginning of the end of that which Martin started all those years ago."

Nathan added, "And it's a big responsibility."

"Indeed it is," the old man confirmed with a sincerity that was clearly evident.

REYKJAVIK – ICELAND
2002

CHAPTER FIFTY-FOUR

Arriving back at Eva's apartment Nathan threw his coat onto the sofa. Fifteen minutes later he had unpacked, tossed his laundry in their washing basket, freshened up and changed his shirt. By the time they both settled in the lounge, exhausted after the journey, the heating had already taken the chill off the place and dispelled the musty smell.

There was a knocking at the apartment door which Eva answered and, after a short conversation, she returned with a stack of mail.

"Do you want something to eat?" Nathan called out, heading for the kitchen.

"It's funny," Eva replied, "all I've done is sit around but I do fancy something.

"What have you got there?" he asked as he brought in the coffee.

"The mail. My neighbour takes it in for me when I'm away. She's good like that."

"I'll fix us a sandwich," Nathan said returning to the kitchen.

As Eva moved his coat to one side of the sofa a copy of *The Copenhagen Post* slipped out of one of its pockets onto the floor. Picking the tabloid up, the paper half opened to reveal a black and white picture causing her to instantly freeze.

"That's impossible!" she cried out. Concerned, Nathan hurried in. "Where did you get this?"

"What, get what?"

"The paper," she said, holding it up.

"It's this week's *Post*, I picked it up at the airport . . . why?"

"Take a look at the photo," she handed him the paper. "That's the man, isn't it? The man I bumped into at The Castle, the one at Martin's funeral."

Nathan found himself staring at the face of the stranger, the man who days earlier had admitted to the part he had played in the cover-up. He collapsed onto the sofa beside her. The headline read: *'MINISTERIAL OFFICIAL FOUND DEAD The body of Gunnar Ingelsson was found yesterday, washed up on the west bank of the harbour here in Copenhagen, close to the statue of The Little Mermaid. The police stated, "There is no evidence to indicate foul play at this time although the body had been in the water for at least two days making it harder to identify any superficial injuries, should they be present." A spokesperson added that a suicide note was found on his person. Gunnar Ingelsson, seventy-two and a member of the Social Democrats Party, had held a senior post within the Justice Department since the 1968 government of Otto Krays. His wife pre-deceased him by three years and they had no children'.*

Gunnar's face seemed to stare out at Nathan, who couldn't help but wonder what it was that had driven this man to take his own life.

Reading over his shoulder Eva gasped, "That is him, isn't it?" she said, resting her hand on Nathan's shoulder.

"Yes," he said.

For a moment a deathly silence hung in the air before Nathan spoke.

"He seemed low when I saw him, but not that low."

"What are you going to do?" she asked as he fumbled with the telephone.

"I'm ringing Gudrun at the paper."

"Then I'll get some food," Eva said disappearing into the kitchen, taking the pile of mail with her.

The switchboard of the *Today* newspaper answered after a minute. "Put me through to Gudrun on the news desk please, tell her it's Professor Nathan Trent . . . and urgent."

"Nathan," her warm voice came back. "I thought you were heading home to Iceland?"

"I am, I mean we're back. I've just read the news of Ingelsson's death in *The Post*. What else can you tell me Gudrun?"

"Hold on. I'll see what I can find." Then, as if thinking things through, she said, "He wasn't your stranger, was he?"

Nathan uttered, "Yes."

Two or three minutes later she said, "We've more just come over the wire." Nathan could hear the tapping of her computer keyboard.

"From what I can see," she continued, "he would have been one of those government officials implicated in the Thule cover-up; anyway that's how the story is being headlined. Strangely enough the police have taken the unprecedented step of releasing the content of his suicide note," and, as if an afterthought, added, "although now I think of it, they did that once before, releasing the words from a serial killer. I'll read Ingelsson's note to you if you like?"

"Go ahead," Nathan said.

"*I thank the Lord for my happy marriage and giving me thirty-four years of exciting challenges within government. The recent sustained onslaught by people conjuring up theories of conspiracies and deceit within our country's government, along with the bombardment of the media by such journalists as Martin Poulson, has been more than I can bear. I have become a victim of unsubstantiated persecution by them. My personal and political life now hold nothing for me.* And he signs off, *Say goodbye to my friends and colleagues for me. Gunnar Ingelsson.*"

"That's it, Nathan." Nathan made no response. "Did you get that?" Gudrun asked.

"Yes, I got it, but I don't believe it," he said.

"Look Nathan, I must go now, I've a meeting, but we must talk soon. Email me if you've got anything and I'll see what I can dig up this end. We must discuss our piece for next weekend's edition, okay?" Gudrun said with a degree of anxiety evident in her voice.

"Thanks Gudrun," he replied, his thoughts elsewhere.

Passing Nathan a plate of sandwiches balanced on top of a large brown envelope, Eva explained, "That's for you, it looks like a Copenhagen post-mark." As he took them, she said, "I suppose people can drown by accident, but I must admit it seems very odd."

It could have been that Nathan was wrong, but something told him that this time he wasn't. He ripped open the end of the envelope and, sliding out its contents, spread them out on the coffee table. Picking up the top sheet he started to read.

Sitting opposite in an armchair sifting the mail, Eva looked up and said, "What have you got there?"

Without glancing up Nathan said, "A letter from a dead man."

"What does it say?" Eva said.

"I'll tell you in a minute," Nathan countered.

For fifteen minutes he examined the wodge of reports and letters that Ingelsson had sent him, then he spoke. "The man never killed himself."

"How can you be so certain?" she said.

"Does this sound like a man who was contemplating suicide the next day?

Dear Professor Trent,

For so long I was lost, not knowing what I should do that was best for the country I loved. Times with Poulson and then our conversations changed all that. I, for the first time, saw the way people had been treated wasn't right, fair or just and realised I had only one option: to step up and do something to change it. The documents I have sent you in some measure go to help bring that about. I have no intention of refuting the part I played in this whole sinister affair or to avoid the consequences of my actions which I undertook in good faith, albeit in hindsight, misguided. Nor do I regret the measures I am now party to in exposing the full story and hope to be able to send you more material that I believe will help in our endeavours.

Glad you are now safely in Iceland. The very best of greetings to your young lady and thank you for all you are doing for so many people.

Hope we can meet in the near future,

Your friend – Gunnar Ingelsson."

Eva had discarded her letters, concentrating as Nathan read.

"No, it doesn't," she said emphatically, "and it's just occurred to me, he never calls Martin 'Martin', does he?"

"What?" Nathan said.

"Well, in that letter when he tells you he's going to send you more material in the future he refers to Martin as Poulson: he's always referred to him as Poulson. But in Ingelsson's so-called suicide note didn't it say Martin Poulson? Did you ever hear him call him Martin? He didn't at the graveyard and he didn't when he spoke to Mia on the phone."

"You're right," Nathan said, "and the papers he's sent blow open the entire affair and all who had a part in it, including the Americans."

Eva stood, "That's amazing. At last we have the evidence, the truth from an insider."

"Discovering the truth is one thing, it's what you do with the truth that matters. Do you believe that?"

"Yes," she said with conviction.

Nathan looked at her lovingly, the woman who had resolutely stood by him.

She stretched. "I'm shattered and going to turn in." Nathan didn't respond. "Okay?" she said.

"Sure . . . you go on," he replied, seeing the tiredness in her eyes.

"And you?"

"I need to jot down a few notes. I won't be long, I promise."

Eva kissed his cheek, "In case I'm asleep when you come to bed," but Nathan was far from ready for bed, his mind was racing over all he had read.

Taking up a lined note pad he began to scribe: 'EVEN DEATH COULD NOT SHUT UP GOVERNMENT OFFICIAL. New evidence from within the Danish government blows open the parts Danish and American governments played in the secretive Thule Affair, and the death of so many innocent people.'

For forty minutes or more he wrote feverishly while referring to the documents. Finally he closed his pad and placed it and the pen on the table. Easing himself out of the sofa, he switched off the lights. The moon's bright glow filled the bedroom as he undressed and slid in beside Eva. Content, he snuggled up close to her and slept.

DEDICATION

This book is dedicated to those who seek the truth no matter at what cost to themselves.

AUTHOR'S NOTES

In the process of my research I have discovered eye-witness accounts and an abundance of facts, some quite extraordinary. Bringing a measure of accuracy, a sense of importance or semblance of order to these has at times proved challenging. I have striven to be as truthful as possible, however, as with most factual accounts, there is usually more than one version and interpretation.

In the interest of the novel I have changed the name and identity of the Danish investigative journalist, as well as exercising artistic license regarding some details of his life (1953 – 2002), including his collaboration with Nathan Trent, the reported conversations within DR and Risø National Laboratory, the incident of the photograph, the televised debate, speculation concerning his death and events surrounding his burial. With a regard to privacy, specifics concerning his family have been altered.

Finally, I would add that the significant part this journalist played in bringing before the people the reality of the Thule incident cannot be over-stated. His unrelenting work for almost two decades, endeavouring to highlight the difference between the sins of the past and the righteousness of the future, is indeed his legacy.

Many wait, with trepidation, to see whether there will be a new Cold War – colder than before.

HISTORIC NOTES

The author has attempted to feature the relevant events as they happened, subsequent to the time the story is set. However, the reader should seek confirmation of the same from appropriate sources where necessary.

2002 – A legal challenge for the Inuit people to reclaim their land on the Dundas peninsular, next to the Thule Base, will be heard by the Supreme Court in Denmark in the autumn. Vittus Qujaakitsoq, secretary to the Minister of Industry in Greenland, is worried that the nuclear pollution might endanger all living species. He stated, 'We have been finding deformed animals in the area, mainly seals with no fur, and deformities of the entrails, guts and organs. Greenlanders have been given assurances the area was safe after the B-52 crash, in which between 500g and 1.8kg of plutonium went missing in the waters of Bylot Sound, but they had been given no hard evidence.'

Subsequent reports have stated that 6kg or 7.5kg or more of weapons grade plutonium was released. A new report from the Risø National Laboratory in Denmark proves that the Americans, in 1968, left much more plutonium at Thule than scientists previously estimated.

In addressing the risks, the British nuclear engineer and analyst, John H Large, cast doubt on Risø's assessment. He disagreed with the final conclusion that the plutonium content at the bottom of the sea does not pose a risk to humans.

2003 – Footage filmed at the site by a US submarine, searching for remains of the B-52 wreckage in 1968, contained images of a bomb-like object, the Danish Ritxau news agency reported –
An attempt by Greenpeace toxic's campaigner, Jacob Hartmann, to gain access to a key US report, *The Environmental Survey,* was rejected by the Danish Foreign Ministry which said the US authorities were 'resisting publication'.

The Danish Environment Ministry asked the Danish Finance Ministry for £400,000 to commission its own report, saying surface-to-air missile silos had been filled with waste and concreted over, alleging that the American report had concentrated on one dump only, ignoring a second dump and landfill sites and impact on ground water and marine life.

Allegations by former workers bring further concerns regarding dumping of contaminated waste and leakage.

2005 – According to Senate testimony by US Defence Secretary, William Cohen, Washington needs a decision on upgrading the Thule radar should the White House give the go-ahead to deploy the missile defences in building a shield against missiles from what it calls states of concern, such as North Korea, Iraq, Iran and Libya.

Moscow opposes the US missile shield plan and says it breaches the strategic missile treaty between the United States and Russia. Russian President, Vladimir Putin has warned Denmark and other US NATO allies that their participation in the National Missile Defence Initiative could upset global strategic stability.

Leading politicians in Greenland, which has enjoyed limited self-determination under the Danish crown since 1979, do not want Thule to play any role in the National Missile Defence Initiative.

2007 – British MEP, Diana Wallis said, 'this largely forgotten piece of history not only had serious ramifications for the unfortunate workers commissioned to clean-up the radioactive debris, but also uncovered clandestine nuclear activity on Danish soil, despite the nuclear-free zone peacetime policy announced by Denmark in 1957.' (Around fifty nuclear weapons had been stored at the base between 1958 and 1965.) The Petitions Committee in the European Parliament overwhelmingly voted (544 to 29 votes) to support MEP Diana Wallis' report on the public health consequences of the 1968 Thule crash. 'Many Thule survivors have died of radiation illnesses due to the lack of medical monitoring, and current survivors risk contracting such fatal illnesses,' stated the accompanying resolution.

Denmark did not cooperate with the parliament's Petition Committee, and still refuses to release key environmental radiation records made at Thule at the time.

2008 – The Thule workers took their case to the European Courts. They claim that Denmark, in contravention of both the European Court directive from 2000, and a European Parliament resolution in 2007, had failed to monitor their health with regular check-ups, leading to delay in detecting illnesses.

A BBC documentary, providing evidence from a number of sources, revealed that investigators at the time could only account for three out of the four weapons. In an interview with the BBC, Jens Zinglersen, chairman of the Thule Workers' Association said, "I think it's a cover-up. We are getting older and the Danish authorities and the Danish government will wait and keep their mouths sealed for another 15, 20 years, then there's no one left who remembers and who was a part of the accident back in the days of 1968." BBC Radio World Service claimed, '. . . that rumours of a lost bomb are true," and BBC Two's Newsnight explained that, 'The US abandoned a nuclear weapon beneath the ice in northern Greenland following a crash in 1968 . . .'

William H Chambers, former deputy associate director and nuclear weapons designer at Los Alamo's National Laboratory*, who had run a team dealing with the Thule crash, is reported to have told the BBC, "There was disappointment in what you might call a failure to return all of the components," explaining, "It would be very difficult for anyone else to find and recover these sensitive classified components." He was of the opinion that the radio-active material would dissolve in such a large body of water, making it harmless.
(*This was the secret US desert facility where Robert Oppenheimer and his international team of scientists built 'The Gadget', the first Atomic Bomb in 1945.)

Kaare Ulbak, from the Danish National Institute of Radiation Protection, stated unequivocally in the 2008 report on radiation levels in Thule, 'The total radiation for representative persons in the Thule area for plutonium contamination resulting from the 1968 Thule accident is lower than the recommended reference level, even under extreme conditions and situations.'

2009 – It was reported that the Danish Institute for International Studies (DIIS) had recently issued a report ruling out any missing bomb, but leaving open at least one question, whether 1.5kg of plutonium could be accounted for following the systematic examination by a historian of some 348 declassified documents. DIIS believes beyond reasonable doubt that all four weapons broke up in the crash and became non-operational. They highlight the seeming discrepancy with regard to plutonium 239, between 24kg thought to be needed to reach criticality in the four primaries taken together, and the approximately 6kg that the authorities claimed to have been involved in the accident. Some might consider that not all four primaries did explode or the supposed 24kg had not been accounted for properly, meaning that the contamination was worse than admitted. The DIIS stated, 'We cannot however, provide a final material balance.' The report states that it is believed the Americans underwater search in Bylot Sound was looking for the weapons component – the Marshal's baton, the fissile core of a secondary, containing uranium 235 – supposedly 8kg. The hunt for this small object continued to the end of the operation in August 1968. The report concluded if there was something to be found, they did not find it . . .'

2009-2013 – The new Danish coalition parties had long before their election victory signalled a positive attitude to a future US missile defence request on Thule. Minister for Finance and Foreign Affairs in Greenland's government, Josef Motzfeldt, was in charge of negotiations with Denmark and the United States. Elements of a possible 'compensation package' listed customs free exports of products to the US, Washington's assistance in building roads and harbours, scholarships at US establishments of higher education and a demand for rental of about $20 million a year.

2015 – Lars Emil Johansen, ex-Prime Minister of Greenland said, the Thule case must now lead to a new constitution, to ensure that Greenland can maintain an independent foreign policy. The Minister for Foreign Affairs, Vittus Qujaikitsoq, required all files being opened, so that it becomes clear whether there are other cases hiding under the sea ice. Johansen calls the case the darkest chapter of National Community history.

2016 – The US Air Force is working on bringing back into service a B-52H bomber (BUFF; Big Ugly Fat Fella) which originally began service in 1961 and had been left at the famous Boneyard at Davis-Monthan Air Force Base in Arizona for seven years. This will be the first time a B-52 has been regenerated back into active duty. It is expected to be finished and in service in 2016. The B-52 long range, heavy bomber has been the mainstay of the United States nuclear deterrent force for more than sixty years. The US Air Force envisions a lingering role for this aircraft and are planning to modernise the B-52 fleet and suggests the life span of the aircraft could extend beyond 2040. (Of the 744 aircraft built, 76 remained in active service as of 2015.)

Just as the Thule case has resurfaced, many wonder whether one day so too may the lost bomb. We will have to wait and see.

ACKNOWLEDGEMENTS

I owe a debt of gratitude to the following individuals for their expert guidance and advice.

Among them Carol Paige, Leader of the Second Violins in the Bournemouth Symphony Orchestra who enlightened me on both the instrument and on the ways of the orchestra, as well as Margrét Ragnarsdóttir – PR and Marketing Director at the Icelandic Symphony Orchestra for arranging my visit to their old performance venue, as well as fixing it so I could sit in on a full orchestral rehearsal in their fabulous new Harpa Concert Hall in Reykjavik. American veteran Lawrence Barr, who helped me make sense of my research regarding what it was like working in Thule at that time and Aero Commander pilot, Jonathan Drew for giving me an insight into operating a cargo service between Iceland and Greenland. Steering me through the world of journalism and Danish politics were Simon Rye Clausen and Anders Hochheim in Denmark and Rune Salvesen and author Tom Egeland in Norway. I am grateful to Chris Caseldine, Professor of Quaternary Environmental Change and J Roy Sambles, Professor of Physics for their time and expertise, while Dr David Willis aided me on all things medical.

Others who gave generously of their knowledge and time were authors Ryan Callery in the USA, and in the UK, William Sutcliffe and Chris Ewan. In undertaking my extensive research I referred to far too many books, publications and websites to make mention of here but the following organisations proved invaluable – Air Force Historical Research Agency, Maxwell AFB, Alabama, USA; BBC Written Archives Centre, Reading, UK; The Copenhagen Post, Denmark; Scott Polar Research Institute, University of Cambridge, UK; US HQ Air Force Safety Centre, Kirtland AFB, New Mexico, USA and the United States Air Force Museum, Wright-Patterson AFB, Ohio, USA.

Lastly, I wish to thank my readers: Susan, Jeff, Nigel, Linda, Nathan, Jackie, Pete and Sue; and of course my editor Stephanie Daggs, my son Ben, for the cover design, and Keren, for her patience and perseverance.

There may be inaccuracies and inconsistencies, just as there may be in memories that are fifty years old. Any errors, distortions or licence for dramatic purposes is the author's responsibility, not that of any of the above.

BOOKS BY THE SAME AUTHOR

One Day in June

This novel follows a young man who joins the RAF. During a secret mission over occupied France, his aircraft is hit and he is forced to bail out. Escaping with the help of the Resistance he later returns to France in an attempt to find those who had saved him.

A Tale of Two Elephants

A tale for readers of all ages as told by a female African elephant. The story traces her life from the wild savannah to a peaceful sanctuary. A story of ruthless poachers, war torn lands and cruel circus owners, as well as her encounters with those who cared.

Within the Mist

While acquainting ourselves with the strange folk that live in the unusual English fishing village of Doon, a mystery begins to unfold. Even here in this god-forsaken place, secrets still linger.

Silly and not so Silly Verse

A medley of the absurd, the imaginative and the unusual. Every one is simply and wonderfully illustrated in a manner that will make you smile.

Voices

An eclectic mix of twenty short stories celebrating a range of genres, times and places. Each story is fronted by an original illustration by a different artist.

All books are available as paperbacks and e-books from Amazon or direct from www.fourboysbooks.com